Henry Allon, John Eimeo Ellis

Life of William Ellis

Missionary to the South Seas and to Madagascar

Henry Allon, John Eimeo Ellis

Life of William Ellis
Missionary to the South Seas and to Madagascar

ISBN/EAN: 9783337316891

Printed in Europe, USA, Canada, Australia, Japan

Cover: Foto ©Raphael Reischuk / pixelio.de

More available books at **www.hansebooks.com**

LIFE

OF

WILLIAM ĔLLIS

MISSIONARY TO THE SOUTH SEAS
AND TO MADAGASCAR

BY HIS SON, JOHN EIMEO ĔLLIS

WITH A SUPPLEMENTARY CHAPTER
CONTAINING AN ESTIMATE OF HIS CHARACTER AND WORK

By HENRY ALLON, D.D.

With a Portrait

LONDON
JOHN MURRAY, ALBEMARLE STREET
1873

PREFACE.

By the present generation the name of WILLIAM ELLIS is associated almost exclusively with Madagascar, and many will, perhaps, expect a history of his life to be occupied chiefly with details of mission work in that country, forgetting that it was not till he had attained his sixtieth year that he had any personal connection whatever with the Malagasy. For many years previously he had been actively engaged in other fields of labour. From 1816, when he first entered on his missionary career, till 1825, he took part in the work, and shared in the exile of those faithful men who introduced the gospel among the South Sea Islands. He was then employed, first as agent, and afterwards as Foreign Secretary of the London Missionary Society, till 1841, when, his health failing, he was compelled to seek its restoration in comparative retirement. The subsequent years of seclusion and leisure, if they could be so called, were yet devoutly consecrated to his

Master's service ; and during his pastorate at Hoddesdon—which terminated only when, in 1853, he was sent
forth to enter upon the crowning work of his life—while
discharging the duties of a faithful minister at home, he
was gathering strength, energy, and wisdom for a
grander work abroad.

With these facts in view, it will, I trust, be deemed
not unreasonable that a large portion of the following
memoir should be devoted to the missionary's earlier life,
with which the reader is probably least familiar, and that
those recent events, the story of which has been so fully
told in current missionary publications, and in Mr.
ELLIS's own narratives, should be more briefly noticed.

The chief sources from which I have gathered
materials, besides my own personal recollections, have
been my father's journals, letters, and books ; and I
have not hesitated to make free use of his earlier works,
because they were written long ago, and because the
quotations I have ventured to introduce contain much
interesting autobiography, and illustrate, moreover, in
a very striking manner, the rapid mental development
of one who, without any literary training, could so
readily exchange the mechanical manipulations of the
garden for the facile and graceful use of the pen.   I
have carefully avoided, however, any transcript of what
has appeared in later publications.

My very cordial thanks are due to the Secretaries of the London Missionary Society for their ready courtesy in granting access to the printed and manuscript records of the Institution, and in affording me every facility for obtaining desired information.

I would also gratefully acknowledge my obligation to Dr. ALLON, for much kind encouragement and counsel ; and for the valuable ' Estimate ' of my father's ' character and work,' which, notwithstanding the multiplicity of his pastoral and literary engagements, he cheerfully consented to write, in compliance with my request—a request that I had ventured to prefer because I knew no one better qualified by intimate personal acquaintance to undertake the task.

Fully sensible of the inadequacy of the portraiture I have attempted, but with a reverent love, such as a parent so worthy could not fail to inspire, and which has deepened as, in the prosecution of my task, I have, as it were, read his heart and studied his goodness afresh, I now offer to the public this plain record of a noble life, whose chief and lasting memorial will ever remain in its large and beneficent results.

JOHN EIMEO ELLIS.

TORONTO, CANADA :
  September 18, 1873.

CONTENTS.

PAGE

INTRODUCTION . . . XV

EARLY LIFE—1794-1816.

CHAPTER I.

EARLY LIFE.

Parentage and Birth—Removal to Wisbeach—Early Characteristics—
Love of Plants—Thirst for Knowledge—Employment as a Gar-
dener—Removal to London—Temptations—First Religious
Impressions—Desire to become a Missionary—Application to the
London Missionary Society—Acceptance, and Designation to the
South Seas—Preparation—Ordination—Marriage—Embarkation   3

SOUTH SEAS—1816-25.

CHAPTER II.

VOYAGE OUT.

Impressions on leaving England—Discomforts of the Voyage—Arrival
at Rio—Re-embarkation—Detention at Sydney—Continuation of
the Voyage—Visit to New Zealand—Encounter with Natives off
the Island of Rapa—First Sight of Tahiti—Introduction to
Pomare and his Queen 29

CHAPTER III.

EIMEO.

Harbour of Oponohu—Reception by the Missionaries and Chiefs—
First Impressions—Removal to Afareaitu—Erection of Printing

PAGE

Office and Dwelling—Products of the Country—Introduction of Printing—Pomare's Inauguration of the Press—Bookbinding—Eagerness of the People for Books—The Mission Reinforced—The First Vessel Built—Domestic Cares—Formation of a Missionary Society 40

CHAPTER IV.

HUAHINE.

Distribution of the Mission—Settlement in Huahine—Description of the District of Fare—A Bivouac—Erection of a new Dwelling and Printing House—Social Improvements of the People—Establishment of Branch Missionary Societies—Royal Mission Chapel—Baptism of Pomare and other Native Converts—Itinerant Labours—Cultivation of Cotton—Sugar-making. 57

CHAPTER V.

HUAHINE—continued.

Voyages among the Islands—Singular Night Adventure—Imminent Perils—Waterspouts—Providential Deliverance—Night Voyage—The First Code of Laws—Arrival of the Deputation from England—Death of Pomare—Visit to the Sandwich Islands—Protracted Absence—Ill health and Anxiety of Mrs. Ellis—Visit of Escaped Pirates—Return of Mr. Ellis—Cause of Detention, and Proposal to remove to the Sandwich Islands—Farewell to Huahine 70

CHAPTER VI.

SANDWICH ISLANDS.

Arrival at Oahu—Character of the Islands and People—Introduction of Christianity by the American Missionaries—Early Mission Work—Tour of Hawaii projected—Incidents of the Tour—The Guide—Approach to the Volcano of Kirauea—Beautiful Night Scene—Description of the Volcano—Native Superstition—Encounter with heathen Priestesses—Return to Oahu—Death of Keopuolani—Visit of the King and Queen to England—Their Death—Illness of Mrs. Ellis—Multifarious Labours—Surgical Operation—Departure of Mr. Ellis and his Family for America—

PAGE

Huahine Re-visited—Arrival at New Bedford—Hospitality of
American Christians—Precarious State of Mrs. Ellis—Missionary
Tour through the United States—Return to England . . . 88

MISSION WORK AT HOME—1825–1841.

CHAPTER VII.

TRAVELLING AGENCY.

Laborious and Constant Engagements—Notes of a Tour in Ireland—
Powerscourt—Publication of 'Tour through Hawaii'—Vindication of the Mission—Spurious Letter of Boki—Domestic Affliction
—Improvement in Mrs. Ellis's Health—Residence in Gloucestershire—'Polynesian Researches'—Its Influence—Correspondence
with Richard Winter Hamilton—Frustrated Hopes of returning
to the South Seas 117

CHAPTER VIII.

SECRETARIAT.

Death of Rev. W. Orme, Foreign Secretary of the London Missionary
Society—Appointment of Mr. Ellis as his Successor—Fitness for
the Office—The House of Mourning—Letter from J. T. Beighton
—Mr. Ellis's Estimate of Missionary Qualifications—Death of
Mrs. Ellis—Its Influence on the Widower—Increasing Occupations—Preparation of the 'History of Madagascar'—Other Literary Labours—Stirring Events throughout the Missionary Fields
of the World—John Williams—Malagasy Refugees and Ambassadors—Evidence before Parliamentary Committee on the effect
of European Intercourse with the Heathen—Introduction to Miss
S. Stickney—Subsequent Engagement—Death of Mr. Ellis's
Mother—Second Marriage—Illness and Death of his eldest
Daughter—Failure of Health—Suspension of Work—Residence
in the South of France—Resignation of Secretariat . . . 144

HODDESDON—1841–1853.

CHAPTER IX.

PASTORATE &C.

Retirement at Hoddesdon—Continued Work for the Missionary
Society—Preparation of the 'History' of that Institution—

PAGE

Interest in Local Schemes of Benevolence—Temperance Associa-
tion—Schools—Opposition to Church Rates—Visit to Italy—
Return, and Acceptance of the Pastorate—Erection of a New
Chapel—Style of Preaching, and Pastoral Work—Letter to an
' Enquirer '—Lectures on Popery—Close of Pastorate—' Rawdon
House '—Death of his Second Daughter—Illness of the Youngest   177

CHAPTER X.

ROSE HILL—HOME LIFE.

Rural Character of Hoddesdon—Special Features of Rose Hill—
Roses, Orchids—Social Qualities—Versatility—Tact—Kindness
to Domestics—Fondness for Animals—Domestic Pets—Literary
Pursuits—Poetical Tastes—Letter from Southey—A Lyric—
Quotations from Epic Poem—Purchase of Rose Hill .   .   .   193

MADAGASCAR—1853-1872.

CHAPTER XI.

FIRST VISIT.—TAMATAVE &c.

Brief Statement of the Condition of Madagascar—Rupture between
the Malagasy and Foreigners—Rumours of a Change—Mr. Ellis
appointed to Visit the Country—Arrival at Tamatave—Permission
to Visit the Capital Refused—Return to Mauritius—Re-opening
of Trade, and Establishment of friendly Relations with Madagascar
—Interest in Natural History—Outbreak of Cholera in Port
Louis—Second Visit to Tamatave—Unsuccessful Application to
proceed to the Capital—Visit to Mission Stations in South Africa
—Return to England   213

CHAPTER XII.

ANTANANARIVO.

Invitation to the Capital—Third Visit to Madagascar—Journey to
Antananarivo—Introduction to Prince Rakotond—Audience with
the Queen—Intercourse with Christians—Conversations with the
Prince—Letter to Lord Clarendon—Medical Practice—Photo-
graphy—Limitation of the Visit—Departure from the Country—
Return Home   226

PAGE

CHAPTER XIII.

LAST VISIT.—RADAMA II.

M. Lambert's Plots—Last Persecution of the Christians—Death of the
Queen—Accession of Radama II.—Liberal Policy—Religious
Liberty—Protestant Missionaries Encouraged to Resume their
Labours—Earnest Invitation to Mr. Ellis—His prompt Response
—Return to Madagascar—Great Changes in the Country—Journey
to the Capital, and Cordial Reception—Arrival of European
Embassies and Consuls—The Bishop of Mauritius—The English
Missionaries—The Coronation—Treaty between the French and
Malagasy Governments—Account of Mr. Ellis's Missionary Work
by the Rev. R. Toy—The Memorial Churches—Erection of Tem-
porary Places of Worship—Organization of Churches .   .   .   243

CHAPTER XIV.

CHANGES.

Visits to Out-lying Districts—Ambohimanga—Misrepresentations of
the British Consul—Accumulated Work and Anxieties—Death of
his Youngest Daughter—Death of the King's Foreign Secretary—
The Duties of the Office partially and temporarily undertaken by
Mr. Ellis—Groundless Complaints from the British Consul—Letter
of Explanation to General Johnstone—Popular Dissatisfaction
with the King's Administration—His Evil Advisers—Machinations of the Heathen Party—The ' Dancing Sickness '—Plots
against Mr. Ellis's Life—Narrow Escape—Radama's Last Edict—
Assassination of the *Mena-maso* and of the King—Acceptance of
the Crown, with Constitutional Provisions, by Rabodo—Religious
Liberty Assured—Rumours of Radama's being Alive—Responsible and Critical Position of Mr. Ellis—Difficulties with the
French Government—Revolt of Sakalavas—Deposition of the
Prime Minister—Satisfactory Progress of the Mission—Departure
of Mr. Ellis from Madagascar—Death of Rasoherina—Accession
of a Christian Queen, and Final Overthrow of Idolatry   .   .   263

CHAPTER XV.

LAST YEARS.

Welcome Home—Itinerant Services—Reception at Wisbeach—Enthusiastic Consecration to Mission Work—Literary Labours—
Vindication of the American Mission in the Sandwich Islands—
Madagascar Bishopric—Indefatigable Spirit and Multiplied Engagements—Special Appeal on behalf of Madagascar—Life-work

PAGE

Ended—Last Letter—Illness—The Closing Scene—Funeral—
Illness of Mrs. Ellis—Her Death 285

CHAPTER XVI.

GENERAL ESTIMATE OF MR. ELLIS'S CHARACTER AND WORK.

BY HENRY ALLON, D.D.

Position among Missionaries—Distinctive Missionary Qualities—Ser-
vices to Madagascar—Hospitality to Cheshunt Students—General
Excellence—Consecration—Entireness of Religious Life—Special
Faculties 302

INTRODUCTION.

THE HISTORY of modern Christian Missions dates from the end of the past and the beginning of the present century. To the Moravians belongs the honour of being the first to engage in this sphere of philanthropy. The Wesleyans, foremost amongst those who were quickened into more vigorous spiritual life by the eloquence of Wesley and Whitfield, were also early in the same field, labouring chiefly amongst the British Colonies; though it was not till the year 1817 that the Missionary Society in connection with their body was formally organized. The Baptist Missionary Society, under the inspiration of Dr. Carey, one of its first agents as well as one of its founders, was established in 1792. The London Missionary Society was formed in 1795; and that of the Church of England in the first year of the present century. Other kindred institutions were brought into existence about the same time, and notably, the British and Foreign Bible Society, and the Religious Tract Society.

It was the peculiar and honoured distinction of the

London Missionary Society to have been founded, not
by one section of Christians, but by a union of good
men from nearly all the Protestant religious denominations of the period.   Its originators, indeed, were
members of the Church of England ; and though now
supported mainly by Congregationalists, it has never
abandoned its fundamental catholic principles and constitution, as a society whose object was to spread the
Gospel among the heathen, and not to propagate any
sectarian creed or special form of Christianity.   Prior
to the establishment of this society, a periodical, that
has ever since exerted a marked influence on the progress of mission work, was started on the same broad
principles, namely, the ' Evangelical Magazine,' which
was at first edited by an Episcopal clergyman, the Rev.
John Eyre.   The chief promoters of this magazine all
co-operated in founding the London Missionary Society.
Amongst those to whom this institution owes its origin,
no one was more prominent or influential than Dr.
Haweis, Rector of Aldwinkle in Northamptonshire, and
chaplain to the Countess of Huntingdon.   Associated
with him were the Revs. J. Eyre, Dr. Waugh, Matthew
Wilks, Rowland Hill, Dr. Burder, and other ministers whose names are still venerated by the Church, and
will long be remembered with honour.

The glowing accounts of Captain Cook's discoveries

in the South Seas, and subsequently Keate's 'fascinating but to a great extent fictitious' narrative of the Pelew Islands and Prince Leboo, had excited an intense and romantic interest in the people of this hitherto unexplored portion of the world. The mind of Dr. Haweis had been smitten with the general enthusiasm ; and to this circumstance may doubtless be largely ascribed the selection of the South Sea Islands as the first field of missionary enterprise, by the society which he was so prominent in founding. Missions soon after were begun, and at first with far more encouraging results, in India, Madagascar, South Africa, China, and other pagan countries. The names of Dr. Vanderkemp and Dr. Morrison are indissolubly associated with the introduction of the Gospel into the last two populous regions of the globe.

Towards the expenses of the first mission to the South Seas, Dr. Haweis contributed from his own private resources £500. The ship *Duff* was purchased to convey the band of Christian labourers to their destination, and Captain Wilson was engaged as commander. The vessel sailed, with a company of missionaries about thirty in number, in the beginning of September, 1796, and, after a long and somewhat perilous voyage, reached Tahiti on the 6th of March, 1797. The rulers of the island received their visitors in a friendly manner, assured them of protection, and surrendered for their use as much land as they required. Eighteen of the company were left at this station; and Captain Wilson, having seen them comfortably settled, sailed from the harbour about the end of March, steering for the Friendly Islands, where he arrived on the 10th of April. Six of the remaining missionaries, under the promise of protection from the chiefs, were landed at Tongatabu, and the *Duff* proceeded with the other two to the Marquesas. Only one of these, however, Mr. Crooks, was willing to remain. Captain Wilson, after returning to pay a farewell visit to each of the stations, turned his course homeward, and, sailing by way of China and the Cape of Good Hope, reached England on the 24th of June 1798.

Not long after, the ship *Duff* attempted a second voyage; but was captured by a French privateer, the *Buonaparte*, when within a day's sail of Rio. The missionaries, after suffering many hardships, though on the whole treated with consideration, embarked in another vessel to pursue their original destination; but were again captured by a Portuguese privateer, and all of them returned to England.

Disastrously as this second missionary enterprise appeared to have failed, the fate of the devoted men who had been left in the South Sea Islands was far more discouraging, and even tragic. The mission to the Marquesas, if it could be dignified by that name, had been abandoned in less than a year. Mr. Crooks finding the means of subsistence insufficient, and his ignorance of the language, together with the character of the people, proving insurmountable barriers to his usefulness, left by the first opportunity for New South Wales, whence he returned to England.

The career of the men who had been left in the Friendly Islands was brief, and mournful in the extreme. Their greatest calamities were due to the evil influence of abandoned seamen from civilised countries—in this instance, escaped convicts from New South Wales—who surpassed the heathen in wickedness, and instigated the natives to perpetrate every species of outrage on the defenceless missionaries. They were robbed of every article of the slightest value, stripped of their clothing, driven from their houses, and forced, at times, to seek shelter and concealment in woods and caves. Three of their number were barbarously murdered, and the remainder would probably have shared the same fate, had they not been providentially rescued by a colonial vessel, in which they made their escape and were conveyed to New South Wales.

The course of the mission in the Society Islands though not so disastrous and fatal as that of the Friendly

Islands, was fraught with peril; and for many years was equally unsuccessful. Many of these misfortunes also were traceable, directly or indirectly, to the conduct of foreign seamen. Like their brethren in the neighbouring group, the missionaries were robbed, and not unfrequently placed in danger of their lives. Pomare was engaged in continual warfare with rebellious chiefs, and scarcely maintained his supremacy; and in the contentions of rival armies the persons and property of the missionaries were exposed to constant jeopardy. Their position at length became so insecure, and their prospects appeared so hopeless, that all but two left the island, and returned to Sydney.

The mission seemed now at an end; and many of the friends in England, inferring that the field of labour had been injudiciously chosen, counselled the entire withdrawal of efforts from this part of the world. But Dr. Haweis, confident in the scriptural warrant of the course pursued, and holding an unwavering faith in the ultimate triumph of the gospel wherever faithfully proclaimed, urged the Society to persevere, and gave a second donation of £500 to sustain and reinforce the mission.

Those who were unfriendly to the cause of missions pointed with triumph, as a confirmation of their views, to the results of the enterprise in the South Seas. It was

a favourite doctrine with such men that the endeavour
to Christianize a heathen people, without first civilising
them, was a subversion of the proper order of procedure.
But events, both here and elsewhere, have abundantly
proved that there is no agency so mighty in civilizing a
people as the introduction of Christianity; and that to
attempt to effect any permanent improvement in the
condition of a barbarous people, apart from its divine
influence, is to undertake a hard, if not a hopeless, task.
An experiment that illustrates this principle had been
made many years before in these very islands. With
the view of introducing the arts of civilization among
the people, through the instrumentality of one of their
own number, Captain Cook had brought with him to
England an intelligent Tahitian chief, of the name of
Mai, erroneously corrupted by us into ' Omai.' This
individual was introduced to the highest society in this
country. His natural urbanity and tact made him soon
at home in the courtly circles of the land. He became
the pet of the aristocracy, and every attention was
lavished upon him. The arts and manufactures, the
customs and institutions of the British people were
explained to him; and after spending some time in
familiar contact with the highest order of civilization,
but without any attempt, apparently, having been made
to impart religious instruction, he was sent back to his

own nation, loaded with gifts—trinkets innumerable, but no Bible. What was the result? He relapsed into his original barbarism; prostituted his acquirements in ministering to the caprices of the king—his skill as a marksman being not unfrequently tested by his shooting down, at the bidding of his sovereign, some individual pointed out to him in the mere passing humour, or from some vindictive impulse, of the despot. He died without having conferred a single benefit on his countrymen, by whom his memory is held in detestation.

Not long after the missionaries had left the islands, indications of a favourable change appeared; and in 1812, at the invitation of Pomare, some of the former teachers returned from New South Wales. The king himself openly renounced idolatry, and desired to be baptized. His example was followed by some of the chiefs; but opposition to this national revolution was for some time strenuous, and not altogether unsuccessful. Even so late as 1815, a plot to assassinate all the Christians at Tahiti was providentially frustrated by their receiving timely notice, and being able to make their escape to Eimeo. After this, Pomare, who had also taken refuge in Eimeo, was treacherously invited to Tahiti, ostensibly to receive the submission of the hostile chiefs, but the real object was to attack and destroy the royal person and party.

The king and his adherents were engaged in public worship (it being the Lord's Day) when the firing of muskets apprised them of the advance of their enemies. Pomare quietly directed that the assembly should not leave the place till prayer had been offered, a portion of Scripture read, and a hymn sung. They then went forth to meet their foes. The idolatrous party at first appeared to gain the advantage, but received a decided check when they came to the position occupied by Mahino, the chief of Huahine, and Pomare Vahine, his heroic wife, and a faithful band of the king's adherents. The leader of the insurgents was killed, their ranks were thrown into disorder, and they fled in confusion. The warriors were pursued, and many taken prisoners, but were treated with clemency, and, contrary to all former usage, the property and persons of the non-combatants, and all women and children, were un-molested. This battle and the humanity that marked its close were decisive. From that day idolatry virtually ceased to exist in the island.

This important event, and the changes which rapidly followed, awakened peculiar joy among the friends of missions in England, vindicating as they did the grounds of their faith and the justness of their ex-pectations; and the marvellous revolution has afforded one of the most striking instances of the power of the

Gospel, and the efficacy of the simple preaching of the Cross, which the world has seen in modern times.

Among those who entered on this interesting field of Christian philanthropy at this juncture, no one has perhaps been more active or more honoured, than the missionary whose career the reader is invited to peruse in the following pages. Personally engaged in at least three different fields of missionary labour, associated in his official capacity as Secretary of the London Missionary Society with the mission work of the world, and instrumental by his writings, in a greater degree, perhaps, than any other man, in commending the subject to the favourable notice of men of culture and social position, his life can hardly fail to be instructive, and the Church will naturally expect some record of his work.

EARLY LIFE

1794–1816

B

LIFE

OF

WILLIAM ELLIS.

—•◇•—

CHAPTER I.

EARLY LIFE.

VERY LITTLE INFORMATION can now be obtained respecting the childhood and youth of WILLIAM ELLIS; but enough is known to show that, far from starting with all the favouring influences of great antecedents and liberal training, he achieved his success in spite of early disadvantages of no ordinary kind. His parents were poor and in the humbler walks of life. His father was born in Norwich, and came to London when a young man to work at his trade. His mother, whose maiden name was Bedborough, about the same time left her native place, Reading, for a situation in London, where the acquaintance between the two was formed, and they were married at St. James's Church, Clerkenwell, on the 13th of August, 1792.

Of the character of William Ellis senior it is enough to say that, though comparatively illiterate, he was a man of considerable natural powers of mind, great shrewdness, and much ready humour, with a genial and sociable disposition which, added to the possession of a good voice and some skill in singing, made him popular among those of his own class, to whom, both in ability and information, he was generally superior. When work was to be had he was industrious and steady; and although the temptations to the indulgence of a vice so common and seductive must have been great, he does not appear ever to have been intemperate. He was an affectionate parent, and always especially fond and proud of his eldest son. With regard to his religious belief, he seems to have been brought up in what he calls the 'orthodox faith' and 'popular notions of Christianity;' but soon after his marriage he embraced Unitarian doctrines, and upon his subsequent removal to Wisbeach became, to use his own expression, even more '*advanced*' and '*liberal*' in his opinions.

The mother, with a fine person but a frame by no means robust, was distinguished by great tenderness and sensitiveness of spirit, easily depressed and prone to despondency, which ill fitted her to bear up against trouble, or to endure the inevitable hardships of poverty. Her gentleness of disposition, however, and her blameless life gained her many friends, and she continued up to her last days to be very much respected by all who knew her.

During their stay in London the newly-married couple lived in a small tenement in Charles Street, Long Acre. The first child born in this humble household (May 29th, 1793) was a son, who received the name of William. His span of life, however, was very brief, for he died on the 3rd of December in the same year. On the 29th of August following (1794) a second son, the subject of this memoir, was born, and was also named after his father—WILLIAM ELLIS—a name that the Christian church 'will not willingly let die.'

For two or three years after the birth of this son business was prosperous and the circumstances of the parents were comfortable. Then came a decline in the demand for the special manufacture in which the young man was engaged, and a consequent reduction in the amount of wages that could be earned. This state of things was followed by a 'strike' among the 'hands,' and great pressure was brought to bear upon the young journeyman by his fellow-workmen to induce him to enlist as a soldier; but the claims of wife and child were too strong, and he was too faithful to desert them. At this juncture, towards the close of the year 1797, and shortly before the birth of a daughter, an advertisement from a. Mr. Shinfield, of Wisbeach, for workmen in the same line of business came under his notice, was answered, and led to an engagement in that town, which was to be the future home of the family, and was to become closely identified with him whose career will form the chief subject of the following pages. The father at once repaired to his new scene of labour, and the mother, accompanied by her son and infant daughter, followed as soon after her confinement as her recovered strength would permit.

The house in Wisbeach which they now occupied and continued to make their home for many subsequent years was situated at the corner of a small street close by what was then called the Horse Market, and at the back of the residence of Mr. Steed Girdlestone, a gentleman who proved himself a kind friend to the family. In about two years after this change of residence, the business of the new employer also began to decline, and the engagement came to an end. It now seemed necessary to try some other occupation, and abandoning very willingly a brief and unsuccessful experiment to establish a small independent business, the perplexed and discouraged parent was glad to accept employment in the candle manufactory of Mr. Usill. In this situation he remained for many years, indeed until after the return of his eldest son from the South Seas; but though thus provided with the means of subsistence, his earnings were but scanty, provisions were often dear, and as the family increased, and the health of the mother frequently failed, the household was debarred from many comforts, the children had but few opportunities of education, were early inured to toil, and became familiar with the inevitable ills attendant on straitened circumstances.

Such was the introduction to life 'with all its woes' which constituted the missionary's early training for future usefulness. In this school he learned to be helpful, unselfish, and self-reliant. His little hands early ministered to the support of his ·parents, and took their full part in the care of the younger members of the family. It is related of him that when scarcely more than six years old he was employed, at the rate of two shillings a week, probably at the candle factory, in winding cotton wicks with one hand, while with the other he nursed his little brother, thus relieving his mother of a portion of her task, and adding his mite to the family earnings. The traits of an observant and thoughtful mind were also very early conspicuous in him. A love of plants was always a marked feature in his character. When a mere child one of his chief delights was carefully to preserve every seed he could obtain, and sow it in the tiny plot of ground that served as a garden, adjoining the house. Some pet of this kind was nearly always the object of his interest and care. He has himself mentioned a reminiscence of this tender age, which made a strong and lasting impression upon him. 'I remember,' he said, 'sitting one day on a bank in our garden (situated on the north side of Upper Hill Street), with a fine, sweet, rosy-cheeked apple in my hand, and that, as I cut it, I observed the pips inside, and wondered what they were for. I asked the question, and was told that from them the apple trees came. Not satisfied by merely hearing this, I took the pips and secretly planted them, placing sticks above them, and watched for nearly half a year, but they never came up. The desire to know was raised; I felt a strong wish to work in a nursery garden, so that I might learn the secrets of the growth of plants. At length my longing was gratified, and I obtained a place in an orchard, beyond Mount Pleasant Bank, past what was called "Osborne's Foot Fields." There I felt delight in watching the developments of nature, and was

not satisfied till I had stayed out a year, and seen the whole
process—the bud, the flower, the fruit.   Then I aspired to learn
about plants less familiar, the vine, the peach, the nectarine,
and left for another place that I might follow up the study.'

This step in advance did not take place till after his twelfth
year.   Meanwhile the demands upon his services to eke out
the resources of the household, and the limited means at their
disposal, interfered very much with any regular instruction
at school.   The only teaching of the kind which the youth
seems to have enjoyed was attendance for a very short time,
and much interrupted, at a small school kept by Mr. Wright,
the Unitarian minister of whose congregation the family were
members.   It is needless to add that the religious instruction
received here, as well as at home, was in conformity with the
Unitarian creed.   The boy's mind, notwithstanding these limited
appliances, was busily storing information, gathered by a ready
and keen observation, a retentive memory, and a bright intelligence, alive to all that came within its ken, and quickened by
the perusal of any books that fell in his way.   Books of travel
and adventure especially had a wonderful fascination for him.

In an address delivered before the members of the 'Working
Men's Institute,' at Wisbeach, not many years before his death,
he thus refers to the period of his life now passing under review.
' I had not the honour of being born in Wisbeach, but I came
here when about four years old, towards the close of the last
century.   Here my early childhood and early youth were passed,
and here were first quickened and unfolded those latent tenden-
cies of mind and heart, which have shaped the channel of many
of my thoughts, and furnished a large amount of the enjoyment
of my life.   Not a hundred yards from this place, I first became
conscious of that deep interest in those wonderful processes of
nature, by which the germinating seed forces up the blade, the
ear, and the full grown corn in the ear, until the valleys are
covered over with grain.   Here began, when I was scarcely five
years old, that strong desire to understand the processes of

vegetable life, and that unspeakable pleasure in meeting with
new, rare, and beautiful forms of plants, flowers, and fruit, which
through all the intervening changes of life, have been to me a
source of pure, unmingled thankfulness and pleasure. An aged
couple lived next door to my parents' dwelling. They were
intelligent, kind, and in comfortable circumstances. They
bestowed on me much friendly notice and many kind attentions.
One of these was the loan of a little book, containing the wonderful account of four or five Christians, who were slaves of the
Turks or Moors. I went to school at the regular school-hours,
but was so deeply immersed in that book that I never parted
with it till I had read it through. This was the first time I
had ever felt interest in persons and things that I had never
seen—the first time that I had ever felt sympathy with any
beyond those immediately around me. Whilst reading I was
in mind in another country, identified with another people,
living in another world. The impression of this book, though
I have never seen it since, and the feelings it excited, have been
in kind among the deepest and strongest I have ever known.
All this class of feeling I first experienced at Wisbeach.

'Not long after this, my father allowed me in an evening
to look over the pictures in " Captain Cook's Voyages." That
opened indeed a new world, and gave me ideas of other lands,
and other races of men, and invested them with an interest which
began in Wisbeach, but which I have never ceased to feel; and
when, twenty years after, I stood upon the rock on which Captain
Cook fell, the picture I had gazed upon at Wisbeach, was as
distinct in my memory as when I first beheld it, and peopled
the scene of that mournful tragedy with the actors and the acts
of that memorable day.'

The opportunities of attending school, slight as they were,
did not long continue, for before he was twelve years old he went
to work, as already intimated, with a market-gardener, Mark
Bristow, who lived in the neighbourhood. This was in the
month of May, 1806. During a visit to Wisbeach many years

afterwards, in company with his youngest sister and niece, passing by the nurseryman's orchard gate, he observed, 'It was
here I received my first sixpence for myself (what I had earned
before went into the common stock); the money was given me
for holding a gentleman's horse, and I spent it in the purchase
of a small second-hand book of travels. I well remember two
things in connection with this incident—the ambition of independence it awakened, and the strong desire to travel which it
stirred within me.' It is probable that from that time he
never cost his father a penny. Indeed, he did not cease to
contribute regularly from his small earnings to the support of
the rest of the family, the only indulgence that he seems to have
allowed himself being the occasional purchase of a coveted book.

In his first situation he remained for more than a year, when
an opportunity was presented of obtaining a better place.
During his engagement with Mark Bristow he still made his
father's house his home, and was occasionally employed by their
kind neighbour, Mr. Steed Girdlestone, in errands and light
services about the house. That gentleman's daughter-in-law,
the wife of the clergyman of Thorney Abbey, was struck with
the youth's bright intelligence and cheerful and active habits,
and observing, 'That's a shrewd, handy lad—*we* want just such
a young boy at home'—made inquiry concerning him, and
very soon arranged that he should live with them at Thorney.
This village is about sixteen miles from Wisbeach; and thither
the youth was transferred, walking, in company with his father,
to his new place one bright February morning in 1808. He
was light of heart, and little burdened with worldly goods, for
he carried his small stock in a bundle hung from a stick over
his shoulder. In the worthy clergyman's establishment he
enjoyed many advantages, became a favourite in the family,
and won the regard of his master, who long continued to take
an interest in his fortunes; and when his young *protégé* was
afterwards engaged in far different scenes amid the South Sea
Islands, kept up with him an affectionate correspondence.

Not the least among the benefits connected with this change was the altered character of the religious teaching that he now received; and which, doubtless, however slightly it might seem at the time to affect him, was not without its influence on his mind. Referring to this period, in a letter subsequently written to the church at Kingsland, he says—'Before I was thirteen years old, Providence directed me to a church minister's family, in which I lived for three years. His preaching I found very different from the religious instruction to which I had listened at home; but I did not trouble myself much about religion at that time. I thought it was too soon to begin to be over-righteous. I used sometimes to read my Bible on a Sunday evening, and thought myself very dutiful to God; for I went to church once a week, and did not commit half so many sins as some I knew. I did not swear, nor lie, nor steal; so I thought I was safe for the present, always intending to repent and do better before I died; and if I should die suddenly, I thought I should be as well off as many others.'

Another friend who took a lively interest in young William Ellis, was Dr. Hardwicke, a physician of much repute and influence in Wisbeach. Through his intervention, probably, it was arranged, after the boy had remained nearly three years with Mr. Girdlestone, that he should be removed to the service of another clergyman, Dr. Hardwicke's son, the Rev. William Hardwicke, of Outwell. He entered on the duties of this new engagement on the 11th of October, 1810. Here he was employed in much the same capacity as he had filled at Thorney, working principally in the garden, though occupied partially within doors. Mr. Hardwicke's well-furnished library was occasionally laid under contribution to supply food for the youth's eager curiosity and love of reading. The only fault that the master complained of was the studious proclivities of his new servitor—his disposition to loiter in this same library, and 'thumb the books.'

The love of gardening, amounting to a passion, which sprang up so early in the boy's heart, grew with his growth; and he could not long rest satisfied with the limited opportunities afforded at Outwell for indulging his predilection. He aspired to learn the art more thoroughly. He had heard of Mr. Bassington, a nurseryman in a large way at Kingsland, who occasionally visited Wisbeach; and, learning that he was to be in the neighbourhood, the lad came on two successive Saturdays into the town, with the purpose of seeing him and securing for himself employment in his establishment. He was disappointed in obtaining a personal interview, but prevailed upon his father to represent his wishes to Mr. Bassington, and, if possible, negotiate an engagement. The application was successful; and with a buoyant heart the young gardener, now just entering his eighteenth year, left Outwell, where he had remained twelve months, and prepared to bid adieu to his home, and to push his fortunes in a wider field. The parting from his parents and brothers and sisters was a sore trial to them all. It was with extreme reluctance that his mother, especially, gave her consent. William had been a truly dutiful son to her, and more than an elder brother to the younger members of the family. All loved him, and, young as he was, all looked up to him and relied upon him as their sure help and stay. But the necessities of the family, the advantages of the change, and the prospects of advancement it held out, were considerations too weighty to be resisted. Thus, not perhaps without some dim foreboding of the longer and wider separation that was impending, the sorrowful household suffered the ' pride of their hearts ' to go forth on his journey to the great city, followed by their simple benedictions and tenderest love.

A journey from Cambridgeshire to London in those days was a very different thing from the railway travelling of modern times; and those whose pockets were scantily furnished had often to trudge it on foot. Partly by this primitive method of migration, and partly by the aid of a lift in the carrier's waggon, the distance was traversed by the young adventurer in two days, and he reached London on the 21st of October, 1811. A few days after, he entered the service of his new employer in the well-known and extensive nurseries at Kingsland, which were almost as famous at that time as those of Paul and Son, at Cheshunt, in the present day.

This was a crisis, and a trying one, in the young man's history. Alone in a great city, freed from the restraints that had unconsciously guarded him to some extent at home, and still more benignly in the families of the clergymen with whom the last four years had been spent, and exposed to the evil example and solicitations of vicious companions, was it possible for him, undefended as he was by religious principle, to withstand the temptations that now surrounded him? This perilous period of his life—this fierce ordeal of his untried virtue—was happily but of short duration. In a letter from which a quotation has already been made, addressed to the Church at Kingsland, he thus refers to it—' I worked at Mr. Bassington's nurseries for about seven months, during which time I was rapidly hurrying down the broad road to destruction. I was under no control. I forgot God, and was led the willing captive of Satan. I eagerly mingled with all sorts of bad company. I profaned the Lord's day; and was often drawn by my companions to spend its sacred hours in the ale-house. I sometimes attended the chapel in the evening, merely to pass away the time. During all this course of sin, I often felt the stings of conscience, and in the midst of my pleasures my heart has condemned me, and told me I was rebelling against God with a high hand. But I used my utmost efforts to stifle these painful reflections, always intending to do better when I grew older.'

Through divine mercy this downward career was effectually arrested by the young man's admission into a godly family. In June 1812, he left Mr. Bassington's, and entered the service of

Mr. Sangster, an excellent and pious man, who, with his equally estimable wife, resided in Newington Green. Here he was received on the footing of a member of the household, though his chief occupation was the care of the garden. A small chamber over the coach-house was assigned to him as a sleeping room. This humble dormitory, where, at the close, and in the intervals, of the day's work, he could always be private, became invested with a special interest, as the chosen retreat of many thoughtful seasons and studious hours, for he brought with him that thirst for knowledge and love of reading which never forsook him ; and it is memorable especially as the scene of much spiritual conflict—the ' holy ground ' of his first prayer.

In the new home to which Providence had brought him, he was required to be present at family worship daily, and in accordance with the custom of his employers attended Kingsland Chapel on the Lord's day. His father very strongly urged him to hear a Unitarian minister whom he named, and to cultivate his acquaintance ; but, happily, the Unitarian church was at too great a distance, and his master's wish that the whole household should attend the same place of worship, weighed in favour of the sanctuary at Kingsland. It was little more than a month after his entrance into Mr. Sangster's family that the important event occurred, which he has himself recorded in a letter to the Rev. J. Clayton, senior, since published, in which he speaks of a sermon addressed to young persons by that good minister, at Kingsland, as having been the means of awakening religious convictions in his mind.

This impressive sermon, and its effects on the heart of the youthful hearer, are noticed both in letters written shortly after and in a private journal, of which a few fragments only have been preserved. In his first communication to the church at Kingsland, he thus recals this crisis in his life : ' I shall ever remember the first time I attempted to pray. Having retired to rest in my own chamber, I sat down to reflect on the events that had recently occurred. A secret impulse, an irresistible power, compelled me to bow my knee, and approach a throne of grace. I could say but little, scarcely more than " God be merciful to me a sinner." A few precious promises were recalled to my mind, and afforded me much consolation—" Though your sins be as scarlet, they shall be as white as snow ; and though they be red like crimson, they shall be as wool "—" Him that cometh unto me I will in no wise cast out "—" God so loved the world that He gave His only begotten Son that whosoever believeth in Him should not perish, but have everlasting life." ' In another part of the same letter he continues, ' Satan was not an idle spectator of these conflicts and reforms. He plied his suggestions to distress and deter me ; tormenting me chiefly with the fear that I should not hold out to the end. Against these discouragements I was upheld by remembering that where the Lord had begun a good work of grace in the heart, He would carry it on to perfection. God in his mercy did not suffer the enemy of my soul to harass me over much ; for my faith was weak. I have enjoyed much comfort in my attendance on the means of grace ; and when, at times, I have felt my love cold and my faith dead, I have drawn near the mercy seat in prayer, and seldom returned without being relieved of my grief, or having my spiritual strength restored. I felt a strong desire to join a church, but was long prevented by two objections. 1st. That in my unsettled state of life it would not be well to unite myself to any church, as I might at any time leave my place. 2nd. I was deterred from even disclosing my mind, from a fear lest my moral character should not correspond with my profession, and I should thus bring reproach on the cause of Christ.' By reflecting on the positive commands of the Saviour, and by taking counsel with a Christian friend, his doubts and fears and hesitation were at length overcome ; he applied for admission into Christian fellowship, and was received as a member of the church at Kingsland on the 1st of February 1814.

While these important spiritual changes were taking place in the heart of the young convert, he was not unmindful of the

claims of his nearest kindred. Throughout the whole period
of his stay in London, a frequent and affectionate correspondence was kept up with his parents and other members of the
family ; and a considerable portion of the earnings of his labour
was devoted to their relief. The letters of his father—stained
and faded leaves, eloquent of the parental heart, and of the
filial love that had treasured them with such reverent care
through all the years—continually acknowledge, in touching
terms, the dutiful and welcome aid thus afforded. They speak
of the simple joys and sorrows, privations and gains of the
humble household ; of the increase to their store in a prosperous gleaning season, of the dearness of provisions, and other
homely details. They bear witness also to the fidelity with
which the absent son, when his own soul became imbued with
the truths of the Gospel, strove to impress his new convictions
on the hearts of those at home. These efforts, and many subsequent persuasive appeals, were not without their happy fruits.
On the minds of his mother and sisters they produced a lasting
effect, the results of which, if not manifest at the time, were
conspicuous in after years. While thus solicitous for the
highest interests of his near relatives, his exertions for their
temporal advancement were constant and self-denying. He
procured for his eldest sister a situation in Newington, an
arrangement that was highly agreeable to both ; and he furnished the money to apprentice his brother to a trade. In the
month of September 1814, he cheerfully defrayed the expense
of a visit that he persuaded his father to allow his younger
brother to pay him in London. It was a time of high delight
to the three young people when they saw together many
of the sights and wonders of the metropolis. But few things
in connection with this visit remain so impressed on the
brother's memory as the spectacle of William's little chamber,
which he shared during his stay. One side of this room was
entirely occupied with shelves filled with books, all of which
had been procured out of the savings of the young gardener's

wages; this, too, in addition to so much that had been contributed from the same source to the keep of those at home.

Besides being solicitous for the welfare of his own family, it was natural for the young Christian to take his part in spreading the knowledge of the Gospel in his neighbourhood. At that time Sunday schools were not, as now, attached to almost every place of worship. On the contrary, they were a new institution; and one of the earliest ever established was in Silver Street, in connection with the church of which the Rev. E. J. Jones was pastor. In this school William Ellis became a teacher. The pastor of the church was warmly interested in the missionary enterprise, and the annual meetings of the London Missionary Society had usually been held in Silver Street Chapel; but, in consequence of the increasing numbers who now assembled on these occasions, in May 1814, the meeting was held in Surrey Chapel. The Rev. J. Campbell, the pastor of the church at Kingsland, had only a few days before arrived in London, after an absence of nearly two years spent in visiting the stations of the society in South Africa. 'His affecting account of the moral wretchedness of the Africans, their willingness to receive teachers, the prospects of usefulness which invited the labourer to the field, given with all the graphic distinctness which resulted from recent and accurate personal observation, and the glow of feeling produced by his arrival from the scenes of moral degradation which Africa presented, made a strong impression on the minds of multitudes who were present.' Many young people had their hearts stirred by these representations, and among the number was William Ellis. In the same assembly, and glowing with the same aspirations, was Mary Mercy Moor, the future partner of his lot, and the sharer of his missionary toils in the South Seas. The subsequent recitals given by Mr. Campbell in his own pulpit revived the impressions of a sermon preached there at an earlier date by a stranger, to which he refers in his first letter to the London Missionary Society, and tended to stir up and strengthen the missionary ardour of the young convert. The desire, at first confined within his own breast, but afterwards divulged to his Christian friends, was encouraged and directed by his pastor, and at length led to his making application to the society, to be employed by them as a missionary to the heathen. The following is the letter in which, with characteristic modesty and diffidence, he makes known his wishes to the Rev. George Burder, the Secretary of the Society :—

'NEWINGTON GREEN: *November* 4, 1814.

'HONOURED AND REVEREND SIR,—It is now twelve months since my mind was first deeply impressed with a desire to devote myself to the service of the Lord as a missionary to the heathen. But fearing I was not qualified for the work, and thinking myself too inexperienced to encounter the trials to which I should be exposed, I did not make my desire known until some time after, when I ventured to disclose my mind to the Rev. Mr. Burder, of Hackney, whose preaching had been particularly blessed to me during the time he preached at Kingsland Chapel. He advised me to become acquainted with some Christians at Kingsland, that they might be enabled to judge of my ability for the work. Accordingly I associated with some of the members of Mr. Campbell's church, and was admitted into church fellowship with them on the first of February last. When I saw Mr. Burder again, he advised me to consult Mr. Campbell, with whom I have conversed several times, and to whose goodness I am indebted for the chief portion of the information I have been able to obtain. He kindly gave me every necessary instruction, and told me, when I had made up my mind, to write a letter to you, stating my conversion, the difficulties that present themselves, and the encouragements that support me; to give the letter to him and he would forward it to you.

'Agreeably to the advice of my much loved pastor, under the

C

conviction of my own inability, with much reluctance, I submit to your candid perusal the following lines.

'I was but little concerned for my soul's welfare till I had nearly completed my eighteenth year, when the kind hand of Providence placed me beneath the hospitable roof where I now dwell. I soon began to think seriously about religion. About this time I went one Friday evening to hear a lecture to young persons, preached at Kingsland Chapel, by the Rev. J. Clayton, Senior, from 31st Psalm, 17th and 18th verses, 'O God, Thou hast taught me from my youth!' &c. And there, while the preacher spoke to my outward ear, the Lord spoke to my heart, and so convinced me of the folly and ingratitude of devoting all the prime of life to the service of the world and the devil, that the impression will never be erased from my mind. I trust from that time I have been enabled to cleave to the Lord with purpose of heart. I shall ever remember the first time I attempted to pray. Having retired to my chamber, I sat down to survey the goodness of God towards so unworthy a creature as myself. A secret power constrained me to bow the knee with thankfulness to God for his unmerited goodness. I saw myself a guilty sinner, exposed to the wrath of a just and holy God, and earnestly sought an interest in the Saviour, who appeared exceedingly precious; and I thought, if I could but believe that He died for me, and that my sins were forgiven through His atonement, I should care for nothing else but to live to His glory, and to show forth His praise by a life and conversation according with the gospel.

'I had not long enjoyed the pleasures of religion before I felt anxious to impart them to others, and wondered that men should be so indifferent about salvation. The first time I felt a desire to become a missionary was after hearing a sermon preached at Kingsland Chapel on the value of the soul, from Matthew 16th, 26th verse, "For what is a man profited, if he shall gain the whole world, and lose his own soul? or what shall a man give in exchange for his soul?" I then thought

that if the Lord should call me to the work, and I should be
the instrument of converting but one sinner, my labours would
be well repaid. A desire to reduce the sum of present misery
among the heathen, to preach to them the way of salvation
through a crucified Saviour, to teach them to be happy here,
and show them the way to eternal happiness hereafter—this, I
believe, is the ground of my wish to become a missionary. I
can conscientiously affirm that it is not an impatience to be
freed from anything that is irksome or unpleasant in my present
situation that induces me to offer myself as a candidate ; nor
am I influenced by any secular motives, for I am perfectly
satisfied with my present station in all respects, and have
reason to believe that I give satisfaction to my employers. I
should be unwilling to leave my present place on any other
account. But so far as I am able to judge of my own heart, I
am actuated by a spirit of obedience to what appears to me a
duty commanded by the Saviour, when He said, " Go ye into all
the world and preach the gospel to every creature." Love to
Christ and to the souls of my heathen brethren, a desire to be
useful in my day and generation, induce me to offer myself;
and to promote the glory of God, and extend the limits of the
Redeemer's kingdom, are the chief objects which I have in
view.

　' Various are the trials and difficulties that have been presented to me in contemplating this work, and the consideration
of these makes me almost ready to shrink back from my design.
But, thank God, I am enabled to say, " I can do all things
through Christ that strengtheneth me." From the promises of
God alone I derive all my encouragement, and in the strength
of Christ I hope that I trust for support under every trial I
may meet.

　' I have but little to recommend me to the Society, having
had but little education, and most of what I have learned I
have learned from observation. I have been accustomed to
work in the garden, which occupation forms the chief part of

my present employment. I received much encouragement from an article in the *Evangelical Magazine*, under the title of " Qualifications for Missionaries," after reading which I indulged a hope that, although my talents were of the lowest sort, yet I might be accepted. I now declare myself willing to follow wherever Providence may lead me.

' Hoping you will excuse all the faults, as I am ignorant of the rules for writing properly,

' I remain,

' Your humble and obedient servant,

' WILLIAM ELLIS.'

This application was followed, in due course, by a requisition to appear before the Examining Committee of the directors, an ordeal that he met with much timidity and misgiving. On being asked by Matthew Wilks where he had received his education, his reply was, ' in my bedroom,' referring to the well-stocked shelves that had struck his brother's eye, and to the many hours of study, stolen from rest, which he had spent in poring over the pages of his humble library. The result of this examination, which took place on December 7, 1814, was a unanimous recommendation to the directors for the young candidate's acceptance. Their decision was soon afterwards communicated to him, and before the end of the month he received intimation that he would probably be sent out immediately to Africa. Indeed, it was definitely settled that he should proceed forthwith to Theopolis. This arrangement was, however, subsequently revoked, and a year's preparation and training in England were allowed, while his destination was changed to the South Seas. There can be no doubt that this delay, and the opportunity of instruction thus afforded, were of incalculable benefit, and vastly increased the missionary's future usefulness.

It is somewhat remarkable that a similar change of destination was afterwards made in the case of the now venerable

Robert Moffat, who, towards the close of the year 1816, was just on the eve of starting with John Williams for the South Seas, when the directors decided to send him to South Africa—a field of labour where the veteran's subsequent career of Christian philanthrophy presented many striking parallels to that of the enterprising pioneer and explorer of the islands of the Pacific.

Returning to the subject of these memoirs; one of his first trials at this period arose from the reluctance with which his parents consented to part with him. This very natural opposition did not spring solely from parental affection. The pain of separation, to use his father's words, from ' a son so dutiful, so good, and so loving,' was greatly aggravated by the religious views of the parent, who looked upon the mission as a fool's errand, at the best, and open, moreover, to the graver charge of being a wild and infatuated scheme to propagate error among a distant people, who were much better let alone. The old man was a philosopher, nevertheless, and finding the task of dissuasion hopeless, prepared to summon his fortitude to bear the inevitable parting. The mother's trial was a still harder one; but she too learned to school her grief. Her distress was not embittered by any element of reproach, and from the depths of a loving heart she could only follow her beloved with her blessing and her prayers. This amiable woman's extreme fondness for her son may be inferred from a remark he once made to his youngest sister. ' I am afraid,' he said, ' you are like your mother in one thing, in which I do not wish you to resemble her,—you idolize me.' There was not one member of the family, old enough to appreciate the change, who did not share in the common sorrow. William Ellis felt all the pain he was giving; but he was not then, nor was he ever afterwards, a man to be swayed by feeling when the path of duty seemed plain before him.

The gardener's vocation was now to be exchanged for that of the student. With a heart grateful for all the kindness he had received, the young man left the hospitable roof of Mr. Sangster, to pursue his studies at Gosport, under the care of Dr. Bogue. Here he diligently improved his time and opportunities in qualifying himself for the work of the ministry ; yet little more than four months were allowed for this preparatory work. In the month of May 1815, he returned to London, to apply himself to the acquisition of some branches of practical knowledge that were justly deemed essential to his efficiency in the field of labour for which he was preparing. The amount of information and practical skill that he succeeded in acquiring during the few months that remained before his departure from England, is truly amazing. During this brief interval of only six months he made himself acquainted with the art of printing, and became expert in all its processes, from type-setting to imposing the forms and working the press. He also learned the art of book-binding. For some months he, moreover, attended lectures in several branches of medicine and surgery, as well as the medical and surgical practice at St. Bartholomew's Hospital. Nor was scholastic learning entirely laid aside, some portion of the time being spent at Homerton Academy, where, under Dr. Pye Smith, the foundation, at least, was laid for the study of the classics. In fact, he omitted no opportunity of adding to his stores of knowledge. Among the minor diversions of this busy season, he procured a few lithograph copies, and gave some attention to the art of drawing, for which he had a natural aptitude, and which he often turned to good account. From a friend he took occasional lessons in playing the flute, and afterwards made the slight musical skill he thus acquired subservient to the purpose of teaching singing to his South Sea converts and pupils.

An interest of another kind, very nearly affecting the young man's future happiness and usefulness, was at this period the source of much solicitude. During the previous year, while a teacher in Silver Street Sunday School, he had made the acquaintance of Miss Moor, who had been one of the earliest scholars,

and subsequently a teacher, in the same school, and whose heart
had long been filled with an earnest desire to engage in missionary work. An acquaintance formed under these circumstances
naturally ripened into the closest intimacy, and it was with this
amiable and heavenly-minded companion as the partner of his
life and labours, that the young missionary was looking forward
to his distant embassy among the heathen. They were permitted,
indeed, to share together the toils and honours of many eventful
years ; but the early history of Miss Moor had been very
different from that which has been narrated in the foregoing
pages. Mary Moor was the descendant of a godly ancestry.
' Her father, Mr. Alexander Moor, was born near Perth, in
Scotland, and was the child of pious parents. The Rev. Joseph
Hart (who, according to the narrative he has published, " was
born of believing parents"), the minister of Jewin Street Chapel,
and author of a volume of devotional hymns, some of which are
familiar to the Christian Church at the present day, was her
maternal grandfather; her mother, Mary Mercy, being his
youngest daughter. Her parents had not only descended from
Christian ancestors, but were themselves eminently pious.' When
she was scarcely three months old, her father died. Nor was
she favoured long to enjoy the mother's care and example ; for
before the daughter had completed her eighth year, her surviving parent was also removed by death. The orphan was now
committed to the guardianship of a kind and pious friend, who
received her as her own child, and supplied, as far as possible,
the loss she had sustained. In the house of this excellent lady,
who kept a school, she received her own education, and afterwards a training for future usefulness as a teacher. Her
religious impressions date back from her earliest childhood,
while she yet enjoyed the privilege of a mother's teaching.
She remained with her kind friend till the year 1812, when she
went to reside with her only brother. Early in 1813 she was
admitted into fellowship with the Christian Church, with which
she had been so long associated, under the pastoral care of the

Rev. E. J. Jones. Her health, which had never been very robust, was occasionally the cause of much concern to her friends, and during the spring of 1815 her illness became at times alarming. This was, for a season, a source of deep anxiety and severe affliction to him who was to be the partner of her life. Her health was, however, mercifully restored, and the painful apprehensions of friends were removed.

The few pages of a private diary, kept at this period that have been preserved, show that while the subject of these memoirs was indefatigably qualifying himself for his future sphere of duty, his mind was undergoing much inward conflict. He was often depressed, always humble, distrustful of self, and drew all his spiritual strength, as every Christian must, from a growing dependence on divine grace. A single passage from this record of his inner life may serve to indicate the quality of his faith.

'Aug. 6, 1815.—Felt deeply humbled by taking a retrospect of the dealings of God towards me, and the manner in which I had requited His kindness. I hope I enjoyed the sweet influences of the Spirit drawing me to Jesus. Felt much fervour in prayer, and trust I was enabled to draw nigh to God in truth. Oh that His Spirit may keep me near to Him in the observance of His will, and keep Christ near to my heart in love; that daily living upon Him, I may be better prepared for the work I have in view; for which I feel myself unfit, and often fear that when I get into a heathen land I shall make shipwreck of faith and a good conscience. "Hold thou me up, O Lord, and I shall be safe."'

The arduous labours of the week did not prevent him from being still a diligent Sunday-school teacher, and he often found pleasure in addressing the children. His first public address in the presence of adults is thus noticed in his journal.

'Lord's Day, Oct. 15th, 1815.—After having been confined to my room by illness for nearly three weeks, I was once more permitted, by the mercy of God, to attend divine worship

in the morning, and heard Mr. Parsons, of Leeds, preach in the
Tabernacle. In the afternoon went to instruct the children
in the brickfields near Newington. Afterwards addressed the
children and their parents, from Exodus i. 14,—" And they
made their lives bitter with hard bondage," &c. This was
the first time I ever addressed an adult congregation. Felt
peculiar pleasure in this opportunity, though much confused.'

On the 6th of November he left Homerton, to make immediate preparation for his departure from England. On the
8th he was ordained to the ministry, with a fellow-student
and fellow-labourer in the missionary field, L. E. Threlkeld, in
Mr. Leifchild's chapel at Kensington. On this occasion the
pastor of the church gave the introductory address ; the
imposition of hands and the ordination prayer were assigned
to Dr. Waugh, who commended the young men to God with
much fervour ; and an impressive charge was delivered to the
newly ordained ministers by the Rev. John Hyatt, from Acts
xv. 22,—' None of these things move me.'

On the following day, November 9th, William Ellis and
Mary Mercy Moor were united in marriage at St. Luke's
Church, Middlesex. The brief interval before leaving London
for Gosport, where the missionaries were to embark, was spent
in bidding adieu to friends, and receiving farewell benedictions
from the churches at Kingsland and Silver Street, and from
their fellow teachers in the Sunday School. It was a season
of severe trial, and called for the exercise of all their Christian
fortitude. On the 8th of December they parted from their
friends in London, a few of the most intimate of the number, among whom was their future fellow-labourer, Charles
Barff, bearing them company to Gracechurch Street, and bidding
them a last tearful farewell as the stage coach drove off at an
early hour in the morning. The travellers reached Gosport in
the evening. The ship that was to convey them as far as
New South Wales, on their way to their distant scene of labour,
had arrived at Spithead on the previous day, but they did not

embark till the 19th, and after being at anchor during a strong
gale of wind for two days, they returned to shore.   The
passengers were several   times during the next few weeks
required to re-embark, but, partly through the caprice of the
captain, and partly from the violence and direction of the
wind, the vessel did not finally set sail till the 23rd of January
1816.   This trying detention was somewhat alleviated by
the opportunity it afforded of renewed intercourse with their
kind and esteemed instructor, Dr. Bogue, and other Christian
friends.

SOUTH SEAS

1816–25

CHAPTER II.

THE incidents of the voyage, and the history of subsequent missionary operations in the South Seas, have been narrated by Mr. Ellis in the volumes which he published after his return to England, under the title of 'Polynesian Researches.' In this interesting record he says :—

'It was the morning of the Sabbath when we embarked. Our friends in Gosport were preparing to attend public worship, when we heard the report of a signal-gun. The sound excited a train of feeling, which can be understood only by those who have been placed in similar circumstances. It was a report announcing the arrival of that moment which was to separate, perhaps for ever, from home and all its endearments, and rend asunder every band which friendship and affection had entwined around the heart. The report we had heard might have proceeded from some other vessel; we hastened, therefore, to the windows, which commanded an extensive view of the sea, and, looking towards the anchorage, saw the small cloud of smoke rising up among the rigging, and the signal for sailing flying from the mast of our vessel. Instead of proceeding to the place of worship, we directed our steps towards the sea-shore; but, before we left our dwelling, we united in prayer with our friends, and were by them affectionately committed to the guardian care of Him, in obedience to whose sacred injunction, "Go teach all nations," we were about to embark; and on whose protection and blessing alone we depended for safety and success. A number of kind friends attended us to the beach, where, after waiting a few moments, we bade them farewell, and then raised the last foot from that earth which was our native soil, over which we had often trod under all the varied emotions of our earliest and maturer years, but which we never expected to tread again.'

Among the group who walked to the shore were three young men, Messrs. Ince, Mault, and Wilson, who had been fellow-students at Gosport, and were expecting shortly to leave their native country on a similar errand of mercy. These took their seats in the boat, and accompanied their departing friends to the ship. Snow was falling, and the gloom of winter lent the sadness of Nature to the mournful hour, as the little party made their way to the vessel's side ; where, with indescribable emotions, they bade each other a last farewell. Some further delay was experienced ; and it was the Tuesday following when the vessel weighed anchor.

'Towards evening,' continues the narrator of the parting scene, ' I left the cabin for the deck, and enjoyed an hour of solemn, and, I trust, profitable meditation. Our ship was now under way, and proceeding steadily, though not rapidly, through the water. Every headland we passed on the Isle of Wight, and every point of land on the Hampshire coast, as it receded from my view, produced the impression that I should never behold it again. I lingered with intensity of feeling on each passing scene, until the shadows of night gathered thickly around, and the only objects visible from the ship were a few distant lights, glimmering amidst the darkness in which everything besides was concealed. After gazing on these lights until a late hour, I directed, as I supposed, a last glance towards them, and the coasts they illuminated, and retired to rest.

' The next morning I hastened on deck, and looking abroad upon the expanse of waters, distinguished with delight a point of land. It was England : my eye rested on it with strong and painful interest ; the mighty waters, like those of the deluge, appeared to rise higher and higher ; until, at last, the waves of the distant and naked horizon appeared to have rolled over it ;

and our vessel, like the ark, seemed all that remained to us of the terrestrial world. In every direction there was nothing now to be seen but one wide waste of water below and the outstretched heavens above. England, with all its associations and enjoyments, its tenderest earthly ties, and its distinguished religious privileges, had vanished.'

No discouragement, however, no regret, mingled with these emotions of sadness; but with unabated ardour, and in dependence on divine help, the missionaries looked forward to their future work. The vessel in which their passage had been taken was a government transport ship that was conveying a number of convicts to New South Wales. The insubordination of these men, creating a constant apprehension of mutiny, with the rude and unmanly conduct of the commander, Captain Mereton, rendered their voyage more than ordinarily trying, especially to the female passengers, towards whom he behaved with marked incivility and cruelty. The food provided was often insufficient in quantity, of the coarsest kind, and sometimes quite unfit to be eaten ; the meat consisting, on more than one occasion, of the flesh of sheep that had died of disease or starvation. So offensive was this man's behaviour during the latter part of the voyage, that Mrs. Ellis was obliged to absent herself altogether from the Captain's table ; and but for the kindness of their fellow-passengers, Mr. and Mrs. Howe, who spared some of their own provisions, and to the utmost of their power contributed to the comfort of their less fortunate companions, their situation would have been still more deplorable. To warn others from a similar fate, and to prevent a repetition of treatment so outrageous, Mr. Ellis felt it his duty, on their arrival at Sydney, to lodge a formal complaint against Captain Mereton, with the Rev. S. Marsden, both in his capacity of Justice of the Peace, and as the agent of the Missionary Society.

With the exception of these discomforts, the passage, though tedious, was not unfavourable. About three weeks after leaving

Portsmouth, the vessel touched at Madeira, and, proceeding on its voyage to Rio Janeiro, cast anchor at the mouth of its beautiful harbour on the evening of the 20th of March. The scene disclosed by the light of the following morning made an indelible impression on the mind of Mr. Ellis. Many years after, when he had visited every quarter of the globe, and beheld some of the fairest spots in the world, being asked which he considered the most beautiful place he had ever seen, he answered unhesitatingly ' Rio.'

Here the travellers were detained more than six weeks. Indeed, the ill-health of Mrs. Threlkeld compelled that lady and her husband to remain for many months. During their stay on shore Mr. and Mrs. Ellis were most hospitably received into the family of an English merchant, John Scurr, Esq., who resided in a delightful situation about four miles from the port. Mrs. Ellis was for a time prostrated by a severe attack of illness, of the nature of Asiatic cholera, and serious alarm was felt on her account; but, by God's mercy, she recovered and was able to resume the voyage when the vessel again set sail.

At Rio they had frequent opportunities of witnessing the observances of the Roman Catholic religion in a country where Popery is the recognised faith of the people. Some of the ceremonies they beheld were, especially to the minds of an ignorant people, sufficiently imposing. Such was the torch-light funeral of the Queen Dowager of Portugal, which took place shortly after their arrival. Other spectacles, however, intended to serve as the medium of religious teaching, were ludicrous in the extreme. Of this character was the hanging in effigy of Judas, of which they were spectators one morning about the time of Good Friday; and they were not a little surprised to behold the representation of the traitor ' in a fashionable coat, waistcoat, and pantaloons, with a pair of Hessian boots, and a cocked hat!' This figure, after being allowed to hang till noon, was taken down and fastened to the back of a young ox; till the animal, driven to and fro, became infuriated, dislodged its burden, and tore it to pieces with its horns and hoofs. There also, for the first time, they came in contact with slavery in some of its most revolting aspects—the slave ship and slave mart. Their hearts were deeply moved by these scenes of misery.

The missionaries, during their detention in the country, preached occasionally in the houses of some of the English merchants, who, with other Protestant families, earnestly entreated one of them to remain as their pastor; but, as each felt that his life had been consecrated to another service, the invitation was declined.

Early in May the voyagers once more embarked, and the *Atlas* set sail towards its final destination. The remainder of the passage was favourable; the Cape of Good Hope was doubled, the Indian Ocean crossed, and eleven weeks after leaving the coast of Brazil the shores of New Holland were in sight, and the vessel, with a fair wind, approached Port Jackson. But, owing to the ignorance and obstinacy of the captain, the opening was missed; and before the mistake was discovered they had passed four miles beyond the entrance. The ship once more returned on her course, and a second unsuccessful attempt was made to enter the harbour. A violent storm now came on, and exposed them to imminent peril, driving them still further from the haven. Contrary winds kept them out at sea for nearly a fortnight, till at length the tantalizing delay was ended by the aid of a pilot, whom the Governor had sent out to their assistance, and they were brought safely into port, and anchored in Sydney Cove on the 22nd of July.

Here they were kindly welcomed by the Wesleyan Missionaries, and by the Rev. S. Marsden, senior chaplain of the colony. Five months elapsed before they could meet with any conveyance to the South Sea Islands. During this interval they took up their abode at Paramatta, with the family of Mr. S. O. Hassel, one of the first missionaries to Tahiti, who with his companions had been compelled by the hostility of the natives to leave the islands, and had not since returned to the sphere of his early labours. To the newly-arrived guests, after the tedium and the uncongenial companionship of a five months' voyage, this was truly a delightful change; the renewal of Christian intercourse was peculiarly grateful; whilst their domestic happiness was enhanced, and the period of this pleasant residence at Paramatta was still further cheered and rendered memorable, by the birth of a daughter.

Not before the 10th of December could a passage to the islands be secured; when the mission family, bidding adieu to their kind friends, and committing themselves once more to the care of divine Providence, embarked in the *Queen Charlotte*, a brig belonging to James Birnie, Esq., of Sydney, and bound for the Society and Marquesas Islands. Ten days after, the vessel reached New Zealand, and entered the Bay of Islands. They remained in port about a week, enjoying pleasant intercourse with the missionaries of the Church Missionary Society, exploring the magnificent forests of the interior, and making their first acquaintance, in the persons of the natives, with heathen and savage life.

Having refilled their water casks, increased their supply of provender for the cattle and sheep that they had taken from the colony, and procured some valuable timber for building, on the 28th of December they resumed their voyage. On the 26th of January 1817, at daybreak, they came in sight of the island of Rapa. The next morning the vessel approached the shore, and sailed along the coast for some distance. Gradually the islanders came out in their canoes; and, though shy at first, were soon emboldened to climb on board, and, crowding on deck, caused considerable annoyance and trouble by a disposition to carry off whatever they could lay hands on. One powerful fellow seized a youth, and endeavoured to lift him from the deck, but the lad slipped from his assailant's clutch. He then grasped the cabin boy, and attempted to drag him off; but the sailors, coming to the rescue, compelled him to relinquish his hold. Another native would probably have been more success-ful in kidnapping a large mastiff that he fearlessly grappled, had not the animal been chained to its kennel, which was, moreover, nailed to the deck. Another sprang upon a young kitten that made its hapless appearance from below, and, leaping with it into the sea, carried it in triumph to his companions in the canoes. The captain was only by earnest entreaty restrained from firing upon the marauders; but, happily, the counsels of prudence and humanity prevailed. Orders were given to clear the ship; and with some difficulty, for the sailors were un-willing to uset heir cutlasses except in the way of menace, the lawless and turbulent visitors were driven off. The care of a merciful Providence on this occasion was thankfully acknow-ledged by the missionaries, in the preservation of their infant daughter, who just before the savages came on board had been playing on deck with its nurse; but was securely asleep in the cabin when the intruders made their sudden attempts to lay violent hands on whatever caught their eye or took their fancy.

The island of Rapa has since received the Gospel through the agency of native evangelists from Tahiti.

On the 3rd of February the voyagers sighted the island of Tabuai—the first retreat of the mutinous crew of the *Bounty*, who afterwards settled in Pitcairn's Island; and the first of the isles of the Pacific that had gladdened the sight of the messen-gers of mercy who sailed in the ship *Duff*, in 1797. Leaving this island on the next day, the *Queen Charlotte* approached Tahiti, the high lands of which were distinctly visible on the 10th of the month.

The circumstances of the South Sea Mission, at this inte-resting period, were peculiarly encouraging. The first mission-aries, after many years of fruitless toil, had all, with the exception of two devoted men, Mr. Hayward and Mr. Nott, left the islands: some, however, subsequently had been induced, by more favourable prospects, to return; and brighter days had dawned. Their hearts were at length gladdened by the first converts to Christianity; King Pomare himself had openly renounced idolatry, had demolished the temples and burned the idols of his country; the decisive battle between the heathen and the Christian party had been fought; and, consecrated by prayer, the cause of Truth had signally triumphed. The clemency of the victors, imbued with the spirit of their new religion, astounded the vanquished, and, more potent than the arms of Pomare, completed the overthrow of idolatry. The rulers of the neighbouring islands had followed the example of the King of Tahiti; having abandoned their old superstitions, they were earnestly seeking instruction in the principles of a benigner faith. The condition of the people throughout the entire group might be fitly described in the language of the prophet, ' The isles shall wait for thy law.'

Such was the state of the island when Mr. Ellis arrived. The small band of missionaries already on the spot were residing at Eimeo, the original station in Tahiti not having then been reoccupied. His first entrance on the scene of his future labours is thus described in his own words :—

' On the morning of the 11th of February 1817, as the light of day broke upon us, we discovered that during the preceding night we had drifted to a considerable distance from the island (Tahiti); the canoes of the natives, however, soon surrounded our vessel; numbers of the people were admitted on board, and we had the long-desired satisfaction of intercourse with them through the medium of an interpreter. A good-looking native, about forty years of age, who said his name was Maine, and who came on board as a pilot, was invited to our breakfast. We had nearly finished when he took his seat at the table; yet, before tasting his food, he modestly bent his head, and, shading his brow with his hand, implored the divine blessing on the provision before him. Several of the officers were much affected at his seriousness; and though one attempted to raise a smile at his expense, it only elicited from him an expression

of compassion. To me it was the most pleasing sight I had
yet beheld, and imparted a higher zest to the enjoyment I
experienced in gazing on the island as we sailed along its
shores.

'The sea had been calm, the morning fair, the sky without a
cloud, and the lightness of the breeze had afforded us leisure
for gazing upon the varied, picturesque, and beautiful scenery
of this "Queen of the Pacific." We had beheld successively all
the diversity of hill and valley, broken or stupendous mountains, and rocky precipices, clothed with every variety of verdure, from the moss of the jutting promontories on the shore,
to the deep and rich foliage of the bread-fruit tree, the oriental
luxuriance of the tropical pandanus, or the waving plumes of
the lofty and graceful cocoa-nut groves. The scene was enlivened by the waterfall on the mountain's side, the cataract
that chafed along its rocky bed in the recesses of the ravine,
or the stream that slowly wound its way through the fertile
and cultivated valleys ; and the whole was surrounded by the
white-crested waters of the Pacific, rolling their waves of foam
in splendid majesty upon the coral reefs, or dashing in spray
against its broken shore.'

The natives, who came off from the land in their canoes,
continued to board the vessel as she approached the bay, and
long before she came to anchor crowded her deck in great numbers. Their appearance was prepossessing. In person they were of
medium height and well formed, the skin of a dark olive complexion, the countenance open and intelligent in expression ;
their manners frank and unembarrassed, yet perfectly courteous
to the strangers. Their dress was mostly of native fashion and
material, though a few wore articles of European manufacture.

The ship had not long been at anchor before Pomare sent the
captain and missionaries a present of provisions, and soon after
himself came on board. He is described as tall and almost
gigantic in stature and proportions, being at that time about
forty years of age. 'His forehead was rather prominent and

high, his eyebrows narrow, well defined, and nearly straight; his hair, which was combed back from his forehead and the sides of his face, was of a glossy black colour, slightly curled behind; his eyes were small, sometimes appearing remarkably keen, at others rather heavy; his nose was straight, and the nostrils by no means large; his lips were thick, and his chin projecting. He was arrayed in a handsome tiputa (a sort of poncho) of native manufacture.' He appeared to understand the English language to some extent, though scarcely able to speak it. After spending a short time in the cabin he went to inspect the cattle that had been brought from New South Wales, and was especially pleased with a horse which Mr. Birnie had sent as a present to the king. In the course of the afternoon an attempt was made to lower the animal into a large double canoe brought alongside to convey it on shore; but, some of the straps giving way, the poor beast slipped through the slings, and after hanging for some time by the neck and fore legs, in great peril of strangulation, fell into the water. Rising with a snort to the surface, he now swam towards the shore; but the natives, following like a shoal of porpoises, seized him by the mane and tail, and greatly impeded his progress. At length the terrified and exhausted creature gained the strand; whereupon his unwitting tormentors, with other spectators on the beach, alarmed in their turn, fled with precipitation, climbing the trees, and hiding behind rocks and bushes for security. They regained their confidence, however, when a sailor took hold of the halter and quietly led him to a tree, where he was temporarily fastened. The astonishment and delight of the islanders was unbounded when the captain next morning, having previously sent on shore the saddle and bridle, mounted the animal, and exhibited his docile and serviceable qualities as, in the Tahitian phrase, 'a man-carrying pig'—the hog being the quadruped with which the natives were most familiar, and the name serving in their limited vocabulary as the generic designation for every other four-footed beast.

Pomare was followed on board the vessel by his queen and her infant daughter, accompanied by a train of female attendants. The aspect and bearing of the women were peculiarly pleasing. They were shorter in stature and lighter in complexion than the men. They greeted the new comers with animated countenances and a remarkably winning address. Their hair was either decorated with beautiful flowers, or covered with a light and not ungraceful bonnet of plaited cocoa-nut leaves; and their dress consisted of a garment of exquisitely white native cloth, investing the person from the neck to the ankles, and fastened in a knot over the left shoulder, so as to leave the arm on that side free and exposed. The visitors remained on board till evening, when the whole party returned to their homes.

Soon after noon the next day the vessel weighed anchor, and sailed towards the neighbouring island of Eimeo.

CHAPTER III.

EIMEO.

THE entire cluster of these islands has been divided, in accordance with their natural juxtaposition, into two groups; of which the more southerly and easterly, comprehending Tahiti, Eimeo, and Sir George Saunders Islands, is called the Georgian, or, from their relation to the prevailing trade-winds, the Windward Islands. The other assemblage of isles is known as the Society Islands proper, or the Leeward group. This comprises Huahine, Raiatea, Tahaa, and Borabora, besides two or three smaller islets. They are of volcanic origin, mostly mountainous—the loftiest summit of Tahiti being 7,000 feet above the sea level—. rich in tropical verdure, and everywhere presenting a diversity of scenery unique in character and unrivalled in beauty. Each island is bordered by a reef of coral, between which and the shore the water is calm and wonderfully clear, affording secure anchorage for shipping, even when outside the protecting bulwark the sea is agitated with storms. The breaking of the surf on one of these submarine ramparts is thus graphically pictured in ' Polynesian Researches':—' The trade-wind, blowing constantly towards the shore, drives the waves with violence upon the reef, which is from five to twenty or thirty yards wide. The long rolling billows of the Pacific, extending sometimes, in one unbroken line, a mile or a mile-and-a-half along the reef, arrested by this natural barrier, often rise ten, twelve, or fourteen feet above its surface; and then, bending over it their white foaming tops, form a graceful liquid arch, glittering in the rays of a tropical sun, as if studded with brilliants. But, before the eye of the spectator can follow the splendid aqueous gallery which they appear to have reared, with loud and hollow roar they fall in magnificent desolation, and spread the gigantic fabric in froth and spray upon the horizontal and gently broken surface of the coral.'

Opposite the mouth of any considerable stream or river there is usually an opening in the reef, marked by the presence of one or more coral islands. The marvellous transparency of the water within the lagoons is such as clearly to reveal to the passing voyager ' the playful movements of the shoals of the small and variegated rock-fish, of every rich and glowing hue, shining in brilliant contrast with the novel and beautiful groves of many-coloured coral, that render the sandy bottom of the sea, though frequently several fathoms deep, in appearance at least, an extensive and charming submarine shrubbery, or flower garden. The corallines are seen spread out with all the endless variety and wild independence exhibited in the verdant landscape of the adjacent shore.'

In such a harbour as this—the enchanting bay of Oponohu— after a delightful sail along the northern part of Eimeo, the *Queen Charlotte* anchored on the afternoon of the 13th of February 1817, and the long voyage of the missionaries was brought to an end, nearly thirteen months after their departure from Portsmouth. The members of the mission came early on board, and cordially welcomed their new associates to the field of their future labours. The newly arrived missionaries, their hearts overflowing with thankfulness and glad anticipation, were conducted on landing to the residences of their brethren in the settlement of Papetoai, as it is called, and received the cheering and affectionate greetings of the resident English families. During the evening several of the chiefs and other natives came to deliver in person their salutations of welcome. Among the number was Auna, whose striking appearance and manner are thus described by Mr. Ellis :—' His person was tall and commanding, his hair black and curling, his eyes benignant, and his whole countenance beamed with a joy that declared his tongue only obeyed the dictates of his heart. He was a native of Raiatea, formerly an *areoi* (member of an infamous and licentious society) and a warrior, who had arrived, with numbers of his countrymen, to the support of Pomare, after his expulsion from Tahiti, but whose heart had been changed by the power of the Gospel of Christ. He was afterwards associated with us at Huahine, a deacon of the first church established there, and subsequently became my fellow-labourer in the Sandwich Islands.'

The house in which the first night on shore was spent was a bird-cage sort of structure; the sides composed of slender poles or sticks, two or three inches apart, placed upright in the ground; and the roof formed of rafters meeting over a ridge-pole in the centre, and resting at the other end on a sort of wall-plate supported by posts. Over this framework was spread a thatch of leaves of the pandanus, less pervious, indeed, than the sides, but permitting the stars to be visible here and there, and by no means excluding the rain. The novelty of the situation, the excitement of recent events, and the swarms of mosquitoes that seemed always especially attracted by strangers, for a long time prevented sleep; but, notwithstanding, they rose in the morning refreshed, and employed the day in landing their goods from the vessel, and in making their temporary habitation, which they shared with Mr. and Mrs. Crooks, more convenient, by putting up screens and partitions of matting.

One of the first objects of interest claiming attention was the school, in which numbers of adults as well as children were daily instructed. Writing was taught, in the absence of slate or pencil, by tracing the characters with a pointed stick on sand spread on the floor, or contained in shallow troughs. The building, constructed, though sixty feet long, in the same slight and open manner as the ordinary dwellings, was also used as a place of worship. It stood near the sea beach, and under the shade of a clump of cocoa-nut trees. It was with no ordinary emotion that the strangers from England, on the first Lord's day after their arrival in the island, attended divine service in this humble sanctuary, and witnessed the devout demeanour and listened to the prayers and songs of a vast multitude who had but recently emerged from the darkness and bondage of the most debasing idolatry. Mr. Ellis wished to address the assembly, but was so overpowered by his feelings that he could not trust himself to speak, and retired in silence from the impressive and delightful scene.

The missionaries were all residing at Papetoai, and, pending the completion of a vessel they were building, had not divided their strength in order to reoccupy the stations at Tahiti or the other islands. But, with the present and anticipated accessions to their number, it was thought desirable that some of them at least should remove to another settlement, though they still deferred till the arrival of the expected reinforcements the occupancy of other islands. Accordingly a visit of exploration was made to Afareaitu, about twenty miles distant on the opposite side of Eimeo. This district is one of the finest in the country. 'It comprises two valleys, or rather one large valley partially divided by a narrow hilly ridge extending from the mountains in the interior towards the shore. The soil of the bottom of the valley is rich and fertile, well stocked with cocoanut and bread-fruit trees. The surrounding hills are clothed with shrubs or grass, and the lofty and romantic mountains, forming the central boundary, are adorned with trees or bushes even to their summits. Several broad cascades flowed in silvery streams down the sides of the mountains, and, broken occasionally by a jutting rock, presented their sparkling waters in beautiful contrast with the rich and dark foliage of the stately trees and the flowering shrubs that bordered their course. A number of streams originating in these waterfalls pursued their course through the valley, and one, receiving in its way the tributary waters of a number of sequestered streamlets, swelled at times into what in these islands might be called a river, and flowed along the most fertile portions of the district into the sea.

'A small bay was formed by an elliptical indentation of the coast, an opening in the reef opposite the bay admitted small vessels to enter, and a picturesque little coral island, adorned with two or three clumps of hibiscus and cocoa-nut trees, added greatly to the beauty of its appearance. There was no swamp or marshy land between the shore and the mountains; the ground was high, and the whole district not only remarkably beautiful, but apparently dry and healthy. The abundance of natural productions, the salubrity of the air, the convenience of the stream of water, and the facility of the harbour, combined to recommend it as an eligible spot for at least the temporary residence of a part of the missionaries.' Permission to establish here a mission station was gladly given by the principal chiefs, who promised, moreover, to render every assistance in the erection of the requisite buildings and dwellings.

It was arranged that three of the missionaries—Messrs. Crooks, Davis, and Ellis—with their families, should remove to the new settlement; and on the 25th of March the party left Papetoai, and, after a fatiguing journey, took up their abode on the following day in Afareaitu. Until new houses could be built, Messrs. Crooks and Ellis occupied one of the ordinary construction that had been vacated for their accommodation. The site chosen for the printing office and dwelling was beside the principal stream, and was altogether a beautiful and convenient situation. Preparations for building were at once begun, the natives lending willing hands to the work, which was rapidly pushed forward. The printing office, as the most important, was the first finished. The sides were boarded, and lighted with glass windows, a novelty in the island; while the floor was covered, partly with split planks and partly with large flattened basaltic stones, that had formed the pavement of an adjacent marae or heathen temple. The dwelling house was not completed till the 24th of July.

Among the minor inconveniences experienced by the missionaries in their new settlement, one of the earliest to be felt arose from the entire change of food, which at first somewhat affected their health. The scanty supply of wheaten flour brought from New South Wales was soon exhausted; and no wheat was grown in the islands, nor, indeed, is the climate adapted for that cereal. Maize has since been introduced, and flourishes. A number of seeds of oranges, shaddocks, limes, &c., had been left by Captains Cook and Vancouver, and have added materially to the resources of the country. Mr. Ellis brought from Rio some coffee berries, which were sown and found to thrive. He also succeeded in raising several useful English vegetables, as well as Indian corn, pine-apples, melons, water-melons, and a variety of tropical fruits, including citrons, tamarinds, Cape mulberries, grapes, and figs, which have since become valuable additions to the wealth of the islands, and a source of considerable foreign trade.

The natural products of the country, at the time when the missionaries settled in Eimeo, though it required a little use to adjust the European constitution to a tropical dietary, were both abundant and diversified. Swine, fish, and poultry furnished the chief animal food. Cattle and goats have since supplied, not only variety of meat, but the invaluable and wholesome article of milk. Of vegetable productions the bread-fruit has always been pre-eminent in these latitudes, and, indeed, may here be regarded as the ' staff of life.' In the South Sea Islands there is great variety in the kinds of this valuable fruit, ripening at different seasons, and affording sustenance during many months of the year. The missionaries are acquainted with no less than fifty varieties; but the principal are *Artocarpus incisa*, and *Artocarpus integrifolia*. The bread-fruit is not only remarkably prolific, yielding three or four crops in the year, but is a handsome, umbrageous tree, and furnishes excellent timber. Other vegetables used extensively for food are the arum, the yam (*Dioscorea alata*), the sweet potato (*Convolvulus batatas*), and the arrowroot (*Tacca pinnatifida*), besides a variety of useful and palatable roots that are less abundant or less freely consumed. The fruits of the islands also thrive in great profusion and variety. The principal are the cocoa-nut (*Cocos nucifera*), multiform in its uses, furnishing solid food, drink, oil, timber, cordage, thatch, matting, bottles, cups, &c.; the plaintain or banana (*Musa paradisaica* and *M. sapientum*), the vi, or Brazil plum, a species of spondias, the jambo (*Eugenia mallaccensis*), and sundry wholesome edibles of less note. Sugar-cane of excellent quality is also indigenous.

Simultaneously with the erection of the printing and dwelling houses, the study of the native language, under the instruction of the senior missionary, Mr. Davis, formed part of the multifarious engagements of every day. Mr. Ellis, though his residence in Eimeo was only to be temporary, employed himself also in clearing, enclosing, and cultivating a garden plot. His mechanical ingenuity was brought early into use, and, though not equal in this respect to his contemporary, John Williams, he displayed considerable skill; making in Eimeo the first wheelbarrow that had ever been seen in the island, and afterwards building a boat, in which he performed many adventurous voyages. The carpentry required in the construction of the house and furniture was likewise the work of his own hands. In fact, the life of a missionary in these remote stations had in it, barring the solitude, much of the Robinson Crusoe element, and called for like faculties of patience, tact, invention, and fertility of resource.

The building for its reception having been completed, the printing press was at length set up, and all was in readiness for beginning the important work. The few books already introduced, of which the supply was quite inadequate to the needs of the people, had been printed in England or in New South Wales; and both missionaries and natives eagerly hailed the establishment of the press on their own shores. On the 10th of June 1817 all was in readiness, and Pomare, who had come to Eimeo for the purpose of witnessing the first printing, was summoned to Afareaitu. The following graphic account of this

interesting occasion is given by the master workman on the
scene :—

'Soon after Pomare's arrival, I took the composing-stick in
my hand, and, observing the king looking with curious delight
at the new and shining types, I asked him if he would like to
put together the first A B C, or alphabet. His countenance was
lighted up with evident satisfaction, as he answered in the
affirmative. I then placed the composing-stick in his hand;
he took the capital letters, one by one, out of their respective
compartments, and, fixing them, concluded the alphabet. He
put together the small letters in the same manner, and the few
monosyllables composing the first page of the small spelling-
book were afterwards added. He was delighted when he saw
the first page complete, and appeared desirous to have it struck
off at once; but when informed that it would not be printed
till as many were composed as would fill a sheet, he requested
that he might be sent for whenever it was ready. He visited
us almost daily until the 30th, when, having received intimation that it was ready for the press, he came, attended by
only two of his favourite chiefs. They were, however, followed
by a numerous train of his attendants, who had by some means
heard that the work was about to commence. Crowds of the
natives were already collected around the door, but they made
way for him, and, after he and his two companions had been
admitted, the door was closed, and the small window next the
sea darkened, as he did not wish to be overlooked by the people
outside. The king examined, with great minuteness and pleasure, the form as it lay on the press, and prepared to take off
the first sheet ever printed in his dominions. Having been
told how it was to be done, he jocosely charged his companions
not to look very particularly at him, and not to laugh if he
should not do it right. I put the printer's ink-ball into his
hand, and directed him to strike it two or three times on the
face of the letters; this he did, and then, placing a sheet of
clean paper on the parchment, I covered it down, and, turning

it under the press, directed the king to pull the handle. He did so; and when the paper was removed from beneath the press, and the covering lifted up, the chief and attendants rushed towards it, to see what effect the king's pressure had produced. When they beheld the letters black, and large, and well defined, there was one simultaneous expression of wonder and delight.

'The king took up the sheet, and looked first at the paper and then at the types with attentive admiration, handed it to one of his chiefs, and expressed a wish to take another. He printed two more; and, while he was so engaged, the first sheet was shown to the crowd without, who, when they saw it, raised one general shout of astonishment and joy. When the king had printed three or four sheets, he examined the press in all its parts with great attention. He remained watching the printing, and admiring the facility with which so many pages were printed at one time, until it was near sunset, when he left us; taking with him the sheets he had printed to his encampment on the opposite side of the bay.

'When the benefits which the Tahitians have already derived from education, and the circulation of books, are considered, with the increasing advantages which it is presumed future generations will derive from the establishment of the press, we cannot but view the introduction of printing as an auspicious event. The 30th of June 1817 was, on this account, an important day in the annals of Eimeo; and there is no act of Pomare's life, excepting his abolition of idolatry, his clemency after the battle of Bunaïna, and his devotedness in visiting every district of the island, inducing the chiefs and people to embrace Christianity, that will be remembered with more grateful feeling than the circumstance of his printing the first page of the first book published in the South Sea Islands.'

The spelling-book, being most needed, was first printed, and an edition of 2,600 copies was soon finished. An edition of 2,300 copies of the Tahitian Catechism, and a Collection of Texts, or

Extracts, from Scripture, were next struck off; after which, St. Luke's Gospel, which had been translated by Mr. Nott, was put to press.

While this important work was in progress, the hearts of the missionaries were gladdened by the arrival of the expected accessions to their number. The first to reach the island were Mr. and Mrs. Orsmond, who were followed, later in the same year, 1817, by six more brethren with their wives. Among the latter reinforcement were Mr. and Mrs. Threlkeld, Mr. and Mrs. Barff, and Mr. and Mrs. Williams. The *Active*, in which these welcome fellow-labourers had sailed, brought also a seasonable supply of paper, sent out by the British and Foreign Bible Society. By this timely contribution an edition of 3,000 copies of St. Luke's Gospel, in addition to other publications, was soon completed. The composition and press work of all these books were performed by Mr. Ellis, with the assistance of Mr. Crooks, labouring eight, and sometimes ten, hours daily. In the meantime, however, native workmen were instructed in the most mechanical operations, and in the subsequent publications were able to relieve the missionaries of the labour of press work.

As soon as the printing was finished, the next process was binding ; and in this department of the work the missionaries' wives and the natives themselves readily lent their aid. The supply of mill-boards brought for the purpose was soon exhausted ; and the ingenuity of the missionary was taxed to provide expedients. Folds of native cloth, made from the bark of a tree, were beaten together, then submitted to the action of a powerful steam-press, and were found, when afterwards dried, to form a good stiff pasteboard. Sheep skins brought from England were cut into strips, for the backs and corners, and old newspapers stained with the juice of the mountain plantain, which yielded a rich purple dye, were used as covers for the sides. When the sheepskins had all been cut up, other materials had to be procured. 'Leather was now the article in

E

greatest requisition among all classes; and the poor animals
that had heretofore lived in undisturbed ease and freedom,
were hunted solely for their skins. The printing-office was
converted into a tanyard; old canoes, filled with lime-water,
were prepared; and all kinds of skins brought to have the
hair extracted, and the oily matters dissipated. It was quite
amusing to see goats', dogs', and cats' skins collected to be
prepared for book-covers. Sometimes they procured the tough
skin of a large dog, or an old goat, with long shaggy matted
hair and beard attached to it, or the thin skin of a wild kitten
taken in the mountains. As soon as the natives had seen how
they were prepared, which was simply by extracting the hair
and the oil, they did this at their own houses; and in walking
through the district at this period, no object was more common
than a skin stretched on a frame, and suspended on the branch
of a tree to dry in the sun.'

When the books were ready for distribution, the eagerness of
the people to possess copies knew no bounds. The inhabitants
of adjacent islands came in their canoes, and swelled the temporary population of Afareaitu, already crowded with visitors
from all parts of Eimeo; so that the district, for the time being,
had all the appearance of a densely thronged fair or carnival.

It was thought desirable not to furnish the books gratuitously;
but in order that the benefited parties might set the greater
value on their acquisitions, and not be led to expect them
on future occasions as a free gift, a small charge, in cocoa-nut
oil, was made for each copy. The people readily acquiesced in
this arrangement.

When the Gospel of St. Luke was finished, an edition of
hymns in the native language was printed, partly original, and
partly translations from the most approved English composi-
tions. These hymns became great favourites with the natives.

The process of printing gave Mr. Ellis considerable collateral
advantage in gaining a knowledge of the language. He says:
—'I found the composing, or setting of the types for the

Tahitian books the best method of acquiring all that was printed in the language. Every letter in every word passing repeatedly, not only under my eye, but through my hand, I acquired almost mechanically the orthography. The number of natives by whom we were always surrounded, afforded the best opportunities for learning the meaning of those words which we did not understand. The structure of many sentences was also acquired by the same means; and in much less than twelve months I could converse familiarly on any common subject.'

The close of the year 1817 saw the completion of the vessel that the missionaries had for some time been engaged in building, and which the mechanical skill of Mr. Williams materially forwarded. It was named, in compliment to the foremost founder of the Missionary Society, the *Haweis*, and after some accidental hindrances, was successfully launched on the 17th of December. The account of the whole transaction has been given both in Williams' ' Missionary Enterprise ' and in ' Polynesian Researches.'

While the missionaries were thus labouring assiduously in various departments of usefulness, their wives were no idle spectators of their toil; nor did they confine their attention to those necessary domestic duties which the want of help, the absence of ordinary appliances, and the heat of the · climate rendered more than commonly arduous ; but they applied themselves sedulously to learn the language, encouraged intercourse with the native women, taught them needle-work, and in various ways endeavoured to promote the improvement of those of their own sex. Mrs. Ellis undertook, besides, the instruction of Mr. Crooks' six children, and devoted several hours daily to this congenial labour of love.

Early in the year 1818, her cares and anxieties were increased by the birth of a second child, whose illness for several months, during which its life was despaired of, brought to the fond mother, not only much painful solicitude, but many weary hours of unrest and fatigue, such as her female companions, though kind and sympathising, could not relieve, for the charge of a sick infant could not be trusted to the indolent and volatile natives. The child's illness, moreover, caused frequent toilsome journeys to Papetoai, on the opposite side of the island, for medical advice.

'These journeys,' using Mr. Ellis's own picturesque description, 'were exceedingly wearisome: returning from one of them, night overtook us many miles before we reached our home; we travelled part of the way in a single canoe, but for several miles, where there was no passage between the reef and the shore, and the fragile bark was exposed without shelter to the long heavy billows of the Pacific, we proceeded along the beach, while the natives rowed the canoe upon the open sea. Two native female attendants alternately carried the child, while Mrs. Ellis and I walked on the shore, occasionally climbing over the rocks, or sinking up to our ankles in fragments of coral and sand. Wearied with our walk, we were obliged to rest before we reached the place where we expected to embark again. Mrs. Ellis, unable to walk any farther, sat down upon a rock of coral, and gave our infant the breast, while I hailed the natives, and directed them to bring the canoe over the reef and take us on board. Happily for us, the evening was fair, the moon shone brightly, and her mild beams, silvering the foliage of the shrubs that grew near the shore, and playing on the rippled and undulating waves of the ocean, added a charm to the singularity of the prospect, and enlivened the loneliness of our situation. The scene was unusually impressive. I remember distinctly my feelings as I stood, wearied with my walk, leaning on a light staff by the side of the rock on which Mrs. Ellis with our infant was sitting, and behind which our female attendants stood. On one side, the mountains of the interior, having their outline edged, as it were with silver, from the rays of the moon, rose in lofty magnificence, while the indistinct forms, and rich and diversified verdure of the shrubs and trees, increased the effect of the whole. On the other hand was the illimitable sea, rolling in solemn majesty its swelling waves over the rocks which defended the spot on which we stood. The most profound silence pervaded the whole scene, and we might have fancied we were the only beings in existence, for no sound was heard, except the gentle rustling of the leaves of the cocoa-nut tree, as the light breeze from the mountain swept through them, or the loud hollow roar of the surf, and the rolling of the foaming wave as it broke over the distant reef, and the splashing of the paddles of our canoe, as it approached the shore. It was impossible at such a season to behold this scene, exhibiting impressively the grandeur of creation, and the insignificance of man, without experiencing emotions of adoring wonder and elevated devotion, and exclaiming with the Psalmist, "When I consider thy heavens, the work of thy fingers, the moon and the stars which thou hast ordained; what is man, that thou art mindful of him, and the son of man, that thou visitest him?"

'The canoe at length reached the shore; we seated ourselves in its stern, and, advancing pleasantly along for seven or eight miles, reached our habitation about midnight.' Contrary to expectation, the health of the child soon after improved, and before they left the island, the fears of the parents on this account were in great measure relieved.

One event of considerable interest and importance signalized the closing period of their residence in Eimeo. This was the formation of the first missionary society in the islands. An extension of the principle that had dictated the propriety of inducing the people to pay for their books, led their teachers to inculcate further the duty of contributing to the support and spread of the gospel. And this end, it was thought, would be better gained, under existing circumstances, by interesting the new converts to Christianity in the work of the Society, to which they were themselves so largely indebted, than by any direct efforts towards the maintenance of the mission in their own land, the motives of which might be misunderstood, and might compromise in their estimation the disinterestedness of the teachers who laboured among them.   The scheme was fully discussed with the king and chiefs, who cordially approved of the proposal ; and the 13th of May, 1818, being the anniversary of the parent institution in England, was fixed for the establish- ment and organization of the native society.   The forenoon of the day was spent in preparatory devotional services, and the public meeting was to be held at three o'clock in the afternoon ; ' but long before the appointed hour,' Mr. Ellis tells us, ' the chapel was crowded, and a far greater number than had gained admission still remained on the outside.

'Three or four hundred yards from the chapel there was a beautiful and extensive grove.   To this spot it was proposed to adjourn, and thither the natives immediately repaired, seating themselves on the ground under the cocoa-nut trees.   At three o'clock we walked to the grove, and on entering it beheld one of the most imposing and delightful spectacles ever witnessed in the islands.   The sky was clear, the smooth surface of the ocean rippled with the cool and stirring breeze.   The grove, stately and rich in all the luxuriance of tropical verdure, ex- tended from the white beach of coral and shells to the very base of the mountains, whose gradual ascent and rocky projections led to the interior.   The long-winged and interwoven leaves of the trees formed a spreading canopy, through which a straggling sunbeam occasionally found its way, and among whose long and graceful leaflets the breeze from the ocean, sweeping softly, gave a degree of animation to the whole. The grass that grew under- neath appeared like a rich carpet, spread by nature for the interesting ceremony ; pendulous plants, some verdant in foli- age, others rich and variegated in blossom, hung from the projections of the rocks, while several species of convolvulus and climbing plants were twined round the trunks of the trees, or hung in gay festoons among the gigantic and wide-spread leaves of the grove, ornamenting the whole with their large and pink blossoms. Near one of the large cocoa-nut trees, whose cylindrical trunk appeared like a natural pillar supporting the roof, there was a rustic sort of stand, four or five feet above the ground, on which Mr. Nott took his station. Before him, in a large arm-chair provided for the occasion, sat Pomare, with the queen and principal women of the islands, and a number of chiefs seated near him ; while thousands of the natives, attired in their gay and many-coloured dresses, composed the vast assemblage, each one having come, as to a public festival, in his best apparel.'

After the singing of a hymn, the offering of prayer, and a few words of explanation by Mr. Nott, Pomare rose and addressed the assembly. He referred to their past degraded state and their present happy condition, to the efforts and claims of the Society in England, to the example of other recently evangelized portions of the world, instancing especially Africa, and concluded an animated and eloquent speech, that would have been creditable to a trained and accomplished orator, by requesting as many as desired the formation of the proposed society to hold up their right hand. ' Two or three thousand naked arms were simultaneously elevated from the multitude assembled under the cocoa-nut grove, presenting a spectacle no less imposing and affecting than it was picturesque and new. The regulations of the Society were then read, and the treasurer and secretaries chosen. By this time the shades of evening began to gather round us, and the sun was just hidden by the distant wave of the horizon, when the king rose from his chair, and the chiefs and people retired to their dwellings under feelings of high excitement and satisfaction. There was so much rural beauty and secluded quietude in the scene, and so much that was novel and striking in the appearance of the people, and momentous and delightful in the object for which they had convened, that it was altogether one of the most interesting meetings I ever attended.'

The practical results of this experiment may be inferred from the fact that the first contributions of oil sent home from these islands not long afterwards, realized more than £1,700 ; and as the British Government, with considerate liberality, remitted the duty, amounting to £200, the whole sum, without deduction, was paid into the treasury of the parent Society.

CHAPTER IV.

ПUAHINE.

THE time had now arrived when the missionaries were to disperse themselves among the principal islands of the group, and repair to the settlements in which it was expected their residence would be more permanent. It was with no light regret that Mr. Ellis and his devoted partner bade adieu to the interesting people among whom they had wrought their first missionary labours, and to the delightful scenes that for eighteen busy and eventful months had surrounded their humble but happy home. Their grief was affectionately reciprocated by the people of their charge, who saw them depart with undisguised sorrow. The newly-built ship, *The Hawies*, conveyed the party, including, besides Mr. Ellis, Messrs. Davis, Williams, and Orsmond, and their families, to their new destination. Their several household goods, the cattle, and the articles connected with the printing-press, were transported in the same conveyance. The vessel left the Bay of Oponohu on the 18th of June 1818, and anchored in Fare Harbour, in Huahine, the nearest and most easterly of the Society Islands, on the morning of the 20th.

Mr. Ellis's description of the spot where he lived during the remainder of his stay in these islands, will be read with interest in connection with the account of this portion of his missionary career.

'Here I looked abroad with new and mingled emotion on the scene in which I was to re-commence my labours. The clear sky was reflected in the unruffled waters of the bay, which was bordered with a fine beach strewed with various shells. The luxuriant convolvulus, presenting its broad and shining leaves in striking contrast with the white coral and sand, spread its vines across the beach, even to the margin of the water, over which the slender shrub or the flowering tree often extended its verdant branches, while the groves of stately-bread-fruit, and the clumps of umbrageous *callophyllum*, or tamanu trees, and the tall and gracefully-waving cocoa-nuts, shaded the different parts of the shore.

'The district of Fare, bordering the harbour of the same name, is about a mile and a half or two miles in length, and reaches from the shore to the centre of the island. It is bounded on the south by a range of mountains, and on the north by a slightly elevated tract of country, whence a long, bleak point of land, extending a considerable distance into the sea, and covered with tall cocoa-nut trees, adds much to the beauty of the shore and the security of the harbour. A ridge of inferior hills divides the district in the centre, and greatly increases the picturesque appearance of its scenery. A small river rises on the northern side of this ridge, and flowing along the boundary between the two districts, meets the sea exactly opposite the northern entrance. Another stream, more broad and rapid, rises at the head of the principal valley, and flows in a circuitous course to the southern part of the bay. The country is well watered and wooded. The lower hills, at the time of our arrival, were clothed with verdure, and the mountains in the centre of the island, whose summits appeared to pierce the clouds, were often entirely covered with trees. All was rich and luxuriant in vegetation, but it was the richness and luxuriance of a wilderness.' A few scattered huts were the only human habitations to be seen.

The first business of the missionaries on landing was to obtain a temporary lodging; and a house, or rather shed—for it was nothing more than a roof supported on posts—was given up to them by the young chief of the island, the son of

Mahine. Their goods having been landed from the vessel were conveyed to this place of shelter, which stood within ten or twelve yards of the sea, the floor being composed of stones, sand, and clay. Here, as soon as the packages were placed under cover, 'we sat down to rest, and could not avoid gazing on the scenes around us, before we began to adjust our luggage. Large fragments of rock were scattered at the base of the mountains that rose on one side of our dwelling, the sea rolled within a few yards on the other, and in each direction along the shore there was one wild and uncultivated wilderness. A pair of cattle that we had brought from New South Wales, with a young calf, were tied to an adjacent bread-fruit tree; two or three milch goats from Eimeo, fastened together by bands of hibiscus bark tied round their horns, had already taken their station on the craggy projections at the foot of the mountain, and were cropping the herbage that grew in the fissures of the rocks. One of our little ones was smiling in the lap of its native nurse, while the other was playing on the dried grass lying by the side of the boxes on which we were sitting; and the natives, under the influence of highly excited curiosity, thronged around us in such numbers as to impede the circulation of the air.

' Our first effort was to prepare some refreshment. The chiefs had sent us a present of bread-fruit and fish. A native youth, fourteen or fifteen years of age, leaving the crowd, came forward and asked if he should cook us some bread-fruit. We accepted his offer: he became a faithful servant, and continued with us till we removed from the islands. He fixed two large stones in the ground for a fire-place, and bringing a bundle of dry sticks from the adjacent bushes, lighted a fire between the stones, upon which he placed the tea-kettle. While he was employed in dressing our bread-fruit &c., we removed some of the boxes, piled up our luggage as compactly as we could, and, when the food was prepared, sat down to a pleasant repast of fried fish, bread-fruit, and plantains, cocoa-nut milk, and tea. As a beverage we always preferred the latter, although the former is exceedingly pleasant.'

By the time the meal was finished the shadow of the neighbouring mountains of Raiatea was thrown across the valley, and admonished the occupants of the bivouac to prepare their sleeping-place. Screens of native cloth stretched on poles driven into the ground, afforded some privacy at least, if but indifferent shelter, and the beds were spread on boxes. 'We procured,' to continue the autobiography, 'cocoa-nut oil, and when it grew dark, breaking a cocoa-nut in half, took one end and winding a little cotton-wool round the thin stalk of the leaflet of the tree, fixed it erect in the kernel of the nut. This we filled with the oil; and thus our lamp and oil were entirely the production of the cocoa-nut tree; the small piece of cotton-wick gathered from the garden in Eimeo being the only article it had not supplied. These were the only kind of lamps we had for some years, and though rude in appearance gave a good light, when kept steady and sheltered from the wind.'

Such was the introduction to the new scene of labour. The inhabitants of Huahine not having enjoyed the presence of missionaries amongst them, were at this time far behind those of Eimeo. None of them could read, and though the ancient idolatry of the country had been abandoned, and Christianity nominally accepted as the religion of the land, very little was understood of its distinctive principles or moral obligations; and the missionaries had to lay the foundation of their teaching in the simplest elements of religion and general knowledge. The chief of the island was Mahine, a man of decision, courage, remarkable intelligence, and benevolent disposition, who became one of the earliest and most consistent converts to Christianity, and continued throughout the steady friend of the mission.

The selection of a spot for the erection of a printing office and dwelling was no difficult matter, when nearly the whole district was open to their choice. A site was appropriated on a small elevation near the junction of two clear and rapid streamlets, about a quarter of a mile from the entrance of the valley. The residence of Mr. Barff was on the opposite side of the valley. The frame of the building was much the same as those at Afareaitu, but more substantial, and the whole was more carefully finished. Floors were laid of bread-fruit planks, the outer walls and partitions were wattled and plastered with coral lime, and glazed windows were introduced into all the rooms. When finished, the dwelling-house was found most comfortable, and furnished a model for a new style of architecture in the islands, which has since entirely superseded the old birdcage huts. A garden was, of course, cleared and enclosed. A group of stately chestnut trees that grew on the banks of the stream were left, as well as several bread-fruit trees, to shade and adorn the homestead. Place was found for the newly-introduced plants and flowers, in addition to the most useful or beautiful indigenous productions of the soil. Orange trees were planted in front of the house, and a citron hedge enclosed the whole. The writer, though scarcely five years old when removed from this home of his childhood, retains in his memory an indelible picture of the charming scene—the opposite house, with the group issuing from it on the Lord's Day to meet the worshippers in the chapel on the shore ; the mountains, the beach, and the characteristic vegetation of the region, the plumed and towering cocoa-nut, the spreading loaded bread-fruit, and the gigantic-leaved banana; the bay with its liquid crystal, the magnificent ocean beyond, and the mountains of Raiatea, like shadowy cloud-land on the horizon.

The advantages of a garden, and the comfort of a more commodious dwelling, were not the only inducements to the introduction of these improvements. One great obstacle to the instruction and advancement of the islanders was their natural indolence ; and to overcome this their teachers had recourse to the stimulus of example or rivalry, and the creation of artificial wants, which should furnish new objects of ambition and new motives for industry. Nor did they miscalculate the influence of these innovations. First the chiefs, then one and another of the people, adopted the more refined order of living. Plastered houses, neat gardens and cultivated fields became general, and altered most favourably the appearance of the district, and even the character of the inhabitants. With the same object in view, the missionaries' wives, while keeping always foremost in their lessons the great truths of religion, besides instructing their own sex in reading and spelling, taught them the use of the needle and the art of plaiting, for which suitable materials were abundant in natural grasses, rushes, and leaves. Hats and bonnets, first worn by the new settlers and their families, were soon adopted by the natives ; and, as in process of time intercourse with civilised countries became more frequent, and cotton was grown and manufactured in their own land, the European dress displaced to a great extent the perishable though picturesque costume of heathen times.

These were the secondary, the adventitious, results of missionary effort among the people. The grand object in view, the introduction of the gospel, was prosecuted with most encouraging success. Public worship was established, the large dwelling and premises formerly owned by the far-famed Mai (Omai), having been set apart as a chapel and schoolroom, until a more commodious place of worship should be built. The observance of the Lord's Day was most exemplary ; while daily private and family devotion became general throughout the island. With many, of course, these changes were merely the effect of example, the unthinking adoption of new customs and popular fashions. But a large and increasing number were seriously impressed by the truth, and showed an earnest desire to understand ' the way of God more perfectly.' The best evidence of their sincerity was given in their reformed and consistent life.

One principle the missionaries, from the first, kept steadily before them. They gave no presents and offered no inducements of any kind, to persuade the people either to receive instruction in the schools or to attend the religious services, beyond the benefits that the pupils and hearers would receive by the knowledge they would gain. This is, no doubt, a sound principle, though there are often temptations to depart from it. Yet its adoption is the more imperative as an untutored people are slow to believe that the motives of their teachers are purely benevolent and disinterested, and are apt to feel that in complying with their requests or invitations to receive instruction they are themselves conferring a favour. Instances of this impression were frequent and sometimes very amusing. On one occasion, a young woman who had been taught the use of the needle, after receiving a number of lessons and attaining some proficiency, applied for payment. 'For what?' asked the teacher. 'For learning,' was the answer; 'you asked me to learn and I have learnt. What am I to get?' It was explained that she had received, and not conferred, a benefit; that the teacher had not profited by the time, patience, and labour that had been freely given for the sole advantage of the pupil. She was, however, encouraged by the promise that in future, as she had now acquired the necessary skill, she should be paid for any work she might do for the mission family: she was also told that she might fairly earn a suitable remuneration by working for others. Erroneous views of this kind would have become stereotyped in the native mind had the missionaries sought to obtain compliance by gifts or rewards; and as their power to offer such inducements was limited in the extreme, and must soon have been exhausted, so would their influence have as rapidly declined. They judged more wisely; and the payment for books, the voluntary labour in building schools and chapels, the support of native pastors and the establishment of the missionary society, were among the earliest practical lessons and results of their prudent decision.

Not long after the party who had left Eimeo to labour in Huahine had occupied their new station, Tamatoa, the chief of Raiatea, with others from the neighbouring islands, arrived in the settlement, and earnestly entreated that some of the missionaries would remove to his dominions. The invitation was accepted by Messrs. Williams and Threlkeld, who soon afterwards took up their abode in Raiatea. Mr. Orsmond followed late in the same year, and, after labouring for some time in the station with his brethren, subsequently established a mission in Borabora. Mr. Nott and Mr. Davis remained for awhile in Huahine, but ultimately settled in Tahiti, and the field of Huahine was left in the hands of Mr. Ellis and Mr. Barff.

The labour of preaching was at first undertaken by Mr. Davis and Mr. Nott, but as the younger brethren rapidly acquired a knowledge of the language, they soon took their share, and ultimately divided between themselves this department of ministerial duty. Mr. Ellis preached his first sermon in the Tahitian tongue in the month of November 1818, selecting for his text the appropriate passage : 'This is a faithful saying and worthy of all acceptation, that Christ Jesus came into the world to save sinners.' (1 Timothy, i. 15.)

No time was lost in putting the printing-press once more in operation, and before long an edition of St. Matthew was published, followed by the gospel of St. John. A larger collection of hymns was also printed, and in other ways the work of the press was in constant requisition.

Mahine, who had been present at the formation of the missionary society in Eimeo, was desirous of establishing a similar institution in his own domain, a desire in which the missionaries were rejoiced to encourage and assist him. Accordingly, about four months after their arrival in Huahine, a public meeting was held, at which Mahine, Tamatoa, and a number of other chiefs with a large concourse of people were present ; and a society similar to that already established in the Georgian group was formed in the Society Islands. A branch association was afterwards organized in Raiatea.

Early in the following year, a project in which the king had for some time been engaged was completed. This was the

erection in Tahiti of an immense place of worship, known as
the 'Royal Mission Chapel,' which was opened in the presence of
a vast assembly, on the 11th of May 1819. The building was
seven hundred and twelve feet in length, and fifty-four wide.
Thirty-six massive cylindrical pillars of the bread-fruit tree,
sustained the centre of the roof, and two hundred and
eighty smaller ones of the same material supported the wall-
plate along the sides and ends. The walls were composed of
upright planks of the same wood. The roof was thatched in
the usual manner. This enclosure was capable of accommodating upwards of seven thousand people. It was furnished
with three pulpits, and from each of these, on the occasion of
the opening ceremonies, a sermon was preached to separate
congregations of more than two thousand each. The encampment of the multitudes brought together to be present at this
opening, stretched along the sea-beach to the extent of four
miles. The occasions when the full capacity of the building
was required were extremely rare: usually a small space at one
end sufficed for the ordinary services. The structure, though
so vast, was comparatively slight and perishable. It had been
undertaken, contrary to the advice of the missionaries, solely
to gratify the caprice and ambition of its royal architect, and
might not inappropriately have been called 'Pomare's folly.'
It soon showed signs of decay, and not many years after the
king's death, the constant repair of so large an edifice being
too laborious and costly to repay the trouble, it was suffered to
fall into ruins, and not a vestige of it remained.

One of the earliest and most interesting ceremonies for which
it was used was the public baptism of Pomare, the first person
in these islands to whom the rite was administered. This was
on the 16th of July 1819. The subject of baptism had long
been under the earnest consideration of the missionaries, who
wished to act with prudence, and to be guided solely by the
teachings of Scripture. To the majority of their number it
appeared that the warrant to baptize was included in their com-

mission to teach; and that it was their duty to administer the rite to all who openly and intelligently avowed their belief in Christ—their faith in His Gospel. One or two, however, held to the opinion, and guided their procedure accordingly, that evidence of that change of heart which all demanded as essential to admission into Church fellowship, and to the privilege of the Lord's Supper, was equally requisite in candidates for baptism. The practice in Huahine was in accordance with the general view. But it was deemed important as fully as possible to instruct those who desired thus to declare their belief in Christianity, concerning the nature of the ordinance, its spiritual teaching, and the duties incumbent on all who received it. For this purpose a weekly meeting was held with those who came forward as candidates for baptism. These meetings were continued for many months before the ceremony was first performed. It was the opinion of these students of Holy Writ that the ordinance was designed for the children of believers as well as for adult disciples. Carefully warning their enquiring applicants against attaching any saving efficacy to the mere ceremony, apart from the spiritual purification which it signified, they invited those who thus declared their discipleship to bring their children to the Saviour in the same dedicatory service. After much patient instruction in what appeared to be the Scriptural teaching on this subject, the ordinance was administered in Huahine on the 12th of September 1819. Mahine, not on account of his rank, but as one of the earliest, most intelligent, and devout among the Christian converts, was the first to receive this rite; and a very large number, both adults and children, were baptized on the same occasion.

The formation of the first church was a matter of still longer prayerful consideration and assiduous preliminary instruction. It was not till May 1820, soon after the completion of a new chapel, that a Christian church was formally organised in Huahine, and then but fifteen candidates were received into fellowship. These apostles to the heathen endeavoured to act faithfully in their responsible position, and while desiring, above all, to be actuated by a spirit of enlarged and enlightened charity, strove to guard against unscriptural laxity in the terms of communion. So that, while the number of members steadily increased, it is not, perhaps, too much to say, the early Church of Huahine would have compared favourably, in fervour of piety and purity of life, with any contemporary church in more advanced Christian lands. Thus it will be seen that these conscientious and humble-minded men were very far from proclaiming all who renounced idolatry as true converts to Christianity; that they scrupulously avoided exaggerating their success by glowing accounts of 'multitudes added to the church,' or highly-coloured statements of the actual changes that had taken place. Indeed, encouraging as the accounts received at home had been, it was the emphatic testimony of the deputation sent out by the Society to visit these stations in 1821, that 'the half had not been told.' Captain Gambier, who made some stay in the islands, and had full opportunities of becoming acquainted with their condition, and comparing it with that of the Marquesas and other heathen countries, bears similar witness to the magnitude and reality of the change, and declares that 'the accounts of the missionaries were, beyond measure, modest.' Other disinterested observers, not regarded as religious men, have corroborated these statements.

As the inhabitants were at first very much scattered over the island, the two pastors in Huahine, instead of confining their ministrations to the district of Fare, alternately journeyed to branch stations on the coast and in the interior, to hold religious services on the Lord's day. Schools, under the superintendence of intelligent native teachers, were also established at each place. Mr. Barff undertook the charge of the coast stations, and Mr. Ellis of those of the interior. These itinerant labours were truly interesting and delightful. The scene of Mr. Ellis's fortnightly visits was a populous and central village in the district of Mæva, on the border of a beautiful lake of the same

name.   It was a considerable distance from Fare, and the
preacher walked thither on the Saturday afternoon and returned
on the following Monday, journeying through a most enchanting country.   A commodious chapel was built, as well as a
small cottage for the accommodation of the minister.   By
degrees, however, the inhabitants collected together, and per-
manently settled in larger numbers within the precincts of
Fare ; and these branch stations, being no longer necessary,
were at length given up.

The establishment of the church, and the meetings for
inquiry and explanation, brought new duties to the missionaries' wives, who took the special oversight of members of
their own sex.   Indeed, their labours now became abundant,
and taxed their strength and time to the utmost.   Besides the
domestic engagements of their own homes, they taught in the
schools, met at stated periods with female applicants for baptism or communion, as well as with those already admitted
into church fellowship; visited the sick and infirm, and held
regular classes for instruction in various useful feminine accomplishments, such as sewing, platting, &c.

Anxious to promote, next to the spread of the Gospel, the
civilization and general improvement of the people, Mr. Ellis
and his coadjutor had, soon after their arrival in Huahine, paid
considerable attention to the cultivation of cotton, an excellent variety of which is indigenous in the islands, and several
of the best sorts had been introduced from abroad.   The natives
were encouraged to embark in the new enterprise, and several
enclosed fields, which they called cotton-gardens, were stocked
with plants and yielded abundant crops.   The first use of the
new produce was to barter or sell it to the captains of foreign
vessels; but the natives were somewhat disappointed with the
price that was paid, and the industry would probably have been
abandoned, had not the directors of the Missionary Society,
in the year 1821, sent out, with other artisans, a skilled workman, Mr. Armitage, from Manchester, who was thoroughly

acquainted with the manufacture of cotton goods. He was supplied with all the necessary machinery for carding, spinning, and weaving the cotton ; a factory was established, and carried on successfully. The natives were also taught to spin and weave the new fabric in their own homes—an occupation better suited to their indolent and desultory habits than the confinement and rigour, as well as monotony, of factory work. At a still earlier period in the history of the mission, the directors had engaged Mr. Gyles, from Jamaica, to instruct the islanders in the cultivation of the sugar-cane—another indigenous product of the country—and the manufacture of sugar. The work was begun, and was attended for a while with complete success; but some interested traders contrived to prejudice the mind of Pomare, by representing the design and ultimate effect of the enterprise as tending to make the country sufficiently valuable to tempt the cupidity of civilised nations, and that this was but the first step towards the occupancy of the islands by a foreign power. These representations so influenced the king's mind that he prohibited the manufacture, except on the most limited and purely domestic scale; and Mr. Gyles was shortly after persuaded to leave the islands. Before his departure, however, Mr. Ellis obtained from him much information concerning the culture of the cane, and the processes of sugar-making. Some of the roller-presses, boilers, and other apparatus which Mr. Gyles had brought with him, were also transported to Huahine ; and the indefatigable missionary added to his other labours the superintendence of a rude, but very efficient sugar-mill, whereby he was able to supply the English families and the native population with an excellent quality of this indispensable article of consumption.

CHAPTER V.

REFERENCE has already been made to a boat that Mr. Ellis built, and in which he made many voyages to the neighbouring islands. These journeys, though often pleasant, were sometimes, in such slender craft, attended with considerable risk.

Once, during perfectly calm weather, and near shore, the canoe in which they were seated was run down by another that suddenly darted from behind a projecting rock, and the whole party, including the mother and children, were precipitated into the sea, and narrowly escaped a watery grave.

On another occasion, while sailing from Huahine to Tahiti, a heavy gale carried away the sprit of one of their matting sails, and compelled them to land at Eimeo, to replace the lost spar. Towards evening they re-embarked, and stood out once more to sea. ' The excitement of watching, and the fatigue of the preceding part of our voyage,' taking up once more Mr. Ellis's narrative, ' having induced a considerable degree of exhaustion of strength and spirits, we had not advanced far upon the open sea, before I became oppressed with a sensation of drowsiness, which I could not remove. During my voyages among the islands I have passed many nights at sea with the natives in an open boat, and generally found them watchful and alert during the early hours of the night, but wearied and sleepy towards morning; and whenever I have felt rest necessary for myself, have usually taken it before midnight, that I might be more vigilant when my companions should become drowsy. This was my purpose in the present instance. I therefore gave

one of the natives charge of the helm, which I had hitherto
kept during the whole of the voyage, and directing him to wake
me in about an hour's time, I wrapped myself in my cloak, lay
down upon the seat in the stern of the boat, and notwithstanding the motion of the sea, and the rattling and shaking occasioned by the movements of the oars, soon fell into a sound
sleep.

‘ The refreshing and beneficial effects of my repose were,
however, entirely neutralised by the sensations I experienced
at its close.　I cannot describe my emotions when I awoke,
and found it was broad daylight: and, on glancing towards
the stern, saw the helmsman fast asleep, with his hands still
on the tiller ; and then looking forward along the boat, beheld
every individual motionless ; the rowers leaning over their
oars, the others stretched along the bottom of the boat, and
every one in the most profound slumber.　Before I attempted
to awaken any one, I involuntarily looked for the island we had
left ; it was still in sight.　I then looked to the opposite side,
for that to which we were going.　It was also in sight, but the
lofty mountains rising at the head of Matavai were far to the
north, and indicated that the port to which we were bound was
many miles behind us.　In fact, we appeared to be about mid-
way between Tahiti and Eimeo, far away from both, and drift-
ing to the southward as fast as the current could bear us.

‘ Fully sensible of our critical situation, if the breeze, which
just began to ripple the surface of the water, should increase, I
instantly awoke my companions, and asked them how they
came all to fall asleep together.　They looked confused on be-
holding the broad light of day beaming upon them, and replied
that each had imperceptibly fallen under the influence of sleep,
without knowing that any other was under the dominion of the
same sensation.　Recollecting that I had in the first instance
set them the example, I could not much censure their conduct ;
I therefore directed their attention to the mountains of Matavai,
far in the rear ; and as Burder's Point was the nearest part of

the coast, urged them to apply with vigour to their oars, that
we might reach it before the wind became so strong as to
arrest our progress.' The men, refreshed by their slumbers,
and conscious of their jeopardy, pulled strenuously, and after
about five hours' hard rowing, brought the boat safely to land.

At another time, a voyage to Raiatea was attended with still
greater danger, and there was in this instance no element of
the ludicrous to detract from the sublimity of the peril.

'About nine o'clock in the morning, Mr. Barff and myself,
accompanied by five natives and an English sailor, embarked
from Huahine. The wind being fair, we expected to reach
Raiatea in three or four hours. We had not, however, been an
hour at sea, when the heavens began to gather blackness, and
dense lowering clouds intercepted our view of the shore we had
left, and of that to which we were bound. The wind became un-
steady and boisterous, the sea rose, not in long heavy billows,
but in short, cross, and broken waves. We had no compass on
board. The dark heavy atmosphere obscuring the sun, prevented our discerning the land, and rendered us unconscious of
the direction in which the gathering storm was driving us. We
took down our large sails, leaving only a small one in the fore-
part of the boat, merely to keep it steady.

'The tempest increased, the rain came down in torrents, and
the waves, washing over the bow and sides of the little bark,
threatened to swamp it; but, happily, we had a bucket on
board, by means of which we were able to bale out the water.
Most of the natives sat down in the bottom of the boat, and,
under the influence of fear, either shut their eyes or covered
them with their hands, expecting every moment that the waves
would close over us. We were not unconscious of our perilous
situation; and, as a last resort, took down our little sail and
our mast, tied the masts, bowsprit, and oars together in a
bundle, with one end of a strong rope, and fastening the other
end to the bow of our boat, threw them into the sea. The
bundle of masts, oars, &c., acted as a kind of buoy, or floating

anchor, and not only broke the force of the billows that were rolling towards the boat, but kept it tolerably steady, while we were dashed on the broken wave, or wafted we knew not whither by the raging storm.

'The rain soon abated, and the northern horizon became somewhat clear, but the joyful anticipation with which we viewed this change was soon superseded by a new train of feelings. '*Huri, huri, tia moana*' (literally, whirling, whirling of the sea), exclaimed one of the natives ; and, looking in the direction to which he pointed, we saw a large cylindrical waterspout, extending, like a massive column, from the ocean to the dark and impending clouds. It was evidently at no very remote distance, and seemed moving towards our apparently devoted boat.

' The roughness of the sea forbade our attempting to hoist a sail in order to avoid it; and as we had no other means of safety at command, we endeavoured calmly to await its approach. The natives abandoned themselves to despair, and either threw themselves along in the bottom of the boat, or sat crouching on the keel, with their faces downwards, and their eyes covered with their hands. The sailor kept at the helm, Mr. Barff sat on one side of the stern, and I on the other, watching the alarming object before us. While thus employed we saw two other waterspouts, and subsequently a third, if not more, so that we seemed almost surrounded with them. Some were well defined, extending in an unbroken line from the sea to the sky, like pillars resting on the ocean as their basis, and supporting the black and overhanging clouds, others assuming the shape of a funnel or inverted cone, attached to the clouds, and extending towards the waters beneath. From the distinctness with which we saw them, notwithstanding the density of the atmosphere, the farthest could not have been many miles distant. In some we imagined we could trace the spiral motion of the water as it was drawn to the clouds, which were every moment augmenting their portentous darkness.

'The hoarse roaring of the tempest, and the hollow sounds that murmured on the ear, as the heavy billows rolled in foam, or broke in contact with opposing billows, seemed as if deep called unto deep; and the noise of waterspouts might almost be heard, while we were momentarily expecting that the mighty waves would sweep over us.

'I had once before, when seized with the cramp while bathing at a distance from my companions, been, as I supposed, on the verge of eternity. The danger then came upon me suddenly, and my thoughts, while in peril, were but few. The danger now appeared more imminent, and a watery grave every moment more probable; yet there was leisure afforded for reflection, and the sensibilities and powers of the mind were roused to an unusual state of excitement by the mighty conflict of the elements on every side.

'A retrospect of life, now perhaps about to close, presented all the scenes through which I had passed, in rapid succession and in varied colours, each exhibiting the lights and shadows by which it had been distinguished. Present circumstances and connexions claimed a thought, and awakened a train of feelings not to be described. But the most impressive exercise of mind was that referring to the awful change approaching. The parting struggle, with all its attendant agonies, caused scarcely a thought, compared with the appearance of the disembodied spirit in the presence of its Maker, the account to be rendered, and the awful and unalterable destiny that would await it there. These momentous objects absorbed all the powers of the mind, and produced an intensity of feeling, which for a long time rendered me almost insensible to the raging storm, or the liquid columns that threatened our destruction.

'The hours that followed were some of the most solemn I have ever passed in my life. Although much recurred to memory that demanded deep regret and most sincere repentance, yet I could look back on that mercy which had first brought me to a knowledge of the Saviour with a gratitude never perhaps exceeded. Him, and Him alone, I found to be a refuge—a rock in the storm of contending feelings, on which my soul could cast the anchor of its hope for pardon and acceptance before God : and although not visibly present, as with his disciples on the Sea of Tiberias, we could not but hope that He was spiritually present, and that, should our bodies rest till the morning of the Resurrection in the unfathomed caverns of the ocean, our souls would be by Him admitted into the abodes of blessedness and rest.

' The storm continued during the day. At intervals we beheld, through the clouds or rain, one or other of the water-spouts, the whole of which appeared almost stationary, until at length we lost sight of them altogether, when the spirits of our native voyagers evidently revived.'

It was not till evening that the tempest abated ; and though land was nowhere to be seen, a streak of light from the setting sun indicated the course to be taken. The bundle of masts, &c., was pulled in, and the natives taking to the oars, rowed towards the west. The moon at length arose, and, sailing through an untroubled and almost cloudless sky, revealed the coast and southernmost harbour of Raiatea. Weary, famished, drenched with rain, and shivering with cold, but grateful to God for their merciful preservation, the voyagers landed about midnight, and were provided by the hospitable inhabitants with shelter, a blazing fire, dry raiment, and food. Mr. Ellis closes the account of this memorable deliverance in the following words :—' I have often been overtaken with storms when at sea in European vessels, boats, and native canoes, but to whatever real danger I may have been exposed, I never was surrounded by so much that was apparent as during this voyage.'

Such stormy encounters were happily exceptional. In general, the voyages among the islands were safe, and very pleasant ; and when, in order to avoid the heat of a vertical sun and the burning rays reflected from the surface of the ocean, the night season was chosen, as it often was, for the passage, the scene, whether invested with the majesty and beauty of the moon, or lighted only by the stars, was often peculiarly impressive. The return of the boat from the somewhat hazardous sail to Tahiti, already described, was on one of these serene and cloudless nights. The sky was moonless, but studded with stars in unusual brilliance. The surface of the deep was unruffled, and, glowing in the wake of the bark with its own phosphoric fires, reflected around, with marvellous distinctness, the lamps of heaven; so that the voyagers appeared to be suspended between two hemispheres, and gliding, as it were, by enchantment, amid the profoundest silence, to some haven of spirit-land. There was something also very striking in the luminaries of the southern firmament. Many of the more northern stars, so conspicuous with us, were absent, though the splendours of Orion, and the milder lustre of the Pleiades, shed their familiar glories from these heavens as well as from our own. But more than all, the eye was arrested by the 'Cross of the South,' the most remarkable of the southern constellations. 'The two stars forming the longest part, having nearly the same right ascension, it appears erect when in the zenith, and thus furnishes a nightly index to the flight of time, and a memento to the most sublime feelings of grateful devotion.'

The occasion of these voyages was generally to consult the brethren on the affairs of the mission; but sometimes they were undertaken at the request of the king, or principal chiefs, to attend, it might be an important conference on affairs of public interest. The missionaries, considering their proper function to be that of teaching the gospel, very carefully abstained from interference in political questions, or the business of the government. But they could not refuse, when application was made to them, to expound the principles of the Bible in their bearing on civil affairs, or to give information respecting the usages of their own country. Hence they cheerfully gave their assistance, by way of counsel, in framing a code of laws for the country ; which the profession of Christianity, and the general enlightenment of the nation rendered necessary. But they wished that the adoption of these laws should be the action of the king and the legitimate rulers of the land, sanctioned by the consent of the people. Accordingly, the first code was submitted by Pomare to his chiefs, and an immense gathering of his subjects, in the Royal Mission Chapel, in the month of May 1819. These laws were few, brief, and simple, not altogether such as the missionaries would have prepared—for the king was somewhat arbitrary in his notions—but on the whole adapted to the primitive state of society, and calculated to promote the cause of morality and good order. In the same month of the following year, a code of laws was publicly adopted in Raiatea, in which it was sought to obviate some of the defects and deficiencies of the first enactments. Among the improvements of the later statutes was the institution of ' *Trial by Jury.*' Mr. Ellis and his colleague also gave much thought and study in framing laws for the island of Huahine, which received the sanction of the ruler and people at a still later period. A literal copy of these laws is given in ' Polynesian Researches.' One of the most remarkable features in this code, was the omission of capital punishment. Independently of the general considerations that bear on this question, it was submitted that the sanguinary customs of heathen times, and the former savage recklessness of human life, made it desirable that the most humane aspect of Christianity should now be presented, and the sacredness of human life set forth in the strongest manner. It was thought, further, that the present was a favourable opportunity to give the substitution of perpetual banishment for capital punishment a fair trial ; and that it would be easier hereafter to introduce the extreme penalty, if it were found necessary, than to rescind it after it had once been enacted.

The close of the year 1821 was made memorable in the annals of the mission by the arrival of Messrs. Tyerman and Bennett, the deputation sent out by the Missionary Society to visit its stations. The occasion was gratifying and cheering to the little band of devoted men, who had long laboured in this distant part of the world, with rare opportunities of direct communication with the home they had left; it was advantageous to the mission; and most encouraging to the friends in England, by the accounts they received from their accredited messengers concerning the marvellous fruits of the gospel in the morality and civilization of these once heathen lands.

Before the end of the year, and while the deputation were still at Tahiti, another event occurred, which produced a profound sensation. This was the death of Pomare, whose health had long been failing, and who expired on the 7th of December. Though there had been much in his conduct that could not fail to grieve his best friends and all good men, he had done signal service to his country, and had been the most prominent native agent in the abolition of idolatry and the general reception of Christianity. He was succeeded in the sovereignty by his only son—a young child—who himself died a few years afterwards. The supreme authority then passed into the hands of his daughter Aimata, who was married to the young chief of Tahaa, a favourite with her father, who had given the young man his own name, so that Pomare continued to be the regal name. The marriage ceremony was performed by Mr. Ellis just before he left the islands.

The deputation remained some time in Huahine, and Mr. Tyerman, accompanied by his host, paid a visit to Borabora and Raiatea. Shortly after their return, the Colonial Government cutter *Mermaid* arrived in Fare harbour, on her way to the Sandwich Islands, with a small schooner, the *Prince Regent*, as a present from the British Government to the king of those islands. The captain intimated his intention of touching at the Marquesas on his return from Hawaii, and offered a passage to any of the mission party who might be desirous of visiting these islands. This opportunity of extending the benefits of the gospel to the Marquesas—a project which had long been contemplated—was gladly embraced by the Church in Huahine. Two native teachers, one of whom was Auna, with their wives, offered to go and take up their abode in that still heathen land ; and Mr. Ellis was appointed to accompany them, proposing to return in the *Mermaid*, as the captain expected, in about three months.

'The arrangements for the voyage being completed,' this enterprising ambassador of the Church informs us, 'we assembled at the chapel about ten o'clock on the forenoon of the 24th of February ; the native evangelists were animated by kind and appropriate exhortations from the Church and from their pastor, Mr. Barff. I then addressed the people, and commending Mrs. Ellis and our dear children to their care, took leave of them. The meeting was peculiarly impressive and affecting ; and after mutually committing each other, under deep intensity of feeling, to the guidance and the keeping of the God of all our mercies, the whole congregation walked from the chapel to the sea shore, where we exchanged our last salutations ; the Deputation, the two native missionaries and their wives, five other natives, and myself, now embarked, and the *Mermaid* stood out to sea.'

The situation of Mrs. Ellis, left with her four children in a sort of widowhood, and oppressed with anxiety for the safety and health of her husband, who was at this time very far from robust, and appeared to have suffered much from the heat of the climate, called forth the active sympathy of her missionary companions and of the kind natives of the settlement. Her own health, too, had been greatly tried by fatigue and exposure in wearisome and stormy voyages between Raiatea and Huahine. To one of these, especially, undertaken soon after the birth of her youngest daughter, she attributed the foundation of that serious affliction from which she afterwards suffered so long and severely. On the present occasion, at the earnest solicitation of Mrs. Orsmond, who was the only European female in Borabora,

she accompanied Mr. Orsmond on his return to that island, to
share for a season the labours of the station, and afford to her
sister the companionship and attention which were at that time
peculiarly acceptable. The chief object of her visit accomplished, at the expiration of nine weeks she was anxious to
return to Huahine, as the term of her husband's expected absence
was drawing near. The voyage from Borabora or Raiatea to
Huahine, being in the direction contrary to the trade-winds, is
often tedious and difficult. Ten stout natives had charge of the
boat in which Mrs. Ellis and her children started to return home
on the 1st of May; but owing to violent and opposing gales
they were driven back, after having so nearly gained their port
that the houses on the shore were distinctly seen—and forced to
land at Raiatea, where they were detained by adverse winds for
nearly a fortnight. On the morning of the 13th, the weather
being calm, the party again left the shore; but a strong current
and head winds setting in against them, after being out at sea
all night, they found themselves next morning close to another
part of the coast of Raiatea, and were compelled once more to
land. Mrs. Ellis was so weak and ill that the natives carried
her from the boat to the nearest hut. This appeared to be
unoccupied; but on looking round a solitary female was perceived
kneeling beside a scarcely breathless corpse, and offering, apparently in great distress, and with frequent sobs and cries, her
prayer to Him who seeth in secret, and is a very present help in
trouble. As soon as her first paroxysms of grief had somewhat subsided, the poor woman came and tenderly sympathised
with her guest; told her the other inhabitants of the neighbourhood had gone to the missionary meeting, but that she had
remained to attend on her afflicted husband, who had expired
as the boat approached the shore. Weak and faint as she was,
Mrs. Ellis endeavoured to direct her mind to the only source of
effectual support, while she offered from the depths of a loving
soul the comfort of her sisterly sympathy, with a tenderness and
sweetness that no heart could resist. The unwitting intruders

on the hour of bereavement would now have retired to some
other shelter, but the new-made widow constrained them to stay,
and with a beautiful, all-womanly self-renunciation, put aside,
as it were, her own unutterable sorrow, that she might minister
to her weary and suffering guest. Such instances of unselfish
loving-kindness, thank God, are not rare. They come out
brightest in affliction; and if one would know the best of human
nature, let him accompany the physician to the homes of the
poor—to scenes of sickness and mourning; and he will learn, if
he needs the lesson, to respect his kind.

During the whole of the day and the succeeding night the
feeble guest was not able to leave the mat on which she had
been laid; but on the morning of the 15th, being somewhat
recovered and the weather being favourable, another, and
happily a successful attempt was made to reach Huahine;
where the exhausted voyager was cordially welcomed by her
anxious friends.

Troubles of another kind now awaited the mission families.
On the day that the boat landed, a brig approached the island
and anchored about noon. The vessel remained in harbour for
more than a fortnight, the captain frequently coming on shore,
and professing to be deeply interested in religion. On the
arrival of the *Westmoreland* from New South Wales, the
brig took her departure. At Tahiti she met with Captain
Henry, who commanded a brig belonging to the Queen, in
which he was about to sail to Sydney. The strange craft
followed Captain Henry to Eimeo and Tabuai. At this place
the suspicions already excited concerning the character of the
crew were confirmed by trustworthy information that they were
a band of desperate pirates, who had seized the vessel in which
they sailed, sent the captain and officers on shore, and after a
series of acts of plunder and murder on the American coast,
had made their way to the South Sea Islands. Captain Henry,
in concert with the chiefs of Tabuai, captured the men, and
took them as prisoners to Tahiti, where he handed them over

to the chiefs, who put them in custody and hauled their ship on to the beach.   But soon after the departure of Captain Henry, the captives eluded the vigilance of their guards, stole a boat belonging to a vessel in harbour, and made their escape. Four of them found their way to Huahine, where their history and character were not yet known.   Being good mechanics they procured employment ; and one of them, a carpenter, was engaged by Mrs. Ellis to do some work in her own house.   In course of time the men stated that they had been to the Sandwich Islands, and that they had met the *Mermaid* — the vessel in which the Deputation and their friends had sailed— but would give no account of the safety of the passengers. Shortly after, Captain Henry arrived in Huahine, and at once informed the chiefs and missionaries of the true character of their visitors.   This intelligence, coupled with the fact that the pirates had met the *Mermaid* and the unaccountable detention of that vessel so long after the time when its return was looked for, produced an agony of apprehension that no words can describe.   The men were instantly seized; their trunks were examined ; and in one of them were found some British epaulettes, which it was supposed had belonged to Captain Kent, the commander of the *Mermaid*, and this was taken as further evidence that the pirates had plundered and perhaps sunk the vessel.   It was with difficulty that Mr. Barff could restrain the natives from wreaking instant vengeance on the wretched men.

'The chiefs and people of the settlement had always shown the warmest attachment to the missionaries, but their kindness to Mrs. Ellis, during the protracted absence of her husband, was as grateful to her as it was honourable to themselves.   They used to designate her their little lonely widow, and seemed anxious to testify their desire to alleviate the distress which they knew she must feel.   Whenever they were successful in fishing, they always sent her a part of what they had taken ; and frequently, in seasons of tempestuous weather, one or two of the chief women of the island would sleep in the house with her, to mitigate the disquiet which her solicitude must occasion. When a valuable female servant, who married, left her, the chiefs persuaded another pious and attentive native to live with her: and by these and numberless attentions, truly acceptable at the time, manifested a vigilance of benevolence and a strength of affection scarcely to be expected in persons among whom the feelings and offices of Christian sympathy and friendship were of such recent growth.'

Eight months elapsed before the return of the *Mermaid* with their long absent friends removed the torturing suspense which these events and the unaccountable delay had excited. The reappearance of the vessel in Fare Harbour, early in October 1822, created a revulsion of feeling that could find its most fitting expression only in devout and thankful prayer to the Almighty. Gladder hearts than those of the re-united husband and wife on that day the world did not contain.

It was now found that the pirates had been to the Sandwich Islands, that they had met the schooner which sailed with the *Mermaid* and had thus obtained information concerning the names of the persons on board the other vessel. This accounted at once for their partial knowledge on some points, and the vagueness of their information on others, which had so greatly aggravated the distress of the mission family and the chiefs.

The explanation of the cause of detention involved also an important change in the mission. The *Mermaid*, after a pleasant voyage of nearly five weeks, reached Hawaii, the largest of the Sandwich Islands, in the end of March. The governor of the island, in the absence of the king, who chiefly resided in the adjacent island of Oahu, cordially welcomed the new comers, and invited them to his house. Here they remained about a fortnight, waiting for the schooner from which they had parted company in the course of the voyage; but, as she did not make her appearance, Captain Kent, supposing she might have arrived at some other port, made sail for Honoruru, the principal harbour of Oahu. His surmises proved to be correct. His consort was lying at anchor. The party now received the salutations of the king, and of the members of the American mission, all of whom were at the time residing at Oahu. They were kindly accommodated at the mission-house and the residences of the brethren. Auna and his wife were invited by a countryman of their own, who had 'emigrated' many years before to these islands, and who now belonged to the household of the queen dowager, to take up their abode in her establishment. The invitation was accepted. It was soon discovered that their countryman was no other than the brother of Auna's wife, and the meeting was as gratifying as it was unexpected.

It was at once apparent that the language of the Sandwich Islands was merely a dialect of that of Tahiti; and Mr. Ellis found no difficulty in conversing with the people, and, indeed, in a very few weeks was able to preach with fluency in the native tongue. He readily gave all the assistance in his power to the American brethren, who had hitherto made but slow progress in acquiring the language, and had preached and communicated with the islanders chiefly through the medium of interpreters, in the persons of some native youths who had been educated in America. Mr. Ellis also composed a few Hawaiian hymns—the first ever written or sung on these shores, and which gave new animation to the religious worship, and great delight to the people. The king was also pleased to find an efficient instructor in the English missionary, from whom he received daily lessons.

It was not expected that the stay of the party from Huahine would have extended beyond a few weeks; but circumstances entirely beyond their control occurred, which detained them for many months. Among the causes of delay was a voyage on some commercial enterprise that the captain was induced to make to latitudes still further north. This alone occupied some months, and led to the abandonment of the visit to the Marquesas. During the interval of forced detention, the missionary

and the native evangelists were not idle.　Besides the assistance
they were able to render from their knowledge of the language,
their arrival with the Deputation was opportune on another
account.　The minds of the king and people had been prejudiced
by the reports of interested foreign traders and ship-owners,
against the character and influence of the changes that had
taken place in the Society Islands.　Indeed, an expedition of
inquiry, which the king was on the eve of making to his
southern neighbours, had been frustrated by these false statements; while the good work of the resident American labourers
could not fail to be seriously impeded by such misrepresentations.
The testimony that was now given by those who had just left
the scene of these recent changes, confounded the traducers of
Christian missions, satisfied the king and others of the falsity
of the accounts by which they had been deceived, and in no
small measure prepared the way for a cordial reception of
Christianity.

It soon became obvious to all, that great advantage would be
conferred on this populous and inviting field of missionary
labour, if the casual visit of these friends from the southern
islands, could be extended into a permanent residence among
them.　Accordingly, the king and chiefs requested that the
native evangelists might remain; and that Mr. Ellis would return to the Society Islands, and, bringing back his family with
him, come and settle in Oahu.　The American brethren very
cordially and earnestly seconded the invitation of the people;
and, upon mature consideration, it appeared to the Deputation
and all concerned, that this course, marked out as it were by
the finger of Providence in recent events, was the path of
duty.　The view taken by the brethren on the spot was subsequently confirmed by the American Board of Commissioners
for Foreign Missions, and by the London Missionary Society.
When at length the *Mermaid* sailed from the shores of Oahu,
to take back her long absent passengers to Huahine, Mr. Ellis
left with the distinct understanding that on the first oppor-

tunity he would return with his family, and, while still re-
taining his connection with his own society, would join the
American mission in the Sandwich Islands.

When these arrangements were announced to the church and
friends of Fare, although they could not but acquiesce in the
decision, the prospect of parting with their beloved teachers ·
was a severe trial to all; and to none more than to the missionary colleagues with whom Mr. and Mrs. Ellis had laboured
in uninterrupted harmony and the most cordial affection—all
the more valued from the isolated position in which they were
mutually placed. The change, while it thus once more broke
up the dearest ties, offered no prospect of temporal advancement, involved personal sacrifices of no trifling character, and
was made solely from a sense of duty, and in the prospect of
greater usefulness. Proofs of the esteem and attachment in
which they were held by the people flowed in upon them in
almost overwhelming urgency. Among the parting communications addressed to them at this time was one from the Deputation, a brief extract from whose letter may serve to recal a few
of the important changes that had been wrought during the
past four years. It is dated Raiatea, December 9th, 1822, and
begins as follows:—

‘ Having completed our official visit to the important station
which you have occupied, we desire to express the high gratifi-
cation which we have enjoyed during our residence with you.
We have witnessed the effects which your faithful labours have
been instrumental in producing among the people of your charge,
with a gratitude to God as the author of the mighty change,
and with a state of mind too pleasurable to allow of adequate
expression. While the propriety with which the Lord's Day is
kept; the regularity of the people's attention to the duties of
religion; the harmony that prevails in all your public meetings;
the decent appearance of the people; the avidity with which
they receive the word of God; and the attention which they
pay to their improvement in the arts of civilised life; the good

order that prevails in the schools, both of adults and children; the pure religion which obtains in the church, and the morality that characterises the whole congregation; and the affectionate esteem in which you and your beloved partner in life are held by the people among whom you have laboured; while all these things evince a divine approbation, and an influence of an extraordinary nature, they redound highly to your own credit, prove you worthy of the important office with which you are invested by the Great Head of the Church, and deserving of the love and confidence of that great Society by which you are employed.'

A passage was secured in the *Active*, a vessel bound to the Sandwich Islands, for the party appointed to proceed thither, consisting of Mr. and Mrs. Ellis and their children, with a faithful and much attached native female companion, and a native teacher and his wife. The farewell scenes were deeply affecting, and to Mrs. Ellis especially were painfully trying. 'The chief women and others took leave of their kind instructress with much affection; and among the many tokens of attachment few were more touching than those shown by native women who had acted as domestic servants in nursing the children, &c., during her residence in the island. One in particular, who had wept much when the sailors were heaving up the anchor, went out on the rocks at the edge of the harbour, far from the shore, and, though still weeping, stood waiting till the ship should pass into the open sea, anxious to give, by waving her hand, the last token of affection, and obtain the latest possible glance of her beloved teacher and friend.' Thus closed a period which Mr. Ellis loved to recal, and of which he often spoke as the happiest of his life.

CHAPTER VI.

SANDWICH ISLANDS.

THE *Active* set sail from Huahine on the 31st of December 1822, and on the 5th of February she anchored in Oahu. The American Missionaries—Messrs. Bingham, Thurston, and Loomis, with their wives—hastened to offer their affectionate salutations, and received their new associates with a kindness and cordiality most cheering and gratifying at the time, and which continued to mark their conduct through all their subsequent intercourse. The scene upon which they now entered, though possessing many points of similarity with that which they had left, was characterized by special and distinctive features. The natural aspect of the country presented much that was new. The climate, though warm and pleasant, was scarcely tropical, and struck the new comers at first as almost cold. This, of course, on the lower levels of the island could be only by comparison, though in the higher regions of the loftier mountains a degree of actual and intense cold is constant. This lower temperature is combined with a less luxuriant soil, and consequently the productions of the country are not equal in variety and abundance to those of the Tahitian group. The scarcity of fresh water, throughout the entire cluster, is also a serious disadvantage. The general appearance of the islands, if less romantic and beautiful than that of their southern sisters of the Pacific, is perhaps more grand and sublime, owing in some measure to the height of the mountains, and the influence of still active volcanoes. The highest mountains are those of Hawaii, of which the summit probably exceeds 16,000 feet from the level of the sea. 'On approaching the islands,' Mr. Ellis remarks in his 'Tour through Hawaii,' 'I have more than once observed the mountains of the interior long before the coast was visible, or any of the usual indications of land had been seen. On these occasions, the elevated summit of Mouna Kea, or Mouna Roa, has appeared above the mass of clouds that usually skirt the horizon like a stately pyramid, or the silvered dome of a magnificent temple,·distinguished from the clouds beneath only by its well-defined outline, unchanging position, and intensity of brilliancy, occasioned by the reflection of the sun's rays from the surface of the snow.'

The entire group comprises ten islands, of which the four principal are—Hawaii, Maui, Oahu, and Taui. The first is by far the largest and most populous, but Oahu is the more fertile, and has the advantage of the most capacious and convenient harbour, so that it has become a favourite with foreigners. The aggregate population was estimated, in 1824, as exceeding 160,000. The character of the people, as might be inferred from the physical geography of their country, is more hardy, enterprising, and industrious than that of their southern neighbours. The position of the group, the splendid harbours, and numerous population, early attracted the attention of foreigners, especially from the continent of America. An extensive trade was carried on, and the amount of shipping gave to the port of Honoruru, at all times, a busy, thriving, and animated appearance.

The condition of the people was such as peculiarly to invite the benevolent efforts of the Christian Church; and early in 1820 a band of American missionaries had arrived in the islands. They were no less astonished than delighted to find that Riho-riho, the reigning sovereign, had abolished idolatry, and that the superstitions of heathenism at least were no longer a barrier to the reception of the gospel. These excellent men laboured assiduously in their noble work; and, notwithstanding the serious difficulties arising from their ignorance of the language, established schools, preached through the aid of an interpreter, and had even so far mastered the elements of the vernacular tongue as to print the first sheet of an Hawaiian spelling-book.

Immediately on Mr. Ellis's arrival he entered heartily on his work, and his occupations became at once incessant and multifarious. He devoted much time with the brethren, in aiding their efforts to acquire the language, and assisting them with their printing. He preached in the native tongue; and was, besides, daily occupied for some hours with the king, with his prime minister, Karaimoku, and with other chiefs, as well as with Keopuolani—the king's mother—and other eminent women, who showed an earnest desire for instruction. The change of climate seemed to be beneficial to his health; while that of his beloved partner was often interrupted by painful and severe illness, which prevented her from taking so large a share in mission work as she desired.

The first house into which they removed from the hospitable roof of their brethren was a cottage, or hut, covered, like most of the native dwellings, with grass. These buildings were put up, as regards the frame-work, in a manner very similar to those of the Society Islands, but the intervals between the larger posts and between the rafters were filled in with sticks, to which were fastened, very closely together, from the ground to the ridge of the roof, tufts of dried grass, so that the whole structure presented very much the appearance of a hay rick, with low sides. These habitations soon decay and leak, and are, besides, very combustible. A spark will ignite them, and lay them in ruins in the course of a few minutes. A stone house, with boarded floors and glazed windows—the first ever reared in the islands—was soon begun, and in the course of the following year, the family moved into this more commodious abode. Karaimoku built one for himself about the same time on the same plan.

Early in April 1823, the mission received a reinforcement from America in the persons of Messrs. C. Stewart, Richards, Bishop, and others; and it was now thought desirable to establish

and occupy stations in the other islands of the group, especially
in the largest, Hawaii; and with the view of ascertaining the
most eligible situation for one or more missionary settlements
in this populous island, Mr. Ellis was invited to accompany
three of the American brethren, Messrs. Thurston, Bishop, and
Goodrich, on a tour through the country. Mr. Stewart was
prevented by illness from going with them; but Mr. Harwood,
an intelligent mechanic, volunteered, and was permitted to
join the party. The incidents and observations of this most
interesting journey form the subject of the first work Mr. Ellis
published after his return to England, and excited a degree of
public attention never before accorded to any history of missionary operations. To follow the party throughout their
travels with any degree of minute description would extend this
memoir to an unreasonable length; while to give an outline of
the journey, without details, would result in a bare chronolo-
gical record—a meagre itinerary—of little interest. The
reader is therefore referred to the work itself for full information; and in the following narrative a few extracts only will be
presented concerning the principal natural object of attraction,
the great volcano of Kirauea, which they were the first visitors
from civilized countries ever to explore.

The American members of the expedition left Oahu for the
port of Kairua, in Hawaii, on the 24th of June, 1823. Mr.
Ellis was detained by the illness of his wife, but was able to
follow in about eight days after, calling on the way at Lahaina,
in the island of Maui, where his friend Mr. Stewart was
stationed, and where the queen, Keopuolani, was at the time
residing. After a short detention at this place, he resumed the
voyage, and on the 14th of July joined his companions at
Kairua. The governor of the district, Kuakini, or, as he was
commonly designated, John Adams, rendered material service,
not only by entering with much interest into the project, and
giving his counsel as to the best route and plans of procedure,
but by furnishing gratuitously a canoe, an escort to carry bag-

gage, and a guide. The course they pursued was along the coast, making excursions occasionally to visit villages, until they approached the volcano, when they left the shore and proceeded towards the mountain. In the outset of their journey they visited, with emotions of peculiar interest, the spot where Captain Cook fell, and where his bones were for a time deposited. Everywhere they were received by the people, and especially by the chiefs, with courtesy and hospitality; being usually greeted, on requesting accommodation, with some such welcome as the following :—' Our house is large, and there are plenty of sleeping mats for us.' Indeed, the demeanour of these nature's gentlemen was peculiarly gratifying to their guests, and ' indicated a degree of refinement seldom witnessed among uncivilized nations. The usual salutation is " Aroha " (attachment); and the customary invitation to partake of refreshment is—" the food belonging to you and us is ready "; always using the pronoun which includes the person addressed as well as the speaker. On entering a chief's house, should we remark, " Yours is a strong or convenient house," he would answer, "it is a good house for you and me." If, on entering a house, or examining a fine canoe or piece of cloth, we should ask who it belonged to, another person would tell us the possessor's name; but if we happened to inquire of the owner himself, he would invariably answer " it is *yours* and *mine*." '

As the explorers proceeded they did not lose sight of the grand object of their mission. They omitted no opportunity of preaching to the natives, most of whom now heard the Gospel for the first time. The subjects of their discourses and conversations were simple and elementary, adapted as much as possible to the untutored minds of their heathen audience. The new revelations were received with much attention, with wonder, and often with delight. The greater part of the people seemed to regard the tidings of ' endless life by Jesus ' as the most joyful news they had ever heard; breaking upon them, to use their own expression, ' like light in the morning.' Sometimes the character of the occasion, the events of the day, or the features of the scene, suggested the text. Such a passage as this—' Whosoever will, let him take of the water of life freely,' would come home with peculiar force to the dwellers in a land where this precious element was so scantily supplied.

The difficulty of procuring fresh water, and the consequent thirst experienced by the tourists, were among their most serious causes of suffering. Only twice in the whole course of their tour did they meet with a flowing stream. Makoa, too, their guide, afraid to approach the volcano, deserted them when his services were most needed. In some measure, he made amends for his inefficiency by the amusement he afforded to the party. His appearance is thus described :—' Our guide, who had been the king's messenger many years, and was well acquainted with the island, was a singular-looking little man, between forty and fifty years of age. A thick tuft of jet black curling hair shaded his wrinkled forehead, and a long bunch of the same kind hung down behind each of his ears. The rest of his head was cropped as short as shears could make it. His small black eyes were ornamented with tatooed vandyke semicircles. Two goats, impressed in the same indelible manner, stood rampant over each of his brows ; one, like the supporter of a coat of arms, was fixed on each side of his nose, and two more guarded the corners of his mouth. The upper part of his beard was shaven close ; but that which grew under his chin was drawn together, braided for an inch or two, and then tied in a knot, while the extremities below the knot spread out in curls like a tassel. A light kind of shawl was carelessly thrown over one shoulder, and tied in a knot on the other ; and a large fan, made of cocoa-nut leaf in his hand served to beat away the flies, or the boys, when either became too numerous or troublesome.' He was fond of collecting an audience of his countrymen, at the close of the day, and giving marvellous accounts of the foreigners, or of the journey. Sometimes he would turn theologian, and was overheard, on one occasion, during supper, telling the party

around him, 'that heaven was a place where there was neither
salt fish, nor calabashes of *poë.* 'Indeed,' he added, 'we shall
never want any there, for we shall never be hungry. But in
order to get there much is to be done. A man who wishes to
go there must live peaceably with his neighbours; must never
be idle; and, moreover, must not be a glutton.' This last was,
doubtless, thrown in as a hint to his friends to leave him a full
share of the delicacies of the meal. He was fond of good
cheer; and it was a difficult task to persuade him to 'move
on' when there was a feast in prospect.

When it was ascertained that no arguments could induce
their guide to visit the volcano, it was arranged that he should
at least conduct the party of carriers, with the baggage, to a
certain spot within less than a day's journey of the object of
his terror, where the missionaries would meet him; but on
their arrival at the place of rendezvous, no Makoa appeared.
They heard also, after waiting some time, that it was not probable he would arrive for several days. Under these circumstances they were glad to avail themselves of the services of a
party of travellers, who were bound in the same direction, and
who entered the place of temporary lodging while the 'white
men' were vainly expecting their faithless guide. At the house
in which they rested, they were not a little amused to observe
a novel kind of pet belonging to the sisters of their host. This
was not a lap-dog, which almost every native female owns, but
a curly-tailed pig, who was very much at home, and, of course,
in excellent condition. At the supper provided for the entertainment of the guests, the principal dish was baked pig—but
not the pet. He was all right, and a lively partaker of the
feast, being plentifully regaled by his indulgent mistresses with
tit-bits of his brother.

Setting out with their new friends in the afternoon of the
31st of July, the exploring party walked for some miles, till
the approaching darkness compelled them to halt. They
passed the night in a remarkable volcanic cavern. 'The

entrance, which was eight feet wide and five high, was formed
by an arch of ancient lava, several feet in thickness. The
interior of the cavern was about fifty feet square, and the
arch that covered it ten feet high. There was an aperture at
the northern end, about three feet in diameter, occasioned by
the falling in of the lava, which admitted a current of keen
mountain air through the whole of the night. While the
natives were preparing beds of fern leaves, a large fire was
kindled near the entrance, which, throwing its glimmering light
on the dark volcanic sides of the cavern, and illuminating one
side of the huge masses of lava, exhibited the strange features
of the apartment, which resembled, in no small degree, scenes
described in tales of romance.'

As it grew dark the occupants of the cave ascended to the
upper regions to try and discern the light of the volcano. 'The
wind blew fresh from the mountains; the noise of the rolling
surf, to which we had been accustomed on the shore, was not
heard; and the stillness of the night was disturbed only by the
chirping of the insects in the grass. The sky was clear, except
in the eastern horizon, where a few light clouds arose, and
slowly floated across the expanse of heaven. On looking towards
the north-east, we saw a bright column of light rising to a considerable elevation in the air, and immediately above it some
light clouds, or thin vapours, beautifully tinged with red on
the under side. We had no doubt that the column of light
arose from the large crater, and that its fires illuminated the
surrounding atmosphere. The fleecy clouds generally passed
over the luminous column in a south-east direction. As they
approached it, the sides towards the place where we stood became gradually bright; afterwards the under edge only reflected
the volcanic fire; and in a little time each cloud passed entirely
away, and was succeeded by another. We remained some time to
observe the beautiful phenomena occasioned by the reflection
of the volcanic fire, and the more magnificent spectacle presented by the multitude and brilliancy of the heavenly bodies.

' Refreshed by a comfortable night's sleep, we arose before daylight on the morning of the 1st of August, and after stirring up the embers of our fire, rendered, with grateful hearts, our morning tribute of praise to our Almighty preserver.

' As the day began to dawn, we tied on our sandals, ascended from the subterraneous dormitory, and pursued our journey, directing our course towards the column of smoke, which bore E.N.E. from the cavern.

' The path for several miles lay through a most fertile tract of country covered with bushes, or tall grass and fern, frequently from three to five feet high, and so heavily laden with dew that before we had traversed it, we were as completely wet as if we had passed through a river. The morning air was cool, the singing of birds enlivened the woods, and we travelled along in Indian file nearly four miles an hour, although most of the natives carried heavy burdens, which were tied on their backs with small bands over their shoulders, in the same manner that a soldier fastens on his knapsack. Having also ourselves a small leather bag containing a bible, inkstand, note-book, compass, &c., suspended from one shoulder, a canteen of water from the other, and sometimes a light portfolio, or papers, with specimens of plants besides, our whole party appeared somewhat grotesquely *en militaire*.'

A small wood was next entered, emerging from which the travellers encountered a strange, wild, and barren country, sometimes traversing plains of volcanic sand, at others crossing tracts of vitreous lava thrown into ridges, where it was with considerable difficulty they could keep their footing. Resting once or twice for refreshment, and shelter from the burning rays of the sun, they pushed on till about two o'clock in the afternoon, when the CRATER of KIRAUEA suddenly burst upon their view. 'We expected to have seen a mountain with a broad base and rough indented sides, composed of loose slags or hardened streams of lava, and whose summit would have presented a rugged wall of scoria, forming the rim of a mighty

caldron.   But instead of this, we found ourselves on the edge
of a steep precipice, with a vast plain before us, fifteen or sixteen miles in circumference, and sunk from 200 to 400 feet
below its original level.   The surface of this plain was uneven,
and strewed over with large stones and volcanic rocks, and in
the centre of it was the great crater, at the distance of a mile
and a half from the precipice on which we were standing.   Our
guides led us round towards the north end of the ridge, in order
to find a place by which we might descend to the plain below.
With all our care we did not reach the bottom without several
falls and slight bruises.   After walking some distance over the
sunken plain, which in several places sounded hollow under our
feet, we at length came to the edge of the great crater, where a
spectacle, sublime and even appalling, presented itself before
us—

We stopped and trembled.

Astonishment and awe for some moments rendered us mute,
and, like statues, we stood fixed to the spot, with our eyes
riveted on the abyss below.   Immediately before us yawned an
immense gulf, in the form of a crescent, about two miles in
length, from north-east to south-west, nearly a mile in width,
and apparently 800 feet deep.   The bottom was covered with
lava, and the south-west and northern parts of it were one vast
flood of burning matter, in a state of terrific ebullition, rolling
to and fro its 'fiery surge' and flaming billows.   Fifty-one
conical islands, of varied form and size, containing so many
craters, rose either round the edge or from the surface of the
burning lake.   Twenty-two constantly emitted columns of grey
smoke, or pyramids of brilliant flame ; and several of these at
the same time vomited from their ignited mouths streams of
lava, which rolled in blazing torrents down their black indented sides into the boiling mass below.

    ' The sides of the gulf before us, although composed of
different strata of ancient lava, were perpendicular for about
400 feet, and rose from a wide horizontal ledge of solid black

II

lava of irregular breadth, but extending completely round. Beneath this ledge the sides sloped gradually towards the burning lake, which was, as nearly as we could judge, 300 or 400 feet lower. It was evident that the large crater had been recently filled with liquid lava up to this black ledge, and had, by some subterranean canal, emptied itself into the sea, or upon the low land on the shore; and in all probability this evacuation had caused the inundation of the Kapapala coast, which took place, as we afterwards learned, about three weeks prior to our visit. The gray, and in some places apparently calcined sides of the great crater before us; the fissures that intersected the surface of the plain on which we were standing; the long banks of sulphur on the opposite side of the abyss; the vigorous action of the numerous small craters on its borders; the dense columns of vapour and smoke that rose at the north and south end of the plain; together with the ridge of steep rocks by which it was surrounded, rising probably in some places 300 or 400 feet in perpendicular height, presented an immense volcanic panorama, the effect of which was greatly augmented by the constant roaring of the vast furnaces below.

' After the first feelings of astonishment had subsided, we remained a considerable time contemplating a scene which it is impossible to describe, and which filled us with wonder and admiration.

' At the north end of the crater we left the few provisions and little baggage that we had, and went in search of water, which we had been informed was to be found in the neighbourhood of a number of columns of vapour, which we saw rising in a northerly direction. About half a mile distant we found two or three small pools of perfectly sweet, fresh water ; a luxury which, notwithstanding the reports of the natives, we did not expect to meet with in these regions of fire. It proved a most grateful refreshment to us after travelling not less than twenty miles over a barren thirsty desert.

' These pools appeared great natural curiosities. The surface of the ground in the vicinity was perceptibly warm, and rent by several deep irregular chasms, from which steam and thick vapours continually arose. In some places these chasms were two feet wide, and from them a volume of steam ascended, which was immediately condensed by the cool mountain air, and driven, like drizzling rain, into hollows in the compact lava on the leeward side of the chasms. The pools, which were six or eight feet from the chasms, were surrounded and covered by flags, rushes, and tall grass. Nourished by the moisture of the vapours, these plants flourished luxuriantly, and in their turn, sheltered the pools from the heat of the sun, and prevented evaporation. We expected to find the water warm, but in this we were also agreeably disappointed. When we had quenched our thirst with the water thus distilled by nature, we directed the natives to build a hut in which we might pass the night, in such a situation as to command a view of the burning lava ; and while they were thus employed we prepared to examine the many interesting objects around us. . . . .

'Just as the sun was setting we reached the place where we had left our baggage, and where the natives, with a few green branches of trees, some fern leaves and rushes, had erected a hut. At our request they had also collected a quantity of fire-wood, and as night approached we kindled a good fire and prepared our frugal supper. Between nine and ten, the dark clouds and heavy fog that, since the setting of the sun, had hung over the volcano, gradually cleared away, and the fires of Kirauea darting their fierce light athwart the midnight gloom, unfolded a sight terrible and sublime beyond all we had yet seen.

'The agitated mass of liquid lava, like a flood of melted metal, raged with tumultuous whirl. The lively flame that danced over its undulating surface tinged with sulphurous blue, or glowing with mineral red, cast a broad glare of dazzling light on the indented sides of the insulated craters, whose roaring mouths, amidst rising flames and eddying streams of fire, shot up at frequent intervals, with very loud detonations, spherical masses of fusing lava, or bright ignited stones. The dark bold outline of the perpendicular and jutting rocks around formed a striking contrast with the luminous lake below, whose vivid rays thrown on the rugged promontories and reflected by the over-hanging clouds, combined to complete the awful grandeur of the imposing scene.'

The next morning, after making their final examination of the marvellous scene, and endeavouring to ascertain the dimensions of the crater, which they estimated at five miles and a half in circumference and upwards of 800 feet deep, the travellers directed their steps once more towards the coast. Subsequent measurements proved that their estimate was below the reality—the upper rim of the vast abyss extending upwards of six miles, and the inner circuit below the ledge being five miles and a-half, while the depth is nearly 1,000 feet. In the return journey the party separated ; some taking the nearest route, directly across the country, to Waiakea, the principal harbour on the eastern side of the island ; and the rest passing by the more circuitous course along the shore to the same place. When, some days after the volcano had been left behind, Makoa once more made his appearance, he coolly remarked that 'the foreigners must have travelled fast to beat the king's messenger,' giving no other account of the delay than that he had made what speed he could.

Among the superstitions that kept strongest hold on the native mind was their belief in the deities of the volcano, particularly in Pélé, the goddess of Kirauea ; and this lingering vestige of heathen mythology was the last to be surrendered and the most stoutly defended by the votaries of idolatry. The visit of foreigners to the very stronghold of the great Power, and their utter disregard of the observances prescribed for all who approach the fiery domain, excited no little consternation, and stirred up various attempts at opposition. The missionaries were confronted at Waiakea, by one who professed to be a priestess of the goddess, and who, indeed, as the climax of her assumptions, announced herself to be the veritable Pélé in mortal impersonation. This woman pompously upbraided the strangers for their sacrilegious intrusion, giving emphasis to her denunciation by doleful menaces of evil. Her pretensions were quietly exposed by the teachers of the gospel, who also exhorted her to put her trust in the true God, and ' fear Him.' At this juncture Makoa, who had been attentively listening, suddenly, and most unexpectedly entered the lists against the false pretender,—telling her that if she were Pélé, the people had nothing to thank her for : ' It is you who have destroyed the King's land, devoured his people, and spoiled all the fishing grounds. Ever since you came to the island you have been busied in mischief; you spoiled the greater part of the island, shook it to pieces, or cursed it with barrenness by inundating it with lava. You never did any good; and if I were the King, I would pitch you all into the sea, or banish you from the island. Hawaii would be quiet if you were away.' This speech, coming from such a source, astonished all who were present.

A still more formidable attempt was subsequently made to appeal to the fears of the people and prejudice their minds against the new teachers. ' Some months after the visit to Kirauea a priestess of Pélé came to Lahaina, in Maui, where the principal chiefs of the island then resided. The object of her visit was noised abroad among the people, and much public interest excited. One or two mornings after her arrival in the district, arrayed in her prophetic robes, having the edges of her garments burned with fire, and holding a short staff or spear in her hand, preceded by her daughter, who was also a candidate for the office of priestess, and followed by thousands of the populace, she came into the presence of the chiefs ; and having told her name and calling, was asked what communications she had to make. She replied, that in a trance, or vision, she had been with Pélé, by whom she was charged to complain to them

that a number of foreigners had visited Kirauea ; eaten the
sacred berries; broken her houses, the craters; thrown down
large stones, &c.—to request that the offenders might be sent
away ; and to assure them, that if these foreigners were not
banished from the islands Pélé would certainly, in a given
number of days, take vengeance by inundating the country
with lava, and destroying the people. She also pretended to
have received, in a supernatural manner, Rihoriho's approbation
of the request of the goddess. The crowds of natives who stood
waiting the result of her interview with the chiefs, were almost
as much astonished as the priestess herself, when Kaahumanu
and the other chiefs ordered all her paraphernalia of office to
be thrown into the fire ; told her the message she had delivered
was a falsehood, and directed her to return home, cultivate the
ground for her subsistence, and discontinue her journeys of
deception among the people.

'This answer was dictated by the chiefs themselves. The
missionaries at the station, although they were aware of the
visit of the priestess, and saw her, followed by the thronging
crowd, pass by their habitation on her way to the residence of
the chiefs, did not think it necessary to attend or interfere, but
relied entirely on the enlightened judgment and integrity of
the chiefs to suppress any attempts that might be made to
revive the influence of Pélé over the people ; and in the result
they were not disappointed, for the natives returned to their
habitations, and the priestess soon after left the island, and has
not since troubled them with the threatenings of the goddess.'

The 'sacred berries' referred to were small red berries
growing on low bushes, which the natives call *ohelo*. They are
rather insipid, but in the absence of water are a welcome refreshment to the thirsty traveller. Wild strawberries and rasp-
berries are also plentiful in the mountainous regions of Hawaii.
These are very palatable, though, for want of moisture, rather
small.

The district of Waiakea, with its spacious harbour, excellent supply of water, and extensive population, appeared admirably suited for a missionary station; and the chief promised every needed assistance, if he were assured of the sanction of the King. No other locality except Kairua seemed, in the present circumstances, equally adapted for the purpose; and the missionaries, on their return to that harbour, which had been their starting point, were rejoiced to find that their recommendation had been anticipated by the governor, Kuakini, who had already begun to build a substantial chapel, making use of the stones of a demolished heathen temple for the Christian sanctuary.

It was early in September before all the party arrived in Oahu. Mr. Ellis stopped on his return at Lahaina, where he found the king, his queen, Kamehamaru, Karaimoku, and other principal personages assembled in the house of Keopuolani, who was then seriously ill. The king's mother, feeling her end to be drawing near, urgently desired that no heathen customs should be allowed at her funeral, but that the obsequies should be conducted after the manner of the Christians.

Mr. Ellis reached Honoruru on tho 10th of September, grateful to find his beloved partner, though she had been a great sufferer in his absence, somewhat restored in health. Very soon after his arrival, he was summoned once more to Lahaina, to visit Keopuolani, who had become rapidly worse. He immediately set sail for that island, accompanied by his wife. At the earnest request of the dying queen-mother, the rite of baptism was administered to her by Mr. Ellis. Keopuolani was thus the first openly proclaimed convert to Christianity, and the first who received the sacred ordinance in the Sandwich Islands. On the following day she died. And, in accordance with her express wishes, the funeral was conducted, for the first time in these islands, with the simple obsequies of Christian burial. A large concourse of sincere mourners followed her remains to the grave. A brief account of the character of this pious queen, with a narrative of her last illness, her tranquil death, and the ceremonies of the interment, was published soon after, both in England and in America, and excited much interest.

When Mr. Ellis returned to Oahu, he found that, during his absence, the chapel at Honoruru had been burned down, it was suspected by some evil-disposed incendiary. But the malevolent object of injuring the mission was frustrated; for the chiefs and people set to work with vigour, and very rapidly put up a larger and more substantial place of worship.

Towards the end of the same year, 1823, a project to visit England, which Rihoriho had long contemplated, was carried into effect. Passage was secured for him, his favourite queen, Kamehamaru, and their suite, in the ship *L'Aigle*, commanded by Captain Starbuck. It was the earnest wish of the king, of Karaimoku, and the principal chiefs, that Mr. Ellis should accompany them; and this proposal was further recommended by the medical adviser of the mission, who urged a return to England as the only means of benefiting the rapidly failing health of Mrs. Ellis. Captain Starbuck was accordingly applied to for a passage for the missionary and his family; but refused to take them, alleging as his reason, in the first instance, want of accommodation. This objection being removed by the surgeon of the vessel, Dr. Williams, generously offering to give up his own cabin, the captain still peremptorily declined to take any white man. He was waited on by the king and chiefs, who offered to pay any charge he might make, and urgently pressed him to allow their friends to accompany the royal party; but Captain Starbuck firmly persisted in his refusal, saying he would give a free passage to the king and his native suite, but would not be induced by the offer of any amount of remuneration to take a member of the mission. This decision very much dissatisfied the chiefs. The king was taking with him twenty-five thousand dollars, and suspicions were naturally aroused concerning the motives of the captain. Indeed, he had openly declared that he would take no interpreter who would not speak and act just as he was bid. Captain Starbuck was therefore informed that unless he would allow Mr. Ellis to accompany him, the king would not sail in his vessel. He remained unmoved, and the negotiation was apparently given up. But a day or two prior to the time of sailing, the captain invited the king on board his ship, plied him with ardent spirits—a temptation he could never resist—and prevailed upon him, while under the influence of his potations, to accept the terms originally proposed. The king was kept in a state of intoxication, and finally taken on board in the same condition, and set sail with his queen and suite, having been literally kidnapped by the unprincipled master of the vessel. The whole affair was cause of great grief to Karaimoku, who now assumed the regency, and to other influential chiefs. It is well known that both the royal visitors died from measles soon after their arrival in this country, and within a week of each other, not having accomplished even so much of the object of their visit as an interview with the king, or the Directors of the Missionary Society, who were denied access to the party, on a point of etiquette, till they should have been presented to the sovereign. The Government extended every mark of attention to their guests, and after their decease, the highest respect was paid to their remains. A British frigate, under the command of Captain Lord Byron, (cousin of the poet), was appointed to convey to the Sandwich Islands the bodies of the king and queen, that their sorrowing people might have the mournful satisfaction of depositing their ashes among the tombs of their ancestors.

Many months elapsed before an opportunity was offered to the afflicted missionary's wife to return to her native land. Meantime, she could only serve her Divine Lord and Saviour by the gentleness and uncomplaining cheerfulness which she displayed under her severest sufferings; and there is reason to believe that this silent testimony to the power of the Christian faith was not lost. Occasionally, when she was well enough to receive visitors, a few were admitted into the chamber where she was reclining, and she delighted, at such seasons, to tell of

the love and faithfulness of her Creator and Redeemer. Everything that the most assiduous kindness and affection could
prompt to alleviate her pain, was done for her by the American
sisters and friends, whose constant and uniform tenderness and
sympathy elicited from the sufferer sentiments of the warmest
esteem and grateful love.

Mr. Ellis continued to be laboriously employed. Amongst
other duties which he undertook, was the instruction of six
Marquesan youths, who paid a visit to Oahu in 1824. He
spent some time daily with these pupils, took special pains
with them, finding them apt and intelligent scholars, prepared
for their use a spelling-book in the Marquesan language, and
printed a number of copies for them to take back on their
return to their native land. So that this indefatigable toiler
for the good of the heathen was thus instrumental in introducing the gospel, and the first elements of letters, into that
group of the Polynesian islands.

The demeanour of the natives at their public meetings and
religious services in this early stage of their transition from
barbarism to Christian civilization was not always marked by
that decorum which was so striking in the Society Islands.
The people would assume any convenient attitude, and would
sometimes indulge aloud in conversation. Pet animals would
accompany their owners : here might be seen a dog with his
head peeping out of a sort of pouch between the shoulders of a
native ; and in another part a screaming parrot would be perched
about the person of its mistress or an attendant. These incidents
were not a little embarrassing, and sometimes spectacles of
the most ludicrous character, in costume or accessories, very
sorely tried the preacher's power of countenance. On one occasion a woman, high in rank, entered with more than usual pomp
and stateliness, accompanied by a numerous train of attendants,
one of whom, nearest her mistress, carried a *covered pail*, evidently a new acquisition. While the missionary was wondering
what could be the purpose of this receptacle, the lofty dame

made a sign to her waiting maid, who, lifting the lid, plunged
her arm to the bottom, and brought up a white pocket hand-
kerchief, which her mistress, after ostentatiously using it,
returned, and it was once more deposited in the pail ; the happy
woman looking round with amusing complacency at the unpretending reticules of the missionaries' wives, from which she had
borrowed the idea, and in which it was the fashion for ladies to
carry that indispensable article of the toilet.　Mr. Ellis was
preaching at the time ; and with his quick and keen sense of
the ludicrous, would not have been able to repress a smile, had
he not schooled himself, with a wonderful self-control, to curb
every expression of emotion when it was needful.　He gave no
sign.　But the humour and infectious mirth with which he
would afterwards relate the circumstance at home, can only
be appreciated by those who knew his genial nature.　Such
irregularities as the foregoing were only temporary, and in
due time the ordinary observances of civilized life were fairly
established.

During his residence in Oahu, an incident occurred which
elicited a display of heroism as remarkable as it was characteristic, and proved that Mr. Ellis would not shrink from
anything that appealed to him on the grounds of duty
and humanity.　On the occasion of firing a salute, a sailor
on one of the ships in the harbour, while loading a cannon,
had his hand and fore-arm frightfully shattered by the
premature explosion of the gun.　There was no surgeon near,
or anywhere within reach.　Mr. Ellis was sent for, and saw at
once that there was but one alternative—amputation, or morti-
fication and death.　He explained the state of the case.　The
sailor begged that Mr. Ellis would perform the operation.　Thus
urged, and knowing that there was no other means of saving life,
he consented.　It is doubtful whether he had ever seen the operation performed ; he had probably only heard it described, and
read detailed descriptions in surgical books.　He did not, however, hesitate.　The arm was amputated, the arteries duly tied,

the flesh and skin brought together, and secured by ligatures, straps, and bandages. The patient was left comparatively comfortable, and overwhelmed with gratitude. The next day, and for many days, the case progressed as favourably as possible, and there was every prospect of the wound healing, and of a speedy convalescence, when, unfortunately, the sailor obtained possession of some spirits, of which he partook freely, and became intoxicated. In his frenzy he tore off the bandages, and brought on hæmorrhage. No one was near to apply the remedies, and the poor man bled to death. This unfortunate termination detracted nothing, however, from the skill and courage of the operation. The surgical cure would have been perfectly successful, but for the man's own folly.

The long desired opportunity of returning to England came, at length, through the kindness of Captain Coleman, the master of the American whaler, *Russell*, who put into the harbour of Honoruru on the 9th of September. Hearing what it was that the missionary family required, he offered, if they would accept such accommodation as his vessel afforded, to take them without charge to the United States, whence a passage home could easily be secured. The captain only intended to remain in port a few days; the decision, therefore, had to be made at once, and no time could be lost in preparation, if the Captain's obliging offer should be accepted. The American physician at Oahu gave it as his decided opinion that nothing but a return to her native land was likely to yield any permanent benefit to the invalid. It appeared, indeed, to all that this was the right course to take. The accommodations on board the *Russell* proved more ample and convenient than the modest captain had set forth, and it was quickly arranged that the mission family should accompany him on his homeward trip. It happened just at that time that one of the daughters was at Kairua, with Mr. and Mrs. Bishop, and another at Lahaina, with the family of Mr. Richards; these friends having kindly undertaken the charge of the children, in order to relieve their mother of part of her

domestic cares. Captain Coleman proposed to call at Kairua,
and Captain Blanchard, a friendly merchant residing at Honoruru, sent a small schooner to Lahaina, with a note, instructing
Mr. Richards to take the child under his charge, in the same
schooner, as far as Kairua, where they would join the rest of
the family.

The members of the American mission manifested their regret
at parting, and their sympathy with the sufferer by numberless
tokens of affection ; and the native women were scarcely less
assiduous in their kind attentions. The ship was stocked with
provisions to any amount by the presents sent on board by chiefs
and other natives, for use on the voyage. 'The 18th of September, 1824, was the day fixed for sailing : many of the chief
women were in the room in which the sufferer was lying the
greater part of the day ; and shortly after noon the members of
the mission joined them, when all united in fervent prayer for
the Divine blessing on those who remained, and on those who
were about to return in quest of health to a distant land.

'At the close of this interview preparations were made for
departure. The invalid had long been unable to stand or walk,
and as the distance was too far for her to be carried in a chair,
Mr. Hunnewell, a merchant in the settlement, a sincere and
constant friend to the missionaries, had obtained a light sort of
waggon, similar to those used in America, in which a couch was
laid. The chief women, who had been with her most of the day,
stood around her bed weeping, and its covering was wet with
their tears : when she was taken up and carried from her couch
to the conveyance her friend had provided, her two children accompanied her, and on reaching the sea-side a large boat was in
readiness, in which she was laid and conveyed to the ship lying
at anchor outside the harbour. When the boat came alongside
the chair was lowered down ; but as she for whom it was designed was unable to support herself, one of the friends seated
himself in the chair, and holding her in his arms, was hoisted
into the ship, where she was carried to her bed. About half-

past ten the captain and Mr. Ellis came on board, and a short time after, the vessel left her anchorage, with a light wind blowing from the island.'

Four days after leaving Oahu, the vessel reached Kairua, where Mr. Richards, with his charge, had already arrived. A brief stay was allowed here of little more than twenty-four hours, and the *Russell* once more launched forth on the wide waters of the Pacific, steering to the south. On the 24th of October, the vessel reached Huahine, and put into Fare harbour. It was the Lord's-day, and no one had come out to meet the vessel in their canoes, except a pilot. When this man had returned to shore, and reported who were the passengers, the people could not refrain from crowding the landing, to welcome once more their beloved teachers and friends. The captain remained in harbour for a little more than a fortnight; and thus a period of delightful intercourse with old friends was mutually enjoyed. Mr. and Mrs. Williams were sent for from Raiatea, and by their presence added much to the enjoyment of the re-union. It was a melancholy pleasure at this season to revisit once more the spot where they had formerly lived. It was now overgrown with weeds, and desolate in its solitude. The citron hedge had been cut down, but the coffee trees, which have since abundantly supplied the islands with plants, were loaded with berries. Some other importations from Rio were equally fruitful and flourishing. The stately chestnut trees still threw their umbrageous arms across the stream, and spread their coolness and shelter over the old bathing-place. During this pleasant interval, the people held one of their social entertainments, at which about 1,400 were present. At their earnest request, Mrs. Ellis was carried to the place of meeting on a couch, and reclined during the repast by the side of the queen and the young princess, who had been her ward, and still called her guardian or mother.

Here again the natives manifested their attachment by taking supplies of stock (chiefly poultry), fruit, and vegetables

on board, until the captain informed them that he could not
receive any more.   On the 11th of November, after uniting in
prayer with the affectionate brethren and sisters, and many of
the people, Mrs. Ellis was carried in a chair to the sea-side,
through lines of natives, who thronged to behold their departure, and tender their parting salutations.

'When our anchor was raised, and our sails spread,' Mr.
Ellis tells us, 'the vessel moved slowly out of the harbour.
The day was remarkably fine, and the wind light, and both
these circumstances afforded opportunities of leisurely survey-
ing the receding shore.   As the different sections of the bay
opened and receded from my view, I could not forbear con-
trasting the appearance of the district at this time with that
presented on my first arrival in 1818.   There was the same
rich and diversified scenery, but, instead of a few rustic huts, a
fine town, two miles in length, now spread itself along the
margin of the bay; a good road extended through the settlement; nearly four hundred white, plastered native cottages
appeared, some on the margin of the sea, others enclosed in
neat and well cultivated gardens.   A number of quays were
erected along the shore; the schools were conspicuous; and
prominent above the rest was seen the spacious chapel, capable
of accommodating 2,000 worshippers.'

The *Russell* pursued her way over the southern Pacific
without any special incidents to vary the monotony of a long
voyage.   The cooler air of the region, as the distance from the
tropics increased, appeared to have a beneficial effect on the
health of the invalid.   Cape Horn was rounded without en-
countering any very stormy weather, the vessel having her
studding sails set night and day, while crossing this usually
tempestuous junction of the two great oceans.   Throughout
the whole voyage the captain spared no pains to contribute to
the comfort of his passengers, and by his considerate attentions
rendered the voyage as pleasant as possible.   The port of destination, New Bedford, was reached in March, and on the 19th

of that month the voyagers were glad once more to set foot
on firm land. They had not been long on shore, when the
Rev. Sylvester Holmes called on them at the hotel, and with
much importunity besought them to remove to his own habitation.
As soon as the mother was able to leave the hotel, the hospitable invitation was accepted, and in the home of this Christian
brother they passed the brief period of their stay in that
neighbourhood.

The owners of the *Russell* very cordially approved of Captain
Coleman's conduct, and generously refused to accept any remuneration for the passage. After resting at New Bedford for
awhile, the family proceeded to Boston. A kind friend, the
proprietor of the mail coach running between the two places,
had one of his most easy and commodious conveyances expressly
fitted up with a comfortable couch for the invalid, and, in order
to render the journey as little fatiguing as possible, himself
drove the coach from New Bedford to Boston, a distance of
sixty miles. They arrived at the latter city on the 25th of
March, and were met by the officers of the ' American Board of
Commissioners for Foreign Missions,' and other Christian friends,
by whom they were welcomed with every expression of sympathy
and affection. They were received into the household of Mr.
Evarts, and remained under his friendly roof for many weeks.
The state of Mrs. Ellis's health now became very precarious, and
even at times alarming; so that her husband was frequently
summoned from a distance, by the physicians, under the impression that the sufferer was near her end. By Divine goodness, however, she was greatly restored as the summer approached; and in the month of June was able to accept the
kind invitation of the Honourable Samuel Hubbard, of Dorchester, a pleasant suburb of Boston, and became for a season
an inmate of his cheerful and hospitable home.

During this period, and as long as he remained in America,
Mr. Ellis was actively employed in preaching and addressing
public meetings on the subject of Christian missions, and par-

ticularly, in giving information respecting the sphere of labour which he had just left. The *Missionary Herald*, the official organ of the American Board, gives the following concise summary of his work in this department :—

'His first efforts of this kind were in Boston; and the large church in Park Street was twice thronged with attentive hearers. Mr. Ellis next delivered an address in the chapel of the Theological Seminary at Andover; afterwards, accompanied by the Treasurer of the Board, he went on a tour eastward, and made his interesting statements in Salem, Newburyport, Portsmouth, Saco, Portland, North Yarmouth, Brunswick, Bath, Hallowell, Gorham, and Dover. His next tour, in which he was accompanied by the Rev. Mr. Fay, a member of the Prudential Committee, was extended as far as New York city. In this tour he delivered addresses in Worcester, Brookfield, Amherst, Northampton, Springfield, Hartford, and New York. Besides two independent addresses in the last-named city, he took part in the anniversary exercises of the United Foreign Missionary Society, and of the American Bible Society.

'For the service which Mr. Ellis performed while in the United States he was well fitted. His habits of observation, his facilities of recollection, and his descriptive powers, gave to his narrations a fulness and vividness which rendered them remarkably fascinating; while, at the same time, every unprejudiced mind could not avoid receiving them as statements of facts. We believe Mr. Ellis to have been remarkably attentive to exactness in his descriptions, and anxious that the impression made on the hearer might correspond with the truth ; and, so far as our knowledge extends, such is the belief of all who have had the pleasure of a personal acquaintance with him. Hence his statements—corroborated, indeed, by the published testimony of many others—have everywhere been received with great confidence ; and they have exerted an influence upon our churches, which is quite invaluable.'

In the month of July, the health of Mrs. Ellis was so far

restored that her physicians sanctioned a journey to New York, with the view of her taking passage thence to England. On the 9th of the month, an easy carriage having been specially provided, the family left Dorchester, accompanied by their kind friends Mr. Anderson and Mrs. Washbourne. The first night was spent at Randolph. Proceeding by slow journeys they reached Hartford, and then Providence; where the travellers embarked in the steam-boat to New York. In this city they were hospitably received by Anson G. Phelps, Esq. Nothing could exceed the kindness everywhere shown to the English strangers by Christian friends in the United States.

On the 20th of July the family sailed from New York in the ship *Hudson*, commanded by Captain Champlin, a kindly and courteous officer, who won the gratitude and esteem of all who sailed with him. After a pleasant voyage of twenty-one days, the vessel approached the British coast. With what emotions the long absent voyagers once more beheld the shores of England, can be imagined only by those who have been placed in similar circumstances.

‘At Margate, arrangements being made for proceeding to London in a steam-packet, Mrs. Ellis was taken in her bed from the ship to the packet on the morning of the 18th of August, 1825, and reached the landing-place at the Tower of London in the afternoon of the same day. From the packet she was carried on her bed to the conveyance provided at the top of Tower-stairs; and in a little more than an hour afterwards was received once more under the roof of her beloved brother.’ Notwithstanding the afflictive circumstances under which the meeting took place, joy and thankfulness predominated over every other feeling; and all united, with hearts overflowing, and eyes moistened by gratitude, in ascriptions of praise to their heavenly Father.

MISSION WORK AT HOME

1825-41

CHAPTER VII.

TRAVELLING AGENCY.

FOR rather more than five years after his return to England Mr. Ellis was engaged in advocating the claims of the Missionary Society, and presenting statements of its work in the South Seas and elsewhere, before public audiences throughout the United Kingdom. There is not a town of any importance in England, Wales, Scotland, or Ireland, which he did not visit. Those were not the days of railways, and travelling, especially in the remote parts of the country, was often laborious and tedious in the extreme. Journeys on the outside of stage coaches, or in open vehicles of the roughest kind, often in cold and inclement weather, were a severe ordeal to one whose constitution was, doubtless, somewhat enfeebled by his previous residence in a tropical climate. His scrupulous regard for the funds of the institution on whose behalf he was serving made him, moreover, almost penurious in his expenses, and he would expose himself on the outside, when he ought to have taken an inside place in a stage coach. His work was also so fully pre-arranged that he had scarcely leisure for needed rest. Every day for months together had its appointed public service, or journey, or both ; and he sometimes felt, willing as he was to devote himself to the interests of the Society, that his labours were taxing his strength too severely. He was subject to severe colds, to attacks of dyspepsia, and other evils incident to the toilsome and irregular course of life he was compelled to lead. A strong constitution, however, an energetic spirit, and a willing heart, carried him uncomplainingly through all, and made him happy in his work.

It is difficult to estimate the influence he exerted, or the amount of good he effected, during these years of itinerant labour. Religious activity and sympathy with the benevolent departments of the Church's work were quickened and revived in hundreds of places throughout the country. A new impulse was given to missionary zeal and liberality, and an interest in the condition of the heathen, never felt before, was excited by the graphic descriptions of one who had dwelt amongst the benighted races for so many years. Very many, who themselves afterwards laboured as evangelists in foreign lands, ascribed their first impulses towards the work to the effect of Mr. Ellis's addresses; while a vast number at home justly attributed their enlarged sympathy and increased earnestness in the cause of missions to the same inspiration. In the course of his travels moreover, the missionary advocate was always a welcome guest in the families with which he sojourned. His genial, pleasant spirit, the fund of varied information always at his command, his enthusiasm in the object to which he had devoted his life, and the ready flow of his conversation, made him a most interesting companion; and he would often, without apparent effort, and in the most natural and unobtrusive manner, keep a large company for hours together in delighted enthralment by the charm of his fluent discourse.

But few records have been preserved of these journeys; and throughout the whole series of public services in connection with them, there would probably be a similarity of character that would preclude any necessity for particular notice. Amongst the few memoranda left is a 'Journal of a Tour in Ireland,' the details of which reflect great credit on the clergymen of the Established Church, who manifested a liberal and catholic spirit, and were on nearly every occasion the cordial supporters of public meetings on behalf of the London Missionary Society, even setting aside, for the time, the claims of their own Church of England institution. A visit to Powerscourt may be mentioned as affording an illustration of this fraternal feeling and conduct. The 'Notes' of the tour thus refer to it :—

'May 23, 1829—About ten in the morning, Mr. and Mrs. Pollock, Mr. Figgis, Mrs. Urwick, Mr. Grey, Mr. Edmonds, and myself, set off in two jaunting cars to Powerscourt, about fifteen miles distant. The country was level and verdant till we reached a romantic pass between two granite mountains, after which we came to Enniskerry, one of the prettiest rural and picturesque villages I have yet seen. In this village Lady Powerscourt has two schools, and in one of these we found our meeting was to be held. We alighted at the inn soon after twelve, and ordered refreshment. While we were partaking of this, we received a call from the Rev. R. Daly, the rector, and Rev. Mr. McKey, the curate, of the parish. They told us the meeting was their quarterly meeting in aid of the Church Missionary Society; but that the collection on that day should be given to our Society. We walked down together to the Infant School-room, where between two hundred and two hundred and fifty persons, many of them of great respectability, were assembled. Mr. Daly commenced by giving out the hymn, "O'er those gloomy hills of darkness"; after which, he made a short speech relative to the recent intelligence from the Church Missionary stations, and the operations of the London Missionary Society. He then introduced Mr. Edmonds, who detailed the results of his mission in India. I followed with an account of Africa, China, and the South Seas. Mr. Daly then made a brief concluding speech, told the people he should be glad to receive their regular quarterly subscriptions, but that whatever they felt disposed to give to the London Missionary Society would be thankfully received; that any subscriptions to that Society would also be acceptable. He announced his intention to become a subscriber of £1 1s. to that institution, and invited others present to give in their names for the same object. "We have," he said, "no plates or boxes here; but I will hold my hat, and my friend, Mr. R. Magee, whom I see standing at the door, will, I have no doubt, hold his for the same purpose." He then gave out the hymn, "From all that dwell below the skies," and concluded by offering up a most excellent extemporaneous prayer. Afterwards he took up his hat, and said, as he held it, that he did not think it had ever been put to so good a use before. The Rev. R. Magee, a clergyman of high position and considerable property, also held his hat, which was considerably whitened by the powder from his hair. After the company had departed, upwards of £13 was emptied from the hats of the two clergymen. Most gratifying of all was the fine feeling of liberal sentiment displayed, as well as of love and zeal for the glory of Christ, rather than anxiety for the advancement of any ecclesiastical interest.

'Lady Powerscourt, who was present with several other ladies of distinction, invited us to Powerscourt, and had ordered an extra conveyance for us. We therefore proceeded up the hill, through the domain of Powerscourt, to the mansion, and were much struck with the beauty and magnificence of this noble family seat. While standing at one of the windows that commanded an extensive view of a beautiful piece of water, a classic bridge, and all the varied scenery by which the domain is distinguished, we were joined by Mrs. Kelly, the wife of the author of the hymns, with her son, and two lovely daughters. The family expressed the delight with which Mr. Kelly expected us at Athie. After a hospitable entertainment, we took our leave between five and six in the afternoon.' A few days afterwards, a pleasant visit was paid to the beautiful residence of the Kellys.

During this tour the acquaintance of Mr. (afterwards Dr.) Urwick was formed, which subsequently ripened into a friendship of the closest kind. The Irish tour was immediately followed by one in Scotland, in which Dr. Patterson of Edinburgh, another of Mr. Ellis's staunchest friends, was his companion.

At the first annual meeting of the London Missionary Society after his return from the South Seas, in May 1826, Mr. Ellis, with his former colleague in the Sandwich Islands, the Rev. C. Stewart, and Captain Gambier, who had recently visited the islands of the Pacific, were associated together in presenting one of the resolutions submitted to the meeting, and delivered very interesting addresses. In 1831, the subject of these memoirs was appointed to preach one of the annual sermons at Craven Chapel. As one result of this sermon, it may be mentioned, that a fellow-townsman, the Rev. James Wilkinson of Wisbeach, was so impressed by it, that he was induced to devote himself to missionary labour; and a brother of the same gentleman also became a zealous missionary, in consequence mainly of representations on various occasions, and in printed publications, by the same persuasive advocate.

Successful as were Mr. Ellis's efforts on behalf of missions—in pulpits, on platforms, and in social intercourse—he exerted, certainly a wider, and probably a more effective, influence by his pen. Before he had been many months in England, his first work, the materials for which had to a great extent been prepared in the Sandwich Islands, and on the voyage thence to America, as well as during his stay in that country, namely, the *Tour through Hawaii*, was published, and met with a reception unprecedented certainly in the history of missions, and not often surpassed in the history of travel. It presented missionary work and its agents in a new aspect, to men who had never before given the subject a thought; it interested all classes of intelligent readers, and was for a time one of the most popular works of the day. It did good service in removing the prejudices on the subject that prevailed in certain minds. These were, however, in some quarters too deeply rooted to be at once easily destroyed; and hence, while the literary merit of the work, and the interest of its descriptions and details, were frankly acknowledged on all hands, some of the leading critical authorities of the day still maintained and expressed their opposition to Christian missions. Soon after the appearance of the *Tour*, a book was published under the authorship of Captain Kotzebue, a commander in the Russian Navy, containing most glaring misrepresentations in reference to the South Sea mission.

About the same time, an ephemeral production was compiled by a Mrs. Graham, from very doubtful and miscellaneous sources, but which was certain to be extensively read, on account of the recent interest of the events detailed, and the noble name associated with them—Captain Lord Byron. The book was entitled, *A Narrative of the Voyage of the Ship 'Blonde' to the Sandwich Islands*, and was interspersed with much palpable misstatement, unfavourable to the missionaries and their work. To these aspersions, as well as to some unfriendly letters by Captain Beechey, additional point and publicity were given by an article in one of the leading Reviews. Under the authority of the London Missionary Society, a reply to these calumnies was prepared by their Secretary, Mr. Orme, to which Mr. Ellis contributed a large portion of the material, and part of which, as an appendix, appeared in his own name. This reply presented a complete vindication of the mission. The writer of the article in the Review alluded to had supported his unfriendly representations by appending to his strictures the copy of a letter, just before received by an English Admiral, purporting to have been written by Boki, one of the ruling chiefs of Hawaii, and a member of the suite who accompanied the late King and Queen of the Sandwich Islands on their visit to this country. Mr. Ellis had been in communication with the Admiralty, and had furnished the department, at the request of Admiral Byng and Captain Parry, with an interesting and valuable account of the islands and harbours of the South Seas, which had been acknowledged in flattering terms by Mr. Canning. The letter bearing Boki's signature was shown to Mr. Ellis by the Admiral. He unhesitatingly pronounced it a transparent forgery, and satisfied the authorities to whom it had been addressed of the correctness of his judgment. Subsequently the document was unequivocally disavowed by Boki himself. In the meantime it was pressed into the service of the unfriendly critics of missionary enterprise. The letter itself, which is a curiosity, and the temperate reply to the article in which it was published, may be interesting, and will serve to illustrate one phase, at least, of Mr. Ellis's character. The letter is introduced by the following note :—

'Since the preceding pages have been struck off we have been favoured with a literal copy of a letter of Boki (which we pledge ourselves to be genuine), confirming what we have stated with regard to the conduct of the American missionaries at the Sandwich Islands.'

'ISLAND OF WOAHOO, *Jan.* 24, 1826.

'Sir,—I take this opportunity to send you these fu lines, hopping the will find you in good health, as ples god the leve me at present.   I am sorry to inform you that Mr. Pitt (Karaimakoo) has gon thro four opperashons sinc you sailed from here, but thank god he is now much better, and we ar in hops of his recovery, and I am verey sorey to tell you that Mr. Bingham the head of the Misheneres is trieng evere thing in his pour to have the Law of this country in his own hands. all of us ar verrey happy to have sum pepel to instruct us in what is rite and good but he wants us to be interly under his laws which will not do with the natives.   I have don all in my pour to prevent it and I have don it as yet, Ther is Cahomano wishes the Misheneres to have the whol atority but I shall prevent it as long as I cane, for if the have ther will be nothing done in thes Ilands not even cultivation for ther own use.   I wish the pepel to reid and to rite, and likewise to worke, but the Misheneres have got them night and day old and young so that ther is verrey little don her at present.   The pepel in general ar verrey much discetisfied at the Misheneres thinking they will have the laws in ther own hands.   Captain Charlton has not arived from Otiety which makes me thing sumthing has hapned to him.   Mr. Bingham has gone so far as to tell thes natives that nether king George nor Lord Biron has any regard for God, or aney of the English cheefs, that they are all bad pepel but themselves, and that ther is no Redemsion for aney of the heads of the English or American nations.   God send you good heath and a long life.

'Mrs. Bockey sends her kind love to Lord Biron and Mr. Camrone and the Hon. Mr. Hill.

Na Boke.'

Mr. Ellis replied in a letter to the Editor of the Review :—

'Spencer Street, Northampton Square.

'Sir,—While I feel obliged by your flattering notice of my volume on the Sandwich Islands, I am bound in justice to myself, and to my Missionary associates, as well as to the public, to correct several of the unfounded statements which that article contains.

'In the article above referred to, it is stated, "that by my own account, the subjects usually chosen for the discourses are the most unsuitable," "such, for instance, as the Virgin Mary, the Immaculate Conception, the Trinity, and the Holy Ghost." "That we hold out to our disciples little or no encouragement, either by precept or example, to industrious habits;" "that the least that is required from the naked, or half naked converts of Owyhee, is to attend at church five times every day," "that on Sunday they are strictly prohibited from cooking any kind of victuals, or even lighting a fire;" that "the efforts of the few zealous missionaries are tending, as fast as possible, to lay waste the whole country, and plunge the inhabitants into civil war and bloodshed;" "that thousands of acres of land, that before yielded the finest crops are now sandy plains;" that "the apprehension of civil war appears to be owing to the misapplication of a passage of Scripture (which, by the way, does not exist in the Bible,) applied and expounded by the Missionaries, and that the effect it had produced in lowering the authority of the chiefs was visible enough." That, at Tahiti, "it is lamentable to observe the change that has taken place among the natives, who appear to have lost the good qualities they once possessed," and "are become intolerably lazy;" that "the looms that were sent out, have been thrown aside, and weaving discontinued." "At Tobuai," it is also said, "that the indolence of the natives since their conversion has been such, that out of the whole population but 200 remain."

' These assertions, unsupported by anything contained in my volume, though some are said to " appear from my own account," are utterly unfounded, and have nothing corresponding to them in the existing circumstances of the islands, or the conduct of the Missionaries; and I am in possession of such evidence in support of this contradiction, as I cannot doubt would satisfy you that the writer of this article has been misled by the evidence on which he has depended. I will mention only one instance of the inaccuracy of Captain Beechy's information, and the consequent incorrectness of his statements. At Tobuai, he states that " the missionaries have succeeded in abolishing human sacrifices, and the prevailing crime of infanticide," when it is a fact that neither infanticide, nor the custom of offering human sacrifices, ever existed in that island.'

' The letter inserted as a " note to the article on the Sandwich Islanders," bears strong indication of being spurious; and I cannot but suspect that an imposition has been practised upon the British Admiral, to whom it was sent. Boki (who was my scholar until his embarkation for England), was never taught to write English, and probably never attempted it. The style of his sentiments, and the structure of his sentences would have been totally different. To " take " an " opportunity," is a phrase which would have been unintelligible to him. The commencement of the letter is a close imitation of the manner of letter writers of the lower order in this country, and has no resemblance to the native habits of thinking and expression. The phraseology throughout is foreign. No native of the Sandwich Islands would have any idea of *going* " *through* four operations." They never speak of a king as the *head* of a nation, a general as the *head* of an army, or a father as the *head* of a family. Had Boki wished to describe Mr. Bingham as (we should say) the head of the mission, he would have called him the *chief* of the mission. The facts of the letter contradict themselves.

Boki, with his brother, Karaimoku, exercises the supreme authority in the islands, and if it had been his desire that Mr. Bingham should have left the islands, his command would have been sufficient to have enforced at any time compliance with his wishes. The orthography in many instances is certainly such as Boki would not employ. Had he written the letter, he would surely have spelt his own name correctly, according to the orthography established by the printing-press in the island; yet in the last paragraph of the copy sent to England, with a sight of which I have been favoured, Mrs. Boki's name is spelt *Bockey*. Besides this incorrectness, here are two letters, viz., *c* and *y*, introduced, which do not exist in their language. In the next line, Boki's own name is spelt *Boke*, but in your Review both these names are altered, and appear as if they had been properly written, *Boki*.

'In addition to the above brief statement of evidence, that the letter was neither written nor dictated by Boki, I have evidence on his own testimony, dated only three months before this letter is said to have been written. I have also letters of a later date from missionaries and chiefs, containing very different statements. Boki, in the last letter to me, under date of October 1825, observes, " All is smooth and straight here, I am making myself strong in the word of God. Turned have the chiefs to instruction. I speak unto them, and encourage them concerning the word of God, that it may be well with our land."

' Without referring to all the topics alluded to in the letter, I feel myself called upon to state that, from habits of close friendship with Mr. Bingham, and an intimate acquaintance with his principles and conduct, I cannot for a moment suppose he has in any manner interfered with the civil or political affairs of the island.

' I am, Sir,

' Most respectfully yours,

' W. ELLIS.'

In the foregoing reply, the reader cannot fail to observe the temperate tone maintained throughout. This was characteristic of the man; not that he was by any means of a naturally meek or phlegmatic temperament; on the contrary, he was endowed with quick, deep, and strong feeling, easily and often powerfully roused. But, though probably a sense of personal dignity would always have made him self-restrained, the marvellous control he had acquired over his temper was the result of early and strenuous effort, springing from Christian principle. The mastery was complete and unvarying. He was never betrayed by the heat of controversy into intemperate expressions. In discussion, whether social or more public and official, he was always, though firm, quiet and courteous, and careful of the feelings of others. This quality was invaluable to him, and was, perhaps, in no small degree the secret of his success and influence in his official capacity in connection with the Society, and in a hundred difficult and delicate positions in which he was often placed during his eventful life. If in oral controversy, his self-command never forsook him, of course, in writing, when his judgment had full play and leisure to act, he was particularly guarded; and the moderation of his tone often elicited the warm admiration of his opponents. Unbiassed minds were convinced by calm and dispassionate statements, where greater vehemence or severity of language might only have aroused prejudice and strengthened opposition.

These years of public work were chequered by domestic events of very varied character. Before the close of the year 1825 the illness of Mrs. Ellis, after a temporary amendment, once more assumed a serious and painful form, and continued to be the cause of much solicitude and alarm, till the spring of 1827. On several occasions, Mr. Ellis was summoned from distant parts of the country, while engaged in his missionary tours, to attend, it was feared, the last hours of his afflicted wife; but as often the sufferer was wonderfully restored. The following letter, addressed to Dr. Raffles, will give some idea of these scenes of

mournful suspense, and will show how little in accordance with
the joyful and festive character of the season the Christmas of
1826 was spent :—

'LONDON, *Dec.* 30, 1826.

'Dear Brother,—Although not permitted to share the hospitality of your board at this season of the year, or avail myself
of the kind invitation given both by Mrs. Raffles and yourself,
I have often, in imagination, mingled with those warm friends
by whom you may have been surrounded, and the recollection
of the generous treatment I experienced while privileged to be
your guest has been grateful to my mind.   I hope the festivities
of the present period have been participated by yourself and
your friends, not only without alloy, but heightened by that
zest which religion imparts to every enjoyment of life.   To me
and mine it has been a season of severest trial and distress.
Mrs. Ellis is still confined to her bed, and with one exception,
has not been lifted from it since my return, and has once or
twice appeared to be sinking in the arms of death.   On the
24th and 25th instant I scarcely left her bedside for five minutes
together.   The painful post of observation drew darker every
hour.   Our children, who had all come home for the holidays,
gathered weeping round her bed, received her benediction, and
a few memorials of a mother's love.   We then stood watching
night and day the pale and painworn sufferer, expecting every
gasp would be her last.   Through mercy she is now revived in
a small degree; still the medical attendants preclude our indulging any hope of her ultimate recovery; and from the
alarming character of the symptoms still present, we fear it is,
to use her own affecting language, but the revival of a dying
ember, brightened for a moment under a passing breath of air.

'On the morning of the 25th, she repeated, with faltering
accents, the first lines of the "Dying Christian," dwelling on
the words, "Let me languish into life," adding: "It is not to
sink to annihilation, not to perish in the grave, but to glide out

of time into eternity—out of sorrow and pain into joy and happiness— through death into life and immortality."

'Long and severe as the affliction has been, her mind has uniformly enjoyed a peace of God which passeth understanding, and her hopes of an abundant entrance into the kingdom of her Heavenly Father have invariably, even in her seasons of severest anguish, been cloudless and unwavering. This is a blessing which worlds could not purchase, which is not a reward of any merit, but is the free and sovereign gift of Him who hath said, " I will never leave thee nor forsake thee: when thou passest through the floods, they shall not overflow thee ; and through the flames, they shall not kindle upon thee."

'I have relinquished the design of publishing a History of the South Sea Islands, merely out of deference to one or two missionaries, who, I learn from Mr. Nott, are preparing something of the kind. The missionary affairs in the South Seas, as well as in other parts of the world, are daily assuming a more prominent and important character than ever. The South Sea Islands have recently attracted the attention of a number of individuals in France, and even of the French Government. Two ships have been despatched to the Islands of the Pacific, Tahiti and Hawaii, on board of one of which vessels were six Jesuits, missionaries to the Society and Sandwich Islands. They have sailed under the special auspices of the French Royal Family, have taken out all the paraphernalia of Popery—viz. : images of Our Lady, crucifixes, crosses, shrines, banners, dresses, bells, &c., together with all the apparatus necessary for working miracles according to the improvements of modern science, viz. : a galvanic battery, electrifying machine, fireworks, &c. ; a splendid organ so constructed that the person who plays it will be invisible; and lastly, a Roman Catholic temple, in frame, to be set up at short notice. What the end of it will be it is impossible to say. The Society have made Government acquainted with the facts; and I have attended Mr. Hankey in an interview with the Under

K

Secretary of State at the Foreign Office. They appear determined to investigate the matter.

' I had great pleasure in hearing that you were to preach one of the sermons in May next, when, if not before, I hope to have the pleasure of seeing you.

' I remain,
' Faithfully yours,
' W. ELLIS.'

Passing by, for the present, the subject broached in the latter part of the foregoing letter, let us pursue the personal and domestic history. The tranquillity of spirit, and even happiness, enjoyed by the sufferer, were indeed amazing. She seemed to dwell continually, like Bunyan's Pilgrim as he approached the Golden City, in the land of Beulah. Her own expression on one occasion was, ' I feel more like an inhabitant of the celestial world, than of earth; yet I desire to be kept tranquil and resigned, rather than to have rapturous joys.' And at another time, after more than usually severe and protracted pain, she said with great emphasis, ' I would not change places with anybody—not with anybody.' Such evidence of delightful peace of mind, such expressions of heavenly joy, were deeply felt by her sorrowing husband as a merciful relief and solace to his own troubled spirit. To him and the nearest friends the message they seemed to convey was like the apostolic benediction, ' Comfort one another with these words ;' nay, without irreverence, it might be said it was like a voice from heaven, ' Be of good cheer, it is I, be not afraid.' There can be no doubt that this acquaintance with grief had its divinely appointed influence on the heart of God's servant, at once softening and strengthening it, and qualified him for greater usefulness in after years—for intenser sympathy with the afflicted to whom he was called to minister.

Contrary to medical opinion and the patient's own belief, in the spring of 1827, a signal measure of improvement took place in her health. At the earnest solicitation of relatives in Lincoln, she removed in June to that town, to be under the medical treatment of a surgeon who had been very successful in cases of spinal complaint. Her maternal uncle, Mr. Hart, who had assumed the name of Thorold, was residing at Harmston, a beautiful estate in the neighbourhood ; and her cousins were living in Lincoln. The visit to these relatives was divided between the two places. No time was lost in testing the new treatment. The result astonished all. The change was as surprising as it was cheering. The invalid, who had for years been confined to her couch, found herself able to sit up, to be driven in a carriage, and even to walk. She was also able occasionally to bear the fatigue of attending public worship. It was with feelings of inexpressible delight that she beheld once more the long unseen face of nature, and appreciated with new zest the beauty of the world around her, as only a convalescent after long illness is able to do.

> 'The common air, the earth, and skies,
> To him are opening Paradise.'

So complete and satisfactory was the amendment that arrangements were made by Mr. Ellis for returning to their beloved sphere of labour in the South Seas ; and it was confidently expected that in the following year this object of their long and intense desire might be accomplished. The improvement continued through the summer and autumn ; and in the end of October the recovered invalid proceeded to Sheffield, and spent some weeks with Mr. and Mrs. Read, of Wincobank. In the middle of December 1827, a further change of residence was made by removal to Nailsworth, in Gloucestershire. In this pleasant neighbourhood more than two years were spent, for the anticipations of recovered health were once more doomed to disappointment. Yet, though the return to the South Seas was postponed, the hope was not relinquished. Indeed, at the end of the period mentioned, it was again revived in all its force.

It is not necessary to follow minutely the domestic history of this interval ; but one or two matters demand notice. In the

anticipation of returning to mission work in the distant islands
of the Pacific, one great perplexity had exercised the parents'
minds.   This was a suitable provision for their children.   All
who know what heathen society is will understand that it is
almost impossible for a missionary, whose time is fully occupied
with public work, to train up a young family in a godly manner
among the heathen.   While revolving this important question, the parents found their anxieties removed in an unexpected manner by the considerate kindness and generosity of
Christian friends.   Amongst the first to offer a solution of the
difficulty were the brother-in-law and sister of Dr. Chalmers,
Mr. and Mrs. Morton, who resided at Chester Hill—Mr. Morton
being at the time the Agent of Lord Ducie, who owned extensive
estates in the neighbourhood.   These friends, in the most kind
and urgent manner, requested to be allowed to take charge of
one of the daughters, offering her a home in their own family
so long as her parents should remain abroad. But Mrs. Morton's
failing health did not allow the benevolent project to be carried
out.   A similar proposal, pressed with a delicate consideration
that could not offend, was made by Mrs. Norton of Nailsworth,
and her accomplished and estimable daughters.   This offer was
gratefully accepted for the second daughter.   In a like spirit of
disinterested friendship, the charge and education of the other
daughters were undertaken by friends in Dublin—Dr. Urwick
receiving the youngest into his family, and Miss Wright, in
conjunction with Miss Cullin, providing a home and training for
the eldest.   Although the project of resuming missionary work
was ultimately abandoned, these arrangements, which continued
for several years, afforded much satisfaction and relief.   The engagements of the father kept him much from home, and the
state of the mother's health precluded that attention to her
daughters, which was so important at their critical age.   Under
these circumstances, the Christian homes and careful training
secured for their beloved children was felt by the parents to be
a boon of inestimable value; and the results on the characters

of the young people were such as to call forth sentiments of the deepest gratitude.

Of the period spent in Gloucestershire many delightful weeks were passed at Chester Hill, under the hospitable roof of Mr. Morton; and in an equally agreeable visit, the family were guests of Mr. and Mrs. Norton. During the remainder of their stay they lived in one or other of the picturesque hamlets in the neighbourhood of Nailsworth. It was during the time of this pleasant residence in the West of England that Mr. Ellis published his second important work, *Polynesian Researches.* Its preparation had occupied brief and scattered intervals of leisure occurring in the busy missionary tours already spoken of. It had been written under all the disadvantages of constant interruption and distraction ; much of it having been penned at wayside inns, in stage coaches, sometimes under hedgerows and in fields; and, in short, whenever an opportunity could be snatched from the official occupations of this laborious season. The winter months afforded, to some extent, a temporary respite from travelling duties, and the holiday interval was sedulously devoted to the prosecution of the work of authorship. The original copy was written in a wonderfully small yet clear hand-writing, and the whole was transcribed for the printer by two of the Misses Norton. The intellectual intercourse with this accomplished family, enjoyed in connection with the preparation of this work, . and other literary recreations, was extremely pleasant, and, indeed, of essential service, to the author. Whether justly or not, the readers of the book in question may form their own judgment, but the writer himself was modestly conscious of his deficiencies in early education, and was ever ready to listen to the suggestions of a judicious friend. He was, moreover, at this time, disposed to consider his comparative disuse of his mother tongue, during the years he spent in the South Seas, as an additional disqualification for writing English. Curiously enough, he was so impressed with the effect of his long familiarity with the dialects of Polynesia, that he used to assert that speaking English made his face ache—the liquid, flowing, vowel sounds of the languages of the South Seas being much more easy to utter than English words, in which sibilants and consonants preponderate. His friends scarcely sympathised with him in the diffident estimate he formed of his own powers.

The appearance of *Polynesian Researches* very greatly enhanced its author's reputation. It was applauded by the contemporary press in a spirit very different from the reception which missionary records had heretofore too often met. Like its predecessor, it was read extensively by a class of persons hitherto prejudiced against, or indifferent to, those schemes of Christian philanthropy which the book was designed to illustrate and promote. It tended, in no small degree, to raise the character of the missionary to the heathen, and the claims of his work in public estimation. It is scarcely too much to say, that its publication effected a revolution in the general sentiments of all but the most determined enemies of religious enlightenment, and the mission work of the Church. It brought the author into intimate acquaintance with many of the best and noblest men of the day. The favour which it met with surprised none so much as himself. The commendation it received from some of the foremost Reviews of the period may be inferred from the terms in which Southey speaks of it in the *Quarterly Review.* 'A more interesting work than this,' says that able critic, 'we have never perused.' The influence it exerted is indeed difficult to estimate, and will, perhaps, scarcely ever be fully known. Men grown grey in the work of the Christian ministry, veterans who have toiled amongst heathen tribes in distant lands, attribute their earliest inspirations to the perusal of those fascinating pages; statesmen, at home and abroad, read them with interest, and men of science and of letters gathered from them new treasures to enrich their stores of knowledge; while the Christian in every walk of life could not fail to have his ardour quickened thereby in the noble work of bringing all men to the knowledge of the Saviour.

The deep impression which these missionary narratives made upon the mind of at least one good and great man, will be illustrated by the following interesting correspondence, which took place about that time. The circumstances under which the letters were penned were as follows. The custom, since superseded by photographic albums, of collecting in an autograph book, the handwriting of friends or celebrities, was then very common; and Mrs. Ellis possessed one of more than ordinary interest, containing, as it did, autograph contributions from such persons as S. T. Coleridge, Robert Southey, Hannah Moore, Robert Hall, John Foster, William Wilberforce, Rowland Hill, Thomas Chalmers, and other eminent characters. Among the number, Richard Winter Hamilton of Leeds, had written a poetical effusion in which he described the enthusiasm kindled in his mind by the account of missionary life in the South Seas, and the strong desire it had awakened to engage personally in the work—a desire which, the writer averred, nothing but a weak vacillation of purpose, and an unworthy moral cowardice, had prevented him from carrying into effect. Mr. Ellis felt himself constrained by this frank confession to write to his friend, earnestly entreating him to reconsider the subject. This letter, which has apparently not been preserved, called forth the following reply and rejoinder :

From Richard Winter Hamilton.

'LEEDS.

' My dear Friend,—Often have I taken up my pen to answer your apparently long neglected letter, and have as often laid it aside. My mind is still in turmoil, and little able to convey its ideas, or rather shadows of ideas. But I can refrain no longer from expressing my deepfelt gratitude to you for your most affectionate, and, whatever be the issue, your most profitable remonstrance. I hope never to lose the benefit of it—assuredly I can never forget nor undervalue the excellent motives which prompted it.

' I quite forget the few hastily composed lines which I felt it an honour to contribute to your lady's album. To have any place in the memory of one so devoted, to contribute in any way to the momentary relief of one so afflicted, was a privilege I could not forego. The sentiment I well remember. It sprang not up for the first time then. For never could I see a missionary but I envied him; never did I hear of missionary success but I sighed to have had a share in achieving it.

' There is one dear friend from whom I conceal nothing, with whom I have frequently interchanged ideas. Ely of Rochdale and myself have often conversed about the point of duty. And other friends, less confidentially endeared, have been occasionally the depositaries of feelings which I was not only impelled to unbosom but anxious to impart. One thing I may just say has been a favourite topic of mine. I have pressed it again and again. I have thought and said, that if a dozen, fewer or more, settled ministers, *comfortable, useful, established* in *every* sense, would propose themselves for the arduous work—ministers who would have to *tear* themselves from their homes—ministers of rank, influence, and not only talent, but commanding *popular* talent—ministers who have been known as advocates of it long, blowing the trumpet to the host, if such would volunteer their *personal* service, east, west, north, or south—a new movement would be given to the Christian public, a new era would be dated in missionary history. The lurking suspicion that we love to shirk our duty and exonerate ourselves, must be done away, and our portion of the Christian Church assume an aspect of *earnest sincerity* which I fear it too greatly fails to present. Oh, believe me, how have I panted to be enrolled among that few, that happy few, that band of brothers.

' If I know myself, I could not refuse to go forth were my *duty* plain. How am I to know it ? I think that should such a case as this be put—a minister perfectly happy in the kindness and respect of his people, occupying an important station, animated by an increasing audience and church, with three motherless babes looking to him for education and protection—ought he to 'go up'? I suppose the general verdict would negative it. I say not that this quite satisfies me.

'What seems to disqualify me for the glorious undertaking is what I must "speak to my shame." I have not that quick sensitive all-absorbing zeal which must be required. Alas, I have ungodly relatives with whom I often mix, yet I say nothing to arouse them to a sense of their danger. I am surrounded by thousands of most ignorant and vicious persons, and still I am afraid and loth to interfere with them. I see and hear misery on every side—-I want the courage to address the remedy. I love the quiet of my regular duties—my, what the venerable Waugh called, "ignoble anchorage." Should I be fit to go to the high places of the field? And thus I reason with myself; my deceitful heart sometimes offering a sophism which I at once detect, at others imposing upon me one it may be as illusory but which I cannot overthrow. Cannot I pray after all—"show me thy way, O God"? Pray, dear friend, not only this for me, but that I may have disposition, when that "way is shown," to follow—a coincidence which I dare not pledge.

'I promised you but the shadows of ideas. I am afraid you will not understand me. I do not myself. There is a confusion in my soul which I cannot unravel. Oh, for light from Heaven! If you should think me worthy of another communication be sure I shall treasure it; never shall I lose the remembrance of this act of kindness towards one whose constant fear is that he will be cast away as an unprofitable and slothful servant, whose best hope is that he may just be saved from hell, and that so as by fire. But enough: all good be with you; my heart thanks you and blesses you; forget me not to your excellent partner; may God be the guide, strength, and portion of you both.

'Ever your sincere and grateful friend,

'RICHARD WINTER HAMILTON.'

From W. Ellis to R. W. Hamilton.

' MISSION COLLEGE, HOXTON.

' My dear Brother,—The very kind manner in which you have replied to my unbidden, but, I now believe, not unwelcome communication, on the subject of missionary engagements, has been, I confess, truly gratifying to my mind. The apprehension that you might regard my remarks as obtrusive did, though but transiently, possess my mind. I was, however, impelled by a powerful sense of duty to offer, whatever might be the result, not what you have I firmly believe by mistake called a "re-monstrance," but an invitation, that you would review a subject which I was convinced was not unfamiliar to your thoughts, and at the same time replete with all that was important in time and eternity to perhaps millions of your species. Your letter has corroborated my convictions; and under this impression I could now fully pour out before you the whole flow of my own soul—my hopes, and desires, and feelings, and reasons; but I deem it most expedient to forbear, lest I should unduly influence your mind. I feel that in this matter I am acting under God, and would, therefore, offer no remark that will not bear His scrutiny now, and the most mature consideration in any period of trial that might hereafter arrive. Were I to give expression to my feelings and desires, and my own impressions as to the beneficial results that would accrue to the missionary cause and to the heathen world, I should urge upon your consideration every inducement to engage in this work. But in a matter so intimately connected with every earthly interest, and the future destiny in this life and the next, my opinion and desires ought not to be the rule of your procedure. Every missionary should be *satisfied in his own mind* that it is his duty to engage in the work; that, so far as he can determine the Divine will con-cerning him, he is called to it of God. This I deem essential; and it will constitute a foundation for peace and satisfaction amidst the greatest difficulties. Anything that I may offer, therefore, will only be in the humble hope of assisting you in this inquiry.

'I have several times been placed in circumstances under which it was difficult to ascertain the will of God, but in which it was necessary for me to act, and that act has very materially affected my future life. It is our privilege to be encouraged to commit our way unto Him who has promised to direct the steps of his people ; but I need not observe to you that, with the most entire reliance on every promise of Divine guidance, we are not to expect any extraordinary or supernatural manifestations, but are to apply general principles to particular circumstances. One prerequisite to the right understanding of the will of God, I have always considered to be, a postponement or suspension of my own determination, until, so far as I was able, I had endeavoured to ascertain this. Many persons err in this. They make up their minds to a certain procedure, and ask Divine direction, seeking, not so much to know the will of God, as to discover something that will warrant the inference that God will approve the course they have already determined, if possible, to pursue.

'I know it is difficult to contemplate impartially two or more important measures with a strong bias towards one or the other. The means I have usually found satisfactory to my own mind have been—first, the sacred oracles. I need not here refer to the very explicit warrant they furnish for engaging in missionary undertakings. Next to this, I have ever deemed it a privilege to avail myself of the advice of pious, judicious, well-informed and, if possible, unbiassed friends. But the diversity of opinion sometimes given serves often to perplex rather than to direct. Lastly, I have endeavoured to exercise, with the utmost care, my own judgment—to examine the origin and tendency of my motives or desires. I would carefully avoid indulging for a moment the sentiment that impulse is to be the rule of conduct, or that we are to submit judgment to feeling; yet I do think that when it is in accordance with the Word of God, the design of the Gospel, the advancement of the great ends of our existence, and the opinion of good men, a strong conviction of duty to engage in a work—a desire for it from motives such as God will approve—that very impression, or conviction, or bias, is a strong indication of the will of God concerning us.   This is, I think, in most cases, the first secret spring that puts in motion those feelings and deliberations that lead to the work of the Christian ministry at home, and the missionary enterprise abroad.   It was this bias, originating in a circumstance comparatively trivial, that induced me to commence that train of thought and inquiry which resulted in the conviction that it was my duty to tender my services for this work.   It was, my dear brother, the discovery of this impression existing in your mind that prompted me to bring the subject under your review; as it was possible that, by a reconsideration of it, you might receive such light and guidance as should satisfy your mind that it was the will of God that you should go forth.

'I have often felt with you how desirable it would be that a number of ministers, such as those you describe, should engage personally in the work ; but perhaps we must not expect it at once.   Freeman, of Kidderminster, going out to Madagascar, is an illustration ; and he has indeed a most important station. There is a feeling in favour of the work among the students at Glasgow and at Highbury.   I have met with many, in different parts of the country who have expressed a similar desire ; but there has always been something that has marred their extensive usefulness at home, and it has been a kind of alternative experiment they have wished to try.   Others have had such family or pecuniary embarrassments as have precluded the idea of their engaging in it.   I think this the greatest difficulty that many able and well-qualified ministers feel.   I am, however, not without hopes that greater numbers will yet enter the field ; and every fresh instance I consider increasingly valuable, not only for the amount of energy brought to bear on the heathen world, but on account of the influence of such dedications on ministers and churches at home.

'Your own case, as you have put it, is certainly a strong one ; and I agree with you that the general verdict would be a negative ; but I would put a stronger case, so far as it respects the dearest and tenderest bonds that bind you here.   I do not leave an important station, an increasing audience and church, but I expect to leave not three but four dear children—so far as it regards the watchful care in moulding their plastic minds and forming their future characters—motherless. I expect to leave my beloved wife—sharer of my joys and griefs, my toils and my repose on heathen ground—in the midst of kind friends indeed, but confined to a couch of languishing and pain.   I feel convinced that were our case submitted to public decision, that verdict would detain me at home.   Yet my dear wife and myself, after painful deliberation, and intimately acquainted as we are with all left here and to be endured there, think it my duty to go—of course for a limited period only.   For a limited period only would I advise your engagement, were you to devote yourself to the work.   At the expiration of this, if it were desirable, you could honourably continue in the field, or, otherwise, as honourably return.

'With regard to qualifications, we are perhaps seldom the most competent judges of our own fitness for stations that we may be called to fill.   I was struck with the resemblance between your feelings and my own concerning ungodly relatives, and the conduct to be pursued towards those with whom we associate ; and often write bitter things against myself for my inconsistency in this respect.   I could stand up in the midst of a heathen assembly, and tell them to flee from the wrath to come, and, I sometimes hope, lay down my life rather than deny my Lord ; yet, when introduced to a party of friends, or seated for many hours in a stage coach with those whose conversation is often interesting, but who, whatever they possess, plainly want the one thing needful, my dastardly fear of being thought puritanical or conspicuous on account of my religion, will doom me to sit silent and self-condemned during the whole journey.

'The close of your letter deeply affected me. I sympathise tenderly with you. The mind is relieved by sympathy, and by unburdening itself of its sorrows. Your feelings on this point are not peculiar. Often after services that appear to have excited the deepest interest, I return under emotions of keenest anguish. The benefit others may have enjoyed appears to heighten my own pain, that I have declared and described what I do not feel— that after all I shall become a castaway—that even the heathen, whom I may have been employed to bring to Christ, shall at the last day look in vain for me among the blessed. The heart knows its own bitterness: much I have been able to unbosom to one dearest, best, of all earthly friends, and have never done so without relief and comfort; but there is much that is known only to God and my own soul—kept from a mind already suffering too much from sensibility, and whom to distress would augment my own grief. But, my dear brother, though this is often the case with me, I dare not abandon hope. Precious, infinitely precious, are those promises that still invite to Christ. To Him, when other refuge fails, the soul can flee, and find security and strength. Commending you to this " Rock of our Salvation,"

'I remain, faithfully yours,

'W. ELLIS.'

In this correspondence, as in other communications addressed by the same writer to young men who appealed to him for advice, before engaging in mission work, or to ordained ministers on the eve of their departure to foreign stations, the conscientious missionary has emphatically asserted the high estimate in which he held the sacred calling, the purity of the motives which alone should in his opinion justify its assumption, and has especially pointed to the constraining sense of duty which would not listen to any alternative, as the guarantee of fitness for the work. Such was the spirit that moved the Apostle Paul when he wrote to the Corinthian disciples, 'For necessity is laid upon me; yea, woe is unto me, if I preach not the Gospel.'

The reference to his own case in the foregoing letter, shows also how earnestly the writer of it desired to resume his own missionary work; that he was even willing to sever for a season the tenderest ties, and leaving the dearest companionship, to go forth once more to the scene of his early labours alone.　In the spring of 1830, however, a favourable change in the health of his beloved wife once more rejoiced the hearts of both, and re-awakened hopes of resuming together their labour of love. Under these gladdening prospects, they left Nailsworth and returned to London in April of that year.　The amendment in health was so great, that confident expectations were entertained of being able to leave England for the South Seas in the course of the summer.　Mrs. Ellis was strong enough to make short excursions into the country, and the writer well remembers the surprise and delight with which he saw her arrive one afternoon, in an open carriage, at Mill Hill (ten miles from London), where he was then at school.　She was able to attend public services and was present at more than one of the May Meetings.

Towards the end of the month of May, in the hope of gaining strength by a brief residence at the sea-side, the convalescent made what proved to be an ill-advised journey to Brighton. The fatigue of travelling so far, and the motion of the coach, were excessively distressing, and brought on a return of unfavourable symptoms.　Rest and the remedies employed, though they afforded temporary relief, failed to restore her to her former measure of health.　The first attack of illness was followed by others still more distressing and alarming, and the patient was more than once reduced to so critical a state that her husband and children were hastily summoned to her presence under the apprehension of her death.　Again she was restored, as it were from the brink of the grave, but never more so far recovered strength as to be able to leave her couch of pain.

CHAPTER VIII.

SECRETARIAT.

THE disappointment of cherished hopes was bitterly felt, but submitted to with Christian resignation; and subsequent events appeared to indicate that the Master had other work in store, and a nearer field of labour, for His faithful servant. In the spring of the year 1830, the Missionary Society had sustained the loss of an efficient officer in the person of its Foreign Secretary, the Rev. William Orme. The duties of the office were for many months temporarily performed by London ministers, while the Directors were deliberating the important question, whom they should select to fill the responsible post. Early in 1831, Mr. Ellis was requested by them to assist in discharging its duties; and for that purpose, as soon as he had finished the missionary tour in which he was then engaged, he once more took up his residence in London.

The characteristic diffidence with which he undertook the new duties assigned to him, will appear from the following extract of a letter addressed to Mrs. Ellis at Brighton, under date March 3rd, 1831 :—' On Thursday I commenced my duties at Austin Friars, and have just come home after the close of my first week's work. Next week I meet the temporary Secretary, and arrange what duties I am to undertake. It is fixed that I preach at Craven Chapel one of the sermons. Mr. Clayton, Mr. Arundel, and others say the engagement is only temporary, but that there is nothing to prevent its being permanent, if I find myself equal to it. I feel my deficiencies, and trust to be enabled daily to look to the only proper source of all qualification, for every

needed aid. Above all, I fear lest my unfitness should stand
in the way of the usefulness of the institution with which I
am connected. I know I have your prayers, and feel I need
them.'

That this modest estimate of his own qualifications did him
less than justice, and that the Directors had made a wise selection in the choice of their new secretary, was soon apparent to
all who had an opportunity of judging ; and so efficiently were
the subordinate duties of Mr. Ellis's first appointment discharged,
that in the following year he was requested to accept the office
of Foreign Secretary-in-Chief. The appointment was officially
ratified at the annual meeting of the Society in May 1833. The
post, indeed, was one for which he was peculiarly fitted. Having
been himself engaged in mission work in a heathen land, he
knew the heart of a missionary, and could sympathise better
than most men with the difficulties and trials of his lot. The
agents of the Society at their different foreign stations soon
learned to feel that, in corresponding with him they were holding
intercourse with a personal friend, and wrote with more freedom
and unreserve than is usually found in official communications.
His experience, caution, and sagacity rendered him a valuable
counsellor to the directors in the conduct of their affairs, and to
his missionary brethren abroad. His remarkable powers of
memory enabled him to keep always in view the multitudinous
affairs of the Society, and he could at all times be referred to
respecting the details of the past, with as much confidence as
the inquirer would feel in consulting the records of the minute-
book. His conciliatory manners, prudence, and temper admirably
fitted him for taking a leading part in the direction of affairs
where collisions of opinion were inevitable. His industry was
untiring, and heart and soul were engaged in his work with a
zeal that never flagged. The value of such a man, in such a
situation, could not fail to be cordially appreciated.

For some months after Mr. Ellis had entered upon his new
duties in 1831, the health of his wife detained her in Brighton ;

L

and it was not till nearly the end of the year that she was able
to undertake the journey to London. From that time till the
close of the mother's life the family resided in Islington.

In June 1834, the return of Mr. Williams and his family
from the South Seas, while it afforded their former associates
the unexpected pleasure of renewed personal intercourse, gave a
new impetus to the public interest in mission labour. The
stirring addresses of Mr. Williams never failed to produce a
powerful effect, and the publication of his *Missionary Enterprises* revived and augmented the vivid impressions that had
formerly been produced by the appearance of *Polynesian
Researches.* The reanimated missionary zeal of the Church
entailed additional though welcome labour on the directors of the
London Missionary Society, and that year, as well as those that
followed, were very busy ones with the Foreign Secretary.

The state of Mrs. Ellis's health at this time was a constant
source of much domestic anxiety. Its influence on the home,
and on the mind of her husband, may be gathered from the
following letter, written by a missionary's son, who was then an
inmate of the family. It was addressed to the writer in view
of the preparation of these memoirs; and as its touching and
grateful reminiscences present a clearer picture of the tried but
privileged household than anything he could himself have
written, he gladly introduces it here in place of words of his
own.

'LONDON, *March* 3, 1873.

' MY DEAR ELLIS,—You know that in the days of my youth
I was, through the great kindness of your father, brought into
intimate relationship with him, and with the serene and hallowed
home which then included the entire household. Possibly a
few of my reminiscences of those days may prove suggestive to
you in your review of that period of his life.

' It was in April 1834 that I arrived in England. Your father
and mine had been "chums" at the Missionary College at
Gosport, of which Dr. Bogue was tutor. The friendship of their

then life was much interfered with by the oceans that divided the missionary stations to which they were appointed, so that their letters to each other were few, and were six or seven months in reaching their destination; but in consequence of this old friendship, and of your father being the Foreign Secretary of the London Missionary Society, I was accepted by him as his special charge. How my heart thrills with thankfulness and joy as I recal the immeasurable blessings which thus filled my lot! About two years before his death, in a general inspection of letters prior to their destruction, I came to a large bundle from him, and the other dear ones of that home, and after I had read them I could not restrain the impulses of love and gratitude they excited, but poured out my heart to him in a letter of thanksgiving to him and to God. You do not need me to tell you how profound was my reverence for him as the wisest and kindest friend I had in England. His wisdom and godliness filled me with an awe which, notwithstanding his gracious and playful manner, I never lost—so that to the last I always felt that he was on a much higher level than that on which I and my companions stood. Whenever he gave me advice, adding in his kind way the reasons for it, it seemed to be exactly the very thing to do—never for a moment was I able to doubt or question it. There was about him, as I shall ever remember him, all the sagacity and foresight of eminent statesmanship with the gentleness and patience of a tender-hearted woman.

'But to return to the home of 1834. It was my introduction to home life in England. Everything was new, and the impressions I received are indelible. I remember him in his office in Austin Friars, when I was given over to his charge, the morning after my arrival in London, your coming in soon after and taking me to your house. I can recal the features of the servant who opened the door, the two portraits, and the two Polynesian landscapes in the front room, and the welcome to dinner in the room behind from your three sisters, Mary,

Elizabeth, and Annie. And the chamber above! That curtained bed—that white, thin, patient, loving face! The tears gather and drop as I write these lines. You perhaps forget the kindness of your mother to the stranger boy that had drifted to the haven. Do you think I can? With all her pain and weakness, and the cares of her own children, she at once found room for me in her thoughts and anticipations. When the month of May brought to town the late Rev. Thomas Scales, of Leeds, she sent for him, as secretary of Silcoates School, to which I was going, and bade him be a father to me. What a solemn tender hour in that chamber did we spend! Mr. Scales afterwards frequently referred to it.

'Nor was this all. Do you know that her thoughts followed me to school? Not only did she send loving messages in the letters your sisters used to write, but at Christmas how she made glad my heart by a box of schoolboys' cheer! Nearing though she then was the hour when " heart and flesh " would for ever " fail," she remembered the lonely boy in the distant school. That chamber is very memorable to me. It was there that we had family worship whenever the sufferer was not in acute pain. You remember that in the morning we had all of us to repeat a passage of Scripture, and frequently I broke down. So did sometimes your sister Annie, even when the bible from which she had been learning the text was in her hand. Whatever the passage, your father immediately gave the whole, and always finished by repeating an entire psalm or chapter, generally from the prophecies of Isaiah. I know these feats of memory used to astonish me. Nor can I forget the general influence of that sick chamber upon the whole household. There was a gentleness and self-repression of a very refined kind pervading the house. When it was a " bad day " upstairs, the house was hushed, the piano closed, and we spoke quietly and walked softly, and each heart seemed full of sympathy and prayer. Your father evidently felt that the shadow of death was on his home. Sometimes he was able, as he was so fond of doing, to tell us a good story, or quote some funny thing he had heard; but usually he was very serious in spirit, and had a look of settled gravity. He was working hard at the time, for I remember that he generally came home late, and often sat up at night to write. And yet how much he thought about me! He it was who used to plan the sight-seeing for me, in which you were the ever-willing guide and guardian, and caution me every day, as a new arrival, about catching cold. I bless God that that home was the first English home I entered. The wise and godly father, the saintly mother, your affectionate, beaming sister Mary, with the graver Elizabeth, and the mirthful Annie (all now gone!), and you, with your kind and patient ways, how can I be thankful enough that the " lines " fell unto me in such " pleasant places."

'I must not forget your father's preaching. We attended " Union Chapel," and our minister was good Mr. Lewis. But your father often preached there on Sunday afternoons, and the earliest sermon I can recollect was one I heard from him there. I think you were with me. I know Annie was. It was in June 1834. The text was " Thou shalt guide me with Thy counsel, and afterwards receive me to glory." It was treated in a beautifully simple way. I remember the heads: " If you were going a journey into a new and strange country, what sort of a guide would you want? (1). One that knows the way. (2). One that could tell you about the things you saw. (3). One that would be a pleasant companion. (4). One that would keep with you to the end," and so on. Even then I recollect being struck with the ease, naturalness, and fluency of his speech; I don't remember his ever hesitating for a word.

' I cannot conclude without some reference to him in his relation to missionary work. At the time to which I have been referring, he had published his two famous books the *Tour in Hawaii*, and *Polynesian Researches*. These works were the first on missions favourably reviewed in any of our Quarterlies. The *Edinburgh* notoriously only ridiculed *Missions to the Heathen*; but Southey, the Poet Laureate, reviewed the *Researches* in the *Quarterly* with great approval, and this led to your father's visiting him at Keswick. When it is borne in mind that your father's education was of the plainest kind, and that he had been living for years as far off as the South Seas, and his life had been chiefly spent in hard everyday toil of every kind, I think his eminence as a literary man was marvellous. His fluency applied to his pen as well as to his speech, and there was I think in later years a tendency to diffuseness in his style; but in the days to which I am alluding it was generally admitted that he wrote chastely, forcibly, and elegantly. I remember the late Dr. McAll of Manchester telling me when I was a schoolboy, that I could not do better than learn to compose as Mr. Ellis did, and I know I used often to read, as full of beauty, that passage in the " Polynesian Researches " describing a moonlight scene in a journey along the coast of Eimeo with Mrs. Ellis and an infant. But my main purpose in this reference to your father as a missionary is to direct your attention to the letter which is enclosed. Many years after the period of which I have been writing I wrote to him about becoming a missionary. The enclosed letter was his reply. Here is found the secret of his intense dedication to missionary work. No one more fully possessed the specialities he here presents as essential to fitness for it. It was with him an inspired enthusiasm. Not more divinely were Abraham, and Moses, and Isaiah, and Paul called to their special offices and work.

> ' I am, my dear Ellis,
> ' Ever heartily yours,
> ' JOHN T. BEIGHTON.'

The following extract from the letter referred to will serve to bring out once more Mr. Ellis's very decided views on the qualifications for missionary work. After alluding to the

advice of his young correspondent's tutor, Dr. Harris, that he should engage in the work of the ministry at home, in preference to missionary work among the heathen, he writes:—
' I concur in his opinion from other considerations as well as those you have mentioned. 1. I have always feared your temperament was too ardent to bear safely the nervous and mental excitement, and consequent debility, of a tropical climate. 2. Without derogating from the weight of the considerations which you urge in favour of your going, it is my firm conviction, matured by much experience, that something more than a *willingness* to go, something more than a sense of duty, and a readiness to pursue what, under ordinary circumstances, would appear the appropriate sphere of usefulness, is necessary to qualify anyone for entering effectively the missionary field, or to justify the ministers of Christ in sending him forth. There should be a decided and matured predilection for the work—an impression on the heart and conscience, after much consideration and prayer, that the Great Head of the Church has called the individual to that work, that not to enter it unless insuperable objects intervene, and to relinquish it unless from absolute necessity, would be a positive dereliction of duty. There should be a conviction of the judgment, and an attachment of the heart to the work, which would make the individual uneasy in any other sphere, so long as there was any probability of his entering that. It is no fault in anyone not to possess these pre-requisites, but the want of them has, I believe, been one great cause of the disappointment felt by many good men themselves, as well as by the churches sending them forth. Our divine Lord does not appear to have given them to you, and, therefore, though you are a missionary's son, and the missionary field might on that account alone appear your appropriate home, I should say, till you possess them, do not think of foreign service in your Saviour's cause; rather regard the absence of them as an indication of His will that you should seek some other sphere.'

The long period of suffering so patiently borne was now fast drawing to its close. The year 1835 found the whole family assembled at home under circumstances of more than usual enjoyment, and little anticipating the mournful bereavement that awaited them. The health of the beloved invalid appeared somewhat improved, and her appetite had also increased. On the morning of Saturday, the 10th of January, her husband left her without the smallest apprehension of any unfavourable change, little conscious that he should never again hold intercourse with his beloved wife. An engagement to preach in the country on the following Sunday prevented his return in the evening. The children passed the closing hours of the day with their mother, happy to find her more than usually cheerful and free from pain. Before retiring to rest, one of them having read a portion of Scripture, the mother offered, as was her custom in the absence of her husband, the petitions of the family at the throne of grace; and having received her last benediction and kiss, all except the eldest daughter, who slept in the same room, retired to their respective chambers. In the course of the night she rang a small hand-bell, which aroused both her daughter, and her son, who slept in the adjoining room, to whom, on his coming to enquire if his sister had heard the summons, she addressed a few kind words. Her daughter then returned to her couch, requesting to be called at seven o'clock. Awaking in the morning she was surprised to find that hour had long passed, and on approaching her mother's bedside was shocked to observe the change in her appearance, and to find herself unrecognised. Her brother, having been immediately summoned, was equally distressed at the unconscious state of the invalid. The attendance of their usual medical adviser, as well as that of a kind physician from a greater distance, was speedily obtained; but these gentlemen held out no hope of rendering any service. As soon as possible after the visit of these professional friends, her son hired a conveyance and drove into the country to carry the sad tidings to his father, with

whom he returned in the afternoon. The patient was still unconscious and rapidly sinking. All earthly intercourse between
herself and her kindred had ceased for ever. About eleven
o'clock in the evening, while the family were uniting, as well as
their distress would permit, in the customary act of devotion,
the happy spirit was released, and doubtless welcomed by its
kindred in the skies. Even in the first moments of their
keenest anguish the overwhelming conviction of the blessedness of the change was the uppermost feeling in the hearts
of the survivors, on whose souls were impressed, with a power
never felt before, such promises as these: ' And God shall wipe
away all tears from their eyes; and there shall be no more
death, neither sorrow, nor crying; neither shall there be any
more pain.'

On the 19th, her mortal remains were conveyed to Bunhill
Fields, and interred in the family grave, where they repose
with those of her venerated grandfather, her mother, and other
members of her family whose spirits have joined the company
of 'just men made perfect,' and whose bodies rest in the grave
till the morning of the resurrection. On the following Lord's
day, the Rev. Thomas Lewis, of Union Chapel, Islington,
preached a funeral discourse from the very appropriate passage
of Scripture: ' Behold, I have refined thee, but not with silver ;
I have chosen thee in the furnace of affliction.' (Isaiah xlviii. 10.)

Mr. Ellis prepared a brief memoir of his beloved wife, of
which several editions were printed. This simple record of the
patient endurance and loving submission of one who possessed,
in an eminent degree, 'the ornament of a meek and quiet
spirit, which is in the sight of God of great price,' has, doubtless, been a solace and encouragement to numbers of tried and
afflicted Christians. Its touching story is still retained in the
memory of many, on whose minds more stirring histories have
left but faint and faded traces.

The writer feels he cannot better close this portion of the
narrative than by quoting the following tribute to the memory

of his sainted mother, from the pen of a much-esteemed physician :—' Such entire acquiescence in the Divine will; such sweet serenity during acute and protracted suffering, even when reviving hope was again and again disappointed ; such a readiness to mark and thankfully acknowledge every allevia-tion ; such a pervading, unshaken reliance on the loving-kind-ness and faithfulness of God, under the most painful and discouraging circumstances, present a cheering and triumphant testimony to the power of Divine grace, not unlike that which was borne by the Apostle, when he said (doubtless after a faith-ful retrospect), " I can do all things through Christ that strengtheneth me." In truth, the cheerful, uncomplaining, and heavenly demeanour of Mrs. Ellis was so remarkable, that some physicians, not regarded as religious men, have been astonished, and led to inquire what possibly could so sustain the mind under the pressure of such grievous sufferings. Who can compute the amount of good which may have resulted, and may still result, from what may be termed the *second*, the *passive* mission of our beloved friend ? How many, in America and in England, may have had their faith confirmed, and their hopes elevated, by such a convincing display of the power of Christ ! How many, too, inclined to doubt, may have been led to embrace the Gospel as an inestimable reality, from observing its unquestionable influence in the time of need ! The delight-ful union of delicate, exquisite feeling, with the firm, un-wavering constancy of a Christian heroine, is most attractive and most instructive.'

With all its alleviations, this painful bereavement weighed heavily on the spirit of the widower, who thus refers to his affliction in a letter to a very dear friend :—' Our loss, and the desire that it might so be sanctified that we might meet again in a world where separations will be unknown, for a time absorbed every feeling; until, in regard to myself, sadness and mourning had almost become the chief elements of my being.' A letter addressed to his son, under date Feb. 8th, 1835, still more fully discloses the state of his mind at this period :—

' My dear Boy,—It seems to me a long time since I wrote to you, or heard from you, though your dear sisters have always great pleasure in showing me your letters as soon as they have received them. It has been from no want of inclination that I have not written to you very frequently; for every day a thousand thoughts and feelings arise within my bosom associated involuntarily with the desire to communicate them to you, my dear boy, as that would double every emotion of joy, and relieve half the pressure of pain. But why should I write in a manner that may allow you to suppose I have pain, in reference to the past and present circumstances of us both, in regard to one whose image we desire may never be absent from our thoughts? My feelings of pain only regard myself; that I should so long have witnessed such a manifestation of superior Christian excellence, and should have been so long under the influence of such a heavenly spirit—such a bright and pure example—have had so many opportunities of doing more to comfort and promote the happiness of one whose measure of suffering was rarely surpassed, and rarely borne with greater cheerfulness and love, and yet have derived so little benefit myself, have been satisfied with so humbling a distance from the attractive model so continually before me. These are the sources of my sorrow; and my alleviation, next to the hope in the pardoning mercy of the compassionate Redeemer, is found in any attention I am able to give to the known wishes of the dear departed—doing that which she would have done, or which, if still with us, she would have approved. When I turn from myself, and think of her, all is pure and clear and bright. There was in her much that was beautiful in that which survives the grave—the mind and the spirit; and death has rendered the beautiful permanent, and has stamped upon all the lineaments of loveliness in intellect and character the impress of eternity. It will know no change but that of advancement from one degree of ineffable felicity to another, as it contemplates new developments of uncreated perfection before the throne.'

Happily, perhaps, under the circumstances, the pressure of official work was much increased. A few years before, the first Radama, the enlightened but ambitious Sovereign of Madagascar, who, from motives of policy, if not on higher grounds, had been the steady friend of Christian missions, died; and the vacant throne was usurped, after a series of acts of treachery, violence, and assassination, by his unscrupulous widow, Ranavalona. This event was speedily followed by the interruption of the mission, and the persecution of the Christians. Much interest on behalf of the people of the country was excited in England; and Mr. Ellis was requested by the directors of the Missionary Society to prepare a history of Madagascar. To this work he now devoted every spare minute, and laboured to accomplish his task with indefatigable assiduity. He expended in its execution a wonderful amount of faithful and diligent research, and the result was the production of a history that even now is the most complete and exhaustive work that has appeared respecting that interesting portion of the globe. So industriously had the author applied himself to his task, that the copy was ready for the press in 1837, although, in consequence of Mr. Freeman's return from Madagascar, who was able to supply much additional and valuable information, it was deemed expedient to delay the publication till the following year.

Other literary work, of a less arduous kind indeed, yet occupying much time, entailing a large amount of correspondence, and taxing in various ways his already overstrained powers of mind, was pressed upon his hands at the same busy period. Desirous of promoting by every legitimate means the public interest in missionary efforts, he had undertaken to edit an annual, entitled the *Christian Keepsake*, the main object of which was to advocate the cause of missions to the heathen. The literary merit of this periodical was far above that of similar ephemeral productions of the day, and elicited the warm commendations of men whose opinions were entitled to high consideration, and whose praise was no empty compliment—such men as Wordsworth, Southey, and many others of a like stamp.

These literary engagements, however, were not permitted to draw off the attention now increasingly demanded by the duties connected with the secretariat. Political changes of great importance in the countries where the agents of the Missionary Society had been labouring—changes that in some cases embarrassed their operations, but in others, far more numerous, opened out new facilities for the instruction of the people and the spread of Christianity—called for increased energy, activity, and liberality among the friends of missions at home, and brought a large amount of additional work upon the directors and officers of the Society. More 'labourers' were demanded, new stations established, or existing ones strengthened and enlarged, and the most strenuous efforts became necessary to augment the income of the institution that had already effected so much good, if its friends and supporters would not see it halt or fall back in its career of usefulness.

Among the events of this period, in which Mr. Ellis was personally very deeply interested, one of the foremost, already mentioned, was the return of his early friend and colleague, John Williams, from the South Seas. Public attention had begun to subside in regard to the earliest scene of the Society's efforts, and had been drawn off, in great measure, to larger fields and more recent and extensive revolutions in the pagan world. This comparative apathy was due, in part, to the disastrous effect of increased foreign intercourse in demoralising the natives, and lamentably hindering the beneficent influence of the Christian teachers; so that the reports that reached England of the condition of the people ceased to be of the cheering character of former times. The state of public feeling was further affected by the shameful interference of the French, which subsequently culminated in the forced usurpation of the supreme authority of Tahiti, under the hollow pretence of a

' protectorate.' The conduct of the French commander in this instance was a flagrant violation of the principles of honour recognised among civilised nations, if not of international law, and would hardly have been permitted by a British Government less weakly bent on conciliating foreign powers than the ministry of that day. Lord Palmerston, who was not then in office, had expressed himself very emphatically against the French scheme of spoliation, and had given Mr. Ellis assurance, that, so far as his own influence extended, the contemplated wrong should be resisted by an unequivocal protest on the part of England. The course of events was a serious cause of grief and disappointment to one whose strongest associations were bound up with the fate of the beloved scene of his first missionary labours. It is, however, a satisfaction to know that this attempt to introduce the system of Popery into a country where the Protestant faith had already been planted, has, like similar schemes of Popish proselytism, backed either by bribes or by force, resulted in signal failure.

The stirring representations of Mr. Williams re-awakened, in some degree, the flagging zeal of the churches on behalf of the Polynesian races, though, doubtless, it was towards new fields of conquest, awaiting the triumph of the Cross, and islands yet heathen, that public sympathy was chiefly directed. Mr. Ellis entered heartily into his friend's schemes of benevolence, rejoiced in his success, took an active part in the purchase and equipment of the *Camden*, was one of the ministers who delivered addresses at the farewell service, held in the Tabernacle on the eve of Mr. Williams' departure ; followed him with unabated interest throughout the remainder of his career ; and there was, perhaps, no individual beyond the immediate circle of the martyr's family to whom the tidings of his tragic death were a greater shock, or who mourned the fate of his early associate with keener sorrow. Ties of the warmest fraternal affection bound together the members of the little band of voluntary exiles ' for Christ's sake and the gospel's,' who, twenty

years before, had entered upon their labour of mercy in the
remote isles of the Pacific, who had been dependent solely on
each other for civilized companionship, and who, during all the
period of their intercourse and co-operation, had maintained an
uninterrupted spirit of harmony and brotherly love. The loss
of a friend thus endeared, under circumstances so painful, was
therefore a trial of no ordinary kind, and could not but deeply
affect the heart of his former comrade.

Another of the South Sea brethren, Mr. Nott, one of the
veterans of the mission, who had gone out in the ship *Duff*,
and had heroically remained at his post through the long ordeal
of darkness and danger, returned to England in 1836, bringing
with him the translation of the Holy Scriptures into the Tahitian language, for the purpose of having it printed in this
country. This work was undertaken, with its accustomed
liberality, by the British and Foreign Bible Society; and when
it was completed, Mr. Ellis had the honour of accompanying
Mr. Nott to a royal levée at St. James's, where the first copy
of the Tahitian Bible was presented to his Majesty William
IV., and his amiable consort Queen Adelaide.

About the same time, Mr. Freeman, and other missionaries
who had been compelled to leave Madagascar by the edict of
Queen Ranavalona, returned home; and their statements
awakened in the hearts of British Christians the deepest
sympathy on behalf of the persecuted martyrs in that unhappy
country. In the following year, the ambassadors sent by
the Queen of Madagascar, with the view of establishing
amicable relations between the British Government and her
own, paid their visit to England, and were accompanied on their
first introduction to royalty, by Mr. Freeman, as interpreter,
and Mr. Ellis, as secretary of the London Missionary Society.
At a less formal interview in Windsor Castle, Queen Adelaide,
in the course of conversation, sent her memorable message to
the persecuting Queen—a message to which, unhappily, the infatuated sovereign paid little heed. 'Tell the Queen of Mada-

gascar from me that she can do nothing so beneficial for her country as to receive the Christian religion.'

Some time after this the first Malagasy refugees, who had succeeded, after almost unparalleled sufferings and hair-breadth escapes, in reaching the coast and gaining an asylum under British protection, arrived in England, and were cordially received and welcomed by the Missionary Society at a public meeting, held in Exeter Hall, the moving interest of which would not soon be forgotten by those who were present.

In June 1836 a select parliamentary committee was appointed to investigate the effect of foreign intercourse with the aborigines in British settlements, or other countries to which British influence extended. The active members of this committee were Sir R. Donkin, and Messrs. F. Buxton, C. Lushington, W. E. Gladstone, A. Johnstone, Holland, and Wilson. Among a very large number of persons examined, D. Coates, Esq., Secretary of the Church Missionary Society, the Rev. J. Beecham, and the Rev. William Ellis, secretaries to the Wesleyan and London Missionary Societies respectively, gave their evidence. The summary of the unanimous testimony of these gentlemen, supported by a large number of other independent witnesses, and by overwhelming proofs, may be thus briefly stated :—

That the intercourse of Europeans with the native inhabitants of British settlements tends (with the exception of cases in which missions are established) to deteriorate the morals of the natives; to introduce European vices; to spread among them new and dangerous diseases; to destroy female virtue; to decrease the native population; and to prevent the spread of education, commerce, and Christianity; and the effect of European intercourse, apart from Christian teaching, has been, upon the whole, a calamity to the heathen and savage nations. Moreover, it was the opinion of these witnesses, that in all instances of contention between Europeans and natives, the first aggression was on the part of the former.

With regard to the duties of the civilised towards the heathen country, it was further shown that Christian missions, in addition to the highest ends, would promote commerce ; improve the habits of the people ; increase their industry ; and would give security to traders and all foreigners in the prosecution of legitimate transactions. That the civilized nation was not only bound to treat the inhabitants of heathen countries with justice ; but, as the only compensation that could be offered for the evils and injuries which civilised intercourse had inflicted, the wronged and unprotected tribes were entitled to the introduction of ' those arts that tend to improve life, and those truths which will promote their eternal welfare.'

Very decided opinions were also expressed in regard to the futility of any attempt to civilize a people without the introduction of Christianity. Mr. Beecham gave the details of an experiment of the kind that had been made by the Wesleyans in Western Africa, to prepare the way for religious teaching, by prior instruction in the arts of civilized life. The trial had signally failed. So also had similar endeavours to civilize the North American Indians. The principal reasons advanced for this view—though it had been adopted from practical experience rather than from theoretical inference—were, that there was no adequate motive to induce men to undertake and persevere in the task of merely civilizing the heathen ; the love of souls, which Christianity alone supplies, was necessary to sustain the enthusiasm, the self-denial, and the patience so essential in the reformer of the heathen. And further, the advantage of civilization was not obvious or attractive enough to the savage to induce him to abandon his former habits. He preferred his freedom and the wild delight of his primitive mode of life to the restraints and the labour imposed by civilization. The foregoing evidence was not suffered to lie buried in the parliamentary Blue Books, but was published in full in a separate pamphlet by the societies represented at the examination, and widely distributed, in order that greater publicity might be

M

given to the emphatic testimony elicited in favour of the principle, that Christianity is the only foundation of true civilization.

The public events thus briefly noticed were among those in which the personal history and official work of the Secretary were most closely associated. It will be convenient now to resume the story of his domestic life.

The lighter literary labour that filled up to overflowing the time of this indefatigable worker was pleasantly relieved by the intercourse which it involved with many eminent and interesting characters of the day. Of this number was Miss Sarah Stickney, a writer, even then, of no mean reputation, whose most ambitious work, at that time, was a beautifully written series of essays on the *Poetry of Life*. Mr. Ellis met her, for the first time, at the house of their mutual friend Thomas Pringle, the African traveller and poet. Finding that his new acquaintance was warmly interested in missionary enterprises—an interest that had been mainly kindled by the perusal of *Polynesian Researches*—the editor of the *Christian Keepsake* enlisted her services in that publication. She very cheerfully complied with his request, and was an industrious and able contributor to the pages of the Annual as long as it lasted. The mutual regard springing up in this first interview, and increased by the correspondence to which it led, was strengthened by subsequent opportunities of personal intercourse in the midst of Miss Stickney's family connections and friends in Yorkshire, and grew at length into an interest of the deepest character. The subject of a second marriage had been presented to the mind of the widower even before his bereavement, by his loving wife, who in the gentlest and tenderest manner had expressed her wish that, after she was gone, he would seek a helpmate for himself, and a friend to their motherless children, stipulating only, with maternal instinct, that the chosen companion should be one who would be kind to them. This sacred trust no one could have enshrined in his heart with more holy fidelity than he in whom that dying confidence was reposed. When the intimacy already mentioned, brought the subject before his mind, one of the first steps he took in the matter was to consult his children, especially the elder ones, and ascertain their wishes. He found them desirous that he should enter into the new relationship, and disposed to receive their father's friend, whom they then knew only from her writings, with all cordiality and affection. From this source they inferred her kindness of heart and refinement of feeling; and knowing the sensitiveness of their parent's spirit, and how deeply his happiness would be affected by the disposition and character of one who would be admitted to so close an intimacy, the estimate they had formed was high indeed. Writing in reference to this subject to one who knew him well, and who had ventured to suggest a caution, lest his delicacy of feeling and quick susceptibilities might render him too exacting, or expose him to undesigned pain, he thus speaks of himself: 'I fear the quality you speak of is not to be traced to the refining process which you suppose has been going on, but chiefly to my having been for twenty years under the sweetest, strongest influence of one whose form personified all that is delicate and pure, and whose whole career was the exemplification of whatever is elevated and refined—not in external accomplishments, but in sentiment and feeling. To have been associated as I was with such a being, and not to have imbibed some of the transcendent excellencies with which the Father of Mercies so richly invested her character, was impossible. And bright as may be the sunshine with which imagination or hope may irradiate the course of my remaining pilgrimage, I scarcely expect in any other companion what I found in her.'

A long correspondence ensued between those who now contemplated the closest of earthly relationships, the subject of their intercommunication being chiefly the all-important one of religion. That this interchange of ideas had considerable influence on the mind of Miss Stickney, will be evident to anyone who will compare the character of her writings before and after her marriage. Whatever the religious views of the author of the former series might have been, they are more pronounced, and personal piety is more prominently enjoined as the only solid ground of excellence of character, in all her subsequent works. It may be observed, by way of illustration, that while the *Poetry of Life* with all its beauty and pathos, might have been written by a romantic worshipper of the beautiful, the *Women of England* was evidently dictated by the heart of a Christian woman.

The year 1837 was an eventful one in the family. In the early part of it, Mr. Ellis was summoned to Wisbeach, in consequence of the death of his beloved mother. He did not arrive in time to see her alive, a circumstance which caused him much distress, and in reference to which he thus writes to Miss Stickney:—'I know you will kindly sympathise in my feelings of pain on this account; and will unite with me in endeavouring to draw from the event lessons of the highest practical value and importance. I trust the bereavement will in mercy be productive of spiritual benefit to my dear father, and my brother and sisters as well as myself. In regard to my dear mother, we could not wish her to remain in the state of suffering in which she had so long been languishing; and I am cheered by the conviction that she was not unprepared for the change, that her hopes were built upon the only sure foundation for a sinner's trust—the mercy of God in Jesus Christ, and that for her to die was gain. Oh how does this belief irradiate the gloom of the grave!' The following touching passage in another letter to the same correspondent, reveals the filial heart of a loving and dutiful son:—'Late in the evening I went alone to the chamber of death, and gazed on that countenance which had kindled the first joyous emotions of my being, and on that eye which had been the first to meet my glance in the dawn of existence—which had ever revealed so eloquently the yearnings of the purest and tenderest love, and which through all my wayward wanderings had known neither diminution nor change in that love, but which I felt could never beam with affection again. I prostrated myself on the ground, and sought forgiveness from Him who had given me such a mother, for the many instances in which I had failed in filial duty. The midnight hour had long passed before I retired, and, with a very short exception, the night was sleepless, thoughts of the past and of the future keeping me in a state of great excitement. On the following day, at one o'clock, the remains were consigned to the cold and cheerless grave. The evening was a peculiarly solemn one. My brother and his wife, and three of my sisters, with my father and myself, constituted the party. I endeavoured to render the season spiritually beneficial to my poor father; for I found if he had returned to any religious belief, it was to Unitarianism; as he told me there was a new minister, a young man, come to the town, and that he was the most eloquent and liberal man he had ever heard—that he heard him every Sabbath, and no other. My distress you may imagine. I spoke as kindly and softly as possible, for he was exceedingly warm on some points, and I spoke more fully and faithfully, as well as directly and personally, on the necessity of immediate inquiry concerning his own state before God, and the only way of salvation, than I ever remember to have done before—with what effect must be hereafter shown. May the Lord have mercy on him and save him at the eleventh hour.'

Some months after this event, arrangements for the marriage with Miss Stickney were in progress, when the brightening prospects of the household were clouded by a new and severe trial. This was the alarming illness of the eldest daughter, then in her twenty-first year, whose health, indeed, though the family were unaware of the fact, had for some time been undermined by that most insidious of all maladies, pulmonary consumption. The announcement of her danger struck her affectionate parent with the deepest grief, and banished all

other prospects from his thoughts. In a letter addressed to
Miss Stickney on the memorable day when this afflicting
intelligence was first communicated to him, May 6th, 1837, he
thus speaks of the distressing change. Having mentioned the
completion of all the preparations for the new inmate of the
household, he writes :—

'The increased indisposition of dear Mary has damped the
ardour of all our hopes; and the account of the physician this
morning is so unfavourable that I have already written off to
John to come up without delay, as Dr. Darling informed me
that there was but little hope of her recovery; that she might
linger for some time, or might sink very suddenly; that she had
evidently been losing ground for the last seven or ten days, and
that I ought to prepare for the worst. This afternoon she was
brought from the house of the friend with whom she had been
staying, and after showing her over the house, I *carried* her
upstairs to her little room, which Elizabeth and Annie had
nicely furnished, though not without some painful forebodings.
Dr. Darling will see her again to-morrow, and then I shall decide
whether or not I can leave her. I need not, cannot, say more.
I feel struck, as it were, prostrate before Him who is the sole
arbiter of life and death, and whose will is supreme. The
prospect of losing one from whose amiable disposition, whose
unceasing and unwavering affection, I had drawn some of my
sweetest hopes of future happiness, and who, I have always felt
the most entire confidence, would mitigate as far as tender, kind,
and filial love could do it, any affliction I might be called to
endure, is deeply distressing. I have not a doubt that to her
to die will be gain, will be to depart and to be with Christ, with
that throng in which her sainted mother has already found a
place.'

In the postscript of the same letter occurs the following
touching sentence :—'Dear Mary talks much of you, scarcely
of any one else. She does not appear to realize her danger, and
dreams of happiness when you come.'

The immediate fears of the family were removed, as the alarming symptoms in the patient's condition abated, and some measure of improvement ensued. It was not deemed necessary, therefore, to postpone the marriage ceremony. Indeed it was Miss Stickney's wish that no punctilio should be allowed to detain her from the bedside of the invalid, to whom she was anxious to render all the comfort and relief that assiduous and loving tendance could supply.

The reader needs scarcely to be informed that Miss Stickney had been brought up among the Society of Friends, of which nearly all her family connexions were members. She had long ceased to be in strict accord with them in her opinions, and having now formally left them, she was admitted into fellowship with the Congregational Church under the pastoral care of the Rev. Thomas Stratten, of Hull. The marriage was performed on May 23, 1837, in as quiet a manner as possible, at the parish church in the small village of Burstwick, a few miles from Ridgmont in Holderness, the pleasant residence of Mr. Stickney's family. No time was allowed for the customary wedding trip, but anxious to take her post by the side of the invalid, Mrs. Ellis at once repaired with her husband to her new home. Here she was received with unaffected cordiality: and her presence afforded no small pleasure and solace to the patient, during the very brief remainder of her days.

No human care or kindness could now avail to prolong the young life but lately so full of hope and promise, and now drawing speedily to its early close. The warm weather of June proved exceedingly trying, and brought on excessive debility, under which the fatal malady gained rapid ground. Before the month was over the end had come, and the family were once more called to resign one of their dearest into the hands of her Maker. No departure could be more peaceful; no bereavement mitigated by circumstances of greater mercy. The remains were interred in Bunhill Fields burial-ground, beside those of her beloved mother, and other pious ancestry.

Mr. Ellis once more threw his whole energies into the accumulating duties of the secretariat, which taxed his strength more than ever. His evenings, and what intervals of relief from official work he could command, he devoted to the completion of the *History of Madagascar*, which had been for a time suspended. In this labour, as well as in other literary engagements, he received much welcome assistance from his accomplished wife, who was never so happy as when conscious that she was rendering the husband, whom she loved and reverenced, any substantial help. The amount of mental toil which these multifarious occupations involved, and the close application he had given to every task he undertook, began now to tell seriously upon his health; and it would have been well for him had he sooner taken warning, and voluntarily relaxed the strain on his mental powers. He continued staunchly at his post, however, throughout the whole of 1838, and part of the following year. Alarming symptoms of cerebral excitement and nervous prostration compelled him at length to seek for relaxation and rest. His own medical attendant, as well as those officially connected with the Society, emphatically urged upon him the necessity of the entire suspension of all mental work. The Directors, therefore, with considerate kindness, released him for a time from the duties of his office, making such liberal arrangements as should relieve him from all anxiety, and providing for the efficient charge of the Foreign Secretaryship by the services of Dr. Henderson, Dr. Tidman, and Mr. Freeman.

The interval of repose he spent in England, visiting places of interest, and friends, old and new, in various parts of the country. So long as he abstained from mental labour his health improved; but after some weeks' entire relaxation, he found himself still unequal to any serious or sustained mental effort. Under these circumstances, the Directors very readily and cordially extended his 'leave of absence.' Notwithstanding some improvement, the end of the year 1839 still found him

unfit to resume his official duties; and his medical advisers
unanimously concurred in the recommendation that he should
take a year's rest, and spend that period abroad. The Directors
of the Society showed their estimate of the value of their
Secretary's faithful services by the gratifying and generous
manner in which they made provision for carrying out the
recommendation of the physicians.

Among the places recommended as suitable for the contemplated rustication, the Cape of Good Hope had been mentioned;
but, besides the objection on account of the distance, it was
feared that, in the neighbourhood of mission fields so interesting
as those of South Africa, it would be almost impossible to avoid
undesirable excitement, and probably a considerable amount of
active work. The south of France was accordingly selected as
altogether the most eligible resting-place; and in the month of
January 1840, Mr. and Mrs. Ellis took up their winter quarters in the pleasant and picturesque town of Pau.

So much has been written about this and all the resorts of English tourists on the European continent, that it would be superfluous and tedious to detain the reader by any account of the
impressions received, or observations made over this well-trodden
tract. Moreover, Mrs. Ellis herself has published an interesting
account of the country, and their residence at Pau and neighbouring places, in a work entitled *A Summer and Winter in
the Pyrenees*. This book supplies many details which it is not
necessary to repeat here.

Much agreeable English society is to be met with in the
favourite watering-places of France; and the travellers made
here many pleasant acquaintances. Among the number were
some friends to whom they had letters of introduction from
Dr. Hodgkin. Mr. John Warner, of Hoddesdon, accompanied
by his wife, was spending the winter at Pau, seeking, like others,
the restoration of health. The acquaintance formed with these
friends, not only contributed very much to the enjoyment of the
temporary sojourn in France, but led to results that affected the

whole of their future lives. Mr. Warner would often in conversation speak of the attractions of Hoddesdon and the neighbourhood. Mr. and Mrs. Ellis were so favourably impressed by these accounts, that when afterwards it became expedient for them to select a country residence in England, they turned their first thoughts to this locality—more particularly to a charming homestead, of which Mr. Warner had been tenant, and still held the unexpired lease. This was Rose Hill, which, after their return to England, became their home for the rest of their lives.

The town of Pau possesses one advantage over many other French towns, in the number of resident Protestants who have settled there, and for whose accommodation, as well as for that of English visitors, the Duchess of Gordon, at her own expense, erected an Episcopal Church, where English and French clergymen regularly officiated. The stipend of the French Protestant minister, as well as the maintenance of the schools, is provided for by the Société Evangélique de France. The Pastor, Mr. Buscarlet, took an active interest in Christian missions, and frequently invited Mr. Ellis to address his people. At Orthez, situated in the same neighbourhood, where there are said to be eighteen hundred Protestants, a deep interest was felt in missionary operations, attributable in part to the fact that an excellent French missionary in South Africa had gone from that town, where his family still resided. In the month of February at the invitation of the Protestant community there, Mr. Ellis paid a visit to Orthez, and addressed an assembly of about three hundred in the church; and afterwards attended an interesting meeting at the house of Madame Casalis, the widowed mother of the missionary already mentioned. It was a comfort to the minister of the gospel, in his enforced retirement, to be able to do even this much in advocating the cause he loved.

In May, as the warmer season approached, the travellers made an excursion to Eaux Bonnes and Eaux Chaudes, returning for a short time to Pau. They left again in June, and took up their summer residence in the neighbourhood of Bagnères de Bigorre. A family from Devonshire, whose acquaintance they had made at Pau, received them there with a true English welcome, and in the kindest manner constrained them to take up their abode with them during the rest of the summer in their charming house, the chateau of St. Paul, where French elegance was admirably combined with English comfort, and whose genuine and warm-hearted hospitality rendered the visit of their guests altogether the pleasantest period of their sojourn in France. The heat of the season was occasionally trying, and the effect of exposure to the sun's rays, inducing a return of cerebral disturbance, was such as to give warning that the condition of the valetudinarian was not yet thoroughly restored to its healthy standard. Nevertheless, many delightful excursions were made to the grand and picturesque localities in the vicinity, and the general impression of their loveliness was such as had never been surpassed. Mrs. Ellis, in the work before referred to—*A Summer and Winter in the Pyrenees*—thus speaks of her husband's appreciation of their beauty. ' My companion, who has seen as much as most travellers of the loveliest aspects of nature, and who possesses, besides, a more than common share of the quick perception of an artist, mingled with the deep enthusiasm of a poet, exclaimed more than once, " I have never seen anything like this ! " He afterwards explained, that though his memory was filled with pictures which no time could efface, of the verdant, sunny, aërial, and almost heavenly aspect of the Isles of the Pacific, he had never seen before such a combination of fertility and gorgeous colouring, with the hoary grandeur, the massiveness, and the sublimity which we found here.' Mrs. Ellis, who added to her many accomplishments a rare and happy facility in handling the pencil or brush, spent many delightful hours in making sketches of her favourite views among the mountains. Her husband, whose skill in drawing, like most of his attainments, was self-acquired, and who certainly had never received any instruction in the use of colours, could not resist the temptation of trying his hand.   To the utter amazement of Mrs. Ellis, who with all her knowledge of his versatility had anticipated failure, he produced a series of water-colour pictures that suffered no disparagement beside her own, and, as she declared, were even more faithful representations of the scenes depicted than her more artistic drawings.

While staying in their summer quarters they were much pleased to have an opportunity of seeing and hearing the poet Lamartine, who paid a brief visit to Bagnères, and with whose appearance and speech, and the reception given him by his countrymen, they were favourably impressed.

In the end of October, they bade adieu to their kind and hospitable friends at St. Paul's, and after a brief stay at Pau, turned their steps homeward, making a halt at Paris, chiefly for the purpose of consulting Dr. Foville.   The opinion of this eminent physician in regard to the amendment of his patient's health, and the prospect of resuming work, was very encouraging —a circumstance that increased the disappointment occasioned by the subsequent less favourable judgment of the English physicians.

Towards the end of the year 1841 the travellers reached home, sanguine respecting the measure of improvement in Mr. Ellis's health and capacity for work.   His first experience, however, of any arduous mental effort or exposure to excitement, showed that the morbid condition of the brain was not entirely sub- dued ; and the medical advisers agreed in the opinion that it would not be safe for him to undertake the duties of the secretariat even in conjunction with an assistant.   This was a bitter disappointment.   The prospect of being laid aside from active participation in the noble work to which his whole soul had been devoted, was, to one of his ardent tempera- ment, a severe trial, and tested sorely his submission to the Divine will.   But under the circumstances he felt that no alternative was left him but to send in his resignation to the Directors of the Missionary Society.   They, on their part, though they recognised Mr. Ellis's claims on their consideration in the most generous manner, and made arrangements for the future in a liberal spirit, could only acquiesce, leaving their former faithful Secretary free, without any express stipulations, to serve the Institution in the measure and manner that his strength allowed, knowing well that his heart would ever beat warmly towards the cause of missions, and that his chief joy would still be to plead or labour in its behalf. The following extract from the letter which Mr. Ellis addressed to Mr. Arundel, the Home Secretary, with the tender of his resignation, expresses, though but in part, the sentiments with which the step was taken :—

' In thus retiring from official connection with the Society, I beg to assure the Directors of my unabated attachment to its interests, of my most earnest desire to promote its vast and glorious objects, and my growing confidence in the ultimate and universal triumph of that sacred cause which it subserves. The officers, agents, or supporters of the Society may be laid aside, or be removed by death, but He, in obedience to whose command its first efforts were put forth, and in dependence on whose blessing all its subsequent exertions have been made, sees the end from the beginning, will accomplish His purposes of mercy to our world, and will fill the whole earth with His glory.

' I cannot close my letter without expressing the deep and grateful sense I shall ever entertain of the kind and generous consideration, as well as the cordial and affectionate sympathy, which I have received from the Directors during the entire period of my connection with the Society, not less when labouring as a missionary abroad than when associated with them in conducting the affairs of the Institution at home. In this work I have found some of the highest and purest enjoyments I have ever known. It has not, indeed, been exempt from trials, some of them severe and unusally protracted, but it has never excited one feeling of regret; and had I life to begin again, with all the experience I now possess, no walk of life would present attractions equal to those of the missionary field. My only aim would be for higher moral and spiritual attainments—for qualifications more suitable for the work, and endowments more adequate than any which I have ever possessed for the efficient and faithful discharge of its duties.

'Though no longer officially connected with the Society, I shall observe its progress with unabated interest, and shall not cease to pray that the Divine favour may rest in rich abundance upon every department of its work. For myself, I desire to recognise the hand of the Lord in my present circumstances, no less than in those which gave me a place among my brethren, and a share in their labours. I know that I have your sincere Christian sympathy with myself and family. Pray that I may have the presence and blessing of Him whose mercy never fails.'

Men are, no doubt, often guilty of grievous presumption and make great mistakes in their attempts to interpret the mysteries of Divine Providence, but surely, in this instance, we may, in a definite and special sense, 'recognise the hand of the Lord;' we may believe that the enforced rest prolonged the life of His servant, and prepared him for the more important service that was to crown his days. Had Mr. Ellis continued to be the Secretary of the Missionary Society, he never would have been the 'Apostle to Madagascar.'

HODDESDON

1841–53

CHAPTER IX.

PASTORATE, ETC.

AFTER his return from France, Mr. Ellis, preferring the pure air and quiet of the country to the crowded area of London, resided for a short time in a rural part of the suburbs, near Finchley. Here he remained, without troubling himself about more permanent accommodation, till the question of his resuming official work was decided. That matter settled, he turned his attention, as already stated, to Hoddesdon, and both he and Mrs. Ellis were so well pleased with the neighbourhood, particularly with Rose Hill, that they were glad to accept Mr. Warner's offer, and take the unexpired lease of the house and premises off his hands. The requisite preparations were soon made, and early in the summer of 1841 they took possession of their future home.

Charming as the chosen residence proved to be, and much as the new comers delighted in rural occupations, the task of making a pleasant homestead, of planting and adorning the grounds about the house, even when to these were added the ordinary claims of society in a country village, could not satisfy the active minds of the tenants of Rose Hill. Though his official connection with the Society had ceased, not many days passed without some business taking the former Secretary to the Mission House. Indeed, in one way or another, he continued to the end of his life pretty deeply immersed in the affairs of the Institution. At the request of the Directors, he also undertook to prepare a history of the London Missionary Society. This task, involving much laborious reading, research,

N

and correspondence, occupied a considerable portion of time; yet, in spite of many interruptions, the first volume of the book was ready for the press and published in 1844. Its completion was delayed by a variety of circumstances; and up to the very last the author was engaged in remodelling the whole, so as to give it to the public in a briefer and more popular form. Mrs. Ellis was also at this time (indeed, when was it otherwise?) busy with her pen. Neither of them could be idle when there was a motive for exertion, and work to be done.

Hoddesdon is situated about four or five miles from Ware, and an equal distance from the county town of Hertford. On the Ware road, in the outskirts of the village, there was an old and wretched-looking building, which had been long used as an 'Independent' chapel. Its pulpit was supplied chiefly by the students of Cheshunt College. Mr. Ellis was of course happy to lend his occasional aid. His family also took an active interest in the Sunday School. Signs of increased life were soon apparent; the attendance of scholars increased, the congregation became more numerous, and the membership of the Church, which had become almost extinct, was reinforced and reorganised.

Schemes of intellectual elevation and innocent social tendency, especially among the young, met with cheerful encouragement and willing help from one whose sympathies were never contracted, and whose benevolence was at the farthest possible remove from the type of 'telescopic philanthropy' in which some, who decry a virtue above them and sneer at what they cannot appreciate, would include all missionary zeal. The young men of the neighbourhood found at Rose Hill a friend ready with his counsel and co-operation in their plans of mutual improvement. He assisted in organising a 'Young Men's Society for Reading and Sacred Song,' whose weekly meetings were held in the vestry of the 'Old Chapel.' From this, the first association of the kind attempted in Hoddesdon, afterwards sprang the 'Young Men's Mutual Instruction Society,' and other very useful kindred institutions now existing in the neighbourhood.   Towards the establishment and maintenance of these more ambitious enterprises of a later period, Mr. Ellis gave books for the library, delivered lectures, and assisted in the formation of classes.   In the drawing class especially great interest was also taken by Mrs. Ellis, who was imbued with a deep love of art, and was anxious to develop a similar taste in the minds of all young people.

On the temperance question both husband and wife held very strong and decided views.   Both were too clear-sighted and large-hearted to entertain what could justly be called extravagant or extreme opinions, or to sympathise in the illiberal denunciations and ill-judged schemes of many advocates of ' Teetotalism.'   But they could not have their attention drawn, as it was, to the gigantic and all-pervading evils of intemperance without being anxious to join in any remedy that promised amelioration.   They took an active part in the formation and working of a Temperance Association ; and not content with merely advocating sobriety, humanely and zealously extended a helping hand in the task of individual reformation—a service for which many a reformed inebriate, many a heart-broken wife and famished children, to whose homes, through their instrumentality, happiness and plenty were restored, even yet bless their memory.

The members of the Society of Friends in Hoddesdon, and foremost among them Mr. Warner, Senior, were the chief promoters of the ' Boys' British School ' that had been established in Hoddesdon.   The latter gentleman had, at his own private expense, erected the building, and was always an open-handed, and indeed the chief contributor to the funds required for carrying out the project.   Liberal-minded men of different creeds were happy to unite in this Catholic institution for extending the benefits of education ; and Mr. Ellis, as a member of the Committee, took his full share of the work as long as he lived.   A similar scheme of benevolence, the ' Girls'

British and Infant Schools,' was projected and largely supported by Mr. and Mrs. Ellis, both of whom took a warm and
active interest in the institution up to the close of their
lives.

No one who knew the earnest, yet quiet and retiring missionary, would expect to find in him a violent party politician;
yet he knew too well the duties that were inseparable from free
citizenship to evade either its claims or privileges. He could
not stand neutral on questions involving the great principles of
civil and religious liberty. Accordingly, when the subject of
Church rates was submitted to the parishioners for decision, he
resisted, both by protest and vote, the imposition of that unequal tax. His opposition and the public declaration of his
principles, temperate as it had been, brought upon him some
ill-will, and created for a time a coolness towards him in the
deportment of some of his zealous Church of England neighbours. He remained long enough among them, however,
quietly to live down such prejudices; and, especially after his
return from Madagascar, when his true worth and noble qualities had become better known and appreciated, no one in the
parish was more generally respected by men of all classes and
creeds. From the first, indeed, he had been received with
cordiality by the leading Churchmen of the place, and was
always on friendly terms with the clergymen of the parish. He
was a frequent guest at Broxbournbury, the seat of Jacob
Bosanquet, Esq., and was always invited to speak at the
meetings of the Church Missionary Society, and other kindred
institutions, which meetings were usually held in the park.
With the members of the Society of Friends, who formed an
influential portion of the little community of Hoddesdon, he
ever enjoyed the most pleasant and intimate relations. They
had been the means of introducing him to the neighbourhood,
and the agreeable intercourse and uninterrupted friendship afterwards maintained with them, were among the chief attractions
and ties that bound both himself and Mrs. Ellis to the place.

In Mr. Warner, senior, the unobtrusive but kindly and generous supporter of every useful scheme for the good of his fellow men, they met with a kindred spirit ; and among the various branches and members of his numerous family they found a congeniality of tastes, and sympathy in intellectual pursuits, which contributed in no small measure to endear their new home, and render this portion of their lives pleasant and happy. One of the last occasions on which he occupied the pulpit, before his departure for Madagascar, was to preach a funeral sermon as a tribute of respect to the memory of his departed friend, the head and patriarch of the family, who died on the 6th of December 1852.

Having been recommended by his physicians to seek again the benefit of rest and change of climate, by residence or travel on the Continent, he left home once more, in company with Mrs. Ellis, towards the end of 1843, and spent several months in Italy. In this very pleasant visit to the classic ground and garden of Europe, Dr. Harris, who was at that time Principal of Cheshunt College, was their companion, and enhanced very much the enjoyment of their residence in the sunny land. The winter months were spent in Rome. No object of interest was left unseen, and seldom has the ancient city displayed her treasures of art and rich historic memorials to more appreciative visitors. As soon as the season rendered travel desirable, the party went to Naples, and after a brief stay there, made their way to Florence, where they were detained by the attractions of the place for a somewhat longer period. They returned to England towards the end of the spring of 1844. For reasons similar to those which limited to a mere cursory notice the account of the residence in the Pyrenees, the period spent in Italy—every part of which is to English readers and tourists familiar ground—is also slightly passed over. Those who may be curious to know more of the impressions produced on the minds of the travellers by the ' beautiful in Nature and Art' presented to their view, as well as of the exact route pursued, and the places visited, will find a very full and detailed account in a book written by Mrs. Ellis, under the title of *The Bennets Abroad*, in which an exact history of her own course and observations in the country is interwoven with a narrative of fiction, the incidents and characters of which had, of course, no counterpart in fact or reality.

After his return to Hoddesdon, Mr. Ellis, feeling himself settled and likely to remain in the place, which longer acquaintance appeared to render more attractive and eligible, entered with renewed earnestness into the various benevolent and social schemes for the good of the neighbourhood. He interested himself more than ever in the affairs of the Congregational Church, dividing with the students of Cheshunt College the duty of supplying the pulpit. These young men were guests at Rose Hill whenever they came to preach at the chapel, were always kindly entertained, and many of them, doubtless, retain very pleasant and grateful recollections of the intercourse they enjoyed with their host and hostess at this home-like retreat. Those at the head of the household had ever a warm sympathy with youth, and delighted to encourage its good and generous characteristics. They generally won the confidence of their young friends, and were thus enabled to exert a deeper and more beneficial influence. As one natural result of this intimacy with the young men who were receiving their training for the ministry at Cheshunt College, Mr. Ellis took a special interest in the prosperity of that institution.

The wretched condition of the building that had hitherto been used as a place of worship by the Congregationalists of Hoddesdon and the neighbourhood, together with the increasing number of those who now attended the services, forced on the attention of all who were interested in the matter, the necessity of providing better accommodation. It was the wish also of the members of the church and congregation that Mr. Ellis should assume the regular pastorate. As his health was greatly restored, and the duties of such an office, in a quiet country town, were by no means onerous, and fully accorded with his earnest desire to be engaged, in whatever way was open to him, in preaching the gospel, he did not hesitate, when the wish of the people was communicated to him, to accept the invitation; and became the pastor of the church in the early part of the year 1847. In the meantime he had bestirred himself, with his usual energy in raising funds for the erection of a new chapel. For this object, besides contributing liberally from his private means, he undertook many journeys, and wrote a multitude of letters, and in various ways laboured so heartily to attain the desired end that failure was impossible. To the credit of liberal-minded Churchmen, it is only just to state, that the subscription list for the new chapel was headed by Sir Culling Eardley and Mr. Puget, each of whom gave the handsome sum of £100. Mrs. Ellis was an indefatigable and efficient helper in the work, and in conjunction with other ladies of the congregation, and friends of the cause at a distance, raised a considerable sum in aid of the building fund by a very successful bazaar, which was held in the school-rooms connected with Union Chapel, Islington. On this occasion the following stanzas, written by Mrs. Ellis, were printed and distributed as an appropriate appeal in behalf of the new edifice, an engraving of which, in juxtaposition with one of the 'Old Chapel,' appeared on the same page with the verses, and told at a glance the necessity of the change.

THE HOUSE OF PRAYER.

We live in times when swift as light
  The march of mind is moving,
New views of life dawn on our sight,
  And old ones are improving.

We live in times when gold can place
  Within the rich man's dwelling,
All gems of art, all forms of grace,
  The tide of luxury swelling.

Nor here alone, but in the vale,
  Where cottage fires are glowing,
The same aspiring thoughts prevail,
  The same strong tide is flowing.

Our cherished home, our ties of love,
　　All scenes beheld with pleasure,
This impulse of our nature prove,
　　To adorn the choicest treasure.

And shall one scene, the House of Prayer,
　　Alone remain neglected,
As if we found no pleasures there,
　　No blessing e'er expected?

Shall we indulge each favourite taste,
　　In ceilèd houses dwelling,
While God's forsaken house lies waste,
　　Of hearts unthankful telling?

Forbid it, every gen+rous thought,
　　And every deep emotion,
If worth be in the blessing sought,
　　Or love in our devotion.

No longer mourn the timely fall—
　　The change by all things needed—
Of lowly roof, and tottering wall,
　　Where Age has crept unheeded.

But let us bring our gifts, and raise,
　　With hopes and aims united,
A roof to echo songs of praise,
　　Less worthy to be slighted.

And let us build a house of prayer,
　　As if we felt the duty
Which called us forth to worship there,
　　Deserved a shrine of beauty.

The site of the new chapel, in the main street of Hoddesdon, and occupying a conveniently central position, was purchased by Mr. Ellis, and handed over with the rest of the property to duly appointed trustees. The building, a neat and plain erection, with a frontage in the Norman style of architecture, was formally opened for public worship on the 27th of April 1847; and Mr. Ellis preached his first sermon therein, on the following Sunday evening, from the text ' How dreadful is this place, this is none other but the house of God, and this is the gate of heaven.'

The regular routine of pastoral work in a retired neighbourhood presents but little variety, and is seldom marked by any events requiring special record.   The affairs of the church were carried on harmoniously, the pastor's ministrations were acceptable to the people, unity was preserved among them, and generally, in their relations as a religious community, they were prosperous and happy.   The character of their minister's preaching was plain and unpretending, yet such as to interest the attention, while it appealed faithfully and earnestly to the heart and conscience.   His illustrations, and the method of treating a text, might sometimes remind the hearer of the manner of William Jay, though the style of the discourse wanted the finish and sententious aptness of that eminent preacher.   He seldom used more than brief notes of the outline of a sermon, trusting generally to his facility in extemporaneous speaking, for the filling in and amplifying the different parts of the subject under consideration.   His very fluency, combined with his deep earnestness, sometimes betrayed him into diffuseness, and made him oblivious of the lapse of time.   On the platform a friendly twitch of the coat tail, and in the pulpit a fortunate glance at the clock, were sometimes necessary to remind the speaker of the weakness of humanity, and to bring his eloquence to a close. The topics which the preacher most delighted to present, were the gracious attributes of the Deity, the fulness and freeness of the gospel, and the practical duties of Christianity; and though he shunned not to declare, so far as he apprehended it, ' all the counsel of God,' he never indulged in those denunciations of eternal wrath and ghastly pictures of perdition with which some divines delight to terrify sinners.

As a pastor he was judicious, kind, and sympathising; and his visits to the well-furnished houses of the prosperous, or the humble cottages of the poor among his flock, were always hailed with pleasure.   He was never obtrusive in forcing religious subjects, either in conversation or correspondence, without regard to fitness or propriety; yet when occasion permitted, he was a faithful and valuable counsellor.   Very many have been indebted to his affectionate exhortations, or clear expositions of Divine truth, for the removal of their perplexities, an enlightened apprehension of the Gospel, and a hearty acceptance of its heavenly consolations, and its free and ample grace. The fidelity and wisdom with which he endeavoured to help those who sought his counsel in their religious difficulties, will appear from the following extract of a letter written to one who had received much early bias from intercourse with Unitarians, but, utterly dissatisfied with their teaching, was seeking a safer ground of trust and hope.

' I will not now dispute your position that conviction is not a matter of choice : there can, however, be no doubt that with-holding conviction, or resisting evidence when this is supplied, involves all the consequences of a matter of choice: but I will not argue. To me your present state appears to have been con-tinued chiefly from two sources, the head and the heart. In regard to the first I cannot gather that you have received clear and just, that is full scriptural views of the Divine character and the way of salvation. Your opinions seem partly defective and partly incorrect. Your view of the character of God *seems* to have been confined chiefly to His mercy and his purity. It is necessary to remember that, though these perfections in their excellency and operations infinitely transcend the highest esti-mate created mind can form, they are only parts of a complete view : the admission of integrity, or righteousness, and truth are equally essential to all correct conceptions of the Almighty. A partial apprehension of the character of God will materially affect our perception of other parts of Divine revelation, and prevent our perceiving or feeling the influence of that beautiful symmetry and harmony which are manifest in the *whole* system of truth. It is my impression that hence arises one of your difficulties in connection with the doctrine of Atonement; though I believe the difficulty more frequently arises from the heart not being sufficiently humbled, emptied of self, and convinced of the nature and tendency of sin, to feel its need of atonement.

' Your views of the way of salvation appear incorrect, inasmuch as you have deemed it necessary to add to the requirements which God has made, a self-imposed obligation to ascertain "what kind of faith is expressly required," and " *how* the sacrifice of Christ *should* atone for the sins of a guilty world," before you could unreservedly and gratefully surrender yourself to the truth that "God so loved the world that he gave his only begotten Son, that whosoever believeth in Him should not perish, but have everlasting life." And because your enquiries have been fruitless you " dare not call yourself a believer." God has not required this before you believe, in order to your salvation ; and for you to require it is like saying, I dare not sow the seed till I ascertain what it will produce. One of the simplest and clearest illustrations of the faith required of us, has, to my mind, been that of the Israelites in the wilderness, when the serpent was lifted up in the camp. Here was the dim vision of the infant, and the hoary-headed sufferer, upon whose sight the mists of age were thickening, as well as that of those in the plenitude of their strength and vigour, yet the *efficacy* of the remedy did not in the least depend on the distinctness with which the object was perceived, but in obedience to the Divine injunction. So it is with salvation. " *Whosoever* believeth in Him (Christ) shall not perish, but have everlasting life ;" " Believe, and *thou* shalt be saved ; "and other promises equally explicit are Divine declarations, and must be received before any spiritual life can be experienced ; but when received, spiritual life follows, as physical healing did to the camp in the wilderness.

' In regard to the doctrine of the Atonement, I will not attempt to render that plainer than it is unfolded in the Scriptures. Doubts in reference thereto were never permitted to make a lodgment in my mind since I began to think seriously on the subject; and it has always appeared to me so essential a part of the revelation God has given, that I never could see very clearly any ground for doubt, when the Divine authority of the Bible was admitted. I have ever regarded it as the most gracious manifestation of Divine wisdom, by which all the perfections of the Divine character were presented in a degree of harmony that could scarcely be contemplated without admiration and love.   I have always supposed that it atoned for the sins of a guilty world by rendering that obedience to the Divine will, and enduring that suffering on account of sin, without which the truth of God would not have been inviolate ; yet it never occurred to me in the light of a cause, but rather as the fruit, of Divine benevolence.   It never appeared to me that the death of Christ *rendered* the Supreme Moral Governor merciful, or that it was necessary to enable Him to exercise mercy ; but, on the contrary, that the sacrifice of Christ itself originated in Divine mercy.   " God so loved the world that *He gave* His only begotten Son," &c.   " Herein is love, not that we loved God but that He loved us and *gave* himself for us," &c.

‘ But I said your present state was, I thought, traceable to the heart as well as to the head.   Are you quite sure, my dear friend, that a feeling of complacency in mental power, in superiority to the multitude who blindly follow their religious teacher, has not unduly operated in keeping you so long unsettled ? Be this as it may, in your letter you say, " there is a state of holiness of life before God and man, of dedication of heart, of surrender of all things, however dear, that are not acceptable in the Divine sight, which has sometimes been presented to me as a duty, and upon which I have as often closed my eyes with a voluntary conclusion that these things were not attainable to me."   Now, has not this withholding of the heart—this hesitancy or refusal to give up the world, or whatever stood in the way of salvation, been the cause in a great degree of your present state of mind and heart ?   Could the principle of spiritual life exist and operate while this was allowed ? You say in one of your letters that at times you can only pray that through any tribulation, through any fiery trial, you may at last be counted worthy to be a follower of Christ Jesus.   You state that you believe His name the only name given among men whereby they must be

saved ; that were you to deny Him you would seal your perdition. Now, these feelings and views are not from your own
heart. Are you sure they are not the first motions of the blessed
Spirit's influence ? And would you not have had all the fruits of
the Spirit, all the functions of spiritual life, had you unreservedly
yielded your heart to their power, and laid hold on eternal life
by believing the testimony that God has given, that whosoever
believes shall not perish ? Think, my dear friend, if you have
not been resisting the Holy Spirit, and thus grieving Him who
is the comforter of believers, by restraining the grateful feelings
of your heart from flowing forth to Him who has made such
ample provision for your redemption and comfort. Think of
this.

'You said you had read all the books on the subject. I am
somewhat doubtful if you have read some of the best. There is
a little pamphlet, *The Way of Salvation*, by David Russell,
of Dundee, exceedingly simple and clear in pointing out the way
of life. I should like you to read it if you have not, and think
it might aid you in understanding the Scriptures, on which
alone your faith must rest. You should also read, by all means,
Smith on the Atonement and Sacrifice, and Smith's *Scripture
Testimony to the Messiah*, a book not of arguing but of
evidence, written by one who has the best heart that was ever
enclosed in a frail human body.'

It was during the period now under review that the general
indignation of Protestant England was roused by the division of
the country into Roman Catholic Sees, and the Papal assumption
of English territorial titles for Romanist ecclesiastics. While
the minds of the people were thus specially directed to the
subject, Mr. Ellis, with the recollections of his observations in
Rome fresh in his memory, preached a series of discourses, in
a plain and popular style, on the doctrines, the system, and
practical operation of Romanism. These sermons, six in
number, were afterwards published, under the modest name of
"Village Lectures on Popery," and formed a truthful, temperate,

and concise exposition of the errors of that anti-Christian system.

The pastor's connection with the congregation, and his interest in all that concerned its welfare continued to the end of his life ; but his pastorate was brought to a close just before he left England on his first visit to Madagascar, when, anticipating a lengthened and indefinite absence from home, he resigned his charge, in the autumn of 1852, though he did not finally take his departure on his distant embassy till the following April. He preached his farewell sermon to his people on the 3rd of April, selecting for his text the words of St. Paul at Miletus, in his charge to the elders of Ephesus, " And now, brethren, I commend you to God, and to the word of his grace, which is able to build you up, and to give you an inheritance among all them which are sanctified " (Acts xx. 32).

The pastorate of the Church at Hoddesdon was next filled by the Rev. J. E. Tunmer, who was succeeded by the Rev. J. Vine, formerly missionary in Jamaica. His health failing, he was compelled to resign his office, which was then held by the Rev. S. T. Williams, a son of the Martyr Missionary. After a comparatively brief connection with the Church, Mr. Williams was induced to accept an important charge in a more populous neighbourhood ; and his place was filled by the Rev. J. W. Blore, who still continues to preside over the little flock that had been mainly gathered together by the attraction of their first pastor's name and influence.

A retrospect of the years spent in Hoddesdon would be very incomplete without some reference to ' Rawdon House.' Although not a matter which directly and personally related to the subject of this memoir, it was too closely associated with other members of his family to be passed over. Mrs. Ellis's thoughts had long been directed, as her various books abundantly testified, to the subject of female education ; and she wished to give practical effect to her views, by the establishment of a school, in which moral training, the development of the character, and

some preparation for the domestic duties that would naturally
fall to the lot of most girls in after life, and of which, at least,
every mistress of a house should possess a competent knowledge—
a school in which these important and practical interests should
be embraced, as well as the mental culture and lighter accomplishments, which in her opinion were too exclusively regarded in most
'seminaries for young ladies.'   That the success of the undertaking would prove a source of income was, of course, a consideration to which due weight was given in the inception of
the scheme.

A little removed from the main road through Hoddesdon,
and standing in a pleasant and ample plot of ground sloping
towards the river Lea, there is a picturesque Elizabethan
mansion known by the name of ' Rawdon House.'   This was
the property of Mr. Warner, senior, and happened to be vacant
at the time when Mrs. Ellis was looking round for a suitable
building for her school.   It was secured upon a short lease of
tenancy, and for the amount of accommodation, attractive
appearance, and convenience of site, no premises more suitable
could have been found.   An old friend of Mrs. Ellis, well
fitted for the task of instruction, shared in the direction
and care of the establishment, and resided in the building.
Mr. Ellis's two daughters also took part in teaching.   The
health of the elder of the two, however, never allowed her to
undertake more than a very slight amount of work, and even
this she was soon obliged to relinquish.   She had been long an
invalid, and finding the air of Hoddesdon unfavourable, she
was recommended to try the climate of Hastings, where her
uncle (her mother's brother) resided.   Some temporary benefit
was derived from the change to the sea-side, but no permanent
relief was secured.   She returned to Hoddesdon to end her
days in the midst of her own family, and after many years of
illness, passed peacefully from earth to her eternal rest.   She
died on the 30th of June 1858, and was buried in Hoddesdon
churchyard, the burial-ground of Bunhill Fields having been

closed. Her youngest sister was then the only remaining daughter of the family.

The school, if it did not realize all the hopes and plans of its projector, proved from the first decidedly successful ; and many who received their education there, look back with fond regret mingled with pleasure to the period passed at ' Rawdon House,' grateful for the delightful home influences which characterized it, and for the training that developed the best and highest elements of their lives. Mrs. Ellis herself, having fairly started the undertaking, and secured for it a firm footing, gradually retired from the active management; and as Mrs. Hurry, the first superintendent also left, upon the marriage of her daughter, the practical conduct and responsibility of the establishment devolved on Miss Ellis, in conjunction with a lady with whom she entered into partnership. Miss Ellis possessed much natural force of character, and excellent mental abilities, and had, moreover, derived great advantage from the influence of her step-mother, who, from the first, had most conscientiously, faithfully, and kindly endeavoured to discharge her duties towards her husband's children. In undertaking the chief direction of the school, she still enjoyed the counsel and help of Mrs. Ellis, and proved herself eminently qualified for her position. Her health, however, was giving way, and for many months, not to say years, before her death, which occurred during her father's last visit to Madagascar, it became evident to her anxious friends, though she bravely stood to her post, that she could not long take part in human affairs—that the ' measure of her days ' would soon be accomplished. The establishment was, nevertheless, kept up for some time by the surviving partner, Miss Taylor, until the property was sold and passed into other hands. Miss Taylor then removed to the neighbourhood of Finchley, where she carries on the school under the old name.

CHAPTER X.

ROSE HILL.—HOME LIFE.

A MORE charming rural neighbourhood than the country around Hoddesdon, with the thoroughly English character of its scenery, could hardly be found within twenty miles of London. The river Lea, a sluggish and unpicturesque stream indeed, but contributing its share, nevertheless, to the completeness of the landscape, flows through the broad valley of the district. The surface of the ground is sufficiently undulating to redeem its stretches of pasture, meadow, and wood from all tameness ; and though fertile farms are not wanting, the number of gentlemen's residences, and particularly the large estates of such wealthy proprietors as the Marquis of Salisbury and the Bosanquet family, give a more than usually ornamental aspect to the country, together with a large proportion of woodland, including within an easy distance the royal forest of Epping. But the chief attraction and characteristic feature of the neighbourhood are the narrow, winding, tree-shaded lanes that abound in every direction, alluring the traveller on by some fresh charm at every turn,—now shutting out all view but their own secluded beauty, and anon disclosing a cool inviting vista of leafy shade, or an undulating sweep of meadow, relieved by groups of trees, and bounded by hills sufficiently distant to assume the soft neutral tints that an artist would choose wherewith to finish the picture.

Rose Hill itself is situated away from the main road, and far enough from the village to give it perfect seclusion. It is bounded and approached on one side by a narrow and not very

O

inviting street or lane, and on the other by open fields. A high wall screens it from the former, and a hedge interspersed with trees divides it from the latter. The house is a plain two-storied, white brick building—perhaps it would be more correct to say *was*—for already dwelling and grounds are undergoing alterations that bid fair to obliterate the former character of the place, and we must speak of it, like everything else in the lives we are tracing, as of the past. The plainness of the masonry, however, was relieved by a luxuriant Wisteria that almost covered the front, up to the eaves, and twice in the year, with its profusion of bloom, presented a picture of beauty that challenged the admiration of every beholder. Some superb climbing roses mixed their warmer blossoms with the purple clusters that claimed supremacy, while the border at the base of the walls was a mass of rich and varied foliage and flower. The grounds were laid out in excellent taste, all formality being avoided, and the walks and planting so disposed as to increase apparently the space, and to retain some of the wild grace of nature with the order of a well-appointed garden. A picturesque Scotch fir and larch, standing side by side and interlacing their foliage, were the most striking objects that caught the eye, and which the imagination would invariably include in every effort to recal the picture. At one time a magnificent elm overshadowed the dwelling; but trunk and root attaining gigantic proportions, and being so near as to disturb the foundation of the walls, it was found necessary to cut it down. A graceful Deodara and a bed of flowers replaced the fallen chieftain, and, realizing the fate of all earthly greatness, it ceased to be missed, if it was not quite forgotten. But the grand charm—the glory—of the scene was its roses. They were evidently at home in the soil and locality, and as evidently the master spirit of the place loved them, and knew how to grow them. The choicest varieties might be introduced without fear of failure. The endless diversity, the profusion, the beauty, and the delicious perfume which this queen of flowers diffused about the homestead,—meeting the eye at every turn, climbing on walls or trellised arches, spreading a blaze of blossom over beds disposed among the turf, presenting here and there magnificent heads of exquisite bloom on grouped or single standards, or nestling in unexpected nooks and corners,—altogether gave to the comparatively narrow enclosure an attractive loveliness peculiarly home-like in its character. The favoured flower, not content with running almost rampant in its legitimate domain, the lawn and pleasure ground, obtruded into the kitchen garden, where it bordered the walks, and imparted unwonted fragrance and beauty to this usually formal and uninviting plot. These successful results were not due, it should be remembered, to the science or practical knowledge of a hired gardener, but were achieved by Mr. Ellis's personal industry and horticultural skill, nearly every variety having been budded by his own hands; and though, of course, a man was employed about the place, that faithful servant owed his knowledge of gardening and the proficiency he ultimately acquired to the teaching of his master. A small greenhouse, adjoining one end of the dwelling, was originally all the glass about the garden; but this was soon found insufficient, and when, after Mr. Ellis's return from Madagascar, many rare and splendid Orchids were added to the collection, it became necessary to build a house for their accommodation, as well as for the exotic ferns and other tropical plants that required a high temperature. The orchids formed a marvellous assemblage of floral beauty, and, owing doubtless to the skilful management they received, flourished here with rare luxuriance. Indeed, both Sir William Hooker and Dr. Lindley, who more than once visited Rose Hill to see the collection or to examine some special novelty, assured the owner that he succeeded better with this class of flowers than they could do either in Kew Gardens, or in those of the Horticultural Society. His name became familiar both among amateur and professional horticulturists in connection with the new plants introduced by him from Madagascar, particularly that marvel

among orchids, the *Angræcum sesquipedale*, and the curious
and delicate lace plant, *Ouvirandra fenestralis*. He was a
frequent exhibitor at the Flower Shows of the Crystal Palace
and Regent's Park, and never failed to carry off prizes. In thus
indulging his taste for flowers, he did not, like some, embarrass
himself by an expensive luxury, but contrived by the sale of
plants to make the conservatory pay at least its own expenses;
so that there was never on this score an accusing conscience to
upbraid him with extravagance.

Such was the pleasant homestead out of doors. Within there
was an unmistakable air of comfort and elegance, marked by
an absence of all pretension or show. Everything was in good
taste, and good keeping, forming a fair picture of a quiet and
refined English home, in the aspect of which one might read
something of the characters of the presiding inmates. Both
were persons beyond the common order; each distinguished by
strong individuality and superior mental power; yet their dis-
positions, dissimilar as they were, blended harmoniously together,
and each exerted a happy influence on the other. Mr. Ellis,
who had been inclined in earlier life to reserve and melancholy,
seemed to throw off in his later years the sombre mantle that
would, at times, envelope his better self, and became habitually—
not more kind and gentle—but more cheery, social, and commu-
nicative. Much of this change, most advantageous to himself as
well as delightful to those about him, was due, no doubt, to the
good sense, and tact, and genial companionship of his loving
wife. She, on her part, loved and reverenced her husband with
true womanly devotion, and from the impulse of a deep affection
ever made his happiness, and, it should be added to her honour,
that of his children, the study of her life.

Never ostentatious in their hospitality, they were yet genuinely
friendly, and had ever a cordial welcome for a guest. Such
things as formal 'parties' were not to their taste, and they preferred to enjoy the society of their friends, either as visitors
staying in the house, or coming in to their early tea and spend-

ing a quiet evening in unrestrained and unaffected converse. Both were what is commonly understood as 'good company,' with a ready flow of animated conversation, and, what is equally essential, a warm and hearty sympathy with others, which made them excellent *listeners* as well as talkers. Of Mr. Ellis's conversational powers something has already been said in connection with his missionary tours. Scarcely any subject of discourse could be started concerning which he could not give some interesting information, or in the discussion of which he could not take an intelligent part. His memory and versatility were indeed marvellous. An instance in point may be mentioned, that occurred in Lancaster, and which surprised all present, perhaps none more than his own wife. A large number of persons were assembled to hear a lecture in connection with a literary institution, but sudden illness, or some other cause, prevented the appearance of the lecturer. In this dilemma, Mr. Ellis was asked if he would say a few words on any subject he chose. Without hesitation he took up the topic already announced for the evening—one entirely removed from his ordinary experience—and delighted the audience by an easy and fluent address, full of interesting information gathered partly from reading and partly by observation in travel. The wonder was, not the fluent speaking, but his familiarity with a subject so unlikely to have engaged his attention.

Another charm of his social nature was the tact and kindliness that always marked his intercourse with others. Questions were not unfrequently asked of him which betrayed the ignorance of the interlocutor, and might have exposed the latter with a less considerate companion to painful embarrassment or ridicule; but Mr. Ellis was usually ready with an appropriate and truthful reply, without exposing the blunder, and so contrived to spare the other's feelings. One or two instances may be mentioned by way of illustration. Whilst staying once at the house of an Episcopalian, the host, who had no idea that his guest was not a 'good Churchman,' suddenly observed in the course of conversation, 'Mr. Ellis, I *hate* dissenters, especially the *Independents*, don't you?' The unfortunate 'Independent,' thus appealed to, admitted that the name was ill-chosen and objectionable, but good-humouredly deprecated such wholesale denunciation of any body of men, and quietly drew off to safer ground, without enlightening his host, at that time, in regard to his own creed. On another occasion, at a public breakfast, a very simple-minded lady, sitting next to him, inquired if 'Polly Nesia was a pious character.' Mr. Ellis promptly replied 'Not decidedly—not altogether'; and contrived so to engage the lady in conversation as to prevent her noticing the amusement which her question had excited among the company in the immediate neighbourhood, and which the courtesy and good example set them by the speaker tended greatly to restrain.

His self-command on such occasions was the more noticeable as he had a quick and keen appreciation of the ludicrous, and shrewd insight into character. This last quality made him quick to detect, and ill-disposed to tolerate, any form of pretension. Conceit, vanity, and effeminacy were especially repugnant to him. But withal he had a well-spring of charity that made him very forbearing. One of the earliest lessons he used to inculcate on his children was to avoid censoriousness, and particularly to refrain from evil-speaking. He exemplified his teaching in his practice. When he could not conscientiously speak the praise of the absent, he was silent. His kindness was not confined to the members of his family or his guests, but extended to the domestics, towards whom he was ever considerate, and never failed to win their esteem and attachment. Once admitted into the household, (certainly they would be selected with some discrimination) they generally remained; and the establishment continued in many respects the same to the very last that it had been when 'the master' first came to Rose Hill.

It was not to humanity alone that this benevolence was limited; animals came in for a large share of appreciation and kind treatment. With Mrs. Ellis the love of animals was almost a passion, fostered partly by a motherless and somewhat lonely childhood.   If she did not develop the same feeling in her husband, she contrived to overcome a certain shyness in mani-festing it, that had its root, perhaps, in a manly nature, despising the appearance even of silliness or effeminacy.   To elicit a display of attachment to a horse, or a dog of some presence and impor-tance, was no difficult task ; but to induce the dignified man to throw aside his gravity of deportment, if not his dignity, and enter heartily into the humour and frolics of an absurd little terrier or a kitten, was perhaps a triumph of womanly influence. Both Mr. and Mrs. Ellis were exceedingly fond of riding on horseback, and found in this healthy exercise a most desirable relief to their sedentary and literary habits.   There was no end of charming rides in the neighbourhood.   The lanes and woods and parks already mentioned afforded unusual attractiveness and diversity, and hardly ever was the state of the weather, or any ordinary hindrance, allowed to interfere with a daily ride.   The dumb companions of these excursions were not mere drudges : they were regarded as friends, their characters studied and judiciously humoured, their comfort considered, and their con-fidence and attachment effectually won.   The field where they grazed with the cattle in summer was separated from the lawn only by a wire fence, to which the intelligent animals would come at call, or without call, glad to receive some delicacy from the garden or kitchen, but evidently gratified also with merely their owners' friendly recognition and notice.   In addition to the two riding horses, a small pony, trained to draw a light basket carriage, had been procured for Miss Ellis, when her health began to fail.   It was a pretty, symmetrical, though diminutive roan, of a sprightly, sociable and familiar disposition, and soon became a great favourite and pet.   It was in the habit of coming to the kitchen door for morsels of bread, and needed only the smallest encouragement to walk into the house. Indeed, on one occasion, while at pasture in a neighbour's field, in the corner of which there was a labourer's cottage, it was searched for, but could nowhere be seen, but on being called by name, emerged from the cottager's door, with a mouth full of bread and butter—it had been taking tea with the family. After its mistress's death it was still kept, chiefly for her sake, and, in proof of the care and kindness bestowed upon it, is living yet, though more than twenty years old, as fat, as funny, and as happy as any little Shetland in the country.

But among the 'lower orders' *the* character of the establishment was a little black and grey Skye terrier, not one of those big-headed, long-bodied specimens of ugliness one sometimes sees under that name, but a compact, symmetrical, beautiful little animal, that would catch the eye of an artist, and indeed, that has had the distinction of being both painted in oils and modelled in clay. It went by the name of 'Jock,' and between it and 'Brenda,' the pony, there existed a curious mixture of friendship and jealousy, which was not a little amusing. It was the special property of Mrs. Ellis, but became very much attached to 'the master.' It would catch the sound of his step or his horse's hoofs long before ears less acute were able to distinguish any token of his return, and run delighted to meet him. A run with the horses when they went for the afternoon ride, was a source of inexpressible pleasure, only marred by the restraint imposed upon him against chasing the game in the woods. But perhaps the crowning delight of the kind was to accompany 'Brenda' in the pony carriage. When preparations for such a jaunt were in progress, he would become frantic with excitement, and when all was ready for the start, having taken his place on the seat, he would seize the reins, and was evidently possessed with the absurd idea that he was driving, and enjoyed the glory immensely. He considered himself the guardian of the premises, and was zealously watchful against strange cats, though he maintained the most friendly relations with the feline members of his own family. The birds he had been taught not to molest.

The event of his life within doors was a weekly occurrence,

which received the name of 'Jock's Sunday Class.' This was a game with his master, in which he contended for the possession of a fir cone attached to a string, and manifestly believed that he retained his hold, not by sufferance, but by main strength, and that some day he would pull his antagonist from his seat. Whether or no this Sunday recreation had a bad effect upon his morals, certain it is that he was not a 'religious animal'; in truth, he entertained a comical repugnance to family worship. No sooner was 'the Book' produced than Jock's vivacity would suddenly cease, his tail would droop, and he would slowly retire to the furthest corner of the room; then facing round, he would sit erect, and supplicate most imploringly that he might be spared the infliction. No notice being taken of this appeal, he would drop down with a sigh, and resign himself to endure as well as he could the trying solemnity. With all his eccentricities, he was touchingly attached to his owners; and, when his master went to Madagascar, was long inconsolable for his absence; and of all the welcomes that greeted the traveller's return, none was so demonstrative, perhaps none so affecting, as little 'Jock's.'

The other domestic animals in the house were a breed of Persian cats, whose characters and peculiarities were subjects of amusing speculation. 'Tim,' the patriarch of the family, dined like a gentleman, partaking of every dish, and showing quite a human appreciation of peas and cucumber. The mother of the tribe came in with the tea-tray, and, after receiving her daily dole, retired with matronly decorum. The young ones afforded endless entertainment, which even the master of the house could not resist. He would perhaps shake his head at the bare suggestion that he could possibly admit a kitten into his study, but the evidence of fir cone or corks suspended from the bell-pull in that sanctum, obviously for the special delectation of the fluffy gymnasts, was conclusive against him. The whole household, it must be confessed, fully carried out the quaint advice of that pleasant humourist, the author of *My Summer in a Garden*—'Let us respect the cat.'

There was yet another class of the brute creation which claimed high honour and indulgence. This was the birds; and foremost among them, in their season, were the nightingales, that abound in Hertfordshire, and seemed nowhere more at home than in the leafy lanes and woods about Hoddesdon, which they made vocal with their melody. They evidently found a retreat to their taste at Rose Hill, and were so lavish with their song that an old woman living near declared she must emigrate, for she could not sleep for the noise they made. No nest about the premises was ever disturbed. The swallows were permitted to build under the eaves, and even under the porch; and if any mischance happened to nest or young, the accident was, if possible, carefully remedied—the nest replaced, when it had fallen, and the fledglings fed, if prematurely deserted by their parents. The sparrows, on account of their thievish propensities, were perhaps held in least esteem; and Mr. Ellis would keep guard over his pet robin, that was always near the threshold to receive its crumbs after each meal, lest his little friend should be robbed by the cunning pilferers. Long after the hand that had fed it, and the heart that had given it a place in its love, were cold in the grave, this little favourite might still be seen, perched on a twig of the Deodara, or on a garden seat, waiting in vain for the friend that would never return. These are trivial details, scarcely worth noticing, some may think, but they reveal a part, and not an unamiable part, of a character that was at once child-like and manly, gentle and noble.

Intellectual pursuits and literary work formed, as will naturally be inferred, a large portion of the daily life of both the heads of the family. Both were hard workers, but there was considerable diversity in their method and temperament. Mrs. Ellis was always fore-handed and orderly; while her lord was more desultory in his application, and a little disposed to procrastinate; so that he would often be compelled to make up by late hours and the 'midnight lamp' for such lack of diligence as the garden, or some other pleasant allurement, might have caused. The habit of procrastinating sometimes, though not often, resulted in a missed train, or some such inconvenience. When a journey was in contemplation the house was on the alert; for 'the master' would invariably put off his departure to the very last second when it was possible to catch the train, and the rest were anxious that there should be no hindrance on their part. The man stood waiting with the horse at the gate, the boy having been despatched to the station to bring it back; coat, wrappers, hat, gloves, and everything wanted were in readiness, so that there might not be a moment's delay at the last. Mr. Ellis once mounted would ride at full gallop to the station, and generally, not always, managed to arrive just in time. His ordinary pace, both in going to the station and returning, was a gallop; and horse and rider at full speed, even after the latter had long passed his 'three score years and ten,' were familiar to every inhabitant of Hoddesdon.

If he was neither punctual nor methodical, Mr. Ellis was, nevertheless, a diligent worker. His sermons were always faithfully studied; and, besides the books that he published, he penned many valuable contributions to the current literature of the day. Several articles in the last edition of the *Encyclopædia Britannica*, such as those on 'Madagascar' and 'Polynesia,' were written by him; and, in short, he was never without some literary work on his hands.

The mistress of the house was equally distinguished by indefatigable industry, and was far more methodical in her arrangements. Her custom was to rise about four or five o'clock, and settle diligently to her writing till breakfast. She preferred the undisturbed quiet of the morning hours, and felt at that time more fresh for mental labour. After breakfast, household duties having received due attention, she would either resume her writing, or devote the forenoon to painting—an art that she loved, and in which she showed both taste and proficiency. One of the latest tasks of the kind she accomplished was a series of water-colour pictures, full size, of all the orchids in their

collection.   These were most beautifully executed, and, whether
regarded as artistic drawings, or as singularly correct botanical
representations of the flowers, they deservedly elicited general
admiration.   Her skill in art was not limited to the pencil and
brush; she was equally successful in modelling, the material
employed being chiefly wax.   She did not confine her attempts
in this department to flowers, but executed some admirable
busts and figures; and among the number may be included a
small bust of her husband, which was both beautiful in work-
manship and an excellent likeness.   Indeed, Mrs. Ellis was
wonderfully clever with her hands as well as her head.   She
was a most accomplished knitter, not only plying the needles
with precision and rapidity, but designing, as she proceeded,
both form and pattern, with wonderful aptness.   A copy for
such work, unless it were from nature, she never condescended
to use.   In the afternoon (it was the custom of the house to
dine early) both Mr. and Mrs. Ellis would usually ride on
horseback; and the evening was generally free for a quiet chat,
and the society of one or more friends.

Mr. Ellis's poetical temperament has been already mentioned,
and is very evident in his prose writings.   But besides the deep
spring of poetic feeling, which in common with most persons of
sensibility he possessed, he had acquired, few as were his opportunities for practice, some skill in versification.   During the
latter part of his life he was too much occupied with higher
work to be able to spare time for a recreation which, in his
earlier years, had been very congenial to his taste.   While
residing at Nailsworth, and during the preparation of *Polynesian
Researches*, besides producing occasional lyrics, he projected
and very nearly finished an epic poem, entitled *Mahine*, the
main theme of which was the overthrow of idolatry in the Society
Islands.   At one time he contemplated the publication of this
poem, and with that view submitted it to the judgment of men
already eminent in the same walk of literature—Wordsworth,
Montgomery, Southey, and others.   All these poets encouraged

him to publish; and the following letter from Robert Southey in reference to the matter will not be uninteresting :—

From Robert Southey.

'KESWICK, *Aug.* 7, 1830.

'My dear Sir,—If I had not been much employed, and, more-over, very much interrupted, I should be ashamed of dating upon the seventh of this month a letter which it was my intention should have been in London by the first, to await your arrival there.

'Messrs. Longman will send to your publishers two sets of the *History of Brazil*, of the *Tale of Paraguay*, and of the *Pilgrimage to Waterloo*; the one set is intended for your Polynesian library, the other you will do me the favour of accepting in remembrance of me.

'Now, with regard to your poem. You only want to read some of our old authors, with the view of improving your diction and enriching your vocabulary. *Old* authors, I say, because you will find there a purity and strength of language not to be found (or most rarely) in later writers. I have marked in your manuscript some passages which may easily be improved, and here and there you will see that I have shown in pencil how they would read more agreeably to my ear.

'You may improve your speeches by giving them a character of the native oratory, and throwing into them some of their metaphorical expressions and figures of speech, perhaps, even some of their idioms: where a foreign idiom can be preserved it gives a great freshness and strength, as we feel in the Hebraisms of the Bible.

'The old dramatists are the best writers in whom blank verse can be studied, that is, in whom you can learn all that you wish to acquire of its construction and capabilities; because no other writers of that age wrote in that metre; and where those dramatists end, the corruption of our language begins. There is no purer diction than that of George Herbert, who is properly called the saintly Herbert. Daniels is very pure; he is in all respects a beautiful and delightful writer, whom it is impossible not to love; but in admiring him there is some danger of being seduced into a languid style, for he frequently writes below his own powers. The freedom and vigour of our language is nowhere to be seen so fully as in the old dramatists, that is of our poetical language. They will offend you often by their grossness, and still more by their immorality, but these are not of a kind which carry pollution with them, like Lord Byron's poems. The manners of their age allowed of such things, and none of those men wrote with any intention of corrupting their auditors, or of disturbing their moral sense: on the contrary, they abound in passages of the best morality as well as of the strongest sense.

'My wife and daughters beg to be remembered to you. I shall be glad if circumstances should bring you again this way, and I will not be in London, without enquiring at your publishers whether you are in town.

'Farewell, my dear Sir, and believe me

'Yours with sincere respect and goodwill,

'ROBERT SOUTHEY.'

'Inclosed is a note of introduction to Sharon Turner, one of the best as well as most learned of men.'

The original copy of *Mahine*, with Southey's pencil annotations in the margin, is in the writer's possession. Notwithstanding much encouragement, the author was too diffident ever to submit this production of his Muse to the criticism of the public. A specimen of one of the lyrical pieces, and a few quotations from the more ambitious epic, will now be read with indulgence at least, and doubtless with interest also.

'OUR FATHERS, WHERE ARE THEY?'—Zech. i. 5.

The fathers, where are they? No longer in sadness
  Mid scenes of affliction their sympathies flow;
Unheard are the voices that cheered us with gladness,
  Gave strength in our weakness, and solace in woe.

The fathers, where are they? No longer beams o'er us
 The light of their path. like the splendours of day;
No more shall the constant affection they bore us
 Like ramparts surround us, each foe to dismay.

The fathers, where are they? No longer among us
 In front of the battle, these men of renown
Shall wave the bright banner, where dark legions throng us,
 Assure us of conquest, and point to the crown.

The fathers, where are they? Securely abiding,
 From labour they rest in the mansions above,
Where the Saviour exalted benignly presiding,
 O'er banquets divine sheds the smile of His love.

The fathers, where are they? In glory appearing,
 In homage they bow at the feet of their King,
The crown and the white robe of victory wearing,
 His throne they surround, and His triumph they sing.

The fathers, where are they? From lofty seats bending,
 Like angels they follow their children below,
Ard the march of their Leader's bright armies attending,
 As each conquest they hail fresh transport they know.

The fathers, where are they? Advancing before us,
 To realms of the blessed they have led on the way;
Their path may we follow till death shall restore us,
 To meet them again in the regions of day.

The poem entitled *Mahine* opens with a brief reference to
the South Sea Islands, and the story begins with the following
scene on the shore:—

  Beneath a stately tree, at evening hour,
  Mahine, monarch of the reef-bound isles,
  In converse social with his chieftains sat.
  O'er the wide beach beneath them, warrior bands
  Their martial sports pursued,—cast the smooth stone,
  The light lance hurled, the sounding bowstring drew,
  Swift o'er the sands in eager contest ran,
  Or sought with manly strength the wrestler's prize.
  Gay, youthful groups strayed o'er the flowery lawn,
  Weaving new garlands for their flowing hair,
  Or, moving graceful to the plaintive flute,
  In artless dances mingled. The broad sun
  Radiant descending mid the woody isles
  That gem the western sea, new splendours poured
  On the umbrageous canopy that hung
  In sylvan grandeur o'er the monarch's head.

Rich glowed the burnished flood, and on its waves,
Like a pearl ship borne on a golden sea,
A well-manned bark appeared. Her streamers gay
Scarce fluttered in the dying breeze, her sail
Hung idly by the mast, while her broad prow
Was shoreward pointed. This Mahine saw,
And bade Maoni, leader of his guard,
Approach the shore and mark her gliding way.

The advancing canoe brings Pomare's herald, summoning his
friends to aid him against a rebellious conspiracy. Loyal help
is eagerly promised by Mahine and his followers. The picturesque progress of the herald to different chiefs, through
lovely and romantic scenes, is then narrated; and a council of
war is described. The following simile occurs in the answer of
one of the chieftains to his sovereign's summons :—

' Oh monarch brave, and worthy of thy sire,
Our fathers' leader, who illustrious fought,
With triumph sated, on the ensanguined flood,
Command from thee impatient here we wait.
As the trained mastiff, when his generous lord
Points to the loaded thief, through morning mist
At distance seen, firm fixes on the wretch
His steady glance, and terror in his voice
Before him sending, bounds across the plain,
Assails the foe, hears not his threats, nor feels
His blows, nor turns his eye, springs at his throat,
And fastens deep his fangs, his hold maintains
Firm and unyielding, brings him to the earth,
Stains with his blood the flower-spotted turf,
Then by the captured spoils recumbent waits
His master's plaudit;—lo, wave but thy hand.
And hasting o'er the deep, thy friends in arms
Shall swift destruction on these rebels pour.
Too long our stately ships in harbour lie:
Our weapons idly in our dwellings hang :
Our fame, though now supreme in every land,
Shall die, or but adorn a rival's name.
Our arm, unused to grapple with the foe.
Shall in the struggle fail, should we, supine,
Luxurious banquets in the bower of peace,
The striplings' dance, the lover's languid sigh,
Or simpering smile of fickle maid, prefer
To glorious conflict in the field of war.'

One more quotation, describing the midnight visit of the priest of Oro, the Tahitian God of War, to the temple of that sanguinary deity, will be sufficient to show the quality of the composition :—

But yesternight,
When each assisting priest had to his post
Retired—alone, the inmost temple's court
Of solemn shade I entered—lowly bowed
Before his sacred presence—thrice invoked
His name—in accents low my prayer preferred—
Then prostrate on the polished stone, low placed
Beside his altar in the skull-paved floor,
I lay in awe-full silence. No quick glare
Of mortals' torch has ever pierced that gloom
Profound, but lights aërial flitting oft
Through long ranged altar pillars, and the paths
On either side by human skulls defined,
That through the temple's secret labyrinth lead,
Each deep recess illumed. No human foot,
Save those of Oro's priest, e'er trod at night
Those paths, and walked again ; but spirits stood
Around great Oro waiting ; heralds fleet,
With noiseless step, along the mazy walks
Passed to and fro incessant. Mortal sound
Broke not the solemn stillness of that hour—
But from the lofty trellice-woven roof
Of branching palms, and foliage deep of grey
And venerated trees, whose moss-grown trunks
By meteors' transient gleaming shown, appeared
Fantastic pillars in the sacred pile ;
And from the temple's caverns deep and dark,
Were heard the voices loud or low of gods
And spirits mingling. Listening unto these
I lay, till half the reign of night was past ;
When 'neath the power of sleep by Oro sent
I sank unconscious.

Before bringing the notice of Rose Hill to a close, it may be well, though it is anticipating the course of events, to state the circumstances under which the property came into Mr. Ellis's possession. The premises had been held on lease, which had been renewed, but had at length expired, and, by an order in Chancery, the whole was directed to be sold by auction. This was in 1870. The prospect of being obliged to leave a home endeared by so many strong associations, and towards the close of life to remove into a new residence, and probably altogether a new locality, was not a little distressing to those who had passed nearly thirty years in this quiet retreat, and had expected to be permitted here to end their days in peace. They scarcely hoped to be able to purchase the property, since the amount they had been able to lay aside from the earnings of their literary labour, as a provision for old age, was but small, and they feared that the anticipated competition at the sale would raise the price beyond their means. To buy, or leave the place, seemed, however, the only alternative. When it became known that Mr. Ellis wished to purchase the homestead, such was the respect in which he was held, and the sympathy felt for him, that there was not a single individual would bid against him at the auction, and the property was handed over to him at a very moderate reserve price. He was thus spared a painful rupture of cherished ties, and both he and his loved wife had the greater enjoyment in their peaceful home during the brief remainder of their time on earth.

From the foregoing sketch of the missionary's home life, imperfectly as the task of description may have been performed, the reader will gather that there was much about the man to endear him to those with whom he associated in the domestic relationships of life, and which formed as essential a part of the complete character as the higher qualities that fitted him for the important public career upon which, after years of comparative retirement, and at an age when most men are content to spend their days in rest and quiet, he once more entered with all the energy and zeal of a ripened and vigorous manhood.

MADAGASCAR

1853–72

CHAPTER XI.

THE DETAILS of Mr. Ellis's residence in Madagascar, and his connection with missionary operations in that country, have already been so fully and repeatedly set before the public, and the events are of such recent occurrence, that the whole subject must be fresh in the memory of every reader. It will not, therefore, be expedient to do more than give a brief sketch of this portion of the life we are tracing.

Under the rule of the first Radama the people of Madagascar had made extraordinary progress. In consequence of the treaty concluded by that monarch with the English, his countrymen had been instructed in many of the arts of civilisation, large numbers had been taught to read and write, and the superiority in knowledge and in arms acquired by the Hovas, of whom Radama was chief, had enabled that tribe to gain the ascendancy in the island, and had placed the sovereignty of the nation in the hands of their ruler. But the most important benefit connected with the alliance was the introduction of Christianity, which had taken firm root in the country, and was steadily gaining ground towards the overthrow of old idolatries. The death of Radama, in 1828, and the usurpation of supreme power by his widow, Ranavalona, wrought a woful change in the fair prospects of the community. Christianity was proscribed, and the missionaries and foreign artisans were banished from the realm. These measures being ineffectual to extinguish the vitality of the new faith, the bitterest persecution, even to death, was waged against the professors of Christianity. Rasalama, the first Malagasy Christian martyr, was put to death in 1837.

In the following year another devoted Christian perished; while
five of the hunted refugees avoided a similar fate only by effecting their escape from the island. In 1842 nine out of sixteen
who were attempting to make their escape were cruelly slaughtered. But these efforts on the part of the Queen and her
party to exterminate Christianity seeming only to give it new
power and life, the hostility of its enemies was proportionally
increased. In 1849 more than two thousand Christians were
punished for their faith, and many of them gave their lives
rather than renounce their religion. The sanguinary cruelties
of this Malagasy Jezebel ceased only at her death.

To these national calamities were added other disasters, in
which foreigners seem to have been not altogether free from
blame. In 1845, in consequence of the evasion of the Queen's
edicts against the departure of any of her subjects from the
country, and of other alleged infringements of her commands
charged against the foreign residents at Tamatave, all such
foreigners were ordered to leave the island, or conform in every
respect to the laws imposed on Malagasy subjects. This they
refused to do, and appealed for protection to the respective
English and French Governments at Mauritius and Bourbon.

Three ships of war were immediately sent to Tamatave, with
instructions to effect, if possible, a peaceful settlement of the
difficulties; but the commanders, failing to obtain any concessions from the Hova chiefs, commenced hostilities, firing on the
fort and destroying the town. A storming party then landed
and attacked the fort; but though they succeeded in silencing
the guns, they found that the capture of the stronghold was
impracticable without breaching artillery, and were compelled
to return to their ships, leaving behind thirteen of their number
dead. This unfortunate attack had, in short, no other result
than that of exasperating the Queen and Hovas against all
foreigners, effecting their expulsion from the island, and closing
all commercial intercourse between the respective countries.
With a view of restoring amicable relations, Admiral Dacres

was sent by the British Government, in 1849, with presents for the Queen; but these conciliatory overtures were rejected, the Malagasy sovereign adhering to her demand for the payment of a specified sum of money by way of indemnity as the condition of re-opening the ports for foreign trade.

Such was the position of affairs when, towards the close of 1852, reports reached England of changes in the temper and conduct of the Malagasy Government, giving promise of happier mutual understanding between the alienated parties. Under these circumstances it seemed to the Directors of the London Missionary Society highly desirable that some trustworthy person should be stationed at Mauritius, and, if possible, proceed to Madagascar, as their agent and representative, to gain authentic information respecting the real facts of the case, and take advantage of the first favourable opportunity for re-introducing Christian missionaries into the country. Mr. Ellis was selected as the fittest man for this important task, and he very cheerfully undertook the service. It was arranged that Mr. Cameron, at that time stationed at the Cape, who had formerly been a missionary in Madagascar, and was, therefore, well acquainted with the people and language, should be associated with him in the mission.

The interval between receiving the appointment and leaving England was diligently employed in preparation for rendering the service as efficient as possible. That the collateral advantages of the journey might be fully secured, Mr. Ellis made himself practically familiar, as far as limited time would allow, with the principles and manipulations of photography, and provided himself with the requisite apparatus and chemicals. He also put himself in communication with Professor Owen, Sir William Hooker, Dr. Lindley, and other eminent naturalists, receiving from each suggestions and instructions with a view of making his visit to Madagascar subservient in some measure to the advancement of natural history, a branch of study in which he always felt a peculiar interest.

On the 14th of April, 1853, the veteran missionary once more bade adieu to his native land on an errand that was most congenial to his heart.   The passage to Mauritius was made in the steamship *Indiana*, under the command of Captain Lambert. During the voyage the agent of the Missionary Society, being, with the exception of an invalid clergyman, the only minister of the Gospel on board, officiated as chaplain, preaching twice on the Lord's-day in the saloon, besides holding a separate service with the sailors in the afternoon, whenever the weather would permit.   He received from all on board—officers, passengers, and crew—the most marked attention and deference, to a degree which surprised and almost disturbed his modest spirit, as the following extract from a letter to Mrs. Ellis will show :—

'I must not go on prosing about myself much longer; yet you must bear with two or three words more. I cannot tell how it is, but I almost feel frightened about it sometimes, though I don't know why I should.   I am treated with so much kindness and consideration by every one on board, from the captain to the boy who pumps the water for my bath, or the black who cleans my shoes. Whether it is on account of my mission, in which almost every one expresses deep interest, or for your sake, I cannot tell, but so it is. If I ever express a wish for anything, it is provided, or my boxes are got out at any time. If I go to the bath-room, the gentlemen waiting outside for their turn, all beg I will go first. If I go on deck, some one instantly comes and asks me if I am inclined to walk, or they sit down beside me. All seem to wish to make my acquaintance. Even the giddy young men who used to swear, and one of whom I publicly reproved, are amongst the most respectful and attentive in their behaviour to me, while the habit is discontinued at least in my presence.'

The passage was altogether pleasant and expeditious. At Table Bay Mr. Cameron came on board. Port Louis was reached, and the voyage brought to a close on the 7th of June.

It now became clear that much misrepresentation had crept into the reports that had reached England respecting the state of affairs in Madagascar. No relaxation in the rigorous proscription of Christianity, and no immediate prospect of the resumption of trade and friendly relations with foreigners, were apparent. Mr. Ellis, availing himself of letters of introduction with which he had been provided in England, waited on Sir James Higginson, the Governor of Mauritius, on Major General Sutherland, and others in authority, and was received by all in the most cordial and friendly manner. Much interest was expressed in the objects of his mission, and every practicable assistance cheerfully promised. But under existing circumstances, it did not appear expedient that the representatives of the British Government in Mauritius should in any way interfere; nor that an agent of the Missionary Society should proceed to Madagascar in a vessel despatched under their auspices. It was therefore arranged that Mr. Cameron and himself should sail to Tamatave in the *Gregorio*, a vessel sent by the merchants of Port Louis with a 'memorial' to the Queen of Madagascar, praying for the re-opening of trade with that country.

The *Gregorio* set sail on the 11th of July, and came to anchor off Tamatave on the 18th of that month. The accommodation on board this small vessel was of the most miserable description, and the conduct of the captain and crew, who were drunk during the greater portion of the time, was such as to render both the outward and return voyage seasons of extreme discomfort to the two passengers. Soon after the vessel cast anchor, a canoe from the shore was sent with an official to inquire on what business they had come. On receiving the desired information, the officer replied that the letter of the merchants would be of no avail without the pecuniary indemnity which the Queen had demanded; and it was evident that the Hovas were still deeply incensed on account of the combined attack of the English and French ships in 1845. Per-

mission to land was not granted till the following day, when
the two missionaries were invited to come on shore, and more
particularly questioned respecting their errand. They replied
that their visit was purely one of friendship, and requested
that a letter might be forwarded to the Queen, asking permission to proceed to the capital. This was granted, but they
were informed that an answer could not be received in less
than fifteen days. Mr. Cameron was not at first recognised by
any of his former acquaintances, and though Mr. Ellis remembered to have seen the harbour master in England, the recognition was not mutual. The reception was, however, friendly,
and the minds of the Malagasy seemed much relieved by the
assurance which the irvisitors were able to give that the
English had no hostile intentions against Madagascar ; for the
people had been much disturbed by reports, the accuracy of
which, in their isolated position, they had no means of testing,
that the British Government was sending an armed expedition
to attack the country. These visits to the shore were repeated
whenever the weather would permit, during the interval that
elapsed before the arrival of the answer from the capital, and
the missionaries had thus many opportunities of friendly intercourse with the people of Tamatave, among whom were some
Christians ; but with these all communication was necessarily
very restricted and guarded ; for though at the time no active
persecution was enforced, still the prohibitions against the
Christian faith were unrepealed, suspected individuals were
jealously watched, and the position of any persons who should
betray their leaning to the proscribed religion was fraught with
peril. Notwithstanding these difficulties much valuable information was gained respecting the condition of Christian converts in the country, means were devised for intercommunication between them and their friends in Mauritius, and some
little pecuniary assistance was given to the most necessitous of
their number. The hearts of these persecuted people were also
cheered by the promise of a supply of copies of the Scriptures at

the earliest opportunity, and more than all, by the assurance of the sympathy of their Christian brethren in more favoured lands.

At the expiration of the time specified, the answer of the Queen arrived at Tamatave and was communicated to the English visitors by the chief judge. It was courteously worded, but recommended the strangers not to prolong their stay in the country at that season, on account of the risk of fever. This reply, although not altogether discouraging as to the ultimate attainment of their object, left the missionary agents no alternative but to return forthwith to Mauritius. Accordingly, they took their leave of their friends, and sailed from Tamatave on the 9th of August. Contrary winds, an ignorant and drunken captain, a crazy craft, and disorderly crew, combined to protract the voyage, during which the passengers were exposed to every species of annoyance that petty malignity could devise, and it was not till the 1st of September that they were able once more to set foot on firm land, and enjoy the welcome hospitality of kind friends in Port Louis.

The visit to Madagascar was not considered by the merchants by whom the vessel had been sent, in the light of a failure. On the contrary, they were stimulated to raise the required sum—fifteen thousand dollars—without delay; and on the 10th of October Mr. Cameron, having been delegated by the merchants of Port Louis to accompany Mr. Mangeot to pay this money, again set sail for Tamatave. The *Nimble*, the vessel dispatched on this errand, returned on the 19th of November, with the welcome intelligence that negotiations had been satisfactorily completed, and that the ports of Madagascar were once more open to foreign trade; bringing also, as an earnest of the fact, the first shipment of cattle under the new arrangement. This long-desired consummation was hailed with great rejoicing in the colony; while the friends of missions regarded the renewal of amicable relations as a favourable indication of better times in prospect for the persecuted disciples of Christ in Madagascar.

The season for visiting the country was, however, now past; Mr. Ellis, therefore, decided to remain in Mauritius till the following year, and at the most suitable time to attempt once more the journey to the capital. Meanwhile he was not idle. He obtained permission from the authorities to preach in the Port Office, every Lord's-day, to the seamen and others who attended in considerable numbers. This service was regularly continued for many months. In company with Mr. Lebrun, the agent of the London Missionary Society, he visited the various mission stations and schools in the district, and took part in several interesting anniversary and inaugural meetings of old and new institutions.

Soon after his return from Tamatave, an event occurred, which excited deep and general sympathy. This was the rescue by an American vessel, under the command of Captain Ludlow, of the passengers and crew of an English ship, wrecked on the Sechelles, a group of low islands lying north of Mauritius. The sufferers were brought into Port Louis, and the authorities and inhabitants vied with each other in rendering aid and relief, and in doing honour to the brave and humane commander, who, at no small risk, had saved the whole number from impending death. Among the rescued passengers, Mr. Ellis met with two gentlemen whom he had known in England. Another waif of humanity also came most unexpectedly across his path in this remote part of the world, in the person of a sick and dying countryman, to whose last moments he tenderly ministered such comfort and aid as he could, and in whom he recognised the husband of a very dear friend in England. This man had long been lost to his family, who were ignorant of his where-abouts, or even of his existence, and it was no small comfort to them to know that his last hours had thus been solaced by Christian counsel, sympathy, and companionship.

During the greater part of his residence in Mauritius at this period, Mr. Ellis was domiciled in the family of Mr. Kelsey, from whom, as well as from other friends, he received the greatest kindness. He paid a visit to the governor, Sir James Higginson, at Reduit, His Excellency's country residence, and enjoyed very agreeable intercourse with his estimable family— an intercourse which was subsequently renewed in England, and laid the foundation of a valued and lasting friendship. He was also a welcome guest at the houses of men eminent for scientific attainments, who sympathised in his enthusiastic love of natural history. From Dr. Powell, the superintendent of the lunatic asylum, who was an accomplished chemist, he gained much valuable information, and improved his practical knowledge of photography. He took peculiar delight also in visiting the Royal Botanic Gardens at Pamplemousses, and derived much pleasure from the society of Mr. Duncan, the director of that interesting establishment. In company with Lieutenant Gordon, and other enthusiasts like himself, he made several botanical excursions, and collected many valuable specimens of rare plants, most of which he succeeded in transporting safely to England. The details of these interesting journeys, and his general observations in the country, are given, with much graphic force of description, in his *Three Visits to Madagascar*, to which the reader is referred for a full and particular account of matters that can only receive a passing mention in this memorial of his eventful life.

These objects of subordinate interest did not for one moment divert the missionary from the main purpose of his journey. As soon as the season for visiting Madagascar returned, he prepared for another voyage to Tamatave, first sending to the Malagasy authorities an intimation of his intention, and repeating his request for permission to proceed to the capital. At this time the colony of Mauritius, and more particularly the town of Port Louis, suffered an appalling calamity in a most fatal outbreak of Asiatic cholera, which, commencing with two cases at Grande Rivière, spread with alarming rapidity, and in a few weeks almost decimated the population. Before the end of May the number of deaths each day in Port Louis nearly reached a hundred, and on the 5th of June there were said to have occurred one hundred and seventy deaths, and one hundred and thirty on the day following. A panic seized upon the inhabitants; many thousands fled from the town; business was suspended; the streets were deserted by all but funeral vehicles and their mournful attendants, and scarcely could the living bury the dead.

While pestilence and death were thus making havoc around him, Mr. Ellis's own health was mercifully preserved; and, taking leave of his kind friends, with many sad and not groundless forebodings on their account, he once more set sail for Tamatave, in the *Nimble*, on the 8th of June. The port was reached on the 12th, but eight days of quarantine were imposed before any passengers were allowed to land. At the end of that time, no case of sickness having occurred on board the vessel, permission to come on shore was granted, and the missionary was kindly accommodated by M. Provint, a French merchant residing at the port, with a convenient building for his own temporary residence and the reception of his packages. Here he remained, waiting the result of his application to visit Antananarivo. His intercourse with the Christians was renewed, but always under the strictest caution and secrecy. He was able also to introduce and distribute, though not without difficulty, copies of the Scriptures, under circumstances which he thus narrates:—

'I found that among those at Tamatave, and at Foule Pointe as well as at the capital, the great want was the Word of God. I had sent from Mauritius a few copies, and I had brought a number of New Testaments, bound together or in separate portions, as well as copies of the Psalms and other religious books; but as the officers of the Custom House had strict orders to seize all books which there was any attempt to introduce into the country, my great difficulty was to get them on shore from the ship, as the captain was unfriendly; I could only conceal them tied under my dress, and in this way, and in my pockets, I managed to take eighteen Testaments and other books at a time. But my heart sometimes beat a little quicker when the bow of the boat touched the shore, and I had to jump down on the beach amidst three or four custom-house officers, lest a copy should get loose and fall on the ground before them. I generally spoke to them and passed on, breathing a little more freely when I had entered my house, locked my door, and deposited my treasures in the innermost room. By this means I was able, during my successive visits to Tamatave, to introduce about one thousand five hundred copies of portions of the Scriptures and other books among the famishing Christians, some of whom had only a few chapters in manuscript, or three or four leaves of a printed book, soiled and torn and mended, until the original was the smallest part left.'

Foule Pointe is situated about forty-five miles to the west of Tamatave, and was visited during this stay in the district. Many Christians were there met with, and much interesting and profitable intercourse was enjoyed by them with their friend from England. The house in which he lodged at Tamatave was also the daily resort of those who were ' disciples of Jesus, but secretly, for fear.' Of this number were several nobles among the Hovas, and one, the aide-de-camp of the Prince, became personally much attached to Mr. Ellis, and is frequently mentioned in his *Three Visits* as his ' tall friend.'

The brief residence at Tamatave was altogether a busy and by no means a wasted period. The missionary's versatile talents were called into constant requisition, and, unlike his religious office, could be openly exercised. Thus he was called upon to prescribe medicine and render surgical aid to the sick and suffering. This he did always cheerfully, and in many instances with gratifying success. His photographic skill was also in frequent request, enabling him to afford much pleasure to the originals of the portraits, and to carry away with him many interesting memorials of the novel forms and scenes that came under his observation. His researches in natural history were prosecuted with his wonted enthusiasm, and many collections of plants in England have been enriched by his labour in this department. Among the orchids which he gathered at Foule Pointe, and succeeded in taking home, was a fine specimen of *Angræcum superbum*, at that time new in this country. This identical plant, bearing flowers in the spring of 1858, furnished part of the bridal bouquet on the occasion of the marriage of the Princess Royal with the Prince of Prussia.

The answer from the capital, which arrived in due time, once more brought disappointment; for though couched in courteous terms, it refused the desired permission to visit the capital, on the ground of. prevalence of the cholera, the introduction of which into the country was greatly dreaded, and every precaution was taken to guard against infection. With the chief object of the journey frustrated, but much good accomplished nevertheless, the Missionary once more prepared to leave the island, and availed himself of the offer of a passage in the *Castro*, which sailed from Tamatave on the 14th of September, to return to Mauritius. The 'tall friend' and other Christian companions, anxious to prolong the period of intercourse with their guide and teacher to the last, and to testify the regard in which they held his mission and his person, brought their sleeping mats to his house, on the day previous to his departure, and spent the evening and far into the morning, conversing on subjects of deepest interest to all. But little time was allowed for rest; and while yet the moon was shining brightly, and only a faint streak of light in the east proclaimed the coming dawn, the party walked to the beach, and under feelings of more than ordinary intensity exchanged farewells; those who remained on the shore watching their departing guest, till the canoe had reached the vessel which was to bear him from their sight. The ship was soon under way, and after a favourable voyage came to anchor in the harbour of Port Louis on the 30th of September. The return was rendered mournful by the devastation which the pestilence had wrought in the interval. The place seemed sadly altered; scarcely was a family left into which death had not entered; and among the desolated homes was that of Mr. Kelsey, from which both parents and two of the children, besides several domestics, had been removed.

There appeared now no reason for a prolonged stay at Mauritius, and as the Directors of the Missionary Society had expressed a wish that, before returning home, their envoy should visit the stations in Cape Colony, he left Port Louis on the 20th of December, in the *Annie*, a small brig of about two hundred and twenty tons burden, and after a voyage of two and twenty days, reached Table Bay in safety in the beginning of 1855.

The main object of a deputation to the missionary settlements in South Africa was to ascertain by personal inspection the condition and wants of the people, to encourage them by the assurance of sympathy and fraternal feeling at home, and especially to stimulate them to increased exertions among themselves, and in extending Christianity around them; so that the Society might be, in a measure, relieved from some of its pecuniary burdens, and enabled to expend its resources in new and more needy quarters—to foster, in short, a healthy spirit of independence amongst the well-established Churches in this comparatively early field of missionary enterprise. Suggestions and arrangements to this end were met by the people at the various stations in a right spirit; and so satisfactory were the results accomplished that the Directors freely acknowledged that, even had no good been effected by the journey to Madagascar, the advantage of the visit to Africa alone amply justified the expense that had been incurred. Mr. Ellis remained in the Colony till the 14th of June, when he embarked in the steamship *Pacific*, and reached England on the 18th of July, 'grateful to the Almighty for the health and merciful protection he had experienced throughout his wanderings,' and welcomed by loving and appreciative friends.

CHAPTER XII.

ANTANANARIVO.

A LETTER from Madagascar had reached Mr. Ellis at the Cape of Good Hope, conveying the permission of the Government to visit the capital, and another letter to the same purport was received after his arrival in England. This invitation was gladly embraced, and the undaunted ambassador of the Gospel prepared for another lengthened journey, and the perils of travel through new lands, in an insalubrious climate, as well as the possible dangers of solitary encounter with a vindictive, ignorant, and semi-barbarous people.

Before his departure he had an interview with Lord Clarendon, and several communications by letter with other officers of the British Government, including Lord Palmerston, and was authorised to convey to the Queen of Madagascar the most positive assurances of the friendly disposition of England towards the Malagasy Government. He was also made officially acquainted with the part that M. Lambert, and other schemers associated with him, had been acting—that he had sought, ostensibly with the sanction of Prince Rakotond, to gain armed assistance from England and France, to depose the Queen of Madagascar and place her son on the throne—to carry out, in short, a complete political revolution in the island. The French Government had declined to act in the matter except in concert with England, and the English Cabinet had resolved not to interfere, advising M. Lambert to attempt the accomplishment of his objects, so far as they were legitimate, through the medium of a friendly commercial company.

Fully commissioned for his important undertaking, and furnished with presents for the Queen and other members of the Malagasy royal family, Mr. Ellis embarked in one of the Peninsular and Oriental Company's steamers from Southampton, on the 20th of March, 1856. Taking the overland route from Alexandria to Suez, he completed the passage in the *Nubia* by the Red Sea to Aden, and thence across the Indian Ocean to Ceylon. Here he was detained for several weeks, escaping, in consequence of the delay, unpropitious as it had seemed, ' both the perils of the sea, and the ravages of the cholera, which had again visited Mauritius almost immediately before his arrival.' Leaving Ceylon towards the end of May, in the *Star of the East,* he reached Mauritius on the 17th of June. There he was again most cordially welcomed; but resisting all temptations to yield himself to the hospitality of his friends, he allowed only sufficient time to communicate with the Colonial authorities, and secure a passage to Tamatave in the *Castro,* the same vessel in which he had last returned from that port.

He was greatly disappointed that Mr. Cameron did not, as he had expected, accompany him; but keenly as he felt the responsibility of his position, he successfully combated every discouragement, and resolutely but humbly, and in dependence on Divine help and guidance, set himself to the accomplishment of his arduous undertaking.

A pleasant and quick passage of only four days from the time of leaving Port Louis brought him to Tamatave on the 13th of July. Going on shore on the following morning, he found ample preparation had been made for his accommodation and comfort. A newly-built house was assigned to him, domestics provided for the necessary personal attendance, while liberal presents of provisions from the authorities, and from private friends, gave evidence of the cordial welcome with which his arrival was hailed. In short, the most respectful and marked attention and observance were paid to him by the

Government and chiefs during this eventful visit, as to one whom the sovereign ' delighted to honour.' At the same time he was aware that a pretty close scrutiny was kept on his actions and company. Two armed soldiers were stationed at the door of his dwelling, ostensibly to guard his property, but he more than suspected that their instructions were to take note of all who had communication with him, and report what might transpire. The greatest caution was therefore necessary in his intercourse with his Christian brethren. Since his last visit more than one of the most faithful of the number had fallen victims to the fatal fever of the country, and among them was his ' tall friend,' whose loss at this particular juncture he deeply deplored. Whilst he was waiting for the arrival of his escort, and other preparations for his journey to the capital, he was present at a public meeting of condolence on the death of M. de Lastelle, a French merchant who had long resided in the country. Much disorder and intoxication attended the cere-monies and feasting on this occasion.

By the 6th of August all was in readiness for the journey. The party of bearers and attendants, amounting to consider-ably more than a hundred men, formed quite an imposing array. The baggage, divided into small packages, was dis-tributed among them ; while eight of the number were detailed to carry the palanquin, which formed the conveyance of their guest. This contrivance resembled a sailor's hammock, with a light screen fixed over it, to defend the occupant from the sun or rain, and was borne on men's shoulders by two poles projecting in front and behind. On ordinary occasions four men performed this service, whilst other four attended to relieve them at regulated intervals ; but in very deep, steep, rough, or difficult portions of the road it sometimes required the whole number to keep the palanquin in position. The person appointed as guide of the party, and interpreter, spoke English tolerably well, having spent some time at the Cape of Good Hope, where he had been servant to Captain Underwood,

aide-de-camp to Lord Charles Somerset, the Governor of the
Colony. Before the party started, an ox, a present from the
Queen, had been killed and divided, as provision for the company, and others were ordered to be slaughtered for their use
at different villages on the route. It was early in the afternoon when the rear of the procession, bearing the palanquin
with their English visitor, left Tamatave, amid the salutations
of the chiefs and a large concourse of people assembled to
witness their departure. The first stage was reached by three
o'clock in the afternoon, and the party halted on the banks of
a large river till the next morning. One of the bearers being
then missing, his place was supplied by a young man named
Sodra, who from the first had attached himself to Mr. Ellis,
and constituted himself a sort of body servant, remaining
faithfully by his master till he left the country, and weeping
bitterly when forbidden by the native authorities to accompany
him further.

For the details of the journey to the capital, the reader is
again referred to the interesting narrative contained in the
Three Visits. It is sufficient here to state briefly that,
notwithstanding much fatigue, inclement weather, and some
degree of illness, every day brought fresh interest and delight
to the observant and enthusiastic traveller. The people, the
novel scenes, the strange and lovely forms of vegetation, presented in all the luxuriance of tropical profusion, and marvellous in their beauty—a very paradise of orchids and ' Eden of
ferns '—seemed to invest every step of the way with enchantment. Slow and difficult as the progress was rendered, when
the only track was made by the infrequent feet of men and
cattle, the soul must have been dull indeed that could have
found such a journey tedious. Their course lay sometimes
along rivers, but to a greater extent by a more toilsome march
over land, occasionally through swamps and muddy flats, though
more frequently on firm ground, passing on their way through
vast, dense, and intricate forests, crowded with gigantic trees,

ferns, and creeping plants, and intersected by hollows, water-
courses, and steep ravines, so as to render the road almost
impassable—a natural barrier to an approach towards the
interior, in which the first Radama placed much reliance,
boasting that he had two generals—' General Hazo, *forest*,
and General Tazo, *fever*—in whose hands he would leave any in-
vading army.'   To the traveller on this occasion, with a native
escort to whom the way was familiar, there were no hardships
not amply compensated by the enjoyments of the expedition.

Twenty days were occupied in traversing the distance
between Tamatave and Antananarivo.   As the capital was
approached, messengers arrived with greetings from the Prince
and others in authority; whilst parties of men, actuated by
various motives, came out some distance from the town and
joined the advancing cavalcade.   At Amboipo, a small suburban
village, the party were requested to halt for the night, on
the 25th of August, as the following day had been appointed
for making the entry into the town.

Early on the 26th, three officers made their appearance, who
had been sent to conduct the visitor to his quarters in the capital.   These men had been educated in England, spoke English
with tolerable fluency, and were dressed in European style.
Antananarivo, as the reader is probably aware, occupies the
summit of a lofty hill, on the crest of which stand conspicuously
the royal residences.   The streets are narrow and steep, and
many of the houses are built on artificial terraces or embank-
ments.   The guest of the Queen, for such the stranger who
had come by her invitation was considered, was conducted to
an enclosure containing three houses, which were pointed out
as set apart for his accommodation.   The rooms were clean and
cheerful, with an aspect of comfort about them that was truly
inviting and refreshing.

Towards evening visitors began to throng the house, among
whom were many devoted Christian men, such as Prince
Ramonja, who had used their station and influence, to their

own personal risk, in befriending their persecuted countrymen. These men could scarce restrain their expressions of joy at seeing once more among them a missionary from England.   One of the officers of the Government, in particular Ra Haniraka, the Secretary of the Queen, a young man who had been educated in England under the charge of Dr. Clunie, constituted himself the special guardian and friend of the stranger from that 'happy land,' and took every opportunity to supply information, to warn him against the treacherous or evil-disposed, to give hints and suggestions in regard to the customs and etiquette of the country, to see that his wants were supplied, and that his words, especially such as were official or designed for the ears of those in authority, were correctly interpreted; and in a hundred ways rendered frequent and essential service.   It was the second day after the arrival of the visitor at the capital before the Prince Royal, Rakotond Radama, paid his respects, his mother having given him strict injunctions that all courtly observances should be duly regarded, inasmuch as 'this foreigner,' to quote her own expression, 'was not like other foreigners; he was great and wise, and she did not wish her son to meet him for the first time but when well dressed,' that is, in official costume.   The ice of ceremony once broken, however, the Prince was a frequent visitor, and was always most cordial in his demeanour.

This young man had been designated by his mother as her successor in the sovereignty.   He was popular with the majority of the Hovas, and had been a steady friend to the Christians, by whom the event of his accession to supreme power was regarded as their day of emancipation.   His disposition was singularly humane, but he was pliant and fond of pleasure, wanting strength and stability of character.   In his claims to the throne he had a formidable rival in his cousin, Rambosalama, who was chiefly supported by the most violent portion of the heathen party, and by the French influence in the capital.   The friends of Rakotond were in constant apprehension of treachery and even assassination from the partisans of his rival.   Happily he was the

favourite of the people, and had the most powerful members
of the ruling Government, as well as the army, on his side.

Mr. Ellis was favourably impressed with the appearance and
demeanour of the Prince at their first interview, and this good
opinion was strengthened by subsequent intercourse. Visitors,
official and friendly, continually thronged the house from
morning till night, allowing him little leisure or rest. Presents
of provisions, on a truly regal scale, were sent from the palace;
three officers, intelligent young men who spoke English, were
appointed to attend him, and show him about the neighbourhood. He also made several excursions in company with the
Prince and Princess to the country residences of the reigning
family, and to other attractive localities. Thus was the interval
busily filled up till the day appointed for his first audience with
the Queen. This was the 5th of September. At this audience,
which was held in presence of a large assembly and with much
ceremony, in front of the palace, the Queen and royal party
occupying the balcony, the official communications from the
British Government and the Colonial authorities of Mauritius,
were delivered to Her Majesty and the court, who appeared much
gratified and animated by these cordial assurances of friendship.
The details of these and other proceedings at the capital must be
so familiar to almost every reader, that it is quite unnecessary
to repeat them.

The formal introduction and interchange of courtesies was
followed on subsequent days by entertainments at the palace,
and at the residence of M. Laborde. The season was far, however, from being one of mere holiday festivity with the guest.
His work, most diversified in its character, was incessant, and
his position in no small degree responsible and critical. He
was under a constant and not friendly surveillance. He was
credibly informed that M. Laborde had offered to give two hundred dollars to any one who would receive a book from the
missionary, or who would give information concerning persons
who had done so; and infinite pains were taken to entrap him

into speech or overt act that would give offence to the Queen. His sagacity and caution saved him from these snares. At the same time he did not neglect the prime object of his mission. No day—no night—passed without faithful and confidential communion with Christian men and women, by whom his sympathy and counsels were received as 'cold water in a thirsty land.' In his intercourse with the Prince he was frank and explicit, admonishing him of his errors and of the dangers of his facile temper; unfolding, to his extreme surprise and distress, the representations and designs of M. Lambert and his associates; counselling him to seek the union and enlightenment of his own countrymen, and warning him against the specious fiction of a French protectorate. Amongst other recommendations he advised him not to allow any foreigner to hold land, except as a tenant, in his dominions. The character of his suggestions will perhaps best be shown by an extract or two from letters sent to friends in England, and the duplicity of M. Lambert and his coadjutors will appear from the account of the matter which Mr. Ellis communicated to Lord Clarendon.

Referring to one of his conversations with the Prince, he writes:—The Prince asked, "What is best to be done? How can the country be best protected and improved? What is likely to be its future?" I replied, that the alliance and the protection of even the moral influence of England would be one of the best guarantees for its independence. He said the Queen would enter into no treaty unless some emergency should arise; but he added, the first thing he should do when he could act, would be to seek the friendship and protection of England. "I am glad you have come; you have seen the country, seen the state of the people, heard from themselves something of their sufferings, and of the grievous yoke they have to bear. I hope the English will sympathise with us in our troubles. The chiefs wished a few months ago to make me king; they were proceeding with their design, and would have put both Rainjohary, the Queen's paramour, and Rambosalama to death that day, and would have set my mother aside and made her resign; but I alone prevented it: I would not be disloyal to my mother, much as I suffer: I would not consent, but threatened to disclose their plan if they did not desist. I would rather wait till God shall make me king, than be a party to any evil to my mother, though no government is so bad as the government of Madagascar now is." I told him I thought he would not regret having taken no part against his mother, and hoped that God would give him wise and faithful friends in his hour of need; for whenever the administration of the kingdom should devolve on him he would have no bed of roses. He replied, "I am not afraid of my life, God will protect me. I know I shall have difficulties, but God will guide me." I said, "I am not so much afraid of your erring in judgment, as of your being deceived, and overcome by artful intrigue. Your enemies will bend all their efforts towards your subjection, because they will know that if they gain you they have gained all." He replied, "They will not gain me." I said "They will not, if you think that is what they are aiming at; but they will take advantage of your good nature, of your frankness, of your pleasure in society, and of your desire after knowledge and the means of improving your country, and, under cover of promoting these things, they will propose projects that will ensnare you to such an extent that you will be unable to extricate yourself." He exclaimed, with some vehemence, "I know them now, they will not deceive me again." I said, "You are too sanguine and impulsive, you act too promptly on the first representation of things. Don't assent to any proposal whatever when it is first made. Say you will think about it, or urge some objection, and then consult some of your truest friends. If it is a snare, you may escape it; if a benefit, you will not lose by caution. There are but two courses open before Madagascar, either to rise to a position of strength and prosperity that shall enable it to maintain the dignity of an independent nation, or subjection and subordination to some one of the great powers of the present day. If the French assume the protection of Madagascar, it will become what Algiers and Tahiti are—a French colony—and you will act under their authority and for their advantage. On the other hand, great as the difficulties and discouragements are, they are not insurmountable. You may in a few years become sufficiently powerful, with true friends, to protect yourselves. But to this end you must unite the peoples of Madagascar as one community. You must try to make the Sakalavas feel that union with you is better than vassalage to France; for the French now speak of them in the journals of Mauritius as " our allies the Sakalavas." '

In a letter to Lord Clarendon, after detailing the interview with the Queen, reference was made to the French party in the following terms:—' In mentioning the French gentlemen residing at the capital, I refer to M. Laborde, a native of Mauritius, and formerly a slave-dealer, who many years ago came from Mozambique to Madagascar, where he proposed to manufacture arms for the native Government. He has since been employed on several occasions by the Queen, and exercises considerable influence over a few of the chiefs. I also refer to a son of M. Laborde, who has recently returned from France; and to a M. Hervier, alias *Père Finess*, a Roman Catholic priest from Bourbon, who had been taken to the capital by M. Lambert in the dress of a civilian, and in the capacity of clerk or secretary, and had been left with M. Laborde for the alleged purpose of teaching his son mathematics. These gentlemen have since been joined by three others from Bourbon, viz., a young medical practitioner, recently from France, who was accompanied by the Abbé Jouen, principal of the Jesuit College at Bourbon, and another priest from the same island. These two ecclesiastics have gone up as civilians, the former in the capacity of assistant to the surgeon, and the latter as his *pharmàcien*. I do not mention these gentlemen because they are teachers of Roman Catholicism, which I feel they have as much right to endeavour to inculcate as we have to spread the Protestant faith, but because I was told they had been sent for by the priest already associated with M. Laborde, to assist in accomplishing the objects of the latter in Madagascar.

'I have also to inform your lordship that the Prince and some of the officers were exceedingly anxious about the result of M. Lambert's voyage to Europe, and applied to me very soon after my arrival for any information I might possess on the subject. The Prince was greatly surprised and deeply affected on becoming acquainted with the representations that had been made by M. Lambert. He said the papers taken away by that gentleman, so far as he had been made acquainted with their contents, were simply a statement of the grievances of the people. He had repeatedly represented to his mother that the sufferings and burdens of the people were too great; and during the period of M. Lambert's visit had conversed frequently with him and M. Laborde on the same subject, but had expressed no wish that any application should be made to the French Government. He further stated that he did not prepare the letters or papers taken by M. Lambert, and had no knowledge of the intention to prepare any papers of the kind until they were completed; that they were written in the French language, of which he does not understand half-a-dozen words, and were, he believes, drawn up by the priest, assisted by MM. Laborde and Lambert; that when the papers were presented to him, M. Laborde translated verbally the pages containing a statement of the grievances of the people, and then said, "If you think this is true, add your name to it." That after long refusing, he did at length, almost by compulsion, affix his name to the papers, but only as attesting the truth of the statement of the sufferings of his countrymen. He declared emphatically that he had never authorised any application for troops or money, or other means of deposing the present ruler of Madagascar. On my enquiring what was the object of the statement of grievances, if not to seek redress, he replied, that he thought a representation from M. Lambert and his friends, to the effect that the burdens of the people were too heavy, might induce

the Queen to adopt a milder rule.   The Prince further stated
that MM. Laborde and Lambert said *they were determined that
there should be a change*, and that if it could not be effected
by other means, they would apply to the French Government
for troops, and if these were refused, they would themselves
hire troops, for they had twenty-five millions of dollars to
appropriate to the object.

'In reference to their intimation of their intention to bring
troops, the Prince said he thought if they did, the native forces
could arrest their progress; but he added that he told MM.
Laborde and Lambert that he would be the first to fight and
shed his blood in defence of his mother.

'I deem it right to inform your lordship that there is a party
at the capital opposed to the Prince, and in favour of his rival,
a son of the Queen's eldest sister.   The pretensions of this
rival are encouraged by the Frenchmen at the capital; and
some of the secondary native officers are said to have been
parties to the project of MM. Lambert and Laborde for bringing French troops to Madagascar; and when the Prince mentioned them in connection with this part of the plan, he said
they owed their lives to his forbearance in not acquainting the
Queen with their proceedings.   The Queen's secretary also
stated that the papers were signed, and a sort of oath not to
divulge the secret extorted by the priest from the Prince, at
the close of a dinner party; and a decree of compulsion, little
short of absolute force, was used to secure his signature, and
that they held his hand on the Bible while the priest pronounced the oath.

'I am unable to describe the Prince's expressions of gratitude
when I read to him the reply given by your lordship to M.
Lambert's proposal.   He said he had prayed to the Almighty
ever since M. Lambert's departure, that the French troops
might not come, and, he added, "I thank God for His protection."'

It will be evident that, under such circumstances, the position of counsellor to a prince, surrounded by so many perils, was one requiring much prudence and sagacity.

As on former occasions, the missionary's medical skill was in constant requisition. His house was thronged by patients, who had come sometimes from a considerable distance for advice and medicine, and he was not unfrequently summoned at untimely hours to administer relief to some poor sufferer. It became evident to him that a medical missionary would here find ample scope for the philanthropic exercise of his profession, and that much ulterior good might be effected by such an agency.

The camera and photographic apparatus were also soon in full operation. But considerable consternation and perplexity were occasioned by the discovery, at the very outset, that there was no acetic acid among the chemicals. None could be procured in this remote part of the world; and the ingenuity of the operator was taxed to find a substitute. Numerous experiments were made, and, after much perseverance and many failures, he found that he succeeded best with strong vinegar. With this he contrived to obtain very tolerable likenesses and a number of views, which, besides giving great pleasure to those who received portraits of themselves or their friends, furnished interesting and valuable illustrations for the volume he published after his return home.

As the month, which had been mentioned as the term of his visit, drew to a close, he made application to the Queen for permission to prolong his stay—to remain in the country nine months longer. This request was courteously but firmly refused, and though every argument was used by his friends to induce the sovereign to grant the desired courtesy, she would not be turned from her decision. Other counsels, and interested counsellors appealing to her fears, her superstition, and her prejudices, gained the day. The French and Roman Catholic influence, though not openly manifest, had considerable share in bringing about this result. There was no alternative, then, but to prepare for departure. Every hour, with scarcely intermission enough for taking food or sleep, was busily occupied in receiving and conversing with visitors, among them many anxious but faithful Christians, in attending to the sick, or in pursuing his photographic operations. The Prince came oftener than ever to see his 'true friend,' and when the hour of departure had arrived, accompanied him for some distance on the way, with every token of cordial esteem, and even affectionate regard. The Queen also, as if anxious to atone for the discourtesy of the dismissal, was lavish in expressions of respect. Eight officers were sent by her to accompany the missionary to the coast, and a hundred men (more than double the number required) to act as bearers and carriers. Sodra was a volunteer, and nothing but compulsion could separate him from close attendance on his beloved master and friend.

The return journey was begun on September 26, and the party reached Tamatave on October 12. It was the middle of November before any opportunity of leaving the port occurred. During the interval the departing guest received the most hospitable attentions from the authorities of Tamatave, and again enjoyed pleasant intercourse with friends. When the *Castro*, the vessel in which a passage to Mauritius had been provided, was ready to sail, ten oxen, a parting present from the Queen, were taken on board, with those intended for the Governor of Mauritius. Early on the morning of November 18th the ship was under way, and once more, with deep and mingled emotions, the missionary directed his course homeward. Calms and contrary winds detained the vessel at sea, and it was not until December 2nd that she anchored in the harbour of Port Louis.

Mr. Ellis took an early opportunity of calling on the Governor, and giving to him, as well as to the Commodore and general commanding the forces, an account of his mission. By these authorities, the service he had rendered the British and Colonial Governments, in the prosecution of his difficult undertaking, were highly appreciated, and warmly acknowledged. A copy of the letter which he had written to Lord Clarendon was shown to them, and accidentally left on the Governor's table. Almost immediately after, M. Lambert himself, the chief subject of the communication, was announced. In his interview with His Excellency he complained bitterly of the mischief which Mr. Ellis had done at the capital, charging him with having defeated all the plans of the French party, and their schemes for the *good* (?) of the country, and otherwise, generally, with having done grievous harm. As soon as he had taken his departure, the missionary so violently denounced returned in search of the letter, in which M. Lambert's name had been so conspicuous, and was not sorry to learn that the Governor's quick eye had observed it, and that with ready tact he had laid it aside. The Governor informed him that M. Lambert's errand in France had very narrowly escaped complete success. It appeared that the members of the French Government, to whom his scheme had been submitted, were unanimously in favour of an armed expedition against Madagascar; but that Louis Napoleon decided that no step should be taken without the concurrence of the British Government. Thus it was to the Emperor's single veto that Madagascar owed its exemption from the horrors of war, if not of entire subjugation.

During the few weeks that Mr. Ellis remained in the colony, he enjoyed agreeable intercourse with friends, and received courteous attention from persons of influence, and members of other religious communions besides his own, the Bishop of Mauritius among the number. He was again a guest at Reduit, where he spent the Christmas with the Governor and his family.

He embarked on his homeward voyage on board the steamer *England*, commanded by Captain Dundas, on January 13th, 1857. Soon after setting sail they encountered a violent hurricane, which others had not so bravely weathered as their powerful and well-appointed steamer; for a day or two after the subsidence of the storm, they fell in with a frail raft, on which two shipwrecked men, in the last stage of exhaustion, were despairingly waiting for deliverance. These men were happily saved from their perilous position, and in the person of one of the rescued mariners the missionary was surprised to find a Sandwich Islander, a native of Oahu, where he had formerly laboured, and who was overjoyed to meet, not only with deliverance, but with a friend who could converse with him in his native tongue. On hearing the first two lines of a hymn in the Sandwich Island language, his countenance brightened, and taking up the strain, he repeated the concluding lines, wondering who it was that thus addressed him and showed such familiarity with the hymns of his childhood. His pleasure was not abated when he was informed that the friend who addressed him had himself composed those lines when he was residing in the islands. The incident of the rescue, as may well be imagined, produced no little excitement and sympathy among the passengers and crew. The rescued men were left at the Cape . of Good Hope, to pursue their course to America. The remainder of the voyage to England was safe and speedy, and on March 20, 1857, the traveller once again experienced the joy of returning home.

Though well entitled to rest, he was not yet allowed, nor was he satisfied, to remain idle. His services as a deputation at missionary and other public meetings were more than ever in requisition, and intense sympathy with the persecuted Christians at Madagascar was excited by his graphic descriptions of their sufferings and their constancy. The novel and varied information he was likewise able to give on other subjects that had come under his observation, was received with appreciative interest. The Royal Geographical Society requested him to read at one of their meetings a paper on Madagascar, which was published in their annual volume of 'Transactions.' He was subsequently elected a Fellow of the Society. The Horticultural Society, and other scientific associations, were also prompt to do him honour. Amidst a busy round of such engagements he found time once more to apply himself to literary labour, and in 1858 published his *Three Visits to Madagascar*—a book that has, perhaps, been as extensively read as any work on missionary enterprise and travel. In that volume will be found, besides a description of the people and country, their productions, institutions, and customs, a complete and minute account of the incidents and events of which the foregoing narrative is but a brief and imperfect outline.

CHAPTER XIII.

EARLY in 1857 M. Lambert, who had arrived in Mauritius from his European expedition, as already stated, just before Mr. Ellis left the colony, returned to Antananarivo; and though he had failed in securing the armed assistance for which he had applied at home, he lost no time in resuming his schemes for effecting a revolution in the country, and for deposing the Queen in favour of her son. The Prince, however, would not countenance the treasonable design; and before the attempt could be made, the conspiracy that had been formed by the Frenchmen at the capital became known to the sovereign, who, naturally incensed, returned all the presents she had received from M. Lambert, and banished him and his countrymen from her dominions. In his return to the capital the French adventurer had been accompanied by Madame Pfeiffer, who was of course included in the edict of banishment. This eccentric traveller and authoress subsequently published an account of her residence in Madagascar, a work in which she constituted herself the mouthpiece of some of M. Lambert's slanders against the missionary who had done so much to thwart his purposes of selfish aggrandisement, and the injuries he had meditated against the country of his adoption.

Whether or not the Queen's indignation at the discovery of the plot against her throne had any connexion with her renewed hostility against the Christians, and that she suspected the treason had been planned in any measure with a view to their advantage, or with their connivance, it was immediately followed by the outbreak of another violent persecution, more cruel than any that had preceded, and involving a larger number of victims, many of whom were put to death in ways the most revolting and merciless, while many more were condemned to slavery and fetters, or to the ordeal of poison, and other forms of barbarous punishment. Numbers also fled from their homes, and remained in concealment till the danger was past. The Prince exerted himself nobly to befriend these victims of superstitious malevolence, and either by himself providing refuge, or by assisting the flight of the accused, succeeded in saving hundreds of lives.

This persecution, as it was the most severe, was happily the last to which the adherents of Christianity were exposed. The Queen's health, which had long been failing, at length somewhat rapidly declined, and on August 16, 1861, her reign and her cruelties were terminated by death. Sufficient warning of this event had been given to enable the prime minister and commander-in-chief, with other adherents of Prince Rakotond, to take measures for his accession to the throne. Shortly before the Queen died the city was filled with troops, and the house in which Rambosalama, the rival claimant of the throne, was devising with a number of his friends their schemes for securing the sovereignty, was surrounded by soldiers; and the baffled aspirant for the crown, finding himself a helpless prisoner, was among the first to tender his allegiance to his cousin, who, as soon as his mother's death was announced, had been publicly proclaimed king, under the title of Radama II. With a less humane opponent, the life of a rival so formidable and so unscrupulous would at once have been forfeited; but among many other acts of clemency which inaugurated the new reign, the sentence pronounced against Rambosalama was the mild one of banishment to one of his own villages, not many miles from the capital. In this place of exile the young man died early in the following year.

The first measures of the new king, in the exercise of the

supreme power, were, a free invitation for the return of all
foreigners, with fresh encouragements to commerce, the advantages of which, however, were marred by the ill-judged abolition of all customs duties; a considerable diminution in the
amount of compulsory labour, and other burdens, which under
former governments had pressed heavily upon the people; the
liberation of political captives, and exiles or prisoners of war,
especially from among the disaffected tribe of Sakalavas, who
were not only restored to liberty, but sent home loaded with
presents—an act of regal generosity that converted the formerly hostile province into the most loyal and steadfast section
of the kingdom; and, to crown all, the proclamation of perfect
religious liberty, without distinction or favour, throughout the
land.

Tidings of these important events, accompanied with earnest
requests for the return of Christian teachers, were not long in
reaching England, and were hailed with unmingled satisfaction
by all the friends of Madagascar, and especially by those who
sympathised with its ' martyr Church.'

Among the first in this country to gain information of the
changes that had taken place was Mr. Ellis; and the manner
in which he received the intelligence was highly characteristic,
showing at once his quiet self-possession and the promptness of
his decision. He was sitting at breakfast with some friends
who were at the time visitors at Rose Hill, when letters from
Madagascar were placed in his hands. Having opened them,
and rapidly glanced over their contents, he laid them down on
the table beside him, without comment or sign of emotion, and
joined with his usual liveliness in the general conversation.
When the meal was over, he walked into the garden with one
of his guests, a brother minister from London, and opened his
Madagascar news with the quiet remark, ' The Queen is dead,
I must go.' Then, having given his friend the details of his
letters, he returned into the house, to impart the same
information to Mrs. Ellis, whom he had been unwilling to

disturb by a more abrupt disclosure of the facts, and to prepare for an immediate journey to the Mission House, in order to confer with the officers and directors of the Society concerning the steps that should be taken. Before the day closed the arrangements for his last visit to Madagascar had been virtually concluded, and he returned to Rose Hill to commence preparations for another adventurous journey and protracted absence from home. His beloved wife would fain have accompanied him; indeed, nothing but an imperative sense of duty would have reconciled her to being again left behind; but the ill-health of her husband's only surviving daughter, whose life was evidently ebbing fast, the claims of Rawdon House, and other considerations, rendered her presence at home indispensable.

Not many weeks elapsed after the arrival of the Madagascar letters, before the ardent missionary was once more ready to set sail on his interesting and hopeful embassy. Before his departure he was favoured with a personal interview with Earl Russell, then at the head of the Foreign Office, and was furnished with an official letter, assuring the new sovereign of the friendly sentiments of the British Government towards that of Madagascar—a communication that would be most welcome to the young ruler, who desired nothing more earnestly than the friendship of England.

The voyage out, by the same course as that taken on the previous visit, was pleasant and expeditious. The first portion of the route from Southampton to Alexandria, was made in the *Pera*, which left her port of embarkation on the 20th of November, 1861. At Suez, the travellers again took ship in the *Norna*, and the party were joined by six French Roman Catholic priests, on their way to Madagascar, besides a French officer with presents from the Emperor of France to Radama. Mr. Ellis experienced as usual the greatest courtesy from his fellow passengers. The attention and kindness of the commander of the *Norna*, in particular, Captain Bain, contributed greatly to the comfort of the passage. His first words of greeting at Suez were an omen of an agreeable voyage. 'Mr. Ellis,' he said, 'though I have not seen you before, I never received a passenger with greater pleasure.' In reply to enquiries about accommodation, he added: 'The two best cabins in the vessel have been assigned to your use, and in everything under my control your wishes shall be attended to.' The Catholic priests were naturally a little shy of their new acquaintance, and some French ladies among the passengers, who had received their information from M. Lambert's accounts and other equally credible sources, seemed disposed at first to believe they had a Jonah on board; but before the end of the voyage, thanks in no small measure to Captain Bain's warm and honest championship, the Protestant missionary's blackened character was amply vindicated, and he stood fairly in the estimation even of those who had before been disposed to regard him as a very monster of wickedness.

Port Louis was reached on the 27th of December, and Mr. Ellis was once more welcomed by his hospitable friends at Mauritius, as well as by others, not less cordial, whose acquaintance he now made for the first time. He was entertained at Reduit by the Governor, Sir William Stevenson, who received him with much courtesy, informing him that he had instructions from the British Government to afford him every possible assistance in the prosecution of his mission.

Hearing that fever was rife at Tamatave, he did not attempt to proceed on his journey till some months after his arrival in Mauritius, when the unsalubrious districts had become more safe for travellers or visitors, but remained at Port Louis, corresponding with native Christians and others in Madagascar, and devoting much of his comparative leisure to the study of the Malagasy language. During this interval also, having conceived the happy idea that the localities in and about Antananarivo, where the Christian martyrs had suffered, would form most appropriate sites for places of worship, which as long as they stood would be striking memorials of the trials of the early Church of Madagascar, and the sublime constancy of its heroic members, who had sealed their fidelity with their blood; believing also that such a commemoration of events so worthy of indelible record would commend itself to the sympathy and liberality of Christians at home, and fearing lest the land should be otherwise appropriated if any delay occurred in securing it, Mr. Ellis wrote at once to the King, requesting that the sites might be reserved for the object desired. To this application a favourable reply was speedily returned. The simultaneous appeal to English Christians for the necessary pecuniary aid met with an equally prompt response, and it was not long before the work of building churches on these interesting spots was fairly begun.

As soon as the favourable season permitted, Mr. Ellis left Port Louis in the *Jessie Byrne*, which set sail on the 17th of May, 1862, and on the 22nd of the same month came to anchor in the harbour of Tamatave. A most cordial welcome awaited the Christian messenger, who was not a little affected by the evidences of the great changes that had taken place in the condition of the people since his last visit. Then, the disciples of the Saviour scarcely dared to recognise each other, and could meet for devotional exercises only in secret, and under the most careful guard against detection; now, no attempt at conceal-ment was needed, joy beamed in every countenance, and family or public worship was held openly, and with all the more manifest enjoyment and fervour from the long suppression of the privilege.

Other changes of a very different character marked the aspect of the place, and painfully impressed the visitor at this period. Signs of increased activity in business were cer-tainly evident, but the most flourishing trade apparently was the sale of spirits, which since the removal of all customs duties had been imported in enormous quantities, and, as the natural consequence, drunkenness, riot, and licentiousness prevailed to a fearful extent. The people appeared to be entering afresh on that critical phase of their course which unhappily too often marks the first contact of a barbarous community with civilized nations, and which, unless counteracted by the elevating influence of Christainity, leads sooner or later to their extermination. Besides the increase of drunkenness which attended the new order of things, the very leniency of the King's disposition and the laxity of his government, by removing the wholesome check of fear and holding out a comparative immunity for wrong-doing, produced an increase of crime, most disastrous in its immediate effects, and which doubtless even thus early laid the foundation of the weak and indolent monarch's subsequent fall. At present, however, there were no signs of the coming evil. The King was everywhere popular, his accession to the throne gave general joy, and even the least sanguine, though not blind to the young Radama's faults, hoped much from the humane and generous traits in his character, his liberal policy, and the undoubted reforms he had already introduced. To the Christians in the land the change was a revulsion, bringing life and freedom, and bright with promise. No wonder they gave their deliverer credit for goodness beyond his meed.

The arrival of Mr. Ellis in the country had been eagerly looked for; officers from the king were in waiting at Tamatave, and every facility was afforded for his journey to the capital. This was begun on the 31st of May, was conducted by a course only slightly varying from those already traversed and described, and was chiefly distinguished by the number of refugees, who had been slaves or outlaws during the reign of persecution, and were now returning to their homes. A number of these accompanied the party from the coast, and small bands would frequently join them as they proceeded on their way; so that before they reached the capital the company was swelled to quite a host. Within a few miles of the city delegates from the Christians came out to meet him, additional officers from the King also gave him welcome, and conducted him with every demonstration of genuine respect and welcome to the comfortable quarters provided for him in Antananarivo. He entered the city on the 16th of June much fatigued, but thankful and encouraged by the cheering circumstances attending his arrival. On the next day he went by appointment to visit the King, who received him with, if possible, even more than his old cordiality. At this audience he delivered to the gratified sovereign the letter from the English Government, together with letters and presents from the authorities at Mauritius, and a number of acceptable gifts from friends at home. The Queen, Rabodo, was not behind her consort in the heartiness of her reception.

Among the first objects of interest that attracted the missionary's special attention were the martyr sites, which he took the earliest opportunity of visiting, and which he could now examine in the most open manner, very different from the jealous surveillance with which his casual glances that way were formerly regarded. He was glad to find them in every way eligible for the proposed places of worship.

His time was now very much taken up by visitors of all kinds, especially from among the Christians, who crowded his house from morning till night, some of them often coming before he was dressed, and sharing his early cup of coffee. His good nature and desire to be useful were not unfrequently pretty severely taxed to keep down any sense or show of irritation at the untimely hours and inconsiderate persistence which characterized some of these visits. A desire for instruction showed itself amongst the more intelligent classes, and many of the nobles were anxious that their sons, if not themselves, should acquire a knowledge of the English language. He was therefore induced to receive a number of young men for the purpose of teaching them English, and devoted to this class two hours daily. He also, at the King's request, gave one hour each day to His Majesty for reading the Scriptures and conversation. These interesting interviews, as well as a religious service at the King's house, were kept up almost without a single interruption until within a day or two of Radama's death.

With all these demands upon his attention and energies, taxing his physical powers to the very utmost, he applied himself diligently and with his usual success to the acquisition of the language. His progress was somewhat facilitated by a certain correspondence between the language of Madagascar and that of Polynesia. He had always a remarkable power of memory for words, and though he might be deficient in his knowledge of the structure and grammar of a new tongue, his vocabulary soon became almost inexhaustible, and he would manage to make himself understood by the natives, however defective the composition of the sentence might be. He took pleasure in tracing words to their source, which in the case of proper names was not a difficult task. He was informed, while pursuing this sort of enquiry, of the origin of the regal name; the legend concerning which is, that the father of the first Radama, enquiring of an Arab what was the name of the greatest, or first man, was answered Adam : 'Then,' said the King, ' my son shall be called Adam '—a name which, transferred into Malagasy, becomes Radama ; for in that dialect, as in those of Polynesia, every word must end with a vowel, and every personal proper name in Madagascar has the prefix Ra. ' Even my cat,' Mr. Ellis adds, ' the natives call Ra-pussy.' Considerable knowledge of the language was thus acquired with wonderful rapidity, more by conversation with the people than by study in the closet.

Events of considerable importance to the new sovereignty were now pending. Among these were the arrival at the capital of embassies from the French and English Governments, and of resident Consuls from these respective countries, as well as the re-occupation of the long abandoned mission field by English Protestant teachers. The Roman Catholic priests were already on the ground, and in conjunction with the French laymen at the capital plied every means, not always very scrupulously, to influence the King in favour of their religion and their own nation. Especially they strove to prejudice his mind against Mr. Ellis, whose growing influence they viewed

with no little dissatisfaction. Nothing was too black for
M. Laborde and M. Lambert to charge against him, nothing
too gross for the Abbé Jouen, with unblushing mendacity, to
invent in defamation of his character. These enemies of the
English missionary seemed to hope much from the expected
arrival of the British Consul, whom they knew and counted
upon as an ally. 'Let him wait,' M. Laborde would say to the
King, 'till my friend Mr. Pakenham comes, and the old
meddler will soon learn to know his place.' These violent
attacks against one whom the King had good reason to value,
only seemed to raise the traduced man in the young ruler's
esteem. He was, not without good cause, suspicious of the
motives and designs that prompted these evil tongues, and
the violence of their hate convinced him only the more firmly
that in 'his Father,' as he delighted to call his faithful
counsellor, he had at least one true man and staunch friend,
whose statements he could implicitly believe, and in whose
judgment he might safely trust.

The coronation of the King, a ceremony of much signifi-
cance in the semi-barbarous condition of the nation, had been
fixed for the middle of August, but, in order to give the
representatives of distant tribes the opportunity of being
present, was postponed till the following month. The alteration was not made known in time to prevent the somewhat
premature arrival of the members of the European embassies,
some of whom were compelled to return before the great event
took place, and those who remained were detained in the
island at some personal inconvenience for a much longer period
than they had anticipated. The first of these distinguished
visitors to reach the capital were the members of the French
embassy, at the head of which was Commodore Dupré. With
these came the French Consul. Not long afterwards the
English embassy arrived, including General Johnstone, Captain
Anson (since promoted in military rank and official position),
and the Bishop of Mauritius. The prelate was charged with

the agreeable duty of presenting to the sovereign of Madagascar, as a present from Queen Victoria, a handsomely bound copy of the Bible, with Her Majesty's autograph inscribed. The embassy was also accompanied by Mr. Caldwell, with other presents from the Queen. This party was soon followed by the newly-appointed English Consul, and before the day fixed for the coronation the European company was augmented by the welcome appearance, an the 30th of August, 1862, of the expected English missionaries. These were met a short distance from the city by some of the members of the British embassy, accompanied by Mr. Ellis and a number of native Christians. They were in the first instance entertained by Captain Anson, and, much refreshed in mind and body by their kind reception, were afterwards conducted to the comfortable dwellings prepared for them. The securing and furnishing of these houses had been part of the irindefatigable friend's preliminary work. The sites and some of the habitations had been given by the first Radama to the former missionaries, and, on Mr. Ellis's application, were restored to the mission, on the payment to the occupants of their duly appraised value at the time of transfer.

The unexpected detention of the British embassy at Antananarivo, however inconvenient to the gentlemen composing it, was peculiarly opportune and refreshing to Mr. Ellis, who received from each of them much courtesy and kindness, and enjoyed frequent and pleasant intercourse, such as secured for him the privilege of their warm personal friendship to the close of his life. The duties of the Bishop of Mauritius obliged him to return before the day of the coronation; but during his brief stay he visited and surveyed with mournful interest the places where the martyrs had suffered; he also witnessed the worship of the native Christians, and addressed them through the medium of an interpreter. Mr. Ellis, moreover, held earnest conference with him on the position and prospects of the mission; and it was mutually admitted that the interests of the people, and the progress of the Christian religion among them, would best be secured by the missionaries of the Church of England occupying other stations than those already filled by the London Missionary Society, and where their labourers had in former years so long and patiently toiled and suffered. Surely the principle is a sound one ; and the Gospel will better be commended to heathen tribes by co-operation, than by the display of antagonism among rival sections of the Church.

As the time appointed for the coronation drew near, the city became filled with eager crowds from all parts of the country. In the ceremony itself, which took place on September 23, 1862, and in its accessories of circumstance and scenery, there was much that was novel and imposing even to the eyes of the European visitors. Of all these particulars, and of many others connected with them that are not even alluded to in this narrative, very full accounts have been repeatedly given to the public in the missionary periodicals of the time, and full details are furnished in Mr. Ellis's work entitled *Madagascar Revisited*. It would be tedious to go over the ground again.

More than one occurrence, though trivial in itself, threatened to mar the harmony of the auspicious occasion, but the prudence of the parties most nearly concerned prevented any public collision or breach of decorum. Foolish persons endeavoured to sow discord, and perplex the King by suggesting, some, that the English general, others, that the French commodore, ought to place the regal emblem on His Majesty's head. He solved the difficulty by crowning himself. The Catholic priests officiously obtruded on the King's privacy on the morning of the coronation day, and, taking him by surprise, before the bewildered monarch could conceive what they were about, actually placed the crown on his head, and delivered a homily to their unwilling and solitary auditor. They afterwards boasted of their performance as a decisive mark of Radama's favour to the Roman Catholic religion. Another threatened *contretemps* was averted entirely by General Johnstone's forbearance and good sense. A day or two before that appointed for the ceremony, the consuls, British and French, informed Radama that they had conferred together, and agreed upon certain arrangements for the coronation, having regard to order and precedence. The King, in some indignation, replied that he had made his own arrangements, and would admit of no interference. He afterwards sent private intimation to General Johnstone that he intended to abide by his own judgment and decision in assigning to him the chief post of honour among the visitors. It was, therefore, with some surprise that the general heard on the morning of the ceremony that Admiral Dupré had insisted upon precedence, threatening, in the event of any other course, to consider the French insulted, and withdraw from all friendly relations with the Malagasy Government. Possibly the first impulse of the English general might have been to absent himself from the pageant altogether ; but, with better tact, he took no notice of the change in the programme which these threats effected.

A day or two after these events the English embassy took their departure, and the members of the French commission were not long in following. These last had, however, previously completed the execution of a treaty between the French and Malagasy Governments. This document was by no means free from objection, even in the form in which it was ultimately adopted; but in the first draft, besides other indefensible claims, it had been stipulated that French residents in the country should not be subject to Malagasy laws. To this exceptional clause, in particular, the chief secretary and other of the King's advisers were strongly opposed. Mr. Ellis, upon being consulted in the matter, could not hesitate to explain at least the usages of European countries, and to state that in England every foreigner, the moment he set foot on British ground, was subject to British law, and that the same rule applied in France, and every other part of the civilized world. The Malagasy Government accordingly declined to accept the treaty with this unusual and unjustifiable clause. The French were very wroth with Rahaniraka and with his English friend, and at first refused to make any alteration in their terms ; but ultimately conceded the point in dispute, and the treaty was signed. Mr. Ellis's share in the transaction, nevertheless, long rankled in the tenacious and vindictive memories of his baffled antagonists.

Appended to this treaty were stipulations that in effect ratified certain private concessions which the King had made to M. Lambert, granting him most extraordinary powers over lands and minerals in Madagascar, and even authorising his issuing coin with the 'king's image and superscription.' This insane agreement was most offensive to the members of the Government and other nobles, and had been clandestinely extorted from the King by M. Lambert, associated with M. Laborde and a French priest, at one of the King's country houses, and *after dinner*. In his sober senses, Radama repented of the transaction, but, though warned that it would inevitably bring trouble on himself and his kingdom, had not the courage to draw back in time.

It was with extreme reluctance that the minister of the Gospel allowed himself to be mixed up in any way with the political affairs of the country. Radama had urged him, soon after his arrival, to compile a code of laws for Madagascar, but this he had decidedly refused to do. He endeavoured to confine his attention as much as possible to the higher claims of his office ; but his position was peculiar, and he could not consistently with his duty altogether avoid expressing his opinion and giving his counsel when it was directly sought. His influence with the King was certainly great, and in every perplexity the young sovereign appealed to him as to the man in whom he could best trust. In reference to the accusations urged against him on this score by those who regarded his beneficent control with jealousy, Mr. Ellis observes :—' Whatever influence I may have possessed with the King had been honourably acquired, and was used solely for the advancement of the great object of the mission with which I was connected—the improvement and religious benefit of the people. I never sought a single favour for myself personally. I was less with the King than he desired that I should be. With the exception of the day of the coronation, I had declined every invitation to dine with him, though messengers had not unfrequently been specially sent for me ; and I had sedulously endeavoured to render my intercourse with him subservient to his own instruction and benefit, as well as to the good of the people. To the King, or those in power, I never offered an opinion on any but religious subjects, except when my opinion was asked ; and excepting my daily visits to the King to read and converse with him, I never went to the palace without having been sent for, and then I invariably accompanied the officer, and entered the palace with him, in order that the other officers on duty within and without the palace, many of whom were heathen, and did not regard with favour the privileges of the Christians, might see that I had been sent for.'

Direct missionary work was that in which this messenger of the Cross chiefly delighted, and to which he made all other engagements subservient. The following account of his labours in this department has been kindly furnished by one of his associates, the Rev. Robert Toy, and will convey a vivid idea of the energy and indefatigable activity which he put forth in his cherished calling :—

'At the end of August 1862, Mr. Ellis was joined by the new missionaries from England. These comprised three ministerial missionaries, a medical man, a superintendent of education, and a printer. On our arrival at the foot of the hill upon which the capital is built, we met our friend for the first time, in company with numerous Christians who had come to welcome us to the scene of our future labours. We had imagined to ourselves an old man of 65 or 70 years of age, and were surprised to find a hale active man of apparently not more than 55 or 60 years, going about in the hot sun with all the vigour and energy

S

of a young man.   His activity at this time was wonderful, and enabled him during the first few months, and before the younger brethren could render him much help, to do nearly all the work of the mission.   He seemed to be everywhere, and doing himself almost everything, preaching at the different chapels, receiving visitors almost innumerable, explaining passages of Scripture to some, giving counsel and advice to others, listening to tales of trouble or complaint, giving medicine to the sick, and help to the poor, going daily to the Stone House where the King spent his time, visiting and advising the missionaries, corresponding with friends and the Society at home, visiting different parts of the neighbourhood, and taking photographs of the more eminent people and places—always full of occupation from early morn till late in the evening.

'The scheme which he had happily conceived of erecting the memorial churches was warmly taken up by the Directors and the Christian Churches at home, and a sum of money far exceeding the amount he had asked for, was speedily raised.   He secured the sites from the King, who readily granted them, including a fifth at Fiadana on the south-west, where thirteen persons had been stoned to death in 1857.   This grant of the land was confirmed by the succeeding Government, and secured for the use of the Christians in connection with the London Missionary Society in perpetuity, when the English Treaty was made in 1865.   Before he left the country he had the pleasure of seeing the first building begun, and making rapid progress. He lived to hear of the successful completion of this and two of the others, one of which—the Ambohipotsy Church—was opened by the present Queen and Prime Minister in person, and of fair progress being made by the fourth.   They are not so plain and unornamental as was at first proposed, some of them being of considerable architectural pretentions.   Strength and utility, however, have been principally attended to, in all of them, and it is believed that for generations to come they will prove memorials of the faithful deaths of Malagasy Christians and of the generosity of English Christians brought about by Mr. Ellis's happy idea, and earnest appeal.*

'The three congregations which Mr. Ellis found when he reached the capital, were collected on the north and north-west of the town. Soon after our arrival, seeing the importance of establishing a church for the population on the southern end, we prevailed upon the King to give temporarily a piece of ground for the erection of a rough building which might be used for gathering together a congregation, and last till the Memorial Church, to be built close by, should be completed. He asked me at the same time to go and live in that part of the town, and undertake the work of gathering together a congregation. We began by holding services in our own house, and afterwards had a large rough clay building erected on the spot of ground given by the King, to which we removed as soon as finished; and, when the Memorial Church was ready, in November 1868, we took possession of it with a Church of more than 500 members, a congregation often numbering more than 1,500 persons, and country congregations connected with it numbering between sixty and seventy. Thus proving the wisdom and foresight of Mr. Ellis in fixing so early upon this position.

'He next recommended, and did very much to help forward, the erection of a church on the east side of the town, at Ankadibivava. This also is now a flourishing cause, with a large number of country churches united with it. The important Church at Andohalo, situate near the centre of the capital, in like manner owes its origin almost entirely to him, as well as the flourishing Church at Ampamarinana.

'It was Mr. Ellis's opinion from the first that no pecuniary help should be given to the natives by our Society for carrying on Divine worship. While other societies are paying native preachers, we have steadfastly refused, but have shown the

---

* The Memorial Church at Ambatonakanga was opened June 22, 1867; that at Faravohitra (Children's Church), July 9, 1867; that at Ambohipotsy, November 17, 1868; and that at Ampamarinana was nearly completed at the commencement of the present year, 1873.

natives that this was their work, and not ours, and that the
Churches would be stronger and more robust by depending
upon themselves rather than on foreign help. This required
great firmness at the commencement, especially as the people
were poor and had suffered much in the days of persecution.
Moreover, they had been hoping for many years for English
help, and had formed high notions as to what they would do
for them should the missionaries ever be permitted to return;
but he felt that the principle was a right one, and in this, as
in other matters, he was earnestly supported by the missionaries.
The result is, that there is at the present time no one Church
supported by the Society, and no Church officer of any kind
whatever in their pay. We have felt it advisable recently,
on account of the heavy pressure upon the Churches resulting
from the great and rapid spread of Christianity, to subscribe
to the native fund for supporting a large staff of evangelists.
We also give a very small subscription when a new chapel is
being built, and we principally support the native school-
masters, though this we hope to throw more and more upon
the natives themselves. But the Churches are all of them
established and carried on by native agency without pecuniary
support from us. It is to this principle, established by the
advice of Mr. Ellis and approved of by the Society and the
missionaries who were with him, that·we owe in a very great
measure the activity, the prosperity, and the stability of the
Churches throughout the country.

'In a similar way he had, before our arrival, proposed to
the heads of the Christians that Bibles, Testaments, and other
books should not be given away indiscriminately, but that
those who were able should pay a small price for what they
required. This met with warm opposition. They had been so
long accustomed to receive them gratis in times of distress,
that they had taken it for granted that the same practice
would still be continued in the days of prosperity. By a little
firmness the point was carried. The principle having been

thus introduced, it has grown till at the present time scarcely anything besides small tracts, reports of unusual meetings, and catechisms for candidates for Baptism and the Lord's Supper, is given away, but a fair price is always charged, a reduction being made in the case of those who are known to be too poor to pay the full price.

' He was always most anxious that the Churches should be established on a thoroughly independent basis. Every Church member should be qualified to vote, and all matters of government and discipline should be submitted to the Church regularly assembled. Irregularities regarding the appointment of Church officers had naturally crept in during the days of the persecution, when their meetings together were attended with so much difficulty and danger, so that the persons discharging the duties of pastors and deacons had fallen as a matter of course into these positions without any direct vote of the Christians as a body. Mr. Ellis spoke to us on the subject soon after our arrival, and a meeting was soon after appointed, at which rules, previously drawn out, were placed before the leading men among the Christians. These after considerable discussion and a little delay were accepted, and have in principle been adopted by all the Churches ever since. Mr. Ellis then proposed that every office-bearer in the Church should be rechosen by each separate Church, and such as failed in obtaining a majority of votes should cease to hold an official position. It was rather a trying ordeal for some of them to go through, but the thing was done, and nearly all the men were re-elected. Nothing that has ever been done in Madagascar has had a more important bearing on the well-being of the Churches than the introduction of the principle, that all points relating to the government and discipline of the Churches shall be submitted to the vote of the assembled members, and besides closing an effectual door against innumerable irregularities which must inevitably have crept in, it is thoroughly adapted to the character of the people, and forms perhaps the greatest safeguard against any attempted proselytism

on the part of any unfriendly society. The natives see that they
are managing their own affairs, and are in no way under the
power and management of foreign missionaries, for we have made
the same principle hold good as much in relation to our own
dealings with the Churches as in that of the native pastors and
deacons. We have assumed from the first no authority, and it
will be difficult for missionaries with high notions of priestly
dignity and authority, now to make much headway against our
teachings.

'One more matter of importance I may mention as having
been carried out through the advice of Mr. Ellis, and that is the
confining of the first efforts of the missionaries to the capital and
neighbourhood, rather than spreading their strength over a larger
extent in the provinces. By making Antananarivo the centre
of our operations, and concentrating there all the power of the
mission for the first few years after its re-establishment, it has
become now the stronghold of Christianity, and is making still
rapid progress in knowledge and all the essentials of civilized
life, while native preachers and evangelists have become qualified
for carrying the Gospel and establishing Churches among the
distant tribes. Missionaries now settling in distant places have
ready prepared native workers to carry on the main labours of
the district under their guidance and supervision.

'After three years of great anxiety and responsibility he would
leave with the full conviction that the work on which his heart
was set, was steadily going on, and Christianity gaining a hold
upon the people generally, which must soon make it difficult, if
not impossible for any Government again to attempt its overthrow. I had not always seen eye to eye with him, but the more
thoroughly I knew him the more I esteemed him, and this was
the feeling prevalent both among the missionaries and the native
Christians.'

CHAPTER XIV.

CHANGES.

THOUGH he might wish to concentrate the energies of the mission at the capital, Mr. Ellis was far from confining his attention or his efforts to this centre. In the month of November, 1862, he paid a visit to the ancient and interesting town of Ambohimanga. This place was regarded as a stronghold of idolatry, and was in some respects a privileged city, into which no stranger (the interdict had never been restricted to *Christians*) even though he were a native of Madagascar, could enter without special authority or permission. Yet even here there were Christians, who sent to the capital to request they might be allowed a plot of ground on which to build a place of worship. This request the King readily granted, and subsequently, at the solicitation of the same parties, expressed his desire that Mr. Ellis should visit the place and preach there. He sent one of his officers in advance to announce the missionary's approach. Two other nobles, Christian men, and members of the Church at Ambatonakanga, accompanied him, on the 15th of August, to the city. With the view of showing respect to one who came to them as the King's friend, and in conformity with ordinary usage when officers of the royal household were to be received, a small military guard of honour was stationed at the gates, and saluting the party as they advanced, preceded them into the city, where their Christian friends, and the inhabitants generally, gave them a cordial welcome. After an interesting religious service, and much pleasant intercourse with the people, the missionary and his party returned. Shortly after this visit some native preachers, who were sent from the capital to the same place, were roughly and inhospit-. ably treated by the authorities, and returning home made complaint to the king of the usage they had received. Considering this conduct of the heathen party as a direct disobedience of his command, and a violation of the religious liberty that had been proclaimed on the sovereign's accession to the throne, Radama evinced his displeasure by degrading the authorities of the city, and appointing others in their place. These severe reprisals were not even known to the missionaries at the time, and still less were they suggested by them. This very simple affair, and the natural and innocent proceedings of the preacher on the occasion, were, several months afterwards, made the ground of serious accusations against him by the British Consul, in a letter to Earl Russell, in which it was represented that, before making this visit, Mr. Ellis had obtained ' *armed followers* ' from the king, and had ' preached *there by force*'; and that he had afterwards '*induced*' the King to degrade all the officers who ' *in the first instance resisted*,' &c. Other charges, equally without foundation, intended to damage the Christian minister's reputation, and to place on him the grave responsibility of having been the chief cause of the heathen reaction which resulted in the King's death, were contained in the same letter. Earl Russell, with characteristic courtesy and fairness, sent a copy of the statement to Mr. Ellis for 'explanation.' This was neither the first nor the last instance in which the British Consul manifested his personal hostility, if not to the Mission itself, certainly to him who for the time was its recognised leader. What was the ground of this hostility was not altogether clear, but so close a friend of the French party at Antananarivo, was, perhaps, not likely to regard the English Protestant missionary with much favour. He had been formerly connected with the Jesuit College at Réunion, had married a French lady, and entered upon his official position with a clearly pronounced partiality for his French friends. Perhaps the English minister could hardly look for much cordiality in a man with such antecedents and connexions. Let the cause be what it might, it is certain that the conduct of the British Consul added very much to Mr. Ellis's distresses and difficulties in Madagascar.

In the midst of these accumulating duties and troubles, he experienced a severe domestic affliction in the death of his only surviving daughter, which occurred on the 10th of September 1862. The first intimation of his loss was conveyed to him in a very kind letter of condolence from the Bishop of Mauritius, in which, however, no name was mentioned, so that to the grief of positive bereavement was added the torture of uncertainty and suspense as to which member of his family had been removed—her for whose death he was in a measure prepared, or some other whom he had left in health, and who had perhaps, his imagination suggested, been suddenly struck down by some terrible calamity. His distress of mind, and the exhaustion of too arduous labour brought on a severe illness, which for a time entirely prostrated him. About a week after the Bishop's letter, another arrived from Mrs. Ellis, giving the details of his daughter's peaceful end. This communication, though it caused him, he says, ' more tears—irrepressible tears—than any event he could distinctly remember,' was, nevertheless, by putting a period to his suspense, a relief, and he could devoutly thank God for the mercy which tempered the severity of the affliction. Mrs. Ellis, in her letter, gave, with much tenderness of sympathy, the details of the closing scene, and the loved one's happy dismissal. The spirit's eternal peace seemed to have left its parting impress on its frail mortal tenement. There was no trace of pain. ' The countenance after death became inexpressibly beautiful. Youth seemed to come back again to it ; ' and as the worn body was composed to its last peaceful slumber, ' it was quite a spectacle of wonder to behold that strange beauty.' Other letters from sympathising friends, showing the love and estimation in which his daughter was held, were a welcome solace to the father's heart. One friend writes,

and many offered their tribute of respect in similar terms :—
'The loss of dear Annie affects me much ; for though we knew
she had long been hovering on the verge of death, still she
seemed so constantly to escape, that we looked that she should
always escape. Few could be more ready for heaven. She
was in every sense to me a lovely woman, a lovely Christian, a
lovely friend. There was a noble simplicity, an unconscious
power, an unwavering devotion to duty, which few possess. I
believe Mrs. Ellis had largely to do with moulding her character, and beautifying it, and if she is proud of nothing else,
she may justly be proud of all her influence there.' In this
season of bereavement, besides these sources of consolation from
a distance, Mr. Ellis was deeply touched with the unaffected
and delicate sympathy of his Malagasy friends, no less than by
the kindness of the mission families, and was powerfully impressed with the evidence of the benign influence of religion in
refining and softening the heart, and drawing closer the bonds
of human brotherhood.

With domestic affliction thus increasing the burden of
accumulating official responsibilities, it is not surprising to find
the over-wrought exile from home writing thus to his absent
wife :—'At times I long with almost inexpressible ardour for
the quiet of Rose Hill ; then again I often feel that God has
certainly placed me here, in a position and with responsibilities
which no one else could sustain ; not from any merit of my own,
but by a combination of circumstances as unforeseen as un-
avoidable, and I occasionally think I should feel ashamed to
come home well and strong, leaving vacant and exposed such a
post as I here occupy.'

About this time, very soon after the visit to Ambohimanga,
the King's foreign secretary, Rahaniraka, died, and Mr. Ellis
was urgently entreated to undertake, at least temporarily, the
duties of the office. Such a request, under the circumstances,
could hardly be refused, and to the missionary's almost
overwhelming labours, was now added the task of translating

and drafting answers to the English correspondence of the Government.

In the beginning of the following month the treaty with England was, after some little difficulty, duly executed. In connection with this transaction, the British Consul preferred a formal complaint to General Johnstone, at that time acting Governor of the Mauritius, against Mr. Ellis, for his interference in the matter, alleging that after three days' full discussion of the terms of the treaty, and when nothing remained but to affix the signatures, he had publicly started objections, which, for the time broke off the business. General Johnstone, in his official capacity, requested an 'explanation,' which was returned in the following reply:—

' To MAJOR-GENERAL JOHNSTONE.   ' *March 28th*, 1863.

' SIR,—While I regret that Her Britannic Majesty's Consul at Madagascar should have so reported any part of my conduct as to produce an impression that my interference was ill-judged and tended to discredit the Consul in his functions, I am grateful for the courtesy which has asked for an explanation of the cause of my interference.

' Though attending the King for an hour or more every day, I heard nothing of any debate about the treaty, and the circumstances under which I interfered were as follows :

' Early in the morning of the 29th of November, several of the King's officers came to my house to ask me to read over with them and correct the translation they had made into Malagasy of the draft of a treaty with England which the Consul had prepared, and also to request that I would afterwards attend on His Majesty at the palace. I read over the translation, and the officers took it to the palace, whither I followed them shortly afterwards. The treaty was then read, and each article separately considered by the King and his ministers, who suggested several important alterations, which were written either in pencil on the document sent by the Consul or on a separate paper, and the draft of the treaty thus amended was returned to the Consul. On the 2nd of December a messenger from the King required the attendance of the other missionaries and myself to witness the signing of the treaty with England. The French Consul and other foreigners were present with the Malagasy. The King asked me to come to his side while the treaty was read, and to inform him if the English and Malagasy texts agreed. The Consul, when he had finished reading the English document, remarked, that the English text alone was valid, the Malagasy translation being only for those who did not understand English. The King's secretary then read the Malagasy translation, the King followed the reading of both by copies in his hand. The Consul then said the translation made by the King's own officers was correct, and taking up a pen asked His Majesty to sign. The King looked at me enquiringly, and I suggested that His Majesty had better pause a moment, as one important addition which the King had made to the original draft was altogether omitted, viz., the rendering the English and Malagasy texts perfectly accordant, and declaring them of equal value and authority for all the purposes of the said treaty. I said the above stipulation had been included in the recently executed treaty with the Emperor of the French, and the King felt assured that Her Majesty would not urge conditions less favourable than our allies had agreed to. The Consul, addressing me angrily, said all former treaties had been in the English language, and he had no instructions to employ any other.

'I also stated that the Malagasy text was in other respects extremely defective, all the most important amendments proposed by the King having been omitted. When I read the respective paragraphs in which these omissions occurred, the King drew back his chair, and the ministers who stood around said the treaty in its present form could not be signed. The Consul said all the amendments handed to him in English had been inserted, and one of the missionaries to whom he had submitted the Malagasy text told him it was correct. The missionary, whose name the Consul had mentioned, being present, explained that he had said the Malagasy was in point of language correct so far as it went, but that he had told the Consul there were many parts in the one text to which there was nothing corresponding in the other, or words to that effect. The Consul then laid the treaty before me, and asked me if I would introduce the amendments of the omission of which the King complained. I said, if His Majesty wished it, I would do so. The King said, " I wish you to do it." I therefore took the treaty, and the king's secretaries having furnished me afterwards with the omitted paragraphs, they were incorporated, and the amended treaty was read, and agreed to by His Majesty, and publicly signed by him in the presence of his ministers and some of the chief nobles of the nation, on the 5th of December. On that day expressions of approval were uttered by many present, and all seemed to rejoice at the satisfactory completion of this new bond of friendship and goodwill between England and Madagascar.

'Your Honour will perceive some difference in relation to facts and dates between the terms in which the Consul has reported my interference, and the above narrative extracted from my own journal, written daily after my return from the palace. I trust my explanation will secure me from censure for the course which, in compliance with the publicly expressed wishes of the King, I pursued on the 2nd of December.'

['I cherish no unfriendly feeling towards Mr. Pakenham personally, but as explanation has been asked from me of my interference in this part of his public conduct, it would scarcely be compatible with the duty which I feel I owe to my country were I not to state that the spirit and conduct of the Consul on this as well as other occasions has destroyed the esteem and confidence with which the King and his ministers, as well as the nobles in general, anticipated the arrival of the representative of the British Government at the capital, and to whom they were prepared to accord, not a formal, but most cordial welcome. The dissatisfaction has been great, and has rendered the appointment of Mr. Pakenham almost the greatest calamity of Radama's reign, while it has not been favourable to the credit, influence, and interests of England in Madagascar. His Majesty has more than once asked me to write and express his wishes that the British Government would appoint some other gentleman to represent England at Madagascar; but I have always replied that it would be perfectly right for His Majesty himself to express his wishes on the subject to Her Majesty's Government, but very unsuitable for me, even at the request of His Majesty, to write on any such subject.']

'I have the honour to be, Sir,

'Your obedient Servant,

'WILLIAM ELLIS.'

The last paragraph of the above letter, though included in the first draft, was withheld from the reply actually sent to General Johnstone. Mr. Ellis's forbearance towards Mr. Pakenham, notwithstanding all the provocation he received, was in this instance, and indeed throughout, as honourable as it was undeserved.

The year 1863 was in many respects one of the most memorable in the history of Madagascar. The King's mistakes of administration, and the vices of his character began early to show fruit. The policy of abolishing all custom-duties, from which alone many of the government officers had derived their pay, gave great offence to the impoverished nobles, while the people complained that they derived no advantage from the change. Grave cause of dissatisfaction, moreover, arose from the fact that the sovereign surrounded himself with young and profligate associates and counsellors,—men without influence or position, who recommended themselves to their master by flattering his vanity and pandering to his pleasures, while his true friends, entitled to consideration from their age, experience, and rank,

were slighted and set aside.   One of the last appointments he
made, and which it was said was instigated and supported by
M. Laborde and by the English as well as the French Consul,
was particularly obnoxious.   This act of folly conferred the
dignity of His Majesty's principal Secretary of State for Foreign
Affairs on 'an ignorant, profligate, drunken American,' who had
been for some years resident in Tamatave, and was universally
known as a violent and hot-headed opponent of the English,
and as blindly devoted to the French.   This step caused the
resignation of several officers of the Government, who were indignant at the appointment and refused to work with such a man.

This occurrence did more, perhaps, than anything that had
yet taken place in Radama's administration, to damage his
character and destroy confidence in his government, while it
threatened, if carried out to its full effect—(the aim of those
who advised it was to make French influence and the Roman
Catholics paramount in Madagascar)—to inflict serious injury
on the Protestant Mission.   But coming events, scarcely yet
foreshadowed, speedily put an end to the insidious mischief.

At this time the heathen party, taking alarm at the rapid
growth and rising influence of the Christians in the country,
bestirred themselves to revive their waning power by exciting
the King's superstitious fears.   The occurrence of an epidemic
malady favoured their machinations and designs ; and, indeed,
there can be no doubt that a large number of the cases were
feigned and instigated entirely by the chief votaries of idolatry
to further their own plans.   The malady, where it was real,
appeared to be a species of hysteria, which a little firmness
would easily have suppressed.   As evidence of this, one noble,
among whose dependants the disorder appeared, threatened to
flog the next person who manifested the slightest symptom of
the disease.   No other case occurred in that chief's establishment.   Two or three soldiers also were affected with the
epidemic, but after the officers had given orders for the arrest
and punishment of the next patient, the 'dancing sickness,' as

the complaint was called, disappeared from the army. The patients, during the paroxysms of their illness, affected to see visions, and to receive communications from the ancestors of Radama, or from the deities of the country, menacing retribution for the favour shown to the Christians. These representations, acting upon a mind naturally weak and degraded by dissolute habits, produced their desired effect, and awakened the King's superstitious fears. Under the influence of these feelings, he no longer favoured the Christians, and was even charged with conniving at schemes for their destruction. He dreaded the vengeance of the offended gods of his country, and regarding the strange sickness as a manifestation of their displeasure, and the possessed as charged with supernatural functions, treated them himself with timid deference, and ordered all his subjects to uncover their heads whenever they met them.

It was not surprising that the malevolence of the heathen party should be chiefly directed against Mr. Ellis, and but for the overruling care of a merciful Providence, he must certainly have fallen a victim to their fury. For many nights in succession warning emblems of death, believed to be endowed with a malign influence of fatal omen, were laid at his door. On one occasion, while reading with the King, a number of the mad dancers, armed with stones and other weapons, forced their way into the room, and, with savage countenances and menacing gestures, seemed bent on taking the missionary's life ; but the King remained close to his side, leaning heavily against his shoulder, and taking his hand in his own, which trembled violently, and though evidently much agitated, so that he could scarcely articulate, he ordered the intruders to be forced back, and the door barred against them. They still maintained their threatening behaviour for some time before they retired, and it was late before the King would allow his friend to return to his own house, where two soldiers were stationed at the door to keep guard during the night. It afterwards appeared that the

party who had forced their way into the king's presence, had
bound themselves by oath to take Mr. Ellis's life on that
occasion.

At another time his escape from death was equally providential. It was the last time he ever visited the king, and only a
day or two before the monarch's tragic end. Mr. Ellis, in the
midst of the tumult, scarcely knowing whether it was prudent
to pay his accustomed visit—for the whole city was in dismay,
each one dreading some undefined and dire calamity—went to
the king's house an hour earlier than he was wont. He found
seated in the room two Roman Catholic priests, as well as the
leader of the party who had sworn to kill him. Finding the
king engaged with the priests, one of them began to prefer some
charges against him with reference to the Abbé Jouen, he rose
to take his leave, interrupting the priest's mumbled accusation
with a peremptory ' Enough of that ; I cannot listen to it now.
Then, turning to the king and saying, ' If your Majesty pleases,
I will retire ; I have something to do at home,' he shook hands
with Radama (it was for the last time), and bowing to the
priests, left the room. On arriving at his own house he found
two messengers from the prime minister waiting his return,
with a warning from their master that it was not safe for him
to remain at home, and desiring him to remove nearer the
chief's own residence. He accordingly went to the house of Dr.
Davidson, which was close to that of the prime minister. He
was afterwards informed that the man whom he saw sitting in
the king's presence with the priests was under oath to put him
to death on that very day, and that the time selected for the
murder was that in which he uniformly left his own house to
visit the king ; so that his going an hour earlier than usual, and
coming away immediately, was, in God's providence, the means
of his escape.

The impending crisis in the kingdom, and Radama's own
tragic fate, were brought about by an act of madness, the cause
or the motive of which it is difficult to assign, though many

T

asserted that its chief object was the destruction of the
Christians. When the king announced his intention to issue
an edict the effect of which would be to legalise murder—
namely, that if any man had a quarrel with another they might
settle their dispute by combat, and, in the event of the death of
either party, the other should go free and unpunished—when
this outrageous measure was threatened, the nobles, who had
become daily more dissatisfied and alarmed, felt it was time
for them to act with decision. The prime minister, accompanied by a number of the chief men in the land, went to the
king and remonstrated with him against his insane proposal,
using their utmost efforts of entreaty to turn him from his
purpose. He declined, however, to accede to their wishes, and
remained fixed in his mad resolve. When, in answer to a last
and direct appeal, the nobles heard from the king's own lips
his determination to issue the obnoxious order, ' Then,' said the
prime minister, ' we must arm,' and leaving the royal presence
with his followers, they took instant measures for their own
safety and that of the kingdom.

The events which followed are too well known to require any
detailed recapitulation. The city was filled with troops. The
advisers of the king—the *menamaso,* as they were called—were
immediately seized, and a number of them put to death. The
rest fled to their master for protection. The nobles demanded
their surrender, which the king at first refused, but afterwards
reluctantly yielded, on condition that their lives should be
spared. With a treachery not to be excused, this promised
condition was violated, and the wretched men shared the fate
of their associates. The king vowed that he would yet be
avenged on the murderers of his friends. Then, and not till
then, the conspirators were impressed with the necessity of
securing their own safety and the completion of their designs
by putting the king himself to death. This was effected on the
night of the 11th or morning of the 12th of May, only three
days after the last ineffectual appeal of the insurgent nobles to

CHAP. XIV.   CHANGES.   275

their ill-advised and infatuated monarch. Not many hours after this fatal occurrence the vacant throne was offered, under certain conditions, to the widow of the fallen ruler, Rabodo. She accepted the conditions, and agreed to receive the crown from the hands that had so recently taken the life of her lord. Let us not be severe in our judgment. She was a heathen ; perhaps her own life was in peril ; and it was generally admitted that she had interposed to the very last to protect the king, and that his murderers, or executioners, had not consummated the fatal deed till she had been forcibly removed from the room.

The chief features of the new constitution by which the queen was bound, in accepting, under the title of Rasoherina, the supreme authority, were, that the will of the sovereign should no longer be the sole law of the land; that the nobles and heads of the people should be associated with her in the government and in the making of laws; and that without the consent of all these parties no life should be judicially forfeited. The queen herself favoured the heathen party, but the religious freedom of all was assured, and happily remained inviolate; so that, however much the fears of the Christians might have been aroused by these violent changes, they had ultimately no cause to complain of the new government.

When tidings of these events reached England, the friends of Madagascar were not a little startled and bewildered by the tragic close of a reign that had opened so auspiciously, and some might perhaps be disposed to think they had scarcely been dealt with fairly in not having received earlier intimation of the impending revolution. Mr. Ellis, however much he might at first have hoped from the humane and kindly disposition of Radama, had never been blind to his faults, nor represented him other than he found him; though it became him to comment on his vices with a certain amount of reserve and caution, when he knew that every word published concerning him in England would come back to the king's knowledge in Madagascar. Both private and official letters, and the daily entries in the

missionary's journal, give abundant evidence of a clear appreciation of the young ruler's character, of waning hopes and growing
discouragements in regard to any reformation or any fruits of
the religious instruction he received. The favourable opinions
concerning him, and the hopes that were entertained in this
country of his ultimate accession to the ranks of the Christians,
were doubtless more sanguine than Mr. Ellis's guarded statements justified. But the chief cause of the surprise which the
first news of the momentous changes occasioned is to be found
in the fact that, owing to some irregularities in the mail,
and the difficulty of transmitting letters from the capital of
Madagascar, no direct tidings from Antananarivo had reached
England for several months. During this period the king's
character had deteriorated, his dissolute habits had gained
strength, and the dissatisfaction of his friends and the country
had taken decided shape and found open expression. Of all this
the absence of letters had kept the English public in ignorance ;
and the announcement of the catastrophe preceded the explanation of its antecedents. This brief statement may serve to
harmonize Mr. Ellis's representations, and to vindicate his
memory from any lingering suspicion of either lack of sagacity
or want of candour.

One of the first acts of the new government was to depose the
obnoxious foreign secretary ; and almost the first audience with
the queen was given to the missionaries, who were assured of the
friendly feelings of the sovereign and her ministers, of liberty to
prosecute their work as unrestricted as they had hitherto enjoyed,
and of the security and freedom of the Christians throughout
the land. Though thus encouraged, the Protestant teachers felt
it necessary to exercise the greatest caution; for the Government,
scarcely considering their position secure, were suspicious and
jealous of Radama's former friends, and were quick to resent any
sign or expression of dissatisfaction with the new administration.

Soon after the accession of Rasoherina to the throne much
excitement was produced in the city, and indeed extended to

distant parts of the country, from rumours that Radama was still alive, and waiting in concealment an opportunity to reassert his claims. The authors of these reports were sought out by the government, and severely punished, some even by the last penalty of the law. Yet, though it was death even to breathe a suspicion of the kind, circumstantial accounts of the late king having survived the attempt at his destruction, and being still in the neighbourhood, were repeated again and again. Messages purporting to come direct from Radama were sent to Mr. Ellis, announcing the late king's purpose of privately visiting him, or desiring him to repair to some place of meeting. What was the origin or object of these rumours, whether it was to entrap and betray the secret friends of Radama, or merely to excite a tumult, it was difficult to determine. However destitute of foundation they might be, they nevertheless served to unsettle men's minds, and to render the greatest caution necessary on the part of the Christians. In sending home an account of the circumstances, Mr. Ellis deemed it prudent to write in the Tahitian language, requesting Dr. Tidman to apply to some missionary from the South Seas to translate his letter. Though thus critically placed in the midst of hostility and suspicion, the missionaries experienced no unfriendly treatment from the Government. Indeed, their veteran leader seemed to be consulted, and held in as high regard by the members of the existing administration, as he had been by the late ruler. Still his position was one of no ordinary difficulty, and he declares that he never before in his life felt the weight of responsibility pressing so heavily upon him. In a letter addressed to his wife at this perilous period he thus writes :—

'The anxiety of this affair, my apprehensions for Radama— lest, on the one hand, if he were really in concealment, he should be discovered, or lest, on the other hand, the false rumours should create disturbance—and the possibility of conflict from one cause or other, with the dangers threatening our own Mission, pressed for the greater part of three months very heavily upon me. Then I had to bear the rancorous hate of the priests, and of Dupré, which was manifested by statements both in his book published in Paris, and in his letter to the queen, fiercely denouncing me, but which raised me in favour here rather than otherwise, as did also the gross falsehoods propagated against me by Pakenham. The falsehoods were too gross to produce any other effect here than an increased conviction of his utter untruthfulness; and I believe they produced the same effect in the colony, and among the British officers at Tamatave. One of the merchants there, a Swiss, wrote to one of the papers, a long defence of the Mission and of myself, showing up Pakenham. I have not seen it, but understand the Consul is dreadfully mortified by it. The French even went so far as to say they had reasons for believing that I was in the pay of the English Government, and was employed to prevent the carrying out of their treaty; while Pakenham accused me of being the cause, by my rash conduct and ill-judged advice, of the revolution. I need scarcely say to you that I took good care to show no sign of uneasiness or alarm, and adopted a resolution from which I never swerved—viz., to neglect no positive duty, and decline no appropriate service, out of regard to what one or the other might say or do. One of my friends in authority at Mauritius said in his last letter to me, "The priests, the Consuls, and the Devil seem to have united with the heathen party to attack you; but it is God's work in which you are engaged, and He will protect you."'

The queen, anxious to secure the favour of England, amongst the first acts of her reign, sent ambassadors to this country to arrange with the British Government either a ratification of the old treaty or the substitution of a new one. These messengers were well received, and returned to Madagascar before Mr. Ellis left the country, with the draft of a new treaty, which was duly executed.

That the difficulties of the position occupied at this time by the head of the Protestant Mission, the energy he displayed, and the wisdom that guided his conduct, were appreciated even by those who did not favour the enterprise in which he was engaged, and who totally misapprehended the motives by which he was actuated, will appear in the following extract in reference to him from a paper published at Port Louis, entitled 'The Overland Commercial Gazette':—'It cannot fail to strike even his enemies with admiration, this picture of a stern, self-denying veteran ' soldier of the Cross '— a relic of an age gone by ; a very Palmerston in religion; leaving wife, home, beloved Albion, that garden of the world, all that makes life pleasant, all' the luxuries of civilization, and at the age of seventy years ·burying himself in the capital of Madagascar, almost ruling the country, puzzling the Jesuits, guiding his fellow-missionaries, opposing the policy of the British Consul, advancing the interests of the London Missionary Society in a masterly manner, rendering his name a very bugbear to the French party, accused of attempted assassination, revolution, and regicide, holding his position in spite of attacks and misrepresentations from without and within, and finally obtaining a signal triumph in the successful manner in which the ambassadors have made their *début* in England ; and if all this is the result of religious conviction, it is only another instance of the extraordinary force and energy derived from a belief in a future state of reward after death for acceptable and meritorious actions performed here, and we can no longer wonder that the enthusiastic and puritanical hordes of Oliver Cromwell finally triumphed over the chivalrous courtiers of Charles II.'

Radama's rash grants to M. Lambert, mixed up as they were with the French treaty, now wrought their inevitable mischief. The Government and the nobles of the country would not, and dared not, if they would, agree to these suicidal concessions; and the French, through M. Dupré, would neither yield nor modify their claims, but threatened to enforce them, if necessary, by an appeal to arms. After much apprehension of such a hostile collision, and long delay, the matter was ultimately settled by the payment to the French of an indemnity of £48,000 ; a very heavy penalty for a country like Madagascar, the imposition of which threatened another revolution, and inflicted a sense of humiliation and wrong which will not soon be forgotten.

Other troubles, from their own countrymen, menaced the new Government of Madagascar. The Sakalavas, indignant at the assassination of their benefactor and friend, rose in revolt, but were speedily quelled by the promptitude and energy of the Hovas, who attacked and routed them, killing many, and taking a number of prisoners. The women and children among these captives were, with well-timed clemency, sent home by the queen ; and the disaffected tribes, at once subdued and conciliated, gave in their allegiance to the new sovereign.

Internal and domestic embarrassments next arose to threaten the stability of the throne and the quiet of the country. The prime minister, who had married the queen, and was associated with her in the duties of government, under the influence of prosperity and power, succumbed to the baser passions of his character, gave way to habits of intoxication, became arbitrary, vindictive, and defiant of all control, till at length the queen and nobles were compelled to depose him from his rank ; and the king-maker, the man who had successively placed two sovereigns on the throne, was himself degraded, and ended his days in poverty and exile.

The disgraced minister was succeeded in his office by his brother, the commander-in-chief, whose influence and policy were beneficent both to his own people and the Protestant Mission. Soon after his appointment, the ceremony of the coronation was celebrated on the 30th of August, 1863. On this occasion the heathen idols were recognized, but the Christians felt that, so long as religious liberty prevailed, the power of the old idolatry was gone.

With unflagging zeal Mr. Ellis continued his indefatigable labours, through evil report and through good report, in the midst of many discouragements as well as many hopeful and gladdening signs of prosperity and progress. Of the latter character was the intelligence brought by representatives of distant tribes, who came to pay homage to the new sovereign, and who reported that, as the result entirely of native teaching in the times of persecution, when the disciples of Christ were dispersed throughout the land, there were converts to the new faith in the most remote parts of Madagascar. Before taking his final leave, Mr. Ellis paid several visits to distant villages; and more than once he preached at Ambohimanga—one of the exclusive idol cities—the only restriction being that the service should be held outside the gates. At the capital he had the satisfaction of seeing the churches consolidated, the schools flourishing, the sick provided with medical relief and hospital accommodation, and the interests of civilization and religion steadily, though slowly, gaining ground. Much of his time was taken up in superintending the erection of the first memorial church at Ambotonakanga, acting as interpreter for Mr. Sibree, the architect, making contracts for the work, and undertaking journeys to procure lime and other building material. The temporary place of worship erected near his own dwelling had been destroyed by fire in the early part of 1864; but a new building was speedily erected on its site, and was opened on the 15th of August of the same year. His own dwelling narrowly escaped the conflagration. At an earlier period of his residence at the capital the house had suffered from one of the floods to which the island is subject. The accident did irreparable damage to much of his photographic apparatus.

Among other reforms which it was his privilege to introduce, was a greater decorum and sacredness in the ceremony and institution of marriage. In June 1864 he officiated at the first Christian marriage publicly solemnized in Madagascar.

His last public act in connection with the mission was on the occasion of signing the new treaty between the British and Malagasy Governments, on the 27th of June, 1865, when he secured, by an official engagement incorporated with the treaty itself, the validity and perpetuity of the title of the memorial churches to the representatives of the London Missionary Society, and the Christians of Madagascar.

On the 15th of July, 1865, he took his leave of the queen and received, in presence of the Court, the expressions of Her Majesty's regret at his departure, and her good wishes for himself and family. The prime minister also sent a letter expressive of the queen's satisfaction with his conduct in all his transactions with the government. On the 18th of the month he left Antananarivo, accompanied by many of the Christians, and bade an affecting farewell to his missionary brethren and the Malagasy disciples for whose interests he had faithfully and devotedly laboured. On the 3rd of August he finally set sail from Madagascar. After a brief stay at Mauritius, where he experienced the hospitality of the Governor, Sir Henry Barkley, and other friends, he commenced his homeward journey on the 8th of September, and landed at Southampton on the 14th of October.

Tidings of the prosperity of the churches in Madagascar continued to gladden his heart. The heathen Queen Rasoherina, who, notwithstanding her openly avowed preference for the worship of her ancestors, had been faithful to her engagements with the Christians, died in the beginning of the year 1868, and was succeeded by a sovereign of another spirit and another faith. Ranavalona, sister of the prince Ramonja, early showed her leaning to the Christians. At her coronation, on the 3rd of September, all symbols of idolatry were excluded, and the Bible was placed conspicuously at her right hand. On the 21st of February, 1869, she was baptized, and on the 6th of June made a public profession of her faith, and still more closely identified herself with the Christians by being admitted into church fellowship. On the 8th of September following, the idols of the nation were, by her command, committed to the flames.

For the filling up of the foregoing sketch the reader is again referred to Mr. Ellis's works, more especially to the last which he published, *Madagascar Revisited* and the *Martyr Church of Madagascar.*

LAST YEARS

1865-72

CHAPTER XV.

THE welcome which the veteran missionary received on his return to England after his last visit to Madagascar was to one of his modest spirit almost overwhelming. The patience that had sustained him in his work through all discouragements, the fortitude and wisdom with which he had overcome the difficulties and dangers of his position, and the unbending integrity and consecration to the great objects of his mission which had characterised his whole course, were widely appreciated, and elicited the hearty admiration of his Christian countrymen. The reception he met with on his first public appearance in Exeter Hall was a truly noble one, and will long be remembered by those who were present. On that occasion, as afterwards, at many interesting public meetings throughout the country, he exhibited among other objects of interest, some of those massive iron chains which had been worn by the persecuted Malagasy Christians, and which he had brought with him to England as eloquent witnesses of the sufferings endured by those martyrs for Christ and His gospel.

A large portion of his time, even up to his last illness, was henceforward employed in attending missionary meetings, or giving lectures, chiefly on Madagascar, to audiences of every class, and in connection with institutions of very diversified character. The first public address of the kind delivered by him, after his last return to England, was in Wisbeach, before the members of the 'Working Men's Institute,' established in that town, and with whom he was always pleased to identify himself.   His fellow-townsmen, of all classes and denominations, were indeed foremost to 'do him reverence.'   On the occasion of this same visit they entertained him at a public breakfast, at which the vicar, Dr. Howson, presided, and men of various shades of religious opinion laid aside their differences, and met to vie with each other in giving a cordial welcome to their guest.   It may here be mentioned, in passing, that his friends at Wisbeach—the earliest and truest he had ever known—have since his death bestirred themselves, in a manner that redounds to their honour, to perpetuate his memory among them.   In addition to other mementoes of his connection with the town, they have placed his portrait, painted in oil by Maul, in the hall of the 'Working Men's Institute,' and a beautiful marble bust, by William Day Keyworth, in the museum, where it stands beside the memorials of another distinguished townsman, the venerable Clarkson, the associate of Wilberforce in his early efforts to emancipate the slave.   This very interesting and well-furnished museum contains, moreover, specimens of the products and manufactures of the South Sea Islands and Madagascar, contributed by Mr. Ellis or members of his family; and here also have been deposited many of the negatives of the photographs taken by him in Madagascar.

Among other tokens by which men aimed to show the high estimation in which he was held, he was elected one of the Vice-Presidents of the British and Foreign Bible Society; and honours of the like kind were tendered him by various institutions, scientific as well as religious.

Those who have followed his career thus far will scarcely need to be told that he was not even yet content to rest upon his laurels.   He could have enjoyed ease and repose in the delightful retirement of Rose Hill, but his heart was too warmly interested in the condition of the people amongst whom he had laboured so assiduously, and too deeply imbued with the missionary spirit, to allow him to be merely an idle spectator of the Church's conflicts and triumphs.   The interest of Madagascar especially became henceforth the object of his life—the passion of his soul. There was no sacrifice, no effort within the compass of possibility, which he was not ready to make on behalf of the Church of Christ in that country. ' " I will go anywhere for Madagascar," he said, when mentioning some prospective engagements to preach or lecture for the Mission ; and, upon Earl Russell's congratulating him, at one of the Cheshunt festivals, on having returned safely from the island, he immediately replied, "My lord, I am ready to go out again." This was at seventy-six years of age. Quiet and almost un-demonstrative as he usually was in manner, he could be roused into the intensest interest about Madagascar, and in anything that concerned missionary work he was an enthusiast. This subject lay nearest to his heart, and therefore came the most readily and frequently to his lips. Together with a keen intelligence, he had much sympathy, for without this he could never have understood so perfectly as he did the wants of the Malagasy. And down to the last moments of consciousness his heart beat true to the cause he so nobly served.'*

In addition to the publication of *Madagascar Revisited*, and the *Martyr Church*, one of the first literary labours in which he engaged after his return home was preparing for the press an edition of the Malagasy Bible. At this work he toiled most assiduously, shutting himself up, we are told, for weeks together in one of the rooms of the mission house, where he could be most secure from interruption.

Not long after he threw his best powers into a labour of love and the cause of justice, by writing a *Vindication of the American Mission in the Sandwich Islands*. The circumstances which led to the publication of this masterly, though temperate, pamphlet are too well known to need more than brief recapitulation, for the whole affair aroused much attention at the time, and the issue has become notorious. A number of Episcopalians,

* Obituary notice of William Ellis, by the Rev. J. W. Blore, in the *Christian Family*.

resident in Honolulu, the chief port of Oahu, had, with the sanction of the King of the Sandwich Islands, who, it was affirmed, favoured that ecclesiastical system, written to England —to Mr. Ellis among others—for an Episcopal clergyman to be sent out to that island.   In the letter written to Mr. Ellis on the subject, the suitable character of the clergyman, and a decided preference for one of 'Evangelical' views, were very distinctly intimated.   This request received additional attention in consequence of a visit paid to England by Queen Emma, the reigning consort of the Sandwich Islands, who excited much interest in this country.   It so happened that the gentlemen who chiefly moved in the matter, at the head of whom was the Bishop of Oxford, belonged to the Ritualistic party in the Church, who, with their accustomed zeal, and in conformity with their views of ecclesiastical polity, would not rest content with sending a single clergyman to this distant and limited station, but resolved to establish an episcopate in the islands.   The Bishop of Oxford, in advocating his scheme, had very unfairly, if not ignored the labours of the American missionaries, at least represented them as illiterate men, of ascetic and puritanical principles, wholly ill-fitted to present the Gospel in an attractive form to the volatile and sensuous islanders.   These unfounded statements, and the total misapprehension of the condition and character of the heathen evinced in the Bishop's representations, called forth the publication in which Mr. Ellis ably vindicated the worth of the American missionaries, demonstrated the marked success of their labours, and explained the real condition of the people, and the circumstances which led to the request for an Episcopal clergyman.   In the interest of peace and catholic religion the writer of the pamphlet also appealed to Christian brethren of all denominations to adhere, in their dealings with the heathen, to the principle of non-interference with the work of kindred institutions, a principle that had been consistently adopted by the Church Missionary Society.   There was ample field, he contended, for the work of all, without distracting the minds of the untutored heathen with the spectacle of a discordant Christianity. 'The Supreme Ruler of the world,' writes Mr. Ellis, towards the close of this appeal, ' seems by the events of His Providence, to be giving us India, and opening to us China and Africa, as well as other parts of Asia; to be calling the varied sections of His Church to the great work of turning the nations of the earth from dumb idols to serve the living God. Among the band of faithful men whom the Churches are sending forth to this work, the venerable antiquity, the exalted rank, the vast resources, which belong to the Church of England, and the dauntless courage which the adherents of that Church have inscribed on the page of our nation's history, point out the front ranks, the high places of the field, where the difficulties are the most formidable, and the struggle most arduous, as the position which belongs to the Church of England, and which her sons would most appropriately occupy. That Church neither does justice to herself, nor achieves all the good that she might in the world, with such wide and transcendently glorious prospects before her, by using any part of her great resources and influence in following the march of others who have broken the ranks of the enemy, and merely gathering up the spoils of a field already won.'

This plain exposition of facts, by one who knew whereof he affirmed, and this just and forcible appeal to the law of Christian amity, opened the eyes of many well-meaning and right-minded clergymen who had before zealously advocated the scheme, and considerably diminished the number of those who supported it. The plan was nevertheless carried out, and a Bishop with a staff of three clergymen was sent to Honolulu. But the experiment proved a failure ; and after only a brief stay in the island the whole party returned to England, and no attempt has since been made to re-occupy the station.

The unsuccessful innovation did not discourage others from agitating for the establishment of an episcopate in Madagascar, the head-quarters of which, notwithstanding the amicable

arrangement for non-interference which had existed between the
Bishop of Mauritius and the London Missionary Society, it was
proposed to establish in Antananarivo. The project was so far
accomplished that a Bishop for the newly projected diocese was
appointed in the person of the Rev. R. H. Baynes, of Coventry.
The Church Missionary Society, however, and many persons like
minded, considering that in the case of Madagascar there were
peculiar reasons for abstaining from all opposition to the work
of evangelization that had already been carried on with such
signal success, expressed in unequivocal terms their protest
against the design, and with such effect, that Mr. Baynes, having
put himself in communication with that society, and also with
Mr. Ellis, ' who received him,' he tells us, ' with a courtesy he
should always gratefully remember,' resigned his appointment,
and withdrew altogether from the contemplated enterprise.
Earl Granville, also, as the head of the Foreign Department of
Her Majesty's Government, and the Archbishop of Canterbury,
in view of all the circumstances, declined to sanction the creation
of the proposed bishopric ; so that the evil, which in the interest
of religion and harmony Mr. Ellis was always foremost to
deprecate and most strenuous in efforts to avert, was, for a time
at least, warded off.

With the rapid succession of important events in Madagascar,
and the marvellous progress of the Gospel among the people
throughout the country, the interest, the zeal, and the activity
of its ' apostle,' as he has been justly designated, kept even pace.
His energies seemed always to rise with the occasion, and to be
equal to the demand upon them. He virtually ignored the fact,
and every one else unconsciously forgot that he was growing old.
Work was assigned to him, and cheerfully undertaken, which
would have been arduous to most men in the prime of their
power. Witness the following programme of appointments in the
West of England, and which is only a sample of similar crowded
engagements. A friend thus writes from Leominster, under
date November 2, 1867 :—' I have written to ——— to tell

him that you will preach at Ludlow on *Sunday*, the 17th, and
that he may advertise you for two sermons on that day, and
that you are willing to lecture there on *Monday* evening, the
18th. You will then be able to devote *Tuesday*, the 19th, to
us at Leominster, and we will try to get you a good meeting in
the Corn Exchange. I have written to Ross, to offer them
Wednesday, the 20th ; also to Hereford for *Thursday*, the 21st,
to ask them to get you *two* meetings —one in the afternoon and
the other in the evening—as at Worcester. I have also written
to Cirencester, proposing that you should visit them on *Friday*,
the 22nd. Now, would you like a meeting at either Cheltenham
or Gloucester on Friday afternoon ? Or do you think this is
already quite as much work as you incline to undertake ? '

On all matters connected with Madagascar he was, at the
Mission House, the prime mover and the chief authority. He
regularly attended the meetings of the Board, besides special
Committee meetings, and never a week passed without more
than one journey from Hoddesdon to London on such business.
So earnest was he in the interests that lay nearest to his heart,
that his brethren, more moderate in their zeal, and more dis-
tracted by other claims, could not always go along with him ;
and he would occasionally return home from these meetings, if
he had failed in some cherished plan, discouraged and weary,
yet too excited to sleep. His was not, however, a temperament
to be easily cast down ; and disappointment only stimulated him
to fresh effort till success had rewarded his endeavours. The
logic of events came at length in aid of his arguments. Each
mail brought fresh tidings of wondrous changes in the far
country, and among the last efforts he was permitted to make,
he issued, with the full and cordial concurrence of the Directors,
his special plea to British Christians for additional funds to aid
in spreading the Gospel in Madagascar. In this 'statement
and appeal,' dated February 7th, 1872, the condition and claims
of the once heathen land were briefly and powerfully set forth,
and the demand for Christian sympathy and help was enforced

with irresistible cogency. The religious destitution of the province of Betsileo, having a population, exclusive of children
and slaves, exceeding 100,000 persons, and which stood most in
need of enlightenment, is thus described :—' Some of the towns
are supplied with native teachers; but large numbers of the
people meet in places where they have built chapels, and come
and sit in silence every Lord's day, without anyone to speak to
them or pray with them ; at times repeating sentences which
they have heard the Christians use. Occasionally, after sitting
the usual time, perhaps an hour or more, a man will rise, and
lifting his hands will look up and say, " O God, we wish to
worship Thee, but do not know how. Teach us, O God, how to
pray, or send some one to teach us." At other times the chief
will rise up at the time of dispersion and say, " Is it well with
you ? " The people will answer, " It is well with us," and then
all will leave the place.

' No condition,' the statement continues, ' can be more critical, no appeals more moving, than those now presented by
these people. They have built houses for worship, in which
they assemble and wait Sunday after Sunday, willing to pray,
and hoping to hear of that " Lord over all," who is " rich unto
all that call upon Him "; but no desired teacher comes, and
they return in disappointment, and some, perhaps, in sorrow,
without having heard one word about Him who came from
heaven to seek and to save, without having implored one
blessing at His hand. But " how shall they hear without a
preacher? how shall they preach except they be sent ? " '

Besides the issue of this printed document, he wrote with his
own hand countless letters, enclosing a copy of the appeal
with each, to the friends of missions over the country. . Not
many days elapsed before replies came pouring in, expressing
the warmest sympathy with the cause he had advocated, and
giving evidence of the genuineness of the feeling by liberal
contributions for the mission ; so that within a very few weeks
Mr. Ellis had personally collected about £7,000 towards the
special fund.

The money having been thus generously and freely given, the next step was to engage suitable men as missionaries. And with this object in view, the indefatigable friend of Madagascar visited the various Nonconformist theological seminaries in the country, and addressed the students on the claims of the people whose cause he was espousing, and on the grandeur of mission work in general. He conversed also with those who manifested a desire to engage in such work : and as the result of these visits, he had the satisfaction of enlisting several young men for missionary service, who have since gone forth to preach the glad tidings of salvation to the Malagasy, and who give promise of becoming zealous and efficient ministers of the Gospel.

Thus was the servant of the Lord employed—giving every day of his life, every faculty of his being, and every thought of his heart to the cause of his Divine Master—when the summons came, announcing that his work was done, and calling him to his rest and his reward. The end of his earthly course was such as he would have chosen, had choice been permitted—such as, with humble submission to the Divine will, he had prayed for—the power and opportunity to work to the last for Him whom his soul loved—a calm dismissal in the midst of his usefulness—a welcome mandate, bidding him from the service to the ' joy of his Lord.'

No failure of health, no feebleness of mind or body forewarned him of his end ; and while habitually mindful of the vanity of human projects, and holding himself ready for the great change, he was still looking forward to much work and much enjoyment. Only the week before his last brief illness he wrote to his son, telling him that he had seldom felt better or worked harder than he had done during the preceding twelve months, and expressing the pleasure with which he anticipated his projected visit with his wife and daughter to England. Before the letter reached its destination, the busy hand had lost its ' cunning,' the loving heart was for ever still.

The same state of mind is evident in another letter, written a day or two later, and which derives additional interest from the fact of its being the last he wrote. It is addressed to his youngest sister, Mrs. Barnard, residing at Bath, and bears date May 31st, 1872. After an affectionate reference to his sister's children, who were just recovering from a serious illness, he thus proceeds :—

' I thank you much for all you say about my coming to see you, and can only assure you that you cannot more earnestly desire a visit from me than I do to see you, for I have long mourned over the distance that separates us, and our meeting so seldom. I want to see you, my dear sister, I want to congratulate you and your family on the recovery of your dear children, and to sympathise with you, and to tell you how much I have felt for you during this long and heavy trial, and how I rejoice with you all in the goodness of God as manifested towards you in its alleviation. But while I feel all this, I feel also that we must keep our minds prepared for whatever in the Providence of God may occur to prevent my carrying out my wishes. I believe that both you and I desire to look fairly in the face every contingency that may delay or prevent our seeing each other, although at present, I see no cause for either. But I want you, my beloved sister, to be *strong* to *bear* and *true and tender* to feel; I *know* you are the latter, and I believe you are the former too, and this is one great source of the strength of my entire confidence in you. I could confide anything to your keeping, even my life itself, if it were necessary, to the keeping of your strength of character and your love.

' I say nothing to your sister about my wishes and intentions until after Monday next, when I expect to go to the Mission House, and I shall then know definitely about my engagements. I purpose devoting a week to my visit, if that will not be troubling you too much, or intruding too long on your family.

'There is much, my own dear sister, that I want to talk to you about, but I leave it all till we meet again. I am thankful to be as well as I am, for although I have worked very hard lately, and am excessively tired at night, I sleep soundly, my appetite

is good, and I am all right again in the morning.   I am cheered
and gladdened too by the encouraging accounts of your dear
children, and that your own strength is returning and your
spirit reviving after the long season of anxiety and toil that you
have had.

'I expect to be at home every forenoon of next week, and I do
not know of any engagement till I go to Nottingham for the
16th, 17th, and 18th.   After this, I hope to arrange to come to
see you.   Assuring you, my beloved sister, that nothing I can
control will prevent my seeing you; and with kindest regards to
Mr. Barnard, and love to all, *especially* to the invalids,

' Ever believe me,

' Faithfully and affectionately yours,

' W. ELLIS.'

The illness which set in three days after the above letter was
penned, frustrated all these plans, and put an end to all earthly
intercourse.   On Monday, June 3rd, he went, as usual, to the
Mission House, to attend a meeting of Directors.   Having
occasion to go by Lea Bridge and Stratford, he was long
detained, and, the day being cold, was much chilled while
waiting at the stations.   He returned home, somewhat late in
the evening, very weary, and suffering bitterly from cold—a
feeling which the usual appliances failed to relieve.   On the
following morning, after passing a restless night, he received a
visit from his medical attendant, who pronounced him seriously
ill, with congestion or incipient inflammation.   The disorder
rapidly became manifest as pneumonia, and though unattended
by any violent pain, was very depressing in its effects, and mastered the patient's waning strength and exhausted vital power.

During the early part of the week he was able to be removed
for some hours daily to a couch in his study; but was so
oppressed with the malady that weighed him down as to be unable to give attention to passing events.   Even letters from
Madagascar, that arrived at the time, remained unopened.   He
roused himself, however, to hold an interview with two minis-

terial brethren, one of whom had recently returned from that country, and the other was expecting to go there. These visitors were the only persons, besides the members of the family and the physicians, who entered the sick chamber. He was loth to be disturbed, and at times appeared to prefer the quiet of solitude to the presence of even those nearest and dearest to him. He was, however, too ill to be left alone, and the watchers by his bedside merely retired out of sight, but remained within hearing, and could catch the frequent utterances of ejaculatory prayer that fell from his lips—such as 'Lord, grant me patience, self-control, ability not to think of myself, but of those whose sufferings are far greater than my own,' and similar petitions, mingled occasionally with a pitiful prayer for rest, of which the constant and distressing cough deprived him.

Almost from the beginning of the attack he seems to have looked for a fatal result, but was nothing daunted by such a prospect. Conversing on the subject with his niece, who chiefly shared with Mrs. Ellis the duty of attending upon him, he said that on Tuesday he had such assuring and delightful glimpses into the unseen world, that notwithstanding the depressing effect of his illness, his spirit had been greatly refreshed.

On Thursday his mind rambled occasionally, being much occupied with his engagements at Nottingham, and it was at times only by strong persuasion that he could be prevented from attempting to rise. This half-unconscious state increased somewhat on the two following days, the Nottingham Meetings appearing still the chief subject of disquiet, while occasionally his memory would carry him back to the early days at Kingsland. On Saturday night, it became manifest to all that the end was drawing near. Just before dawn on Sunday morning, while his attendants were watching silently and sadly around his couch, after having remained awhile unusually still, he suddenly put himself, as it were, in the position of one addressing an audience, and then with distinct utterance, and in a most collected and impressive manner, delivered a charge, apparently to the Directors of the Missionary Society, begging them to excuse his failing to keep the engagement at Nottingham, as ' the hand of the Lord had laid him on a sick bed,' resigning his trust into other hands, and ending by taking a most affectionate and solemn leave of his ' brethren,' and invoking upon them the benediction of the Almighty. So startled—so awe-struck—were the bystanders, that they could afterwards recal only few of the words that were spoken ; but the strange solemnity and impressiveness of the scene will never be forgotten by any who were present. After this he lay still for some hours, with a sweet expression of peace on his countenance. A little after eight in the morning, his wife and niece had retired from the chamber, but were almost immediately recalled to witness the end. All was calm and serene. The breathing gently subsided into a sigh, and while tearful eyes were looking their last on him they loved, the spirit had taken its flight, and the venerated form was invested with the majesty of death.

Little remains to be recorded. The tidings of the almost sudden removal of one, who, though full of years, had been also full of vigour and work to the last, came upon every one as a surprise ; and a feeling of unfeigned sorrow, of tender respect, and of sympathy for the surviving members of the family, was shared by all who had known the departed servant of God. A deputation from the Missionary Society promptly waited upon Mrs. Ellis, then herself upon a sick bed, to request that the Directors might be allowed to take the charge of the funeral. The proposal was gratifying to the stricken widow, who willingly gave her consent, observing, ' It is right ; it is as it should be ; he deserves all honour at their hands.' It was arranged that the funeral should take place on the following Friday, and the grave in Abney Park Cemetery, where the youngest daughter of the deceased was buried, was selected for the place of interment. On the day appointed a large number of friends assembled at Rose Hill to accompany the funeral procession, and a still larger

concourse gathered at the grave to pay the last tribute of respect
to the dead.   The aspect of the quiet village of Hoddesdon on
the occasion was strangely impressive, and eloquent of the high
estimation in which he who was taken from them had been held.
The streets were almost deserted, the windows of the private
houses were darkened, and the shops were closed ; an air of
solemnity and mourning pervaded the place, while young and
old, rich and poor alike, seemed anxious to testify their love
and esteem for one who had endeared himself to all by his un-
deviating integrity and constant kindness—whose face they
should see no more.

On the following Lord's-day a funeral sermon was preached
at Hoddesdon, in the chapel of which the deceased had been
minister, by the Foreign Secretary of the London Missionary
Society, the Rev. Dr. Mullens, who selected for his text on the
occasion the passage of Scripture in 2 Timothy ii. 21, 22—
' But in a great house,' &c.   The sermon was afterwards
delivered at Union Chapel, Islington ; and in several of the
Metropolitan pulpits, as well as elsewhere, the lessons suggested
by the missionary's holy life and peaceful death were made the
subject of special discourses.

But the story is not yet all told.   The closing scenes of one
life derived additional pathos from another touching yet happy
departure, which closely followed in the same household.
Scarcely was the old man laid in his grave, ere the wife of his
bosom, who for thirty-five years had been the sharer of his
deepest joys and sorrows, the faithful friend and counsellor in
every triumph and trial—the light of his home—keeping near
him, as it were, to the last, passed the same portal to her
eternal rest, and the dear companionship of earth, interrupted
only for a few brief days, was resumed in another and a better
world.

The course of Mrs. Ellis's illness was in every respect very
similar to that of her husband—rapid, restless, and depressing
—and followed closely in its wake.   Soon after the head of the

house had breathed his last, and the sorrowing family had mingled for awhile their irrepressible tears, the chief mourner of the group desired to be left alone in the chamber, and passed some time in the holy presence of her dead. Strengthened, doubtless, by communion with her Heavenly Father, she then roused herself to give attention to some necessary business, principally to writing a few letters to absent members of the family. Having retired to rest, she woke during the night, with an unusual sensation of cold, quickly followed by burning heat; and other symptoms of the fatal malady showed themselves in rapid succession. Her physician, who visited her in the morning, took a serious view of the case, and her own impression from the first was that she would not recover. The disorder was characterised more by oppression and restlessness than by pain. During its progress she retained, for the most part, her consciousness, and even busied her mind with household cares from which others were most anxious to relieve her. She was thoughtful for everyone about her, pitifully watching the pale and wearied faces of her attendants, and prompt to express a most pathetic contrition for the least sign of impatience that might escape her, observing on one occasion—'I always thought myself so brave—so brave—but pain is easy to bear compared with this excessive weariness and oppression.' She could scarcely refrain from giving herself needless concern respecting the arrangements for the funeral; although, through the considerate care of sympathising neighbours, particularly of their long-tried and true-hearted friend Mr. Prior, who was always at hand to tender every alleviation and assistance that thoughtful kindness could suggest, the sorrowing members of the family were spared all trouble and anxiety about such distressing details.

On the day of her husband's burial, Mrs. Ellis was calm and collected, placing her watch on a table by her bedside, that she might calculate and mentally follow the solemn procession on its way to the cemetery. In reference to her own funeral, she

expressed a wish that she might be laid in the 'Friends'' grave-
yard at Hoddesdon—that she might be borne to the grave by
' poor men,' and followed to her last resting-place by true and
loving hearts without any parade of mourning.

On the night of Saturday, the last of her earthly existence,
she seemed for a while slightly delirious, but her imagination
presented visions of beauty, and she spoke of the flowers that
she saw—'oh such beautiful flowers,' she added, 'we shall not
need to wear our little yellow roses there.' The delirium was
only transient, however, and consciousness soon returned. Occasionally, looking upward with much solemnity, and clasping
her hands, she would give utterance to her soul in prayer.
Towards morning she appeared easier, very calm, and much
refreshed by a brief period of sleep. Her heart seemed full to
overflowing of gratitude and love to all around her. She
addressed her weeping maid with touching kindness, commending the value of her devotion to herself, and saying how greatly
she esteemed such faithful service, and how acceptable it was
in God's sight as well as man's.

During the course of the day—Sunday—she received a visit,
which greatly pleased her, from a very near and dear friend, who
had come from a distance to see her. Her nephew also was
admitted into her chamber, and greeted with her peculiar
sweetness and kindliness of welcome. To her medical attendant
she expressed her reluctance to take any stimulant, as she wished
to have, in her last hours, 'a clear mind and an unclouded
spirit.'

All the afternoon her thoughts were busy and seemed to fly
fast and far. She spoke much and cheerfully, now telling her
friend of her beautiful pony, 'her sweet Fanny,' and begging
her niece not to allow her favourite to go where she would be
uncared for or hard worked; then earnestly entreating her loving
attendants to take a little sorely needed rest—tranquil and content as regarded herself, but full of consideration for others.
'Throughout her illness,' observes her niece, from whose memo-

randa this brief account has been compiled, 'her peculiar brightness shone out in every little thing, so that the charm, as well as the sadness, of those few last days will always be remembered by those who were with her.   She spoke much of the love of Jesus.   She dwelt also on the great kindness of all her friends; and in enumerating her blessings, she looked round upon those who were in the room, and added, "and to be surrounded by all of you whom I so much love—it is like a bit of heaven."'   She continued calmly conscious to the last, even expressing her desire that her domestics should attend the evening service at which Dr. Mullens was to preach her husband's funeral sermon. But a little before the usual hour of public worship, she suddenly became very quiet, and in a few minutes gently breathed her last.

The announcement of her death was made to the congregation gathered to hear Dr. Mullens' discourse; and those who were present will not easily forget the solemnity and awe which fell upon the assembly when the tidings reached them.

Thus closed, almost simultaneously, two lives that for half the term of human existence had been united in the closest of earthly relationships.   Death scarcely parted them.   The angel of the Lord opened the gate of Heaven to one, and while the other still lingered at the portal, bade her also enter.

CHAPTER XVI.

GENERAL ESTIMATE OF MR. ELLIS'S CHARACTER AND WORK.

BY HENRY ALLON, D.D.

THE qualities which, in their individual excellence, and their
unusual combination, gave Mr. Ellis a place so distinctive and
eminent among the missionaries of this nineteenth century, will
be sufficiently apparent from the preceding narrative of his
work.   It is only in deference to the modest feeling of the bio-
grapher that this more formal estimate of them is appended.
Above most kindred societies the London Missionary Society has
had a continuous series of eminent men, whose remarkable gifts
and consecration, have not only achieved much in their distinctive missionary work, but have incidentally contributed much
to civilization, science, and commerce.   Some have won a renown
which extends far beyond the circle of their own associations.   It
is sufficient to mention the names of Dr. Morrison, Dr. Med-
hurst, and Dr. Legge, of China ; Dr. Vanderkemp, Dr. Phillip,
Dr. Moffatt, and Dr. Livingstone, of Africa ; and of John
Williams and William Ellis, of the South Sea Islands.   Each
name is apostolic in its missionary achievements, and is connected
imperishably with the Christianity of the country ; while either
in the creation of a national literature, the abolition of slavery,
or the discoveries of travel, it has an honourable place in the
history of human progress.

Mr. Ellis stands in the foremost rank of these illustrious
men, and, among them, occupies a distinctive place.   By

his fervent piety and religious earnestness he did much in preaching and diffusing the Gospel of Christ. By his intellectual endowments and scientific attainments, he achieved works on the history, archæology, and physical characteristics of Polynesia and Madagascar, which are a contribution to the sum of human knowledge, and give him an honourable place among literary and scientific men. By his singular wisdom and statesmanlike qualities he became the trusted councillor of the Government of Madagascar, in the supreme crisis of its transition from heathen barbarism to Christian civilization. His high Christian integrity, and his uncompromising principles of civil and religious liberty, enabled him to counteract unprincipled devices which would have been fatal to the nascent political, commercial, and ecclesiastical freedom of the nation of Madagascar, and to imbue the new constitution with principles of self-government, equity, and freedom, which have probably determined its destiny, and will continue to bear fruit so long as it is a nation. It is not too much to say that to Mr. Ellis alone it is owing that Madagascar is at this moment a free, constitutional, and Protestant country. Christian, in any case, it probably would have become—the seeds of Christianity had been planted and had produced fruit before Mr. Ellis visited the island—but his wisdom in the great crisis of transition largely determined what character its Christianity should assume, whether that of simple spiritual truth and freedom, or that of Romish superstition and bondage; what ecclesiastical organisation its churches should assume, whether that of self-regulated freedom or that of hierarchical authority; and what should be the relations of the latter to the civil government, whether those of subordination and dependence, or those of spiritual and pecuniary independence. Through his counsels and urgencies, the churches of Madagascar have probably been saved from the disastrous history and issue of Established Churches in all nations. Few men in modern times have been called upon to discharge such a mission, few

have possessed such a combination of qualifications for it, and
few have achieved a success so disinterested and noble.   To the
Madagascar of future generations William Ellis will be, only in
a far simpler and nobler character, what Augustine was to
England, what Boniface was to Germany, what Patrick was to
Ireland, with the great distinction that, unlike them, he had
forged no chains to bind the Christian energies and life of the
Malagasy.

My own personal acquaintance with Mr. Ellis began in 1841,
just after his removal to Rose Hill, Hoddesdon, and soon after
I entered the College at Cheshunt as a theological student.
One of the admirable adjuncts of the College is a group of
village chapels and preaching stations, which are under the
care of the students, and at which they conduct religious
services and in some cases Sunday schools.   Besides the
religious benefit to these villages which these services may
confer, they are a very important part of the ministerial training
of the College ; they keep alive the religious sensibilities of the
students, and they are invaluable exercises in the art of preaching.   In 1841 the little chapel at Hoddesdon was thus under
the care of the students, and three or four other of these
stations were within two or three miles of Rose Hill.

With characteristic hospitality, Mr. and Mrs. Ellis made all
the students feel that not only was their house at all times open
to them, but that their presence gave unaffected pleasure to
their host and hostess.

In my own case, some common associations with the north of
England on the part of Mrs. Ellis, soon caused this intercourse to
ripen into a warmer feeling, and a friendship was the result which,
uninterruptedly maintained for thirty years, ended only with
their death ; it was frequent and pleasant in intercourse, always
cordial in feeling, and often confidential in character.   In the
events connected with Mr. Ellis's visits to Madagascar especially,
and in his delicate and various relations to the London Missionary
Society, of which also I was a Director, I had peculiar opportunities

of knowing his most secret thoughts, and of seeing the workings of his high toned principles and feelings.   The result is the impression of a character of wise goodness, unaffected piety, and simple self sacrifice, almost perfect.   I am at a loss to vindicate myself from a too partial estimate of my revered friend by the specification of any defect, or even the suggestion of any qualification.   I never heard from him a word, nor saw in him a feeling that did not deepen my reverence for him, as a saintly man, and a consecrated servant of Christ.   Mr. Ellis doubtless had his defects, but if so, he had so far corrected them, that not only were they not apparent in the intercourse of friendship, but I may venture to affirm they were never discovered by the devoted and gifted wife, who survived him but a single week. Mrs. Ellis was a woman whose intellectual strength and penetration were of a very high order, and whose robust common sense made any kind of weak conjugal sentimentality simply impossible to her.   Her bearing towards her husband was simple, natural, and full of self respect, her judgments were independent, and her deportment was unusually self reliant: but notwithstanding this, and although she was married to Mr. Ellis when both were in middle life, she regarded him with an admiration and affection that were almost a worship.   She watched the formation of his purposes concerning Madagascar with a wifely anxiety that she could not wholly conceal, but at the same time with a reverence that hindered a single word which might influence them wrongly.   She knew them to be so pure, disinterested and noble, that they were to her almost as inspirations of God ; the process of their formation was so purely religious, that she felt they ought not to be intermeddled with.   Again and again I have heard her say, and especially when the peculiar circumstances of the family caused her an anxiety, which was almost an agony, that ' nobody could know how good he was.'

As an illustration of the noble feelings of both, I must be permitted to refer again to an incident already mentioned in the biography.   My wife and I were the guests at Rose Hill re-

x

ferred to on page 245, when Mr. Ellis received information concerning the death of the Queen of Madagascar.   It was on
October 8, 1861.   The letters were brought in when we were
at breakfast.   He read the one from Madagascar with the rest,
and put it down upon the table, not so much as a glance indi-
cating to us that there was in it anything extraordinary; although I fancied even at the moment that Mrs. Ellis looked
enquiringly if not anxiously, when he was reading the suspicious
looking foreign letter.   The conversation which had been bright
and jocular was resumed.   Soon after breakfast was finished, I
found myself alone with him in his orchid house, I do not remember how.   He was very grave.   His first words were, 'I have
received a letter from Madagascar, the Queen is dead, I must go.'
After a few particulars concerning the event and its bearings,
he began to speak about his family circumstances, the critical
state of his daughter's health, Mrs. Ellis's responsibilities at
Rawdon House, and the impossibility of her accompanying him,
as I had ventured to suggest.   He knew that in all human
probability he would see his child no more.   He knew that he
was leaving to Mrs. Ellis a heavy burden of domestic responsibility and sorrow, but the conclusion at which he had intuitively
arrived never for a moment wavered.   'And now,' he said, 'I
must go and tell Mrs. Ellis.'   What passed between them during
the half-hour of secret confidence which followed, no one knows.
Our own hearts were full of highly wrought reverence for him
and of sympathy for her, which could find expression only in
prayers for both.   Mrs. Ellis appeared full of deep emotion, the
frequent tear gathering and falling as she spoke; but with a
noble appreciation of the crisis, and with a faith and self sacrifice equal to his own, she had accepted the conclusion to which
he had come, as the only one possible.

Within a couple of hours, Mr. Ellis and myself were on our
way to London to convey the intelligence to the Mission House,
and to proffer to the Directors the service which he purposed,
and which of course they thankfully and joyfully accepted.

Every member of the board felt that God had given us, for the work that was now to be done, not only a man whose qualifications were pre-eminent, but one whose spirit of simple unhesitating self-sacrifice had scarcely ever been surpassed in the annals of the Church.

As the basis of Mr. Ellis's qualification for his missionary work must be recognised, the peculiar simplicity and entireness of his piety. No doubt he had his spiritual struggles and his religious imperfections; his remarkable letter to Dr. Hamilton indicates his own deep sense of them; but religious principles and affections had taken possession of him in an unusual degree. In many religious men, we see a certain inchoateness and vacillation—alternations of spiritual and unspiritual feeling, of church habit and worldly habit—which indicate, not insincere, but very partial religious life. In Mr. Ellis, religious life was deep and pervading; it was the inspiration and sentiment of everything that he did; it ruled with apparent entireness and ease every consideration and purpose of his life. His son intimates that constitutionally, he was warm in temper. It is difficult for those who knew him only in the latter half of his life to imagine this: so completely was every word and feeling subdued to gentleness of bearing, thoughtfulness of meaning, and kindly considerateness for others, that he seemed incapable of provocation or resentment. Probably this was the result of religious discipline; if so, the victory was a remarkable one. Hence in the great questions of service that came before him, the manifest solicitude that dominated every consideration was—What was his duty to his Divine Master and what were his obligations to his fellow-men? It often seemed to me as if he never had to struggle with the selfish considerations that are so powerful in other men, and cause them to hesitate about duty when it is the most unequivocal; his only difficulty seemed to lie in the determination of duty itself—once this was clear to him, his obedience was unhesitating and instinctive. Because debate seemed impossible effort seemed unnecessary. This is the great characteristic of entireness. Few men have brought their entire nature under religious control more completely than Mr. Ellis did. To the same pervading religiousness of feeling and purpose may be attributed the clear and prompt spiritual discernment that so eminently characterised Mr. Ellis. Robert Hall once said of Paley that he never would put his foot into the other world if he could find a place for it in this. Exactly the reverse may be said of Mr. Ellis. Instinctively he judged all things in the light of spiritual principles; they were regarded by him as means and influences of spiritual things. His Biblical teachings were of spiritual principles, and aimed at spiritual results: his ecclesiastical polity was in order to the realisation of the highest spiritual truth, worship, freedom, and life: his political counsel sought the moral elevation and self-government of the people. A man who accustoms himself thus to look at the principles and influences of things rather than at their traditions or forms, will estimate them most justly, and will be the wisest counsellor in all things, even in the most secular things of life: his 'eye being single, his whole body will be full of light.' Mr. Ellis was full of calm, clear, practical wisdom. He carried every question into the domain of great principles, and thus solved it in the truest, most catholic, and most permanent way.

Mr. Ellis's patient industry, ready acquisitiveness, and versatile aptitudes very signally contributed to the greatness of his work. His passion for Botany, cultured by his early occupation as a gardener, enabled him to turn his opportunities of observation to good account, and to make important contributions to botanical science, as well as to introduce into different places important food plants. He was a good archæologist. He taught himself the arts of printing, carpentry, cotton culture, and photography. He possessed some knowledge of medicine and surgery, of the latter enough successfully to amputate a limb. He was no mean linguist, and easily acquired languages. In his mental composition there was, too, an imaginative vein, which found expression in poetry of considerable excellence, and in those rich pictorial descriptions of the people and places that came under his observation, which make his books so charming. The historical faculty was strong in him, and gave peculiar and permanent value to his works on Polynesia and Madagascar. In addition to his 'Polynesian Researches,' which won for him the recognition and friendship of some of the most eminent literary men of the day; and his account of his visits to Madagascar, he wrote a history of the latter island before he had any anticipation of visiting it; as also the first volume of a very interesting History of the London Missionary Society. These various aptitudes were combined with a quiet energy which gave him peculiar qualifications for his work. To these characteristics must be added unusual wisdom, perfect self-control, and much Christian magnanimity, as specially evinced in his delicate and difficult relations to the Malagasy Court, to the French authorities there, and especially to Mr. Pakenham, the English Consul, of whose undisguised hostility to him he had many proofs of which he made no public use. Few men would have escaped shipwreck among so many breakers, or would so prudently and magnanimously have used their success. As a preacher, Mr. Ellis was less successful than as a writer. His preaching always excited interest, but a certain monotony of voice and manner was scarcely overcome by his intellectual independence, his spiritual simplicity, and his intense earnestness; while his extemporaneous speaking betrayed him into long, involved sentences, considerable repetition, and sometimes inordinate length, especially in his later years. His quiet, affectionate, steadfast disposition made him a gentle and loving father and husband, and a warm and faithful friend—some degree of social taciturnity and a slight tendency to excess of gravity notwithstanding. The London Missionary Society has had few agents who have done greater service to the people to whom they have been sent, and the Church of Christ has rarely known a more saintly and consecrated man. His character was undemonstrative while it was determined and persistent; his temperament was modest, and yet ardent and enthusiastic; his work was unobtrusive and various; but so far as comparative moral estimates can be formed, there are few concerning whom it could be more emphatically said—' He served his generation according to the will of God.'

LONDON: PRINTED BY
SPOTTISWOODE AND CO., NEW-STREET SQUARE
AND PARLIAMENT STREET

MR. MURRAY'S
LIST OF NEW WORKS.

The NATIONAL MEMORIAL to the PRINCE CONSORT.
Illustrated by Engravings in Line, Mezzotint, Colours, and Wood, of the Monument, its Architecture, Statues, Mosaics, &c. With Descriptive Text. Folio, £12. 12s. half-bound ; large paper copies (only 50 printed), £15. 15s. half-bound ; or special copies in full morocco, £18. 18s.

The SPEAKER'S COMMENTARY on the BIBLE, EXPLANATORY and CRITICAL. By BISHOPS and CLERGY of the ANGLICAN CHURCH. Edited by F. C. COOK, M.A. Canon of Exeter.
VOL. IV.—JOB, PSALMS, PROVERBS, ECCLESIASTES, SONG of SOLOMON. Medium 8vo. 24s.

PERSONAL RECOLLECTIONS, from EARLY LIFE to OLD AGE, of MARY SOMERVILLE. With Selections from her Correspondence. By her DAUGHTER. With Portrait. Crown 8vo. 12s.

The LIFE and DEATH of JOHN OF BARNEVELD. Including the History of the Primary Causes and Movements of 'The Thirty Years' War.' By J. LOTHROP MOTLEY, D.C.L., Author of the 'Rise of the Dutch Republic' &c. With Illustrations. 2 vols. 8vo. 28s.

The MAINTENANCE of the CHURCH of ENGLAND as an ESTABLISHED CHURCH. By Rev. C. HOLE, Rev. R. W. DIXON, and Rev. J. LLOYD. Three Essays, to which the Prizes offered by HENRY W. PEEK, M.P., were awarded. 8vo. 10s. 6d.

The MINOR WORKS of GEORGE GROTE. With Critical Remarks on his Intellectual Character, Writings, and Speeches. By ALEXANDER BAIN, LL.D. With Portrait. 8vo. 14s.

The NATURALIST in NICARAGUA ; a Narrative of a Residence at the Gold Mines of Chontales ; Journeys in the Savannahs and Forests ; with Observations on Animals and Plants in Reference to the Theory of Evolution of Living Forms. By THOMAS BELT, F.G.S. With Illustrations. Post 8vo. 12s.

The MOON. Considered as a PLANET, a WORLD, and a SATELLITE. By JAMES NASMYTH, C.E., and JAMES CARPENTER, F.R.A.S. With numerous Illustrations. 4to. [*Nearly ready.*

MEMOIR of WILLIAM ELLIS, Missionary in the South Seas and Madagascar. By His Son. With an Estimate of his Character and Work. By HENRY ALLON, D.D. With Portrait. 8vo. 10s. 6d.

The SHADOWS of a SICK ROOM. 16mo. 2s. 6d.

The MOSEL ; a Series of Twenty Etchings, with Descriptive Letterpress. By ERNEST GEORGE, Architect. Imperial 4to. 42s.

WORDS of HUMAN WISDOM. Collected and arranged
by E. S. With a Preface by Rev. H. P. LIDDON, D.D., Canon of St. Paul's.
Small 8vo. 3s. 6d.

LECTURES on the GEOGRAPHY of GREECE. By
H. F. TOZER, M.A., Tutor of Exeter Coll. Oxford. Post 8vo. 9s.

The TEN PLAGUES of EGYPT ; or, Signs and Wonders
in the Land of Ham. With Ancient and Modern Parallels and Illustrations.
By Rev. T. S. MILLINGTON. With Woodcuts. Post 8vo. 7s. 6d.

UNIVERSITY SERMONS. Preached at Cambridge,
1845-51. By the late J. J. BLUNT, B.D., Margaret Professor of Divinity.
Post 8vo. 6s.

A CABINET EDITION of Canon ROBERTSON'S HIS-
TORY of the CHRISTIAN CHURCH, from the Apostolic Age to the Reformation, 1517. Vol. I. Post 8vo. 6s. (To be completed in 8 vols.)

HISTORY of the MODERN STYLES of ARCHITEC-
TURE. By JAMES FERGUSSON, F.R.S., D.C.L., Fellow of the Royal Institute
of British Architects. Second Edition. With 330 Illustrations. Medium 8vo.
31s. 6d.

HORSE-SHOEING ; AS IT IS, and AS IT SHOULD
BE. By WILLIAM DOUGLAS, late of 10th Hussars. With Illustrations. Post 8vo.
7s. 6d.

A HISTORY of the ROYAL ARTILLERY. Compiled
from the Original Records. By Captain DUNCAN, R.A. Vol. II. Completing
the Work. 8vo. 15s.

PERILS in the POLAR SEAS: True Stories of Arctic
Adventure and Discovery, for Children. By Mrs. CHISHOLM. With Illustrations. Post 8vo.

An HISTORICAL ATLAS of ANCIENT GEOGRAPHY,
Biblical and Classical. Compiled under the Superintendence of Dr. WM. SMITH
and Mr. GEORGE GROVE. Part III. Folio, 21s.

The HARVEST of the SEA. Including Sketches of
Fisheries and Fisher Folk. By JAMES G. BERTRAM. 3rd Edition. With 50
Illustrations. Post 8vo. 9s.

ADVENTURES on the RIVER AMAZONS. With
Notices of Brazilian and Indian Life during Eleven Years of Travel. By
H. W. BATES, F.R.G.S. Third Edition. With Illustrations. Post 8vo. 7s. 6d.
(Forming the New Volume of 'Murray's Series of Popular Travels and Adven-
tures.')

JOHN MURRAY, Albemarle Street.

ALBEMARLE STREET,
November, 1873.

MR. MURRAY'S
FORTHCOMING WORKS.

THE NATIONAL MEMORIAL TO THE PRINCE CONSORT AT KENSINGTON.

ILLUSTRATED by first-class Engravings in Line, Mezzotint, Colours, and Wood, of the Monument, its Architecture, Decorations; Sculptured Groups, Statues, Mosaics, Metalwork, &c., designed and executed by the most eminent British artists; engraved under direction of LEWIS GRUNER. With Descriptive Text.

24 Plates. Folio. 12 Guineas, half bound. Large Paper (only 50 printed), £15 15s., half bound; or Special Copies in full morocco, £18 18s.

LIFE AND DEATH OF JOHN OF BARNEVELD.

INCLUDING THE HISTORY OF THE PRIMARY CAUSES AND MOVEMENTS OF "THE THIRTY YEARS' WAR."

BY JOHN LOTHROP MOTLEY, D.C.L.,
Author of the "Rise of the Dutch Republic," &c.

With Illustrations. 2 vols. 8vo.

THE ORIGIN AND HISTORY OF THE FIRST OR GRENADIER REGIMENT OF FOOT GUARDS,

From Original Documents in the State Paper Office, Rolls' Records, War Office, Horse Guards, Contemporary Histories, and Regimental Records.

BY LIEUT.-GEN. SIR FREDERICK W. HAMILTON, K.C.B.,
Late Grenadier Guards.

With many Illustrations. 3 vols. 8vo.

A BRIEF MEMOIR OF
THE PRINCESS CHARLOTTE OF WALES,

WITH SELECTIONS FROM HER CORRESPONDENCE AND OTHER UNPUBLISHED PAPERS.

BY LADY ROSE WEIGALL.

With an Original Portrait from a Miniature by Stewart. Post 8vo.

SHADOWS OF A SICK ROOM.
Small 8vo. 2s. 6d. (*Ready.*)

THE
SPEAKER'S COMMENTARY ON THE BIBLE.
BY BISHOPS AND CLERGY OF THE ANGLICAN CHURCH.
EDITED BY F. C. COOK, M.A.,
Canon of Exeter.

VOL. IV.—JOB, PSALMS, PROVERBS, ECCLESIASTES, SONG OF SOLOMON.
By G. H. S. Johnson, M.A., F.R.S., Dean of Wells;—F. C. Cook, M.A., Canon of
Exeter;—C. J. Elliot, Vicar of Winkfield;—E. H. Plumptre, M.A., Prebendary of
St. Paul's;—W. T. Bullock, M.A., Queen's Chaplain at Kensington Palace;—and
T. Kingsbury, M.A., Trinity College, Cambridge.

Medium 8vo.   (*Ready.*)

LECTURES ON THE GEOGRAPHY OF GREECE.
BY H. F. TOZER, M.A., F.R.G.S.,
Exeter Coll., Oxford; Author of "Researches in the Highlands of Turkey."

Post 8vo. (*Ready.*)

UNIVERSITY SERMONS AT CAMBRIDGE.
PREACHED DURING THE YEARS 1845-51.
BY THE LATE J. J. BLUNT, B.D.,
Margaret Professor of Divinity.

Post 8vo.   6s.   (*Ready.*)

NEW JAPAN; THE LAND OF THE RISING SUN:
ITS ANNALS DURING THE PAST TWENTY YEARS : RECORDING THE REMARKABLE PROGRESS OF THE JAPANESE IN WESTERN CIVILIZATION.
BY SAMUEL MOSSMAN,
Author of "China; its History, Inhabitants, &c."

With Map.   8vo.

THE MOON.
CONSIDERED AS A PLANET, A WORLD, AND A SATELLITE.
BY JAMES NASMYTH, C.E.,
AND
JAMES CARPENTER, F.R.A.S.,
Late of Royal Observatory, Greenwich.

Numerous Illustrations.   4to.

A CONCISE DICTIONARY OF THE ENGLISH LANGUAGE.
8vo.   Uniform with "Dr. Wm. Smith's Dictionaries."

"It is desirable that the present needs of the average Englishman should be promptly supplied. He should be provided with a Concise Dictionary in a single volume, neither too heavy nor too costly, close shorn of superfluous detail and speculative fancy, registering compact precise information from the best sources, and always ready to keep him straight and firm in handling the most copious, versatile, and powerful language of the modern world."
—*Quarterly Review.*

*** A STUDENT'S AND SCHOOL-ROOM ENGLISH DICTIONARY.   12mo.

LITERARY REMAINS OF THE LATE EMANUEL DEUTSCH, D.C.L.

CONTENTS.

The Talmud.	Semitic Palæography.	Semitic Languages.
Lectures on the Talmud.	Renan's "Les Apôtres."	Samaritan Pentateuch.
Islam.	Worship of Baalim in Israel.	The Targums.
Egypt, Ancient and Modern.	The Œcumenical Council.	Book of Jasher.
Hermes Trismegistus.	Apostolicæ Sedis.	Arabic Poetry.
Judeo-Arabic Metaphysics.	Roman Passion Drama.	

8vo.

THE MINOR WORKS OF GEORGE GROTE.

WITH CRITICAL REMARKS ON HIS INTELLECTUAL CHARACTER, WRITINGS, AND SPEECHES.

BY PROFESSOR ALEXANDER BAIN, LL.D.

With Portrait. 8vo. 12s. (*Ready.*)

MEMOIR OF WM. ELLIS, MISSIONARY

IN THE SOUTH SEAS AND IN MADAGASCAR.

BY HIS SON.

WITH AN ESTIMATE OF HIS CHARACTER AND WORK BY REV. HENRY ALLON, D.D.

With Portrait. 8vo. (*Ready.*)

PERSONAL RECOLLECTIONS, FROM EARLY LIFE TO OLD AGE.

BY MARY SOMERVILLE.

WITH SELECTIONS FROM HER CORRESPONDENCE.

By her DAUGHTER, MARTHA SOMERVILLE.

With Portrait. Crown 8vo. (*Ready.*)

THE EARLY HISTORY OF INSTITUTIONS,

MORE PARTICULARLY AS ILLUSTRATED BY THE IRISH BREHON LAW.

BY SIR H. SUMNER MAINE, K.C.S.I., D.C.L.,

Corpus Professor of Jurisprudence in the University of Oxford, and formerly Reader in Jurisprudence and Civil Law at Middle Temple.

8vo.

SCHOOLHOUSES FOR THE PEOPLE.

DIRECTIONS FOR ARRANGING AND BUILDING SCHOOLROOMS, &c.

BY E. R. ROBSON.

Architect to the London School Board.

Copiously illustrated with Plans drawn to scale, &c. Post 8vo.

SIGNS AND WONDERS IN THE LAND OF HAM.

A DESCRIPTION OF THE TEN PLAGUES OF EGYPT, WITH ANCIENT AND MODERN
PARALLELS AND ILLUSTRATIONS.

BY THOMAS S. MILLINGTON,
Vicar of Woodhouse Eaves, Loughborough.

With Woodcuts.   Post 8vo.   (*Ready.*)

THE SECOND AND CONCLUDING VOLUME OF

HISTORY OF THE ROYAL ARTILLERY.
Compiled from the Original Records.

BY CAPT. FRANCIS DUNCAN, R.A., LL.D.,
Superintendent of the Regimental Records.

With Frontispiece and Index.   8vo.   15s.   (*Ready.*)

THE MOSEL:
A SERIES OF TWENTY ETCHINGS.
With Descriptive Letterpress.

BY ERNEST GEORGE, ARCHITECT.
Imperial 4to.

THE MAINTENANCE OF THE CHURCH
OF ENGLAND AS AN ESTABLISHED CHURCH.

BY REV. CHARLES HOLE, B.A.—REV. R. W. DIXON, M.A.—
AND REV. JULIUS LLOYD, M.A.

THREE ESSAYS, TO WHICH THE PRIZES
OFFERED BY HENRY W. PEEK, M.P., WERE AWARDED.

8vo.

A SMALL COUNTRY HOUSE.

A BRIEF PRACTICAL DISCOURSE ON THE PLANNING OF A RESIDENCE
TO COST FROM £2000 TO £5000.

BY ROBERT KERR, ARCHITECT,
Author of "The English Gentleman's Home."

12mo.

A CABINET EDITION OF

CANON ROBERTSON'S HISTORY OF THE
CHRISTIAN CHURCH,

FROM THE APOSTOLIC AGE TO THE REFORMATION, 1517.

To be completed in 8 vols.   Post 8vo.   Vol. I., 6s.   (*Ready.*)

ENGLAND AND RUSSIA IN THE EAST.

A SERIES OF PAPERS ON THE POLITICAL AND GEOGRAPHICAL
CONDITION OF CENTRAL ASIA.

BY MAJOR-GEN. SIR HENRY RAWLINSON, K.C.B., F.R.S.
Member of the Council of India.

With Map. 8vo.

PROVERBS OR WORDS OF HUMAN WISDOM.

COLLECTED AND ARRANGED BY E. S.

WITH A PREFACE BY THE REV. H. P. LIDDON, D.D., Canon of St. Paul's.

Fcap. 8vo. (*Ready.*)

PERILS OF THE POLAR SEAS.

STORIES OF ARCTIC ADVENTURE FOR CHILDREN.

BY MRS. CHISHOLM.

Illustrations. Small 8vo.

THE NATURALIST IN NICARAGUA.

NARRATIVE OF A RESIDENCE AT THE GOLD MINES OF CHONTALES; JOURNEYS IN
THE SAVANNAHS AND FORESTS; WITH OBSERVATIONS ON ANIMALS AND PLANTS
IN REFERENCE TO THE THEORY OF EVOLUTIONS OF LIVING FORMS.

BY THOMAS BELT, F.G.S.

With Illustrations. Post 8vo.

MISSIONARY WORK IN EAST AFRICA.

A LETTER TO THE ARCHBISHOP OF CANTERBURY.

BY SIR BARTLE FRERE, G.C.S.I., K.C.B., D.C.L.

Small 8vo.

THE GEOLOGY OF YORKSHIRE.

VOL. I.—THE COAST.

BY JOHN PHILLIPS, D.C.L.,
Professor of Geology at Oxford.

Re-constructed and re-written. With many additional Illustrations. 4to.

A DICTIONARY OF CHRISTIAN ANTIQUITIES AND BIOGRAPHY.

FROM THE TIMES OF THE APOSTLES TO THE AGE OF CHARLEMAGNE.

EDITED BY WM. SMITH, D.C.L., & REV. S. CHEETHAM, M.A.

Medium 8vo. Uniform with "Dr. Wm. Smith's Dictionary of the Bible."

HORSE-SHOEING;
AS IT IS, AND AS IT SHOULD BE.

BY WILLIAM DOUGLAS,
Late of 10th Hussars.

With Coloured Plates and Woodcuts.   Post 8vo.   (*Ready.*)

The object of this book is to show that Horse-Shoeing is no mystery, and that masters and owners of horses and grooms may effectually avert injury to the horse and suffering to the animal, by knowledge of a few simple rules.

THE TRAVELS OF MARCO POLO.
A new English Version.   Illustrated by the Light of Oriental Writers and Modern Travels.

BY COLONEL HENRY YULE, C.B.
Second Edition.   With Maps and Plates.   2 Vols.   Medium 8vo.

BRICK AND MARBLE ARCHITECTURE OF THE MIDDLE AGES.

BY GEORGE EDMUND STREET, R.A.
SECOND EDITION, WITH NOTES OF TOURS NORTH OF THE APENNINES, INCLUDING AQUILEI, UDINE, VICENZA, FERRARA, BOLOGNA, PIACENZA, MODENA, AND VERCELLI.

With Illustrations.   Royal 8vo.

Uniform with Street's "Gothic Architecture of Spain."

PRINCIPLES OF GREEK ETYMOLOGY.
BY PROFESSOR GEORGE CURTIUS, OF LEIPZIG.
Translated from the German

BY A. S. WILKINS, M.A., AND E. B. ENGLAND, B.A.,
Professors at Owens College, Manchester.

8vo.

THE FRENCH PRINCIPIA.
A FIRST FRENCH COURSE FOR SCHOOLS, CONTAINING GRAMMAR, DELECTUS, EXERCISES, AND VOCABULARIES.

On the plan of Dr. William Smith's "Principia Latina."

12mo.

A MEDIÆVAL LATIN DICTIONARY.
Based on the Work of DUCANGE.

Translated into English and Edited, with many Additions and Corrections,

BY E. A. DAYMAN, B.D.,
Prebendary of Sarum, formerly Fellow and Tutor of Exeter College, Oxford.

Small 4to.

⁎ A Specimen Sheet may be obtained from any Bookseller.

HISTORY OF THE MODERN STYLES OF ARCHITECTURE.

BY JAMES FERGUSSON, D.C.L., F.R.S.,
Fellow of the Royal Institute of British Architects.

Forming the Fourth Volume of the New Edition of the "History of Architecture."

Second and Revised Edition. With 330 Illustrations. Medium 8vo. (*Ready.*)

POETICAL WORKS OF LORD HOUGHTON.

New Edition. 2 vols. Fcap. 8vo.

THE THIRD PART OF

DR. WM. SMITH'S ANCIENT ATLAS.

CONTENTS:

THE WORLD AS KNOWN TO THE ANCIENTS.
HISPANIA.
NORTHERN GREECE.
CENTRAL GREECE.

HISTORICAL MAPS OF ASIA MINOR.
THE HOLY LAND (Southern Division).
MAP OF ASIA, to Illustrate the Old Testament and Classical Authors.

Folio. 21s. (Ready.)

A MANUAL OF ECCLESIASTICAL HISTORY.

BY PHILIP SMITH, B.A.,
Author of "The Student's Old and New Testament Histories."

Post 8vo.

MURRAY'S EUROPEAN HANDBOOK FOR TRAVELLERS.

A CONDENSED GUIDE TO THE CHIEF ROUTES AND MOST IMPORTANT PLACES ON THE CONTINENT.

With Map. 1 Vol. Post 8vo.

THE NATURALIST ON THE RIVER AMAZONS;

A RECORD OF ADVENTURES, HABITS OF ANIMALS, SKETCHES OF BRAZILIAN AND INDIAN LIFE, DURING ELEVEN YEARS OF TRAVEL.

BY HENRY W. BATES, F.L.S.,
Assistant Secretary Royal Geographical Society.

A New and Popular Edition, with Illustrations. Post 8vo. 7s. 6d. (*Ready.*)

Forming a New Volume of Mr. Murray's Series of "Choice Travels."

MAETZNER'S ENGLISH GRAMMAR.

A METHODICAL, ANALYTICAL, AND HISTORICAL TREATISE ON THE ORTHOGRAPHY, PROSODY, INFLECTIONS, AND SYNTAX OF THE ENGLISH TONGUE.

TRANSLATED FROM THE GERMAN

BY CLAIR J. GRECE, LL.B.,
Member of the Philological Society.

3 Vols. 8vo.

A WORD-BOOK OF THE ROMANY, OR ENGLISH GYPSY LANGUAGE;

With many pieces in GYPSY illustrative of the way of speaking and thinking of the ENGLISH GYPSIES; also SPECIMENS of their POETRY, and an Account of certain GYPSYRIES, or places inhabited by them, &c.

BY GEORGE BORROW,
Author of " The Gypsies of Spain," &c.

Post 8vo.

A DICTIONARY OF BRITISH HISTORY.
Medium 8vo.

HUME'S HISTORY OF ENGLAND TO THE REVOLUTION OF 1688.
NEW EDITION, *Annotated and Revised.* 7 Vols. 8vo.

METALLURGY;
BY JOHN PERCY, M.D., F.R.S.,
Lecturer on Metallurgy at the Government School of Mines.

VOL. I.—FUEL, WOOD, COAL, COPPER, ZINC, &c.

New Edition. With Illustrations. 8vo.

BOSWELL'S LIFE OF JOHNSON.
EDITED BY THE RIGHT HON. J. W. CROKER.

WITH NOTES BY LORD STOWELL, SIR WALTER SCOTT, SIR JAMES MACKINTOSH, DISRAELI, MARKLAND, LOCKHART, &c.

A new and revised Library Edition.

Prepared by ALEXANDER NAPIER, M.A., Editor of " Isaac Barrow's Works."

With Portraits. 4 vols. 8vo.

THE HARVEST OF THE SEA.
INCLUDING SKETCHES OF FISHERIES AND OF FISHER FOLK.

BY JAMES G. BERTRAM.
Third Edition. With 50 Illustrations. Post 8vo. 9s. (*Ready.*)

ALBEMARLE STREET,
November, 1873.

MR. MURRAY'S
NEW WORKS NOW READY.

THE
SPEAKER'S COMMENTARY ON THE BIBLE.
EXPLANATORY AND CRITICAL,
WITH A REVISION OF THE TRANSLATION
By BISHOPS AND CLERGY OF THE ANGLICAN CHURCH.

EDITED BY F. C. COOK, M.A., CANON OF EXETER.

VOL. 1.	VOLS. 2 & 3.
GENESIS—BISHOP OF WINCHESTER.	JOSHUA—CANON ESPIN.
EXODUS — CANON COOK AND REV. SAMUEL CLARK.	JUDGES, RUTH, SAMUEL—BISHOP OF BATH AND WELLS.
LEVITICUS—REV. SAMUEL CLARK.	
NUMBERS—CANON ESPIN & REV. J. F. THRUPP.	KINGS, CHRONICLES, EZRA, NEHE- MIAH, AND ESTHER—CANON RAW- LINSON.
DEUTERONOMY—CANON ESPIN.	

Medium 8vo.

THE LAND OF MOAB.
TRAVELS AND DISCOVERIES ON THE EAST SIDE OF THE DEAD SEA AND THE JORDAN.

By H. B. TRISTRAM, M.A., LL.D., F.R.S.,
Author of "The Land of Israel," "Natural History of the Bible."

AND A CHAPTER ON THE PERSIAN PALACE OF MASHITA.

By JAMES FERGUSSON, F.R.S.

With Map and 40 Plates. Post 8vo. 15s.

THE PERSONAL LIFE OF GEORGE GROTE,
HISTORIAN OF GREECE.

Compiled from Family Documents, Private Memoranda, and Original Letters to and from Various Friends.

By MRS. GROTE.

Second Edition. Portrait. 8vo. 12s.

THE GEOLOGICAL EVIDENCES OF THE ANTIQUITY OF MAN.

WITH AN OUTLINE OF GLACIAL POST-TERTIARY GEOLOGY, AND REMARKS ON THE ORIGIN OF SPECIES,

WITH SPECIAL REFERENCE TO MAN'S FIRST APPEARANCE ON THE EARTH.

By SIR CHARLES LYELL, F.R.S.

Fourth Edition, Revised. Illustrations. 8vo. 14s.

MONOGRAPHS—PERSONAL AND SOCIAL.

By LORD HOUGHTON.

SULEIMAN PASHA—ALEX. v. HUMBOLDT—CARDINAL WISEMAN—WALTER SAVAGE LANDOR—THE BERRYS.—HARRIET, LADY ASHBURTON—REV. SYDNEY SMITH—HEINRICH HEINE.

Second Edition. Portraits. Crown 8vo. 10s. 6d.

THE EASTERN CAUCASUS, THE CASPIAN AND BLACK SEAS.

DAGHESTAN, AND THE FRONTIERS OF PERSIA AND TURKEY IN 1871.

By LIEUT.-GEN. SIR ARTHUR CUNYNGHAME, K.C.B.

Map and Illustrations. 8vo. 18s.

THE TONGUE NOT ESSENTIAL TO SPEECH.

WITH ILLUSTRATIONS OF THE POWER OF SPEECH IN THE CASE OF THE AFRICAN CONFESSORS.

By THE HON. EDWARD TWISLETON.

Post 8vo. 6s.

LETTERS, LECTURES, AND REVIEWS.

INCLUDING THE PHRONTISTERION, OR OXFORD IN THE 19TH CENTURY.

By H. L. MANSEL, D.D.,

Late Dean of St. Paul's, and Author of "The Limits of Religious Thought Examined."

EDITED BY HENRY W. CHANDLER, M.A.,
Pembroke College, Oxford.

8vo. 12s.

RECORDS OF THE ROCKS;

A SERIES OF NOTES ON

THE GEOLOGY, NATURAL HISTORY, AND ANTIQUITIES OF NORTH AND SOUTH WALES, DEVON, AND CORNWALL.

By REV. W. S. SYMONDS, F.G.S.

With numerous Illustrations.   Crown 8vo.   12s.

HISTORY OF THE REIGN OF QUEEN ANNE UNTIL THE PEACE OF UTRECHT, 1701—13.

By EARL STANHOPE.

Cabinet Edition, with Portrait of the Author.   2 Vols.   Post 8vo.   10s.

SOCIETY IN FRANCE BEFORE THE REVOLUTION OF 1789,

AND ON THE CAUSES WHICH LED TO THAT EVENT.

By ALEXIS DE TOCQUEVILLE,
Member of the French Academy.

TRANSLATED BY HENRY REEVE, D.C.L.

New Edition, containing Additional Chapters.   8vo.   14s.

ANCIENT HISTORY,

FROM THE EARLIEST RECORDS TO THE FALL OF THE WESTERN EMPIRE, A.D. 1455.

By PHILIP SMITH, B.A.,
Author of "Student's Manuals of the Old and New Testament History."

Fourth Edition.   3 Vols.   8vo.   31s. 6d.

HISTORY OF THE CHRISTIAN CHURCH.

VOL. IV., COMPLETING THE WORK.

FROM THE DEATH OF BONIFACE VIII. TO THE REFORMATION, 1303—1517.

By J. CRAIGIE ROBERTSON, M.A.,
Canon of Canterbury, Professor of Ecclesiastical History, King's Coll., London.

8vo.   18s.

THE LONGEVITY OF MAN; ITS FACTS AND ITS FICTIONS.

INCLUDING AN ENQUIRY INTO SOME OF THE MORE REMARKABLE INSTANCES, AND SUGGESTIONS FOR TESTING REPUTED CASES, ILLUSTRATED BY EXAMPLES.

By WILLIAM J. THOMS, F.S.A.

Deputy Librarian, House of Lords.

Post 8vo.　10s. 6d.

ETRUSCAN INSCRIPTIONS.

ANALYZED, TRANSLATED, AND COMMENTED UPON.

By THE EARL OF CRAWFORD AND BALCARRES,

Author of "Lives of the Lindsays," "Progression by Antagonism," &c.

8vo.　12s.

AN HISTORICAL ATLAS OF ANCIENT GEO-GRAPHY—BIBLICAL AND CLASSICAL.

Compiled under the superintendence of

DR. WILLIAM SMITH and MR. GEORGE GROVE.

CONTENTS :

PART I.

THE HOLY LAND. (Northern Division.)
HISTORICAL MAPS OF THE HOLY LAND.
GREEK AND PHŒNICIAN COLONIES.
GALLIA.
ITALIA SUPERIOR.
ITALIA INFERIOR.
GREECE AFTER THE DORIC MIGRATION.
GREECE AT THE TIME OF THE PERSIAN WARS.

PART II.

JERUSALEM. (Ancient and Modern.)
MAP. To Illustrate the New Testament.
PELOPONNESUS. With Plan of Sparta.
SHORES AND ISLANDS OF THE ÆGEAN SEA.
GREECE AT THE TIME OF THE PELOPON-NESIAN WAR. [LEAGUE.
GREECE AT THE TIME OF THE ACHÆAN
EMPIRES OF THE BABYLONIANS, LYDIANS, MEDES AND PERSIANS.
EMPIRE OF ALEXANDER THE GREAT.

To be completed in Five Parts, with Index of Reference, Folio, 21s. each.

RUDE STONE MONUMENTS OF ALL COUNTRIES:

THEIR AGE AND USES.

By JAMES FERGUSSON, D.C.L., F.R.S.,

Author of "The History of Architecture."

With 230 Illustrations.　Medium 8vo.　24s.

A CHARGE DELIVERED TO THE CLERGY AND CHURCHWARDENS

At the General Visitation, held in 1873.

By ARTHUR CHARLES, BISHOP OF BATH AND WELLS.

Second Edition. 8vo. 1s.

YARKAND, KASHGAR, AND THE KARAKORUM PASS.

A NARRATIVE OF A JOURNEY TO HIGH TARTARY.

By ROBERT SHAW,

British Commissioner in Ladak.

With Maps and Illustrations. 8vo. 16s.

THE LETTERS AND JOURNALS OF THE LATE EARL OF ELGIN,

Edited by THEODORE WALROND, C.B.

With a Preface by the DEAN OF WESTMINSTER.

Second Edition. 8vo. 14s.

ARISTOTLE.

By GEORGE GROTE, F.R.S.

Edited by ALEXANDER BAIN, LL.D., and G. CROOM ROBERTSON, M.A.

2 Vols. 8vo. 32s.

MOTTOES FOR MONUMENTS.

A SELECTION OF EPITAPHS FOR GENERAL STUDY AND APPLICATION.

By F. & M. A. PALLISER.

With Illustrations from Flaxman and others.

Crown 8vo. 7s. 6d.

HISTORY OF THE GALLICAN CHURCH;

FROM THE CONCORDAT OF BOLOGNA, 1516, TO THE REVOLUTION.

WITH AN INTRODUCTION.

By W. HENLEY JERVIS, M.A.,

Prebendary of Heytesbury, and Author of the "Student's History of France."

With Portraits. 2 Vols. 8vo. 28s.

THE EXPRESSION OF THE EMOTIONS IN MAN AND ANIMALS.

By CHARLES DARWIN, F.R.S.

Eighth Thousand.   With Illustrations.   Crown 8vo.   12s.

THE HISTORY OF SICILY

DOWN TO THE ATHENIAN WAR, WITH ELUCIDATIONS OF THE SICILIAN ODES OF PINDAR.

By W. WATKISS LLOYD.

With Map.   8vo.   14s.

NOTES OF THOUGHT.

By the late CHARLES BUXTON, M.P.

Preceded by a Biographical Sketch.   By REV. LLEWELLYN DAVIES, M.A.

Portrait.   Crown 8vo.   10s. 6d.

HISTORY OF THE ROYAL ARTILLERY.

COMPILED FROM THE ORIGINAL RECORDS.

By CAPT. FRANCIS DUNCAN, R.A.,

Superintendent of the Regimental Records.

With Frontispiece.   VOL. I.   8vo.   15s.

THE HISTORY OF ANCIENT POTTERY,

EGYPTIAN, ASSYRIAN, GREEK, ETRUSCAN, AND ROMAN.

By SAMUEL BIRCH, LL.D., F.S.A.

New and Revised Edition.   With coloured Plates and 200 Woodcuts.

Medium 8vo.   42s.

Uniform with "Marryat's Modern Pottery."

AT HOME WITH THE PATAGONIANS.

A YEAR'S WANDERINGS OVER UNTRODDEN GROUND FROM THE STRAITS OF MAGELLAN TO THE RIO NEGRO.

By CAPT. G. CHAWORTH MUSTERS, R.N.

New Edition.   With Map and Illustrations.   Post 8vo.   7s. 6d.

THE INSCRIPTION OF PIANCHI MERAMON,

KING OF EGYPT IN THE EIGHTH CENTURY B.C.

TRANSLATED BY F. C. COOK, M.A.,

Canon of Exeter, and Editor of the "Speaker's Commentary on the Bible."

8vo. 2s. 6d.

HANDBOOK TO THE WELSH CATHEDRALS.

LLANDAFF, ST. DAVID'S, BANGOR, AND ST. ASAPH.

BY R. J. KING, B.A.

With Illustrations. Crown 8vo. 15s.

THE ADMINISTRATION OF JUSTICE UNDER MILITARY AND MARTIAL LAW.

BY CHARLES M. CLODE,

Of the Inner Temple, Barrister-at-Law, and Solicitor to the "War Department."

8vo. 12s.

HANDBOOK FOR TRAVELLERS IN ALGERIA, ALGIERS—CONSTANTINA, ORAN, &c.

WITH SOME ACCOUNT OF THE CLIMATE, AND ITS FITNESS FOR WINTER RESIDENTS AND INVALIDS.

Maps and Plans. Post 8vo. 6s.

THE DUKE OF WELLINGTON'S CIVIL AND POLITICAL CORRESPONDENCE.

(IN CONTINUATION OF THE FORMER SERIES.)

VOL. V. SEPTEMBER, 1828, to JUNE, 1829.

EDITED BY HIS SON.

8vo. 20s.

NOTES ON BANKING.

IN GREAT BRITAIN AND IRELAND, SWEDEN, DENMARK, AND HAMBURG,

WITH SOME REMARKS ON THE AMOUNT OF BILLS IN CIRCULATION, BOTH INLAND AND FOREIGN.

BY R. H. INGLIS PALGRAVE,

Member of the Council of the Statistical Society of London.

8vo. 6s.

HANDBOOK FOR TRAVELLERS IN SCOTLAND,

EDINBURGH, MELROSE, ABBOTSFORD, GLASGOW, DUMFRIES, GALLOWAY, AYR, STIRLING, ARRAN, THE CLYDE, OBAN, INVERARY, LOCH LOMOND, LOCH KATRINE & TROSACHS, CALEDONIAN CANAL, INVERNESS, PERTH, DUNDEE, ABERDEEN, BRAEMAR, SKYE, CAITHNESS, ROSS, AND SUTHERLAND.

New and entirely revised Edition. Maps and Plans. Post 8vo. 9s.

RESULTS OF CHRISTIAN MISSIONS IN INDIA.

By SIR BARTLE FRERE, G.C.S.I., K.C.B., D.C.L.,
Member of the Council of India, and President of the Royal Geographical Society.

Second Edition. Small 8vo. 2s. 6d.

THE CONSTITUTION AND THE PRACTICE OF COURTS MARTIAL,

With a Summary of the Law of Evidence, and some Notice of the Criminal Law of England with reference to the Trial of Civil Offences.

By CAPT. T. F. SIMMONS, R.A.,
Formerly Deputy Judge Advocate.

Sixth Edition, revised to 1873. 8vo. 15s.

HANDBOOK FOR TRAVELLERS ON THE CONTINENT.

Part I.—HOLLAND, BELGIUM, RHENISH PRUSSIA, AND THE RHINE UP TO MAYENCE.

Portable Edition, Revised. On thin paper. With Maps and Plans. Post 8vo. 6s.

THE HANDBOOK FOR TRAVELLERS ON THE CONTINENT.

Part II.—NORTH GERMANY, PRUSSIA, SAXONY, HANOVER, AND THE RHINE FROM MAYENCE TO SWITZERLAND.

Portable Edition. With Maps and Plans. Post 8vo. 6s. *(Nearly ready.)*

BRADBURY, AGNEW, & CO., PRINTERS, WHITEFRIARS.